Memories of the Future

Also by Siri Hustvedt

FICTION

The Blindfold

The Enchantment of Lily Dahl

What I Loved

The Sorrows of an American

The Summer Without Men

The Blazing World

NON-FICTION

Yonder

Mysteries of the Rectangle: Essays on Painting

A Plea for Eros

The Shaking Woman or A History of My Nerves

Living, Thinking, Looking

A Woman Looking at Men Looking at Women:
Essays on Art, Sex, and the Mind

The Delusions of Certainty

POETRY

Reading to You

Memories of the Future

Siri Hustvedt

Drawings by the author

SCEPTRE

First published in Great Britain in 2019 by Sceptre
An imprint of Hodder & Stoughton
An Hachette UK company

1

Jacket and interior illustrations by Siri Hustvedt
Illustration on page 156 by Fonds Marc Vaux © Bibliotèque Kandinsky

A CIP catalogue record for this title is available from the British Library

Hardback ISBN 9781473694415
Trade Paperback ISBN 9781473694422
eBook ISBN 9781473694439

Printed and bound in Australia by McPherson's Printing Group

Hodder & Stoughton policy is to use papers that are natural, renewable and recyclable products and made from wood grown in sustainable forests. The logging and manufacturing processes are expected to conform to the environmental regulations of the country of origin.

Hodder & Stoughton Ltd
Carmelite House
50 Victoria Embankment
London EC4Y 0DZ

www.sceptrebooks.co.uk

Memories of the Future

CHAPTER ONE

Years ago I left the wide, flat fields of rural Minnesota for the island of Manhattan to find the hero of my first novel. When I arrived in August of 1978, he was not a character so much as a rhythmic possibility, an embryonic creature of my imagination, which I felt as a series of metrical beats that quickened and slowed with my steps as I navigated the streets of the city. I think I was hoping to discover myself in him, to prove that he and I were worthy of whatever story came our way. I wasn't looking for happiness or comfort in New York City. I was looking for adventure, and I knew the adventurer must suffer before he arrives home after countless trials on land and sea or is finally snuffed out by the gods. I didn't know then what I know now: As I wrote, I was also being written. The book had been started long before I left the plains. Multiple drafts of a mystery had already been inscribed in my brain, but that didn't mean I knew how it would turn out. My unformed hero and I were headed for a place that was little more than a gleaming fiction: the future.

I had given myself exactly twelve months to write the novel. If at the end of the following summer, my hero was stillborn or died in infancy or turned out to be such a dullard that his life deserved no comment, in other words, if he was not a hero after all, I would leave him and his novel behind me and throw myself into the study of my dead (or failed) boy's ancestors, the denizens of the volumes that fill the phantom cities we call libraries. I had accepted a fellowship in comparative literature at Columbia University and, when I asked if I could defer my admission until the following year, the invisible authorities had sent me a long-winded letter agreeing to my request.

A dark room with a kitchenette, an even darker bedroom, a tiny black-and-white-tiled bathroom, and a closet with a bulging plaster ceiling at 309 West 109th Street cost me two hundred and ten dollars a month. It was a grim apartment in a scraped, chipped, battered building, and had I been just a little different, a bit more worldly or a touch less well read, its sour green paint and its views of two dirty brick walls in the stinking summer heat would have wilted me and my ambitions, but the degree of difference that was required, however infinitesimal, did not exist at the time. Ugly was beautiful. I decorated the rented rooms with the charmed sentences and paragraphs I lifted at will from the many volumes I kept in my head.

> He had filled his imagination with everything that he had read, with enchantments, knightly encounters, battles, challenges, wounds, with tales of love and its torments, and all sorts of impossible things, and as a result had come to believe that all these fictitious happenings were true; they were more real to him than anything else in the world.

My first moments in my first apartment have a radiant quality in memory that have nothing to do with sunlight. They are illuminated by an idea. Security deposit down, first month's rent paid, door closed on my squat, grinning super, Mr. Rosales, sweat soaking the underarms of my T-shirt, I hopped about on the floorboards in what I believed to be a jig and threw out my arms in triumph.

I was twenty-three years old with a BA in philosophy and English from St. Magnus College (a small liberal arts institution in Minnesota founded by Norwegian immigrants); five thousand dollars in the bank, a wad of dough I had saved while I worked as a bartender in my hometown of Webster for a year after graduation and bunked at home for free; a Smith Corona typewriter, a tool kit, cooking equipment donated by my mother, and six boxes of books. I built a desk with two-by-fours and a plywood sheet. I bought two plates, two cups, two glasses, two forks, two knives, and two spoons in anticipation of the future lover (or series of lovers) with whom, after a night of delirious banging, I planned to eat a breakfast of toast and eggs, which, because I had no table and no chairs, would be consumed on the floor.

I remember the door closing on Mr. Rosales, and I remember my jubilation. I remember the two rooms of the old apartment, and I can walk from one to the other in my mind. I can still see the space, but if I am honest, I cannot describe the precise configurations of the cracks in the bedroom ceiling, the lumpy lines and delicate flowerings I know were there because I studied them, nor am I absolutely certain about the dimensions of the refrigerator, for example, which I believe to have been smallish. I'm quite sure it was white and it may have been round at its corners, not square. The more I focus on remembering, the more details I am likely to provide, but those particulars may well be invented. And so, I will not expound on the appearance, for example, of the potatoes that lay on the plates in front of me thirty-eight years ago. I will not tell you whether they were pale and boiled or sautéed lightly or au gratin or fried because I do not remember them. If you are one of those readers who relishes memoirs filled with impossibly specific memories, I have this to say: those authors who claim perfect recall of their hash browns decades later are not to be trusted.

And so, I arrive in the city I have dreamed about since I was eight years old but do not know from Adam (as a child, I thought the expression was "from atom" and that it bore some relation to the terrifying physics of the bomb).

And so, I arrive in the city I have seen in films and have read about in books, which is New York City but also other cities, Paris and London and St. Petersburg, the city of the hero's fortunes and misfortunes, a real city that is also an imaginary city.

I remember the eerie illumination that came through the broken blinds the first night I slept in apartment 2B on August 25. I told myself I needed a new shade or it would never be truly dark in the room. The hot air didn't move. My sweat turned the sheets damp, and my dreams were harsh and vivid, but by the time I had made coffee and taken the cup back to my foam mattress to drink it the following morning, I had forgotten what I dreamt. During my first week in New York, I wrote in the mornings and traveled on the subway in the afternoons. I had no destination in mind, but I know that as the train rumbled through the bowels of the city, my heart beat more quickly, and my newfound freedom seemed nearly impossible. A token cost fifty cents, and as long as I didn't take an exit and climb the stairs, I could change from one train to another without paying another fare. I chugged uptown and downtown on the IRT, and flew express on the A, and I crossed from the West Side to the East on the Shuttle and investigated the curious route of the L, and when the F rose up into daylight at Smith and Ninth Street and I had a sudden view of steaming Brooklyn with its jazz of jutting cement blocks, warehouses, and billboards, I found myself smiling out the window. As I sat or stood in one of the cars, jostled and jolted by its stops and starts, I paid homage to the ubiquitous graffiti, not for its beauty but for its insurrectionist spirit, one I hoped to imbibe and emulate for my own artistic purposes. I rejoiced in the screeching trains and in the voice of the man whose announcements turned to an unintelligible but sonorous scratch over the loudspeaker. I celebrated the press of the crowd as I was pushed out the door in a collective swell of movement, and I recited Whitman's lines "myself disintegrated, every one disintegrated, yet part of the scheme." I wanted to be part of the scheme. I wanted to be everyone. I listened to all the languages spoken, some of them recognizable—Spanish, Mandarin, German, Russian, Polish, French, Portuguese—and some that I had never heard before. I reveled in the varieties of skin color near me, having been sated in Webster, Minnesota, by enough Lutheran pallor and its inflamed shades of pink to red to burnt farmer brown to last me a lifetime.

I studied the bums and panhandlers and bag ladies at various stages of descent into the indignities of the street. Years before my arrival in New York City, the powers-that-were-at-the-time had opened the doors of psychiatric wards and released their patients into a dubious freedom. Mad people skulked on the platforms, picking at their sores. Some shouted verses. Some sang or whined or preached about Jesus coming or Jehovah's wrath, and some sat silently in black corners, reduced to husks of despair. I inhaled the stench of their unwashed bodies, an odor wholly new to me, and held my breath.

The rhyme and reason of Manhattan's streets would have to wait. How one neighborhood related to another could be traced on the map I carried around with me, but it still had no carnal logic. When I leapt up the steps into the sun and the crowds, and my shoes hit the baked asphalt and melting tar, and I heard through the talk and traffic and general roar the cacophony of music from boom boxes hoisted on shoulders or swinging at thighs like suitcases, my skin bristled, my head felt light, and I prepared for the coming sensual assault. I remember my first walk down pushy, pungent Canal Street, the bronzed ducks that hung by their feet through greasy glass, the tubs of shining whole fishes, the baskets and cardboard boxes laden with grains and vegetables, and the fruits I would only later learn to name: star fruit, mangosteen, breadfruit, and longan.

There were the squalid pleasures of walks through Times Square—the signs that lured patrons with X and XX and XXX and burlesque, also spelled burlesk and bur_esk (due to fallen l), peep shows and the Paradise Playhouse and Filthy's and Circus Circus with live girls onstage for just a quarter and "$10 dollars complete," and the silhouettes of naked women with jutting breasts and long legs above the marquees, and views of pizza parlors and game rooms and grim little laundry shops with brown paper packages tied with string piled high and the litter that leapt and twirled when the wind blew and three-card monte cheats who set up on the sidewalk to scam the suckers and the men with their shirtsleeves rolled to their elbows in the hot air who paused on the sidewalk, held captive for a moment by the promise of jiggling flesh and speedy relief, before they either walked inside to get some satisfaction or turned left or right and went on their way.

I trekked to Greenwich Village for its Bohemian mythology in search of Dada's brilliant company. I was looking for Djuna Barnes and Marcel Duchamp, for Berenice Abbott, Edna St. Vincent Millay, and Claude McKay, for Emmanuel Radnitzky, alias Man Ray. I was looking for William Carlos Williams and Jane Heap, for Francis Picabia and Arthur Craven, and the astounding character who had popped up in my Dada research, a woman I had chased to the archives of the University of Maryland, where for three days I had laboriously copied out in pencil her mostly unpublished poems: the Baroness Elsa von Freytag-Loringhoven, née Elsa Hildegard Plötz, artist as proto-punk, fuck-you riot, who struck poses with birdcages on her head and headlights at her hips and wrote poems like howls or burps that came from deep in the diaphragm.

"No one asks for these papers," the archivist told me before she hauled out the boxes. I'm No One then, I thought. The Baroness's papers arrived in Maryland in 1970 because Djuna Barnes, author of the intoxicating novel *Nightwood*, had saved her dead friend's letters and manuscripts and drawings and stored them in her New York apartment. When the university acquired the Barnes papers, the Baroness came along for the ride. Hour after hour, I sat with Elsa's yellowing papers, lined and unlined, studying one draft after another of a single poem until I became confused and my eyes hurt. After the day was over, I sat on my bed in my room at the Holiday Inn to read over what I had recorded and to feel the percussive jolts and jerks of the Baroness rock my body. She lived in the pages I took with me to New York, but there was no trace of her downtown. She wasn't even a ghost. There was nothing left of her in the narrow, off-kilter byways of the Village.

Christopher Street was vibrant then, an open-air theater I liked to walk down incognito and peek in windows at erotic paraphernalia and costumes of a sort I had vaguely known existed but had never seen, and I wondered what my old friend Pastor Weeks would have thought of it all and what he might have said if he had been walking beside me, and I answered in the words he would have chosen: "We are all sisters and brothers in the Lord." I admired the proud couples that resembled twins, lean and trim in matching blue jeans and fitted T-shirts and perfect posture with a little sway in their hips and maybe a dog on a leash between them as they strolled to show off their perfect beauty, and I liked the tall girls in plumes and heels, and I tried not to stare at the men I silently referred to as "leather threats," the big muscle boys in black regalia with silver studs and spikes and intense expressions that made me look down at the sidewalk.

I loitered in bookstores, in the Coliseum and Gotham Book Mart and Books and Company and the Strand. In the Eighth Street Bookshop, I bought *Some Trees* by John Ashbery, and I read it on the train and then aloud in the apartment over and over again. And I discovered the National Bookstore on Astor Place, jammed with tantalizing scholarly books wrapped in plastic to prevent fingerly invasions from people like me, overseen by a tyrant with white hair who kept time with his tapping pencil and barked if you lingered too long over a volume, and I had to save my money, so I usually left empty-handed, but old man Salter, not so friendly himself, let me sit on the floor of his bookstore back in my own neighborhood just across the street from

Columbia, and I would lean against a shelf and read until I knew I truly wanted this book or that one, mostly poets new to me, but before the year was over, I had bought the whole New York School and beyond, more Ashbery, as well as Kenneth Koch and Ron Padgett and James Schuyler and Barbara Guest and Frank O'Hara, the latter killed by a dune buggy on Fire Island twelve years before I arrived. And I still remember Guest's words, the ones that prompted me to buy her book: "Understanding the distance between characters." I am still trying to understand that.

And when I wanted the city to stop, I bounded up the steps between the stone lions and passed through the doors of the New York Public Library and walked swiftly to the grand reading room, fit for kings, and I seated myself at one of the long wooden tables under the vast vaulted ceiling with a chandelier dangling high above my head, and I ordered a book as the silent daylight from the great windows fell upon me, and I read for hours and felt as if I had become a being of pure potential, a body transformed into an enchanted space of infinite expansion, and as I sat and read to the dull sound of pages turning and to coughs and sniffs and footsteps that echoed in the immense room and the occasional rude whisper, I found refuge in the cadences of whichever mind I was borrowing for the duration, immersed in sentences I couldn't have written or imagined and, even when the text was abstruse or gnarled or beyond me, and there were many of those, I persevered and took notes and understood that my mission was one of years, not months. If I could fill my head with the wisdom and art of the ages, I would over time augment myself, volume by volume, into the giant I wanted to be. Although reading required concentration, its demands were not those of the streets, and I relaxed in the reading room. I breathed evenly. My shoulders fell from their hunched position, and I often allowed my thoughts to play in reverie over a single phrase, "The irrationality of a thing is no argument against its existence, rather a condition of it." In the library I had wings.

Before I left the building, I would always stop by the Slavic Reading Room, open the door, and peek in at the old men who resembled ivory carvings of themselves, their skin the color of gray-tinted eggshells and their long beards a paler shade of the same color. They dressed in black and at first appeared motionless as they sat over the old books. Only their long forefingers moved with deliberation as they turned the pages, a uniform gesture that proved to me the statues were alive. The old men must be long dead now, and the Slavic Reading Room is no more, but I never failed to look in on them and inhale that special dry odor of aged scholar and precious paper, which together seemed to me to carry a faint whiff of smoking incense and the mystical philosophy of Vladimir Solovyov before the revolution. I never dared cross the threshold.

The library is an American palace, built by Lenox and Astor money to show snooty European money that it had nothing on us. But I can say this: no one measured me up and down or gave me an intelligence test or checked my bank account before I walked through the door. In Webster, Minnesota, there were no truly rich people. We counted a few turkey farmers and store owners as wealthy, and doctors, dentists, lawyers, and professors, however modest their means, were given a class bounce by their years in school and were often resented by the poor farmers and mechanics and myriad others in and around town who had no letters after their names. But in New York, money was there to gawk at, money the likes of which I had never seen. It strolled down Fifth and Park Avenues, alone or in pairs, and it laughed and conversed behind the windows of restaurants at tables with wine bottles and pressed white linen napkins and low candles. It stepped out of taxis in shoes with soles that appeared never to have touched a sidewalk, and it slumped gracefully in the backseat of chauffeured limousines. It sparkled in displays of watches and earrings and scarves in stores I was too shy to enter. And I couldn't help but think of Jay Gatsby's beautiful shirts in many colors and stupid, empty Daisy, and the sad green light. And I thought of Balzac, too, how could one not, of the grubby, glittering human comedy and of Proust dining at the Ritz with the friends he robbed of their traits with such terrifying exactitude, and of Odette's "smart set," which is not so smart at all, vulgar, in fact, and I struggled to feel beyond it all, to be my own character, that noble, young if poor person with high, refined literary and philosophical tastes, but there was power in the money I saw, a brute force that frightened me and which I envied because it made me smaller and more pathetic to myself.

I am still in New York, but the city I lived in then is not the city I inhabit now. Money remains ascendant, but its glow has spread across the borough of Manhattan. The faded signs, tattered awnings, peeling posters, and filthy bricks that gave the streets of my old Upper West Side neighborhood a generally jumbled and bleary look have disappeared. When I find myself in the old haunts now, my eyes are met with the tightened outlines of bourgeois improvement. Legible signage and clean, clear colors have replaced the former visual murk. And the streets have lost their menace, that ubiquitous if invisible threat that violence might erupt at any instant and that a defensive posture and determined walk were not optional but necessary. In other parts of the city in 1978, one could adopt the ambling gait of the flaneur, but not there. Within a week, my senses had gained an acuity they had never needed before. I was ever alert to the sudden creak or whine or crack, to the abrupt gesture, unsteady walk, or leering expression of an approaching stranger, to an indefinable odor of something-not-quite-right that wafted here and there and made me hasten my steps or dodge into a bodega or Korean grocery.

I kept a journal that year. I found my hero in it, the homunculus of my traveling thoughts, and I tried out passages for his novel in the notebook. I doodled and drew and recorded at least some of my comings and goings and my conversations with others and with myself, but the black-and-white Mead composition book with its account of my former self disappeared not long after I had filled its pages. And then, three months ago, I found it packed neatly in a box of miscellany my mother had saved. I must have started another journal and left the old one behind me after a visit to my parents in the summer of 1979. When I spotted the slightly creased-at-one-corner notebook beneath a box of loose photographs with the absurd title *My New Life* handwritten on the cover, I greeted it as if it were a beloved relative I had given up for dead: first the gasp of recognition, then the embrace. Not until hours later did the image of myself clasping a notebook to my breast take on the ridiculous appearance it surely deserves. And yet, the little book of two hundred pages has been invaluable for the simple reason that it has brought back, to one degree or another, what I couldn't remember or had misremembered in a voice that is at once mine and not quite mine anymore. It's funny. I thought I had begun every entry with "Dear Page," an invocation I found witty at the time, but, in fact, I called my imaginary interlocutor by a couple of names and sometimes by no name at all.

My sister and I were going through every object that belonged to our mother because she was leaving the five-room independent-living apartment that had been hers for almost a decade after our father died. Her destination was a single room in the assisted-living wing of the same retirement complex, which meant we had to travel yards not miles, but the move required that our mother's possessions be drastically pruned. While not a joyous event, the change was less painful than it might have been because in between her nine and a half years of "independence" and her new location that required "assistance," our ninety-two-year-old mother had been the frail, recumbent resident of the third wing on the same property known as the "Care Unit." Ten months earlier, the medical man on my mother's case had declared her nearly dead, without using those words, of course. Dr. Gabriel had told us to prepare for her demise, without choosing that word either. Instead, in early October of last year, he had pointedly asked us to consider an "early Christmas," Christmas in late October or early November, the implication being that our mother was unlikely to find herself anywhere in December, so if she was to suck some small pleasure from her favorite holiday we had better hurry it up.

Although neither of us said anything to him in response, my sister and I found the suggestion that we finagle the calendar year to accommodate our mother's probable death preposterous. The months follow each other one after the other, and if she died in October or November, we weren't going to pretend Halloween or Thanksgiving was Christmas, and, although our mother had become confused about time in general and had forgotten the series of health emergencies—the broken foot, the broken arm, the congestive heart failure, the pseudo-gout that bloated her thin legs into excruciating red logs, and finally, the infection that entered her bloodstream and caused her to hallucinate dead friends, children's choirs, and elves with top hats that waved at her from outside the window—she would have strongly disapproved of us tampering with the seasons. She has always regarded herself as "philosophical." My mother's idiosyncratic definition of the word is the following: we all suffer and we all die. "Never, ever," my mother said to me when I was eleven, "say 'pass away' for 'to die.' People die. They don't evaporate."

Our mother lived through Halloween and she lived through Thanksgiving and she lived through Christmas and she lived through Easter and by the time summer had come and gone and the leaves of the trees beyond the Care Unit had begun to rust, she was no longer dying, and because she had pulled herself back from the ultimate threshold and the administrators of the Care Unit needed her bed for a person who truly stood, or rather lay, "at death's door" (words also never spoken aloud), they bumped her up to assisted living but did not approve a return to her old independent quarters, which precipitated the move, my discovery of the notebook, and the writing of this book.

My mother is now well settled in her new room, and I wouldn't be surprised if she lives another decade, but she forgets. She forgets what I have just said to her on the telephone. She forgets who it was that just entered her room with a pill or glass of water or raisin toast. She forgets that she has taken the pill for her arthritic pain and she forgets whether she has had any visitors, and she speaks to me instead about the orchids on her windowsill. She describes their colors and the number of blooms that remain on individual stalks and how the light hits them, "some clouds today, so the light is even." She is articulate, and she remembers much about her life, especially her early life, and these days she likes to revisit the old stories. Yesterday, she told me one of my favorites, a tale I asked her to tell me again and again when I was a child. She and her brother had seen Eva Harstad's face in the second-floor window of the house at the end of Maple Street in Blooming Field where she grew up. "Oscar and I were walking home at sunset. There were pink streaks in the sky and a strange light. We both saw her in the window. Impossible, you know, because she had hanged herself the year before, poor Eva. We didn't know her well. There was a baby on the way, you see. No one ever found out who the father was. Her death saddened everyone in town who wasn't mean-spirited, sanctimonious, or hypocritical, but there she was, her long blond hair hanging around her face. I know I've told you this many times before, but there was something wrong with her lips. She was moving them crazily, the way some singers warm up their mouths to get them ready to sing the song, but nothing came out. We didn't run, but our hearts froze, if you know what I mean. We walked fast. Oscar never liked to be reminded of it. I think it scared him more than it did me. I should ask him. Shouldn't I? Now, where is Oscar?" Uncle Oscar died in 2009. My mother is aware of this fact on some days but not on others.

The past is fragile, as fragile as bones grown brittle with age, as fragile as ghosts seen in windows or the dreams that fall apart upon waking and leave nothing behind them but a feeling of unease or distress or, more rarely, a kind of eerie satisfaction.

September 2, 1978

My dear Page,

I have waited for this *now*, the *now* that will disappear if I don't seize it, shake it, and drain it of its bursting presence.

My heroic boy has become more than an itch in just a few days! He has a shape—tall and thin—and a permanent location—Marginal to the Concerns of Most People. So we are alike, he and I. Ian Feathers. His initials: I.F., as in "if" . . . a subjunctive character of wings and flight, of quills and pens and typewriters. My own Midwestern knight, addled by mystery stories and the seductions of logic.

And something strange: My next-door neighbor chants every evening. She may be a Hari Krishna or belong to the cult of that foolish-looking fat boy maharaja whose picture I've seen around. She says amsah, amsah, amsah, over and over and over. Yesterday, she paused from moaning amsah and said loudly, "They wanted someone else." The misery in her voice closed my own throat for an instant. I couldn't help but wonder who "they" were, and the sentence hasn't left me. It's as if it has some special and terrible meaning. I think she may have yelped and gasped in the middle of the night, too, but I was not awake enough to monitor the sounds.

Chapter 1. Ian Is Born Between the Covers

Ian Feathers read so much detective fiction as a boy that his mother worried his eyes would be strained to blindness and his sunless limbs would wither from inactivity. Mr. and Mrs. Feathers, as the Greeks before them, believed in "moderation in all things." The American version of this ancient adage was "well rounded." The Feathers' loved their tall, skinny, smart, near-sighted, hyperlexic boy, but they worked hard to file him down and round him off—for his own good. They knew, as all God-fearing Midwesterners knew, that the ideal, well-rounded boy was never *too much* of anything. He did well in school but not so well that he could be accused of freakish brilliance. He strayed into trouble now and again (to demonstrate he had pluck), but the trouble he found himself in was never dire and usually involved fisticuffs with a less-than-ideally well-rounded boy. His moral compass was set due north but wavered periodically because no one likes a prig. He was modest, of course, benevolent to his many inferiors, and rather tall, but not too tall. On Ian's part of the plains and America in general during the middle of the twentieth century, it went without saying that the ideal well-rounded boy was Caucasian (although he tanned nicely in the summer), was non-fanatically Christian, and, as presented in the popular literature, anyway, had sandy hair and 20/20 vision. If the ideal boy were to be assigned a temperature, it would be lukewarm. In fact, there was only one arena of extremity open to that paragon of mediocrity, one the Greeks themselves would have approved of: sports.

Although Ian aspired to a pleasant roundness or at least the appearance of it from time to time to please his parents, his passion for mysterious circumstances, unsolved crimes, theft, larceny, and murder, especially murder, fell into that un-American category of the too much. Ian's "real" life was lived in books, not out of them. And yet, the border between inside the covers and outside the covers was not decisive. Murders were rare in the Feathers' hometown of Verbum, Minnesota, but Ian trained rigorously for the future case. He studied lint and wrinkle formations on jacket sleeves and trouser legs and noted the cat and dog hairs that clung to pet owners. He stared at the soles of shoes (on and off potential suspects) for soil and debris and chewing gum and recorded their color, consistency, and humidity. He noted the varying degrees of human perspiration and its effects on the underarms of shirts. He spent hours memorizing tire tracks from bicycles, tow trucks, station wagons, and pickups. He began to induce personality traits from cigarette butts, those that were smashed in half, for example, as opposed to those left in an ashtray to drift to nothing. The boy lived in a world built entirely of clues.

Over the years, Ian graciously accepted his parents' birthday and Christmas gifts that were intended to redirect his fanaticism—the basketball (for which they had high hopes on account of their offspring's looming stature), the baseball and bat; their later offerings of tennis racket, skis, swimming trunks and goggles; and their final pitch in the direction of the Someone Else they hoped he might become—a badminton net and birdies—but Ian not only refused to take up sports, he did not even like them. If he had been a geometrical figure rather than a boy, he would have been a great cubicoboctahedron with multiple protruding points, points he had been sharpening ever since he discovered his calling in life through that inimitable genius of analysis and logic, the splendid S.H.: Sherlock Holmes.

For many years, I recalled my initial weeks in New York City as the Period of Nobody Real. I knew I had spoken to the flesh-and-blood Mr. Rosales, of course, whom I always greeted with a hello, but whenever I talked to him, his eyes darted in all directions and then moved to the floor. I think he was worried I would ask him for repairs. I read poems and novels and books of philosophy, all of which had people in one form or another inside them, and my hero slowly began to find himself, as did his all-important confidante, his Sancho, his Watson: Isadora Simon, I.S., initials of being—present tense. I roamed Manhattan, but I had no friends or acquaintances. When I told the story of my urban initiation, I would always say, "I must have been one of the few people who moved to New York and didn't know a soul." This is true. No friends, no friends of friends, no third cousins twice removed and therefore no telephone number to call. Then I would add for poignant effect, "For the first three weeks I spoke to no one." This turns out to have been a blatant falsehood, although I had never intended to lie.

September 3, 1978

This afternoon I returned to the Hungarian Pastry Shop, my new hangout. Read for two hours over one coffee with refills. Smoked too much. Book: Bergson's *Laughter: An Essay on the Meaning of the Comic*. Took notes, and then started conversation with girl named Wanda—large eyes, small mouth, dark blond hair, studying Russian history at Columbia. We discussed Symbolism. I talked a lot, gesticulated, blurted out pent-up thoughts. Days of solitude have made me garrulous. Symbolism led to dinner at the Ideal (Cuban-Chinese on the corner of 107th and Broadway). I asked her about Gogol's *Dead Souls* and parataxis, told her I wished I had studied Russian, and then I asked her about herself and, after some preliminaries, she told me her mother had had a stroke last year. The left side of her face drooped and she dragged her arm and leg on the same side. "Just cut me in half and talk to the good side," she told her daughter, but she slurred the words. A second stroke killed her. Dry, blank, and stiff, Wanda told me the story in a voice that had no feeling at all, but I noticed she addressed the wall behind me, not me, which I guessed was a way to avoid the sympathy that must have shown on my face. It was awkward, and I think she regretted telling me. When she finished the story, she flushed. She had to leave right away. I felt the urge to kiss her goodbye on both cheeks, but when I saw her lips pressed tightly together, I withdrew and didn't get my face anywhere near hers. We shook hands and exchanged numbers.

I have no memory of Wanda.

I remember Ian Feathers, and I remain fond of him to this day as an invention I hoped would soar beyond me and into the world, whereas Wanda isn't even a vague mental image, and, believe me, I have tried to summon her large eyes and small mouth and dark blond hair, but the student of Russian history is beyond my recollection. How many other people, events, conversations, and stories of dead parents have I forgotten? How many Wandas are there? Hundreds, I would guess. Memory is not only unreliable; it is porous. For all I can recall, a stranger might have written those words about

Wanda or my former self might have made up the whole story. The latter is doubtful. I remember my young self well enough to know that, despite my ripening sense of irony, on the subject of dead mothers I remained sincere.

I hover above the self that met and then wrote about Wanda. I am somewhere near the cracked ceiling of the shabby, nearly empty apartment, the sprite of what-will-be who looks down with a mixture of wonder and pity on the young person hunched over the notebook. The journal passages remind me that I smoked then—I add a cigarette to my mental scenery and watch the smoke drift upward from the white weed held between her two fingers. A young woman sits and smokes and produces page after page of prose, some good, some bad, but soon finds herself lost in a labyrinth of her own making, although she had some help from Feathers, who wasn't sure where he was headed either.

The story goes on.

According to my journal, on September 5, two days after I met Wanda, I understood that my neighbor was not a member of an Eastern cult. I wasn't sleeping well. Although the worst of the heat was over, the apartment's rooms were not yet cool, and my nights were alive with the city's noises, a clamor that took some getting used to because I had grown up with such different sounds. In summer at home, a single plaintive mosquito hovering by my ear at night could keep me awake, but I liked to listen to the cricket choruses at dusk and the katydids that sang into the small hours. I slept to their songs and to the winds of varying magnitudes that crackled tree branches and shushed the long grasses outside the house. When the June storms came, it thundered up close and it thundered far away and my heart beat with excitement as the sky dropped rushing water onto the roof, and in winter when a blizzard hit, I would listen to its hoarse roar and intermittent wails and then to the near silence that followed it—a paralysis of sun and snow. I hear nostalgia in my description, but I was not nostalgic at twenty-three. I embraced the urban din. My neighbor ceased to drone at around ten, but the elevator opened and shut at all hours and sirens blasted from Broadway. I listened to other voices carry through windows that had been left ajar across the airshaft. My neighbors' televisions talked and wept and sang jingles. Drunken shouts arrived from the street and the muted guttural rumble of garbage trucks woke me at about five in the morning. I would hear the engines idling and then the sound of metal cans as they rattled to the sidewalk. One morning, I heard a woman scream and, still in a state of half sleep, I bolted upright in bed to listen. Not until the next morning did I wonder if it was the person next door. In my notebook, I described the shriek as "a harbinger of terror and glee." Below this Romantic twaddle, I jotted down a line from Baudelaire's *Fleurs du Mal*: "*Si le viol, le poison, le poignard, l'incendie . . .*"

On the evening I have been making my way round to, I sat at my desk, stared at the page in front of me, and pondered the fourteen-year-old Ian and the mystery he intends to solve: the frequent sightings of Frieda Frail's face in the window of the house where she had died of an epileptic seizure a year before. My note to myself in the composition book: "Ian's Sherlock worship leads him straight into the world of propositional logic and valid and invalid inference. Our not-so-ideal boy lives for cleaving true from false and busies himself with p's and q's and r's as well as with the signs for not [¬], and [∧], or [∨], if then [⇒], and if and only if [⇔]. He proceeds step by step. His reasoning is perfect, but our hero will be misled by his deductions. Isadora Simon, Ian's Watson, will take another more effective route."

While thinking about Ian and Isadora and the symbolic logic I had studied in college, I heard my neighbor start up her chant again, amsah, amsah, amsah. Her intonation had a dirgelike quality, and I realized that her sorry repetitions had begun to work on me. They slowed my thoughts and turned them in an unhappy, wounded direction, as if someone had taken to methodically rubbing my chest with sandpaper. I walked to the wall, pressed my ear against it, wished I had the old stethoscope my father had given me when I was ten that lay in the top drawer of my dresser at home, and I listened, my strained body alert to the incantation. "Amsah, amsah, I'm sad, I'm sad, I'm sad, I'm sad." And on it went with a single variation, "Lucy's sad, she's sad, I'm sad, I'm sad, I'm sad." This was worse than a mantra. I was living next to a woman so sad she proclaimed her sadness aloud every night. I could almost see her rocking back and forth in her room. In the notebook, I wrote, "I have to block her out. I've decided to buy a cheap radio and turn it on in the evenings. I know if she keeps it up, I'll go insane. I stuck toilet paper in my ears and hit the foam."

"Hit the foam" was code for self-induced rumpty-rumpty.

I did a lot of masturbating in those days, but I was discreet then and reluctant to commit my onanistic fantasies to paper. That modesty has vanished. I would lie back on the foam mattress that sat on top of the platform bed I had devised from discarded orange crates I found on the street and another cut-specifically-to-your-measurements piece of plywood and generate a lover as my hand became his hand or her hand, depending on my predilection of the moment, and I twisted and turned and panted in the sheets my mother had bought for me at Sears as a stranger with black hair that fell onto his forehead and extremely narrow hips and a nice round butt entered the sleeping compartment of a train on its way from Berlin to Paris and undressed on the floor below me and crawled into my upper bunk and pressed my shoulders against the hard pallet, and as he regarded me intently, I noticed the shine on his upper lip because it was warm in the train, and he turned me over abruptly and fucked me from behind, and I loved it, or a blond girl that resembled Marilyn Monroe mounted me in that same compartment and slowly unbuttoned her blouse as the car we were in rocked on the tracks and the whistle sounded, and then I pushed her onto her stomach and pulled down her panties and took in the beauty of her wondrous ass and, in one position or another, I fingered her clit until she came and I came—we all came—sometimes the three of us came together as a chorus when I had decided on a trio. I took every part. I was man and I was woman. I was woman with man and sometimes the man with the woman and then again the woman with the woman. I have no problem recalling my masturbatory fantasies today because they are oddly fixed. The rest of me has matured and changed. I am a wise old bird now, leavened by the pains and understandings that arrive over the years, but the erotic gymnastics that took place in my head then and the ones that play out now are remarkably alike. Sexual fantasy is a machine, not an organism. I continue to have a weakness for sex on trains. It must be their rhythms.

"To write a book is for all the world like humming a song—be but in tune with yourself, Madam, 'tis no matter how high or low you take it." I kept the quotation from *The Life and Opinions of Tristram Shandy, Gentleman* by the Reverend Laurence Sterne taped to the wall above my desk as inspiration and a pointed reminder that novels did not come in a single variety. As my great-aunt Irma used to say, "It takes all kinds."

When I looked at the mailbox for 2C in the small entryway to the building, I found the single name L. Brite. Surely L stood for Lucy: Lucy Brite. It was a pretty name that might belong to a pretty woman, if a sad one. Brite generated associations, brightness as in the sun, but also the so-brilliant-I-have-to-blink smiles of advertisements for toothpaste, exactly the opposite of what my neighbor was communicating through the wall. There is metaphorical brightness, too, as in a person's intellectual shininess or momentary great idea, made concrete by the image of a lightbulb above that someone's head with little lines emanating from it that onlookers were meant to read as rays. The name inspired me, and I made a little drawing of an imaginary Lucy glowing in the darkness of her sorrow. I had forgotten the drawing, too, until I came across it in my old composition book.

During the day, my neighbor did not sing out her sadness. She tapped and pounded on what I guessed was a small carpentry project and, while she worked on it, she whistled. Lucy Brite whistled well, a gift that reminded me of my father, who had sung tonelessly but whistled in perfect tune, something that had always astonished me as a child. How was it that in church my father moaned out hymns in a voice so flat I had to stop myself from grimacing, but he could whistle like a messenger from heaven? Whistling from my father was a declaration of high mood, a sign that for the moment, anyway, life was good for him, which made it good for us, his children, the two girls who listened to wordless renditions of "Camptown Races" or "I've Been Working on the Railroad" or "There Is Power in a Union" from the backseat of the car, which is why I associate whistling with a picture of my father from behind—the rim of dark hair beneath his bald pate and his ears "that lay nice and flat against his head," the only way ears should lie, according to our mother.

We liked it when he whistled and drove the first family car I can remember, Clunky, a brown-and-white 1959 Chevy with a dent in the fender that was never fixed because "it in no way interfered with a smoothly running engine." My father viewed the slightly squashed metal from a purely utilitarian perspective, a view my mother did not and still does not share. She would glance at Clunky's flank in dismay before a car trip but remain silent about the affront to her aesthetic values out of respect for the patriarch, who had priority when it came to all things out-of-doors, a border that began with the garage (paradoxically, since it technically constitutes a kind of indoors), the car it sheltered, the many tools hanging from its walls, and emanated outward to the road and the mailbox in the direction of town and beyond. The single exception to the outdoor rule were the flower beds of marigolds, zinnias, and roses that hugged the side of the house and belonged exclusively to our mother.

As a child, I thought the entire world was organized in this fashion, with mothers mostly inside and fathers mostly outside, but I was never quite sure how I fit into that scheme of things or how my sister, Kari, born two years after me, fit into it either because Kari was a cartwheeling, fence-hopping, tree-climbing, horse-loving girl who, when it was necessary, could defend the family honor. I can still see Daryl Stankey's face as he pushed himself onto his elbows and stared up at us from the gravel of Old Dutch Road where Kari's punch had landed him. I can see his grubby cheeks striped clean by tears and the pale green blob of snot just below his left nostril. I was so proud. Although all the credit belongs to my sister, the image of the defeated, blubbering Daryl inspires me to this day. It inspires me as much as Shandy's digressions, as much as Marilyn Monroe, as much as the mordant prose of the seventeenth-century philosopher Anne Conway, whom I have been reading lately. Kari's fist met Daryl's chin because he had called our physician father "a quack."

In my memory, those days of paternal whistling are warm, not cold, and the car windows are rolled all the way down, and the wind rushes in on me and Kari, and I allow only my nose to cross the threshold, careful not to "stick my head out," knowing it could end in decapitation. I repeatedly imagined losing my head to a speeding truck coming in the opposite direction. I would watch my head fly onto the road after it had parted company with my neck, now a bloody stump attached to a pathetic little girl's body fallen over onto the backseat never to stir again, and the anguished pity I felt for Kari and my father and my mother who were left with the dead me in two ghoulish parts caused spasms in my stomach and a feeling of faintness and nausea so intense I would have to lean forward in the seat, close my eyes, and breathe deeply to recover. The drafty delights of being blown like crazy at sixty miles an hour competed with my imagination, which raced ahead of me into possible horrors. I firmly controlled my urge for momentary gratification—my head stayed in the car. Over my fantasies, on the other hand, I exercised little or no governance.

It would be false to say that I was reminded of my father as I sat at my desk on 109th Street smoking cigarettes and trying to write my Quixotic story. I have no memory of thinking of my father then, and I wrote very little about either of my parents in the journal. The whistling connection between the first man in my life and my invisible neighbor occurs to me only now. My father has been dead for twelve years, but in 1978 he was still vigorous, still practicing medicine, still disgusted by Republicans. His whistling was welcome because my father was subject to what his aunt Irma called "black moods," during which he seemed to disappear. At these regular junctures he neither saw nor heard any of us. It seemed to me that he roiled with unspoken torments and that they might blast out of him, that my father might spew lava, but he never did.

Exactly what he thought about the daughter who had left home on a literary mission remains his secret and is buried with him, along with countless other secrets, in the cemetery of St. Paul's Church in Webster, but I suspect that he disapproved of my writing year without ever uttering a word about it. The son of a country doctor who had gone from house to house by car in summer and by horse and sleigh in winter when the roads were blocked by snow, my father had clung tightly to rural truths, as opposed to urban truths, to the idea of neighborliness without fences, to Depression-style frugality and a suspicion of wealth, to farmers and workers (and the occasional doctor) in cahoots to build a better world, more socialist than capitalist, to collective labor of all kinds, including family weeding of the vegetable garden, and to an eternal idea of a useful life. Art for art's sake made no sense to my father.

Lucy Brite was partial to whistling Irish ballads, which are usually sad, some of which I recognized. "The Wind That Shakes the Barley" was one. Her songs drooled with melodic sentimentality and, despite the absence of lyrics, made me think of bonny lads and drowned darlings and missed assignations and winding roads in that greenest of green countries that were never taken or taken but reached a dead end in noble rebellion and tragedy because when the young die, whether to lost love or political turmoil, it is awful, and these unspoken, but melancholic subjects augmented the ache just beneath my rib cage I carried around with me everywhere, although I never knew what had caused it—a physical reminder of my vulnerability and never-ending guilt, I suppose, a physically implanted token of innumerable nameless hurts inflicted on me in the past and which I had inflicted on others, hurts that would surely return in the future. There is a false idea abroad in the West that the human being is an isolate who decides on his or her path and presses forward alone. In fact, we are always somewhere and that somewhere is always in us. Listening to Lucy's repetition of "I'm sad" over and over was bad enough, but listening to music, even the thin clear sounds of a whistler, goes deeper. Music penetrates skin and muscle and finally settles in the bones. It can sway a mood from optimism to gloom and nudge a thought from airy contemplation to hip-jiggling, sweaty lust. In this, music is like the weather—sunlight buoys the soul, and days of rain beleaguer it with gathering thoughts of dejection. When it comes to music, human beings are helpless, rocked and rolled and lifted up and pressed down and turned around in dizzy confusion. It all depends on the melody.

If Lucy Brite had, in fact, been someone else and had selected less mournful songs to whistle, I might not have been overcome by feelings that bled into Feathers' story and the vivid dreams that began to muddle his logic. I wasn't sure where in the story the dream would go, but I composed it for him anyway and put it in the notebook.

Ian Feathers opens a door in his dream and finds himself in Frieda Frail's bedroom at night. How he knows this room belongs to the dead woman is the dream's secret. He does know it, however, and he surveys the room with the cold detachment of an experienced detective and searches for clues. The single bed, the night table, the lamp, and the rag rug on the floor are imbued with a quality that disturbs him. "Too perfect," he thinks. They have the unreal smoothness of a picture of a room in an advertisement. Ian walks to the window to look outside at the lawn and the sidewalk and notices a key lying on the sill. As he looks at it, the key shudders slightly, as if it is alive. He slaps his hand over it, feels a tremor under his palm, but closes his fist tightly around it. When he turns around, he discovers a door that had not been there earlier, opens it with the living key, and sees a girl with a cardboard sign on her back that says I.F.F. The sign confuses him, and from it he suddenly understands that he has committed a crime and is seized by a terrible sense of guilt. But what crime? What have I done? he thinks. The girl leaps up a staircase four steps at a time, and with each flying hop her dress blows over her head, and he glimpses her naked body beneath. He has an erection. The dream becomes a wet dream, and Ian Feathers wakes up.

Lucy didn't pipe "lone lorn" ballads every day. Thank God. On the evening of September 6, her "I'm sads" were interrupted by a sudden outburst I recorded in the composition book as I stood at the wall. She seemed to be talking to someone in a loud, angry growl, and I wondered if she might be on the phone, but when she had finished her brief accusation, I did not hear her put down a receiver. "You thought you had the right, the right, the right to hurt me. You thought I was your bitch to kick. I thought so, too. I didn't say a word. It's back at night. You're back. It happens again. I can't breathe! And Lindy's dead. The window. I see the fall." I do not need the notebook to remember what I heard or felt. My body stiffened against the wall. And then Lucy said in a loud, emphatic voice, "Are you listening?" I jumped away from my post. I was listening, and, as her listener, the sentence coursed through me as if it were an electric shock.

CHAPTER TWO

The young woman who whiled away her late afternoons at the Hungarian Pastry Shop in early September of 1978 did not go there only to escape the confines of her small, dimly lit apartment or her chanting neighbor or to plan the rest of her novel or to try to make sense of Edmund Husserl, whose mysterious sentences in *Logical Investigations* she read over and over again. She went to the Hungarian Pastry Shop and seated herself at a table she regarded as well situated because it had a clear view of the door and every person who entered or left the establishment. From that felicitous spot, she could easily glance up from her coffee and her book and take note of any and all interesting strangers. She whiled and idled and was known to waste her money on cappuccinos and croissants because she lived in a state of perpetual suspense. She, like her hero, Feathers, spent much of her time in the subjunctive tense, projecting herself into "as if" cases and the innumerable illustrious possibilities that awaited her: charming company at the least, torrid passion at the most.

In this respect, we differ, my former self and I. It was impossible for me to know at twenty-three that the dreadful phrase "life is short" has meaning, that at sixty-one I know there is far less ahead of me than behind me, and that while she wasn't terribly curious about herself as herself, I have become curious about her as an incarnation of hopes and errors that had or seem to have had a determining effect on what I am now. While she was intent on rushing ahead on that imaginary timeline, the one that moves from left to right on the page and chronicles the evolution of organisms over millennia or Roman emperors or the life of Napoleon (as if time were space and not something wholly ineffable, an invisible motion so enigmatic that to think hard about it means to lose it altogether), I am interested in understanding how she and I are relatives, which means turning around and following the timeline in the other direction because I can't imagine time without spatial metaphors—without backward and forward, without roads behind me and ahead of me, as if I am walking through it—but then my space has only three grubby Euclidian dimensions. Time, the physicists tell us, is the fourth. In our plain old human world, the young woman who lifts her eyes when she hears the door open at the Hungarian Pastry Shop in September 1978 becomes the aging woman who sits here now in September 2016 in her study in a house in Brooklyn and types the sentence you are reading in your own present, one I cannot identify. But over there in Minkowski spacetime, the still girlish "I" and the much older "I" coexist, and in that startling 4D reality, the two of us can theoretically find each other and shake hands or converse together because in the block-universe time doesn't flow or dribble or leak, and it makes no difference whether you travel into the past or into the future. My husband, Walter, tells me the mathematics work out beautifully. And when he explains it to me, as he has many times, I say to him: The idea is that the motion of time is a cellular delusion? What is memory if my earlier self is still out there somewhere unchanged? And then he likes to mention the story Rudolph Carnap reported about Albert Einstein in his memoir: "The problem of Now worried Einstein seriously. He explained that the experience of the Now means something special for men, something different from the past and future, but that this important difference does not and cannot occur in physics." And Walter finishes off this famous anecdote by noting that Carnap had little sympathy for Einstein's anxiety because he was a hard-assed logical positivist of the Vienna Circle and Einstein's concern for human feeling mystified him. And I always say to Walter, but that meaningful *now* is nothing. It is as elusive as *was* and *will be*, and there is much to be gained from thinking beyond mathematics, and he agrees because he isn't a hard-ass, and the problem of time is not resolved and that is just one of the reasons why I remain so fond of my husband after all these years.

But the frozen block of Walter and his physicist cohorts is rather like a library, is it not? Karl Popper's World 3 out there for all of us. In it we can leap from *after* to *before* at will. If I choose, I can remove Plato's *Apology* from the shelf or pluck up the Baroness Elsa von Freytag-Loringhoven's poems, now printed in a beautiful edition, and, if I devise an eccentric system for my library, the two might be neighbors. Socrates explained himself in 399 B.C. and then he killed himself, as everyone knows, but only a very few know even now that the Baroness referred often to suicide in her writings and that she came from a family of suicides and that, tired and poor, she may have killed herself with a newly bought gas stove in her cold Paris flat in 1927. Therefore in my library Plato's Socrates can kiss the Baroness with the hemlock still on his lips because time is not a problem in the library, despite the fact that the ugly sage preferred boys and would, no doubt, have regarded the Baroness as a monster. Temporal coexistence is true of every single book as well. You can hop to page 137 and then back to page 7 twenty times over, but the story or the argument is fixed, determined from first word to last. And in this particular book, the book you are reading now, the young person and the old person live side by side in the precarious truths of memory. Here

"THE PROBLEM OF NOW WORRIED EINSTEIN SERIOUSLY."

I am free to dance over decades in the small white space between paragraphs or linger over one bright minute in my life for page after page or toy with tenses that point backward or forward. I am free to follow the earlier self with interruptions from the later self because the old lady has perspective the young person cannot have. I meet myself on the page, then, on the pages she wrote years ago and the ones I am writing now. A young woman sits in the Hungarian Pastry Shop on Amsterdam Avenue at 111th Street and raises her eyes from her book when she hears the door open and they fall on a handsome stranger as he walks through the door. My guess is that any onlooker, if she or he had bothered to glance even for an instant at the young woman's face, would have seen hope in her expression.

September 10, 1978

Dear Page,

Hungarian Pastry Shop today, 4:15: Grinning young man with short, neat beard comes in and gets a coffee. Sits down at table next to me, gives me a significant nod and smile. I feel a constriction in my breathing, that pleasurable tightness of possibility. Good-looking, brown hair, slender, slightly freckled straight nose with delicate nostrils that flare to reveal pale pink interior. Smallest overlap of two front teeth—a fetching flaw. He begins. Names exchanged. Aaron, Aaron Blinderman. My turn. That's an unusual name, he says. What is it? Norwegian, I say. Oh, Norwegian, he says. Brief explanation by me of immigrant history on both sides out there on the Minnesota prairie. Aaron seems pleased by my Nordic roots and launches into description of his anthropology thesis. Good start. I am interested in everything. Aaron is immersed in the Hua of New Guinea. I know nothing of the Hua and say so. My ignorance pleases him, although I can't say why. His head bobs. He smiles. I can see his chest expand. Aaron takes some time setting the Melanesian stage—living arrangements, food, and tools. I am bored. I am not entirely ignorant of anthropology. I have read Lévi-Strauss. Then he speaks of something called Nu, a dynamic traveling force among the people, a kind of life principle. This idea enlivens me. I ask questions. He uses his index finger to answer and make his points, shaking it at me. The finger is rarely still. I don't like the finger. He tells me that in Hua culture, women are pollutants, to which I say, "Oh." He is lecturing me now, and I notice he cannot keep his eyes on my face, despite the insistent finger. Hua women are semen stealers. They sap men's strength. With each drop of the precious fluid the women grow stronger, more vital, more dangerous. Hua men strenuously battle the urge for sex because it will drain the life out of them. They have to hoard their goo just to stay alive. Aaron is adamant my breasts should know about this all-important sex-death connection. I begin to say something, but he continues. I think Aaron may want to smother himself to death between my very own tits, which is probably not a Hua practice. I cannot say, Please look up at my face, Aaron. He probably doesn't even know he is speaking to my boobs. I am patient, but after a bit more of the Hua hooey, I feel pressure in my chest, a suffocating discomfort so strong I have to flee. I tell him I have an appointment and must run. It was so nice talking to you, so interesting, good luck, yada, yada, yada. I begin to stand up, and Aaron reaches across from his table and grabs my wrist. He hisses, "You're beautiful, do you know that? Really beautiful."

I recall that my cheeks felt hot, and I stuttered, but now only a few hours later, I'm not sure what I said to him. He loosened his fingers from my arm, looked up at me with a pleading face, and I felt bad—that little tug beneath my ribs. I thanked him again for the conversation. I smiled. At the door I gave him a wave. I could see the disappointment in his face and it pierced me. I had been kind, but I felt as if I had been mean. I felt bruised—guilty, ashamed, humiliated—as if those various feelings were not distinct as they should have been but had merged into an amorphous blob in my upper gut. I stood on the hot street and wondered if in an hour or so Aaron might not have improved. Maybe it would have been better to listen a little longer to stories about the Hua just for his company. I am pining for a real conversation. And here's the truth: If he had kept his mouth shut and his eyes straight ahead, I might have jumped in bed with him just because of those adorable teeth.

The bad feeling stuck inside me, and I decided to walk it off. I went over to Broadway and headed downtown, feeling hungry, not for food, but for something else, someone close, someone I already knew and loved. Aaron and the Hua had made me feel much lonelier, and I recited the poem by the Bad Baroness I had discovered in the archive:

And God spoke kindly to mine heart—
So kindly spoke he to mine heart—
He said: "Thou art allowed to fart!"
So kindly spoke he to mine heart.

And I smiled and walked and talked to myself: *The Narration of Perambulation*. (I thought of that as a title for something.) Words and phrases surfaced and retreated, and within a block or two I was telling Kari all about Blinderman and making him funnier than he was for her, and then thoughts of my mother arrived, no, not thoughts. I felt her hand on my shoulder and the sympathetic pat of her hand. The words "Mama, I'm afraid" rose up, and I shook them off. But my fellow pedestrians began to undulate in liquid, and I decided not to go back to the apartment. I knew my head would explode if I read more today. To hell with Husserl! I decided I would not go back to the apartment and read, and I would not sit in another café and read, and as I walked fast and kept time with the hard, even beat of my feet on the cement, I realized my thoughts had hovered onto Lucy Brite and from Lucy Brite to Lindy's fall and Lindy's death, to that fragment of a story I had heard through the wall. I tried to supplant Lucy and Lindy with Ian and Isadora, but it didn't work and instead I saw a window and a man push a girl out of it, and I watched her fall to the ground and land in an empty space between two buildings—a no-man's-land with a few weeds on the parched, untended ground struggling feebly upward in the direction of the thin sunlight—and the more I walked, the more I saw, and time moved backward so the story could begin earlier.

For some reason, the room where the terrible thing takes place is bare. It has no furniture. A tall man with thinning dark hair and a flushed angry face shoves a small girl in overalls against the wall. She cries out and another girl, somewhat older—she has long braids—comes running, and she throws her arms around the man's waist to pull him away from the younger girl, and there is a struggle. The girl in braids bites the man's arm and leaves vivid teeth marks, after which his blood begins to run from each sharp indentation on his skin and down his hand in brilliant red lines. The children are screaming. The man picks up the younger girl to restrain her, but she escapes his grip, runs to the window, and he pushes her out. Her body lies two floors beneath them. One of her arms is twisted in the wrong direction and her thin legs in the striped overalls are splayed out. The sight made me wince as I walked, but I kept walking and, as I kept walking, I understood that I had imagined the murder in the front room of my apartment, the one with no furniture, and that I had seen the little girl's body lying in the small, ugly patch of land between my building and the one next door. I tried to expel the fantasy.

If I hadn't found the Thalia movie theater, everything would have been different, but when I hit Ninety-Fifth Street, I saw its marquee and the name of an old movie, *Cluny Brown*, directed by Ernst Lubitsch, and I went in and bought a ticket, and the movie took me right up and out of myself and away from the sadness and the terrible merged feelings and from Aaron Blinderman and Lucy Brite and the dead Lindy, who seemed to have become Lucy's sister. I sat next to an older woman with an enormous plastic shopping bag on her lap. When we walked out of the theater, I noticed her hard red curls had white roots and she was dressed entirely in purple. She even wore a watch with a violet band. A real character, Aunt Irma would have said. But while we sat there together watching the immense people on the screen, we laughed at the same time and we were quiet at the same time, and I felt that the purple lady and I were friends in the near dark of the cinema. I smiled at her afterward but she gave me a hard, unfriendly look in return. For an instant, I felt pained, but that twinge had no more resonance than a single guitar string after it has been plucked. I left the theater and trotted home reinvigorated for my on-my-own-all-alone battle, and I made myself chicken livers with onions for protein, 39 cents a pound, and I drank two big glasses of milk. I am now writing to you about my strange day with cotton balls in my ears, but I can still hear you-know-who through the wall, and I'm still titillated and disturbed, and I hope she doesn't chant too loudly or scream in the middle of the night.

Good night, my dear P. Libellus.

S.

I only vaguely remember Blinderman. I certainly couldn't describe him from memory, and I couldn't have reported on his wagging finger or his lecture on the Hua's misogyny. I trust the notebook for those details. What I have not forgotten about that day are the distress and confusion I experienced after I left the anthropology student, my tormented walk down Broadway, and the movie I saw at the Thalia that made me feel much better. I also remember the purple woman vividly, although I have no explanation for why she made a lasting impression. The unappetizing dinner I seemed to enjoy of chicken livers and a quart of milk has gone the way of Wanda. But I can say this: Although I don't remember young Aaron Blinderman with any precision, he was one of many, and the many have been conflated in my mind to become one, one sort of man I encountered again and again, a man, younger or older, whose eyes continually strayed from my face to parts below, a man who talked and talked and talked and asked me no questions, a helpful, smiling, knowing man who for reasons that baffled me seemed to believe I was incompetent in all matters large and small, a man who, by the end of the evening, when I had risked dinner in my irrepressible hope for company and perhaps love, was all hands and saliva and urgent needs and who now and again had to be forcibly pushed away. He, that reduction of many men into one man, inevitably looked betrayed and puzzled or betrayed and miffed as he stood on the street or outside the door to my apartment, or sat beside me in a taxi, or had squeezed against me in a corner of a night-club as the strobe lights flashed above us.

Surely, if that plural man remembers me at all, he remembers as I remember, not me but my type, a tall blonde whose face he can no longer decipher. And if he remembers a person, it is unlikely he will recall what attracted him to me beyond my type. I, too, have become an absence or a blur in the mind of that multiple man—one of many comely young women who shut the door in his face.

Sometimes memory is a knife.

As I read through the pages of my old notebook in the guest room of the retirement complex after a day of garbage bags and boxes and the screech of packing tape and chortling with Kari over our early drawings we scrutinized for identifying characteristics—"it's yours, I know it's yours. I never drew dog noses like that"—there were moments when I had to place the notebook facedown on the night table beside me and stare at the dresser with its paneled veneer that had been made to look like oak but wasn't oak and at the wax apples in a bowl that sat on top of it to collect myself. When I reached the words "Aaron reaches across from his table and grabs my wrist," I began to tremble. I do not mean this figuratively. My hands shook as I read. What made that asshole think he had the right to seize my wrist? And I, or she (easier to say she), why did she protect the oh-so-delicate feelings of someone whose hectoring ways and pointed descriptions of the practices of that New Guinea tribe already counted as hostile acts? Rather than yank her wrist away from that pompous nincompoop and bark at him, she runs out the door and, once on the street, cannot comprehend why she feels wounded.

Nudge it—
Kick it—
Prod it—
Push it—

The Baroness wrote those lines in a poem called "A Dozen Cocktails, Please." And as I lay there in the guest room of the retirement center, I nudged, kicked, prodded, and pushed Aaron Blinderman into the back wall of the Hungarian Pastry Shop, and I waggled my finger at him and stuck out my tongue and farted for good measure and roared into his amazed face that he should keep his goddamned hands off me without my express permission, and the rebellious fantasy relieved me. We are all wishful creatures, and we wish backward, too, not only forward, and thereby rebuild the curious, crumbling architecture of memory into structures that are more habitable. I know I never backed young Blinderman against the wall, but I also know I have countless memories that must be wrong, memories I have dressed up with wishes. Kari remembers differently from me or she remembers and I forget or I remember and she forgets. She is certain she saved our turtle, Dinky, from the jaws of the Harringtons' sheepdog, Laurence, and I am certain I held the dog's mouth as he slavered over my hands and I plucked Dinky from his jaws. It is indisputably true that although each of us wished to have been the agent of that daring exploit, only one of us was the hero, and in the annals of our childhood, it is also true that the hero was usually Kari, not me.

Lucy didn't stop talking. I bought a radio for music, but when she began her "I'm sads," I turned it off, and I listened. I had mentioned my tender feeling for the stethoscope in a letter to my parents, and my mother sent it to me in a small package with a note:

> *My Dearest Darling,*
>
> *I am glad you are doing so well. Your father smiled when he read about the stethoscope. We still have tomatoes and squash, and I am picking the late raspberries. Yesterday I had coffee with Rosemary Petersen, who sends her best to you. Ellen is in law school. When I took my walk yesterday, I felt the change in the air, the fall snap. The season changes so fast these days—winter will be here in a blink. I brought home a bouquet of long grasses and arranged them in one of Lila Hernke's ceramic pots. They look lovely.*
>
> *Be careful. I love you. Mama*

The stethoscope amplified every sound. It was as if I were a blind woman inside Lucy Brite's apartment. I heard my neighbor breathe and sigh and walk across the room. I listened to her whistling, her brief ejaculations, her monologues, and sometimes to her TV when she watched it, reruns of *Kojak* mostly. I would settle myself on the floor with a pillow for my head, a blanket underneath me to cushion the oak, and the stethoscope plugged into my ears. I had both my notebook and Smollett's *The Adventures of Peregrine Pickle*, the novel I was reading in the evening for entertainment and inspiration, but when Lucy began to speak, I would fling Pickle to the side and plant the chest piece against the wall with an eagerness that embarrassed me. If someone had seen what I was doing, I would have been more than embarrassed, I would have been ashamed, but my secret act of auditory spying—an oxymoron that nevertheless fits the behavior—brought me a voluptuous pleasure I had never known before and which I have never forgotten. Over the years, I have tried to pick apart my motives and analyze the almost erotic feeling that accompanied my eavesdropping (a word from the Old Norse, *ups* for "eaves" and *dropi* for "drop." Water drips from the eaves of a house, and over time transmutes into words picked up by a clandestine listener.) My neighbor dribbled drops of a larger story, a frightening story I wanted to know, but more than that, on hindsight I believe my listening had an aggressive quality I failed to understand at the time. I crossed a threshold and entered Lucy Brite's rooms by ear alone, and this unseemly invasion excited me.

Sometimes Lucy spoke directly to a "you." He had a name, Ted. He was the one who had felt he had the right to treat her badly—"your bitch to kick"—and sometimes she moaned or gasped out little fragments of her past or what I guessed were childhood stories. But sometimes her "you" was herself, it seemed. She also changed her voice. It fell deep and rose high, as if she were embodying different people as they spoke. I recorded all of them to the best of my ability, but I wished I knew shorthand, the mysterious dashes and squiggles I had seen Mrs. Stydnicki use in my father's office. I devised my own system of abbreviation so I could write fast. I left out articles and prepositions and filled them in later. My handwriting was slovenly. When her voice fell so low that I couldn't hear her, I used ellipses. Years after the notebook disappeared, I began to long to see those entries again. Although I remembered their gist, I had lost memory of their exact content.

September 11, 1978

For Page Libellus: A Lucy Brite Monologue:

Wedding . . . wedding, oh my God. [Laugh.] He was in me then. You didn't want it. You said it. It, it, it, well, it was an IT. Mistake! Wrong! Bad Seed! Big Dealmaker. Real Estate Paradise. The thing had to be hidden. Appearances matter. You bet they matter. You kept stopping the car to make a call, get gas. You turned around twice. The big visit to your parents. Your dad was an ass, Ted. Do you know that? And your mom, poor Barb in that awful blue dress with the corsage and her skinny legs and pinched little wrinkled face and so sad in that house with all the doilies. The woman never smiled. I'm sad. I'm sad. I'm sad now. Good Mom was dead, so she didn't have to see it all. No optimism. That's what she would have said. Look on the sunny side of life, Barb. Dad . . . his legs . . . like a shell-shock victim in that crummy suit. Barb Brite made me sick, too. You didn't know that, Ted, did you? I was so nice to her. All right. I was sweet to everybody, for God's sake. Get me a drink, Barb [deep voice]. Holy Christ. And she runs to the bar like a dog fetching a stick. You were a chip, his chip, chippy. Luce [deep voice], it's a mess around here. What are you doing with yourself all day? Luce this and Luce that. You pulled out the goddamned vacuum cleaner? We have a maid! What do you do? Throw dirt around after she leaves? You said I trapped you. There were nights you loved me, though. Oh, you loved me, couldn't get enough of me, could you? I'd wake up and there you were on top of me, gnawing at my tits. The doctor said to lie in bed so it doesn't come. But your son came. Ugly baby . . . Incubated [shrieking voice]. Why didn't I hate you then? No, I loved you. I did. Be honest. Be honest. I was trapped. You had it backwards. The club. The golf. Shoes. Golf shoes. Where are my golf shoes? Slamming doors. Fits. He cried and cried. You know what I think, Ted? I think you warped him before he was even born. You shriveled little Ted's character into a prune. All the yelling and screaming. You blamed me. The bad mother. Put it in writing. I do my best. I do my best. [Crying.] He hated Lindy. [She whistles "Ring Around the Rosy."] You scared her. No one knew but us. We were the insiders. You were so smooth, so neat, and that laugh you saved for the boys, that sick laugh. Big man. Big Bad Wolf. [Again the whistling: Ring around the rosy / Pocket full of posy / Ashes, ashes, we all fall down.] You didn't like my volunteering. You didn't even like my book club. You don't read the books, Luce. You pretend to read them. That's what you said to me. You were mean, Ted. Why were you so mean? [squeaking voice]. Then you would get all sorry. Honey, honey, honey. [Silence for a long minute.] After my baby fell—

our beautiful girl dead, dead in the courtyard—you didn't come to see me in the hospital. Yes, once. Pull yourself together, Lucy, [deep voice]. I think you were already with her. Her! You were fucking her in our bed. Twenty-five years, and I signed away everything 'cause I was tired, Ted. Lindy died, and I didn't give a crap anymore. You took advantage. I had to take the pills. No pills. No Lucy. I had the doctors. You had the lawyers. And you're right across town with that slut and those goddamned kids. [More whistling "Ring Around the Rosy."]

September 12, 1978

For Libellus: Another Lucy Brite Monologue:

I'm sad. I'm sad [about a hundred times]. I'm not going to talk to you anymore. Shut up! I'm hungry. [Footsteps, rustling, unidentifiable noises, sighs, whistling ballad.] Mom was grouchy. Don't make that noise, Lucy. It hurts my head. Well, she was sick, for heaven's sake. You have a future. You're so pretty, Lucy. [Laughs.] Such a nice figure. You have a future. Who was that boy? Lucy, can I touch your hair? I want to touch your hair. Wasn't it nice back then? Dancing days. Think about that. The movies. Lana Turner in a white turban. You had one and wore it with passion-red lipstick. Just a kid. I was just a kid. It was swell, baby, swell. [Silence.]

Don't go over there. Don't go [tough low voice].

Why can't you stay out of the kitchen? [Pause.] She screamed, that's why. Falling. [Pause.] His face. No. Shocked. [Pause.] He could have grabbed her. Say it. I can't say it. Running. The elevator. I have to say it. I have to say it. Look. Don't look. It was an accident. No, Lucy, you think you know. But what do you know? [in deep drawled-out voice]. Dr. Stone, I don't know [high false girlish voice]. If you talk about it, Lucy . . . [deep again]. [Laughter.] I'm talking about it now, you old coot! [Silence for twelve seconds.] She was afraid of her own son. There. There, I said it. There, there, now. Don't cry. I'm not crying.

I don't know anything. [Coughing fit, mumbling, the sound of steps, the click of the TV. Sound of siren on TV.]

P.S. A cockroach the size of Gregor Samsa just ran across the floor.

September 13, 1978

Dear Page,

I'm trying to think more Isadora, less Lucy Brite. What happened to Lindy? Last night I was afraid the bug would come back. Stupid. I lay awake worrying about bugs, money (it will never last), Lindy, and the police report. How old was Lindy when she died? "She is afraid of her own son." Is Lucy afraid of her own son or is it someone else's son? I take refuge in the town of Verbum.

Chapter 2

Ian met Isadora in biology class over a piglet they were destined to dissect together. It was Isadora's steely temperament that impressed him, her steady eye and the precision of her hand as she sliced open the porcine corpse on the table. He admired the way she kept the instruments between them—clean and in the prescribed order—and he liked the way her eyes narrowed when she gently cut skin and muscle to reveal an organ beneath. Although he did his best to hide his feelings from Isadora, Ian preferred the cleanliness of mathematics and astronomy to the muck and slime of biology. His first sight of the animal's intestine made him gag, and he had moments of nausea throughout the semester. He much preferred the conversations he had with his friend when the ever-dwindling piglet was no longer in view. Isadora had no such qualms. She was a passionate investigator and explicator of the anatomical systems she listed in alphabetical order: blood, cardiovascular, digestive, endocrine, integumentary, lymphatic, muscular, nervous, reproductive, respiratory, skeletal, and urinary. Ian began to feel certain that when Isadora's expertise on the highways and byways of the mortal body was coupled with his own refined logical skills, together they could solve even the most puzzling murder. That murder had not yet happened, of course, but Isadora was astute on Frieda Frail's epilepsy, and Ian hoped she might be able to shed scientific light on the problem of the dead woman's regular visitations. Could they be caused by a virus roaming about Verbum that brought with it hallucinations of the dead?

Ian's growing affection for Isadora was enhanced by his admiration for her whole family. He basked in the oddities of the Simon household, so different from his own. The Simons, husband and wife, were both English professors, of Chaucer and Milton respectively, and a good deal of quoting went on upstairs and downstairs from *The Canterbury Tales* in Middle English, which to Ian sounded a lot like growling and chewing ("The droghte of March hath perced to the roote"), and from *Paradise Lost*, a work that exercised the throat less and the lips and teeth more (with mighty wings outspread / Dove-like satst brooding on the vast abyss"). The two scholars had spawned four daughters and nurtured them in an atmosphere of Chaucerian and Miltonic declamation without noticeable damage to a single one of them. Professor (Mr.) Simon was an especially affectionate parent and regularly sang out from his study: "Where, oh where, are the darling Doras?" He extended the "dah" in "darling" for two to three seconds and then followed it with a lower-pitched "ing," after which he would rise up in a climactic "dohr" to fall again in a final long "ah" as he summoned his offspring.

The father's shorthand was made possible by the fact that Isadora was the oldest of four Doras: Isadora, 14, Theodora, 12, Andora, 11, and just plain Dora, 9. They had organized their sisterhood by discipline: Isabiology, Theophysics, Anhistory, and Doralit. Although little Dora had been stuck on *Alice's Adventures in Wonderland* for quite some time, hopes in the family ran high for her thesis on *Finnegans Wake*. Professor S. (Mrs.) had pushed out her girls over the course of six years without it dampening her excessive love for the blind poet, but Ian noticed that unlike his own mother, the Simon matriarch had a casual attitude toward housekeeping, made evident by her habit of kicking various playthings under sofas and chairs and throwing damp towels that had somehow found their way into the living room into the coat closet. She was also prone to ordering around the Chaucer specialist in a way he found surprising. "Percy," Professor S. (Mrs.) would say, "dishes!" Or "Percy, the floor!" Although these curt directives were clearly intended to move Professor S. (Mr.) to take action in domestic trouble spots, their effects were less than successful. For example, if the wife said, "Percy, cushions!" the husband would freeze at the sound of her voice, nod his head sagely, as if he were listening to the pronouncement of an oracle, and then hurry off in one direction or another, only to reappear a moment later with a book in his hand or a parakeet on his shoulder.

The family had an immense Old English sheepdog, Monk, who produced masses of saliva and lumbered about the house shaking his great wooly head, but Mr. Simon also kept rabbits and birds and white rats in large cages in the living room, who were often on the loose, either by design or by accident, which meant caution had to be exercised when traveling from wall to wall. The Doras further claimed that their father housed an alligator named Geoffrey in the basement, a reptile Ian wasn't sure he believed in, although he did notice the girls scrupulously avoided the door that led to the damp murky region where Geoffrey supposedly lived.

The lover of the Canterbury pilgrims had driven a tank during the war in Europe, and Isadora confided to Ian that the rigors of the experience had jolted his brain, which caused her father to "float outside of himself" from time to time. The family policy was to ignore the occasional excursions Mr. Simon took beyond the confines of his corporeal boundaries. It was only "when he went too far," when he headed down the block with a confused expression on his face or hid under a bed, that one Dora or another would retrieve him and lead him back to his study, where he usually fell peacefully back to work on the thing the girls referred to as his "opus." "He is perfect on Chaucer, you know," Isadora told Ian. "You put him in front of a class and it just rolls out of him."

Mr. S's hair had turned prematurely white, and he wore it fluffed and ruffled and ragged, a hairstyle Ian admired and began to imitate, to his mother's mortification. "Do you want to look like an inmate from an insane asylum?" she asked him. Ian blushed, but his mother's rhetorical question prompted him to ponder his motives. Perhaps, despite his love of logic, a part of him did want to resemble a mad poet or even an innocuous lunatic. Hadn't Holmes injected cocaine and played the violin between cases? Didn't severity in one thing call for lassitude in another?

And then, one afternoon, Ian found himself rocking in the rocking chair Theodora had decorated with the periodic table. He surveyed the wonderland that was the Simons' living room and inhaled the strong smell of bird and beast that pervaded the air, and just as his eyes fell on the pretty breasts of the oldest Dora, who was his own particular friend, breasts that seemed to grow larger every day, Roger, the Simons' cockatoo, squawked out three immortal words the bird loved to repeat, three words Ian had been told appeared somewhere in the *Tales:* "thy stubbel goos!" At that very same moment, Just Plain Dora rushed into the room, panting and red-faced, to declare to anyone who would listen that she had seen the ghost in the window with her own eyes, that it wasn't a lie, and they had to listen to her. Either Frieda Frail was still alive or ghosts were real!

I remember the Simons and the pleasure I took in their company, but the story on the other side of the wall had crawled inside me to become a kind of parallel, if disjointed, narrative to the story of the still untitled novel I was writing. Lucy's whistling rendition of "Ring Around the Rosy" had particularly upset me. The stupid little song brought back my own bewildering days on the grade-school playground in Webster, but as feeling only—a kind of muddy, pained confusion that vaguely summoned gravel, tar, sunlight through clouds, singsong voices, and the mob Kari and I referred to as "the other kids." I was closer to my childhood then, but I thought about it less. Now it returns to me often in what my mother calls "snippets," not stories at all, but sensual fragments—holding up the barbed wire so Kari can slide beneath the fence, my own view of the sky when she does the same for me, squatting with a stick to prod the cow pies so desiccated in midsummer they had turned to powder and in time would disappear in the winds, the swollen creek noisy in the spring, and my hands, red from cold, as they grasped the loose gray bark of the fallen tree trunk that served as our bridge to the other side, and the culvert that ran beneath Old Dutch Road with its curved ribbed metal walls we scaled partway up, a foot wobbling on one metal rivet and then the next, the echoes we could make inside the tube as we called out each other's names or the names of the characters we were playing, and the magic in our games that leaked into the brambles and grasses and pebbles beneath the running water. I remember the powers of telekinesis I had in my dreams as I lifted a fork from the table and directed it to fly out the window and the joy I felt in my power, and I remember my waking awe, too, when I went to sit on the throne behind the house. The oak's roots that protruded from the steep cliff behind the house curled to make a royal seat, where a potentate could sit and survey her kingdom and lose herself in reverie and let her thoughts sail toward the inexpressible and the sacred, and then I wasn't "I" any longer but a creature disseminated into the sound of leaves moving above and the moist odor of creek soil and the sodden decaying branches and the points of sunlight that jumped in the snake grass. That transcendent being had a head as weightless as a helium balloon and was lifted up, up, up into clouds with ignited sparklers in them. But the strange trips I took out of myself remained secret. I kept them in a special pocket beneath my ribs, one only God and the angels could see.

But I had fears, too. Perhaps my flights and my terrors were linked. I knew a thing hovered at the bottom of the stairs, was certain of it because I felt it, a hard, malevolent presence that wanted me dead. And so, as I stood at the top, I would scold myself in a maternal voice, count to ten or to twenty, depending on the degree of my fortitude, and, holding myself strictly to the vow, I would stop breathing, rush down the stairs, and leap over the last three steps, as if that hop would prevent him from striking—yes, it was he, I remember now. It was a he.

On September 14, I wrote, "The horrible tune is in my head and it makes me feel itchy and crazy, as if I want to remember something but can't. Today the last lines, 'Ashes, ashes, we all fall down,' made me think of dead children lying between the slide and the swings. How grotesque. I play the radio to get it out of me, but it comes back. Hit the foam twice today." Maybe the child and the young woman were not so far apart.

I had never set eyes on Lucy Brite, and this surely made her far more mysterious than if I had first run into her on Riverside Drive or met her in the library. The woman was literally all talk. Further, although I had friends elsewhere, I was still friendless in New York, which meant all my distractions from the lady next door, my books and my novel, were also bodiless. I wanted to see the woman who railed at Ted and mourned for Lindy, so I kept an eye out, and, finally on the afternoon of September 16, I saw her.

Dear Page,

I heard steps in the hallway, walked out, and ran into Mr. Rosales, who was balancing three packages in one arm outside Lucy Brite's apartment, while he knocked on the door with his free hand. I mentioned I was going down to check my mail, but instead I lingered beside him. I was, in fact, happy to see Mr. Rosales, who greeted me politely and seemed in a better mood than usual because he looked up into my face with a quizzical expression I chose to interpret as friendliness. He was wearing a tie for the first time, a startling violet garment covered with tiny brown puppies, pale pink tongues hanging out of their mouths. He must have felt my glance because he pointed at the neckwear and said, "My daughter, Bianca. Father's Day."

I mumbled a few words intended to convey that by wearing the tie he was demonstrating a rare strain of benevolent paternity. I glanced at 2C and said to my super in a near whisper: "She talks a lot, and she whistles. Are you aware of that?"

Mr. Rosales grinned, nodded, and answered me with a non sequitur, "Nice lady. Nice lady." He knocked again, and Lucy Brite opened the door. I worked hard to behave as if I were not agitated by her presence, made a conscious vow to turn myself into Ian Feathers for the duration and examine her with his disaffected, searching gaze. Midforties—a guess. What the world calls "an aging beauty." Fine wrinkles around her eyes and mouth, lipstick, softening chin, brown hair tied back in short ponytail, voluptuous body, and a jacket that buttoned to her neck and fell to her hips, narrow pants, scuffed ballet flats. "Luis!" she crowed, as if he had brought her roses. "My mail!" She took the packages from him and smiled as if the two of us were a hundred adoring fans.

I realized later that I had half expected an unfamiliar voice to emerge from the well-groomed body, but the voice was the voice of the monologues, that is, the voice she used when she wasn't imitating someone else. It struck me that Lucy Brite did not look at all crazy and that some piece of me had assumed she was, that I may have expected a disheveled wild-eyed mental patient or at least a worn-out woman with misery stamped on every feature, but she did not appear to be a person tormented by a child's death or agonized by a husband's betrayal. Although my view lasted only seconds, I glimpsed a densely furnished room behind her—rugs and lamps and bookshelf, handsome table and two chairs, at least one painting, a room that must have been a near mirror of mine, but appeared as a domestic jungle to my desert. It was then that she turned to me, and Luis

Rosales, whose first name I had just discovered, said, "Meesis Brite, your neighbor." He did not make an attempt at my name. He might not have remembered it. Lucy Brite gave me a fast, hard glance and a smile that did not include teeth. "Nice to meet you," she said coldly and vanished behind the door.

I felt disoriented. Back in my apartment, I remembered Simone Weil's sentence "Imagination and fiction make up more than three quarters of our real life." Weil was a genius, a sage, a starving saint, and a truth teller. Was I disappointed I hadn't found Miss Havisham living next door to me? Is that what I wanted? For some stupid reason, "Ring Around the Rosy" was in my head again, and I had an urge to box my own ears. I took a breath and decided to think rationally about the brief encounter. I called Ian to the rescue yet again. I had recorded Lucy's words, hadn't I? She might appear "normal" in the doorway, whatever that word might mean. Mr. Rosales might think of her as a "nice lady," but she did spend a significant part of her evenings chanting, "I'm sad," and she did chatter to herself in at least a couple of voices about an accident, suicide, or—murder. There, I said it. Then I saw the image of a child lying on the ground in the space between my building and the next, and I walked over to the window and looked down. Did I want to check to make sure no body had fallen from above? Am I the one who is crazy? I turned away from the window, walked to my kitchenette, newly decorated with roach baits, and, as I stood there contemplating vermin, I heard Lucy Brite laugh. It was one of those gasping staccato laughs that nevertheless had real volume. And for some reason, a reason that was unreason, her laughter made me feel at once frightened and abandoned.

CHAPTER THREE

September 17

Dearest, darling, beloved P,

Went to the reading. Just came home. Two thirty in the morning. Joy! A friend! Artist! Poet! We talked into the night and she hugged me when we parted. I will tell you more tomorrow. S.

When I wrote that giddy message in the composition book, I had been a resident of Manhattan for exactly twenty-two days. What the number fails to express is the feeling of time spent, a time that in memory has gained the distended quality of an era or epoch, a period of yearning for someone who would open a door, walk into a room, and bring the Age of No One Real to an end. But it is only on hindsight that I am able to make sense of my "three weeks and a day" because while I was living them, I never once admitted to myself that so far my adventures in the city had had a largely imaginary quality. My characters IF and IS had been launched into their mystery. I had neatly inscribed the titles of all the books I had read into the pages of Mead Comp, and I had eavesdropped on Lucy Brite. My writing and reading could have taken place anywhere. Lucy was a real, living being in 2C, but her rambling monologues had spawned pictures of violence and turmoil that had no known reality beyond the confines of my skull.

On September sixteenth, between the time I heard Lucy laugh and the time I departed for the evening, I looked out the window of my front room several times to make sure no dead person was lying among the weeds. Had I actually spotted a corpse I'm sure I would have lost consciousness instantly; I did not *expect* to see one. And yet, I was drawn to the window in order to verify what I already expected—no body. The urge, a psychic tic, may have bloomed in my isolation, but it was rooted in some speechless fear I couldn't name. The young woman who had settled into her rooms on West 109th Street to embark on her new life would have regarded the conscious acknowledgment that things were not going as planned as a defeat.

Whitney Tilt, the artist-poet or poet-artist, walked into the Ear Inn downtown on Spring Street on the evening of September 16 in a pair of green high heels, black stockings, a tight cobalt-blue dress, and a yellow beret to listen to John Ashbery read his poems with another poet named Michael Lally, whose work neither of us knew but expected to admire because he had been given a spot beside a living master, and she seated herself next to me, and I thought she was a marvel from the first second I saw her, or, as I wrote to Page the next day in a swell of enthusiasm, "She is beautiful, sophisticated, a being touched by a fairy wind." Although we later joked that winds or at least the stars must have been aligned in our favor, neither of us believed in fate. There is chance and there are random sequences of events out of which some probability can be established. The odds for us were narrowed by poetry. In a city of seven million people, poetry was still a passion for the happy few.

Every afternoon, I read poems aloud in 2B. My own voice became the voice of my familiars, and these incantations brought me comfort.

I read Ashbery along with my old loves, Thomas Wyatt and Shakespeare. I read Donne, Clare, Dickinson, Moore, Stevens, Riding, and Plath. I read Stein's prose as poems. I sang out Goethe, Hölderlin, Trakl, Celan, and Bachmann in my high-school-turned-college German; Baudelaire, Rimbaud, Verlaine, and Mallarmé in my three years of college French. I chimed out Anna Ahkmatova and Marina Tsvetaeva in translation and they sounded grand in English, and I returned to the sputterings of the Baroness because I regarded her as my own archival rescue job, almost annihilated back then, and I wanted to protect her from oblivion with my voice. "Say it with— / Bolts! / Oh thunder! / Serpentine aircurrents—Hhhhphsssssss! The very word penetrates."

Sometimes I swayed in an iambic side-to-side as I read. Sometimes I rocked from my waist or jerked to the uneven patterns of the moderns. I sat and I read poems, and I stood and I read poems, and I paced back and forth and read poems. I wanted the meters of the greats to take me over, to enter my walk and direct the kinetic music of my thoughts. I wanted Ian and Isadora to move on poetic legs, and I wanted them to swing poetic arms. I wanted melodious prose, not the dead sentences of the bad novels I remember buying during that first year in New York because they had golden stickers plastered on their fronts and notables barking on their backs about "riveting" and "lyrical" achievements, books which I then put down after ten or twenty pages because I discovered that these touted works thumped along on two wooden legs, and I was forced to surmise that either mutual backs were being scratched or the notables were ignoramuses.

I dressed up for John Ashbery that evening. I wanted to look as if I had lived in New York all my life, but my dressing up was not Whitney Tilt's dressing up. I had been schooled in the Minnesota dogma that no one should stick out or put herself forward or be overly proud of her accomplishments, much less her face or figure. To flaunt one's "God-given assets," as Aunt Irma called them, was unseemly at best, whorish at worst, and I probably chose a simple shirt and jeans for my evening at the Ear Inn, fully conscious that my assets were not hidden. My wardrobe was meager, but I know that my general idea was to look at once serious and fetching. I wanted to smolder with intelligence. This makes me laugh now. Men can smolder with intelligence. Women aren't allowed such subtleties, but I was naïve, and I imagined that people would listen to me as well as look at me, that they would hear in my sentences the cadences of a strong mind hard at work. It took me years to understand that such an assumption is false, at least much of the time, that expectation is the better part of perception, and a young woman's face acts as a barrier to her seriousness, especially when the face is accompanied by an unaggressive manner.

I was young well before the craze for self-documentation took over every country on earth, and only a few photographs of me exist from that period. Except for the mirror, the photograph is the only way to view oneself from the outside, and the mirror can no longer show me what I looked like then, but I recall that in those early years in the city, I would, every once in a while, come as a surprise to myself. When I left friends at a restaurant for the toilet and had washed my hands and was greeted by my reflection in the mirror, I remember thinking, I had no idea you were as pretty as all that. There is often a mismatch between inside and outside. We lose our faces completely in the swing of living, and our former faces are even more elusive. If I hadn't been told, could I point to myself as the baby in the photograph?

We keep company with an inner voice, one that began long ago in early childhood and falls silent in unconsciousness, in dreamless sleep, and in death. When we are alive and awake it is the mouthpiece of the self, and she or he is the chattering person we know best, often deluded, it is true, but endlessly explicating events as they happen. It is poignant now to remember the young woman not long out of her girlhood whose own face surprised her because the features, lovely as they may have looked, had an alien, perhaps insipid, quality. The internal narrator I carried around inside me then had already been formed by hundreds of books, by their stories and characters, by their arguments and concepts and categories, by authoritative voices pronouncing on this and that and by less authoritative voices interrupting the stream of that consciousness to get a word in here and there, and because of the indisputable truth that no one's words are her own in any genuine sense of the word *own*, I always wonder who is actually speaking in there.

Nevertheless, face and voice may constitute cacophony, not harmony, and sometimes the world conspires to annihilate the speaker within to force a match between the two. When I surprise myself now, I am startled by a countenance that has raced ahead of me: Am I really so old? But in those days, when I left my apartment to take a walk and think through a question by listening to, not a single voice, but two inner voices engaged in lively dialogue, and I had forgotten the mirror and its contents entirely, I was often roused from my amnesia by the ubiquitous stare that belonged to no man in particular but to many men all at once, and which accompanied me down the street, and I remember that all that gazing at my body in motion had a stiffening effect on my limbs because it turned a simple stroll into an unwilling performance, and I feigned deafness when bursts of obscene commentary came from one side or the other. I supposed they wanted me to blush. I didn't. I remember, too, that I was sometimes commanded to smile by a stranger on the sidewalk. "Why so glum, baby? Smile!" I would grin obediently and move on.

One evening, however, I was caught off guard. I was heading home down Broadway, and a man coming toward me politely lifted his forefinger to stop me, a question in his eyes. I thought he was going to ask for directions or the time. Instead, after I had paused in front of him, he pushed his face close to mine and, teeth bared, growled at me in a voice of unfathomable rage, "Fucking cunt, evil, filthy, disgusting bitch!" I can't remember what the man looked like, except that I think he was white and middle-aged, but I'm not entirely certain. I recall the block. It happened between 114th and 115th on the west side of the street. I have a strong memory of the time of day and the darkening sky, the uninterrupted gait of pedestrians on either side of us as they pressed forward, most of them on their way home, and I can still feel the shock. I jerked my head backward, leapt out of his way, and began striding down the block, my heart pounding. I did not run. I know I asked myself why I had been singled out. Was there something in me that he had seen and hated? Had I looked like a vulnerable mark or did the man simply pick out women at random and scream horrors at them? I did not write about it in the notebook.

I can be sure only of two things when it comes to my appearance on the evening of September 16. When I left my apartment for the Ear Inn, my lips were blood red—a brashly painted mouth was one small sign of personal rebellion against the never-stick-out-anywhere-for-any-reason rule, adopted well before I arrived in Manhattan—and I was wearing a pair of black snakeskin cowboy boots Kari had helped me buy, and which, after I had pulled them on, gave me a feeling of toughness and masculinity, and I recall that when the elegant Whitney Tilt slid into the chair beside me, I felt glad that at least I had those fancy boots.

I retain a clear memory of walking through the door that night. The murky bar-smells of alcohol, old and new cigarette smoke, and Pine-Sol cleaner. I can almost bring back the odor. There are hazy lights to my left as I look ahead at the chairs haphazardly set up for the reading. I am shy, but I seat myself near the front because I am also eager. Whitney arrives, and I take her in from top to toe and think to myself how lovely she is. She sits down. We smile at each other. She stretches out her legs straight in front of her. They appear to be almost as long as mine—she is tall—and she stares at the green pumps and wheels her heels around and clicks her toes together several times. Such a small business, and yet, I remember the toe clicking perfectly, just as I remember the smooth skin of her neck and the dark curls that seem to float out from under the yellow beret and her perfume that might be described as umbral.

When the man of the hour begins to talk, he explains that the poem he is going to read, "Litany," runs in two columns. Because the work is cut in two, he has not yet decided how to read it, but he begins. Ashbery has a rather high nasal voice, and someone behind me shouts "louder" after he has read two or three lines, but the poet replies that he can't read louder, which is puzzling, and as he continues, I am forced to admit I am disappointed in this flat voice reading a poem I can hear is a good poem, a very good poem, and I am forced to acknowledge that when I read aloud at home to myself, I read his words better than the author of the poems himself. I adjust to the thin, wheedling timbre, close my eyes, concentrate on the words, and make my way through the poems in a state of determined compromise. But there is this, too: I can feel the young woman next to me listening intently without my even looking at her. I feel her acute, tight presence as a human force field.

I can't remember which of us spoke first, and my ten-page journal entry the following day does not supply that detail. I know that after several minutes of polite talk back and forth, she said, "Let's blow this Popsicle stand." And I agreed and tried to disguise the explosion of excitement I felt as we walked south to Magoos and sat down at a small table opposite the bar. It was still early and the place wasn't crowded, but it was there our friendship began. It has never stopped although Whitney is now living in Berlin, and many months may go by without a word between us. Our daughters are friends. We each had one. My child is Freya. Hers is Ella, after Ella Baker, not Ella Fitzgerald. The intervening years have both clarified and obfuscated what we were to each other then. After I found the notebook, I sent her an e-mail with the words I had written about her the day after we met:

"Whitney Tilt. Graduated from Radcliffe. Student in Columbia's MFA writing program. Grew up in Philadelphia. Hazel eyes lined with kohl. Held mine longer than is usual between two almost strangers. I had to look away often. Shaped brows, as if painted in two perfect strokes by a master calligrapher, a rather flat nose, and a full mouth that turns up regularly in ironic disdain, and when she laughs, head back and eyes skyward, she is magnificent. She gestures with her long fingers while she talks, as if she is dismissing so many idiots from her regal presence, and after she lights her cigarette, she shakes out the match with a single snap of her wrist. She is a staccato being all around. Her clipped precise syllables accumulate into nicely shaped sentences with full stops. I could almost see them hovering before me as she spoke. I felt awkward and unpolished. She is the city. She is New York. I have found her."

She wrote back: "This is what I wrote about you in *my* diary, not the next day, but maybe a week later: 'I had coffee with Minnesota today. When I first laid eyes on her I thought she was one of those cold, vapid blondes trawling the town for culture. My misperception. Today she went on about Simone Weil in that funny Midwestern accent of hers with the dragged-out vowels and got so worked up about something that mystic wrote about grace, her voice got all croaky with emotion. Once she had pulled herself together, she apologized for being moved, and then she apologized for apologizing because why "the heck" shouldn't we be moved by what we read?' Your old, and I mean OLD, friend, Whit."

I see myself as an absurdity.

Whitney's father was a lawyer who became a judge. James Tilt died last year at the age of ninety. According to his daughter, the judge remained lucid and formidable until the end. He had the sonorous voice of an actor, definite liberal opinions, and, like my own father, when he spoke he expected your full attention. With the single exception of an aunt who had become a professional gambler, Whitney regarded the Tilts as a boring lot. "That's what my mother hungered for: no excitement and no eccentricity." Whitney's mother, Clara, is still alive, but weak, querulous, and alert to her daughter's guilt, which, as Whitney puts it, "she plays like a piano." Clara grew up coddled, wealthy, and confused because Clara's mother, Mini, lived her life as an adventuress. Mini was born into a spectacularly wealthy family in Buffalo, New York, at the turn of the century. She married at eighteen and divorced, fled to Italy, where she became infected with radical politics and a particular brand of anti-modernism—that yen to return to the intensity and purity of a world stripped of its neurasthenic "civilizing" layers. She met her second husband in Rome, another American, and the couple returned to New York and settled on Park Avenue, where Mini hosted a salon that attracted bohemians and eggheads and artists of all stripes and colors. She indulged herself in lovers, clad herself in flowing robes and floral headdresses, tired of her spouse, divorced him, and within a few months rashly married a minor French painter, Jean-Claude Lefebvre, whom she took with her to Taos, New Mexico, a fashionable destination for gallivanting society types and a promising landscape for a man with a paintbrush. It was there she met a Pueblo Indian whose name was Charles and was also married. Mini and Charles fell hard for each other, which caused a scandal in the tribe but had an invigorating effect on Jean-Claude, who threatened Charles with a pistol, an act that so impressed Mini she threw herself back into the thin arms of her third husband and headed home for New York. Not long after the Taos debacle, during her parents' euphoric, if brief, conjugal period, Clara, their only child, was conceived.

I didn't learn these stories that night, only a flying fragment or two. Jean-Claude died before Whitney was born. She remembers her grandmother as a small, elegantly dressed person who reeked of perfume and liked to go barefoot in the warm weather. "Oh, the grass between my toes," she would sing out to her grandchild. "I love the feeling of grass between my toes." Mini died when Whitney was eight.

"One thing I know," Whitney said to me years later, "Mini's life was made of money. Without money, her story is impossible."

We all have our ghost stories. Mine features rugged Norwegian farmers come to till the prairie soil with their hearty, axe-wielding wives and blond, red-cheeked children and chests filled with fortitude and so on and so on, and it was all true up to a point, but one of my great-grandmothers on my father's side went mad out there in the summer of 1872 under the vast and turbulent Minnesota sky. Helga believed her husband was poisoning her and, although she cooked all the family meals, the delusion held fast. She stirred and sniffed and served the food but remained convinced that Ulf had secret, perhaps supernatural, methods of doing away with her. To ward off the inevitable, she stopped eating altogether, fell ill with bronchitis, and only days later was "carried off into the next world."

I am quoting old Mrs. Heglund, who used those words one afternoon as I sat next to her with a cup of tea in my lap at my mother's Nordic Arts meeting. I was fourteen. Mrs. Heglund was ninety-six, "clear as a bell," and had heard the story from her mother. The Heglunds had been neighbors about a mile down the road from Helga and Ulf. "My mother said she was a delicate woman with a fine head and a slim figure who read the newspaper front to back and cut out the articles she liked and knew a thing or two about politics and embroidered the tiniest, most perfect stitches you ever saw. She and my mother were friends, you know." My teacup rattled only once as I listened to her tell me what I had never heard before, and rather than say, Oh my God, what an awful story, I nodded sadly and said nothing.

I didn't tell Whitney about my psychotic relative until later. Instead, as the bar began to fill up with a talking crowd of various ages dressed casually or with a highly self-conscious quality that interested me—a woman in a hat with a veil—I amused my new friend with stories about our neighbors, the two Professor Harringtons who lived a little farther up Old Dutch Road, with their dog, Laurence, after Laurence Sterne, and their cockatoo, George, after George Eliot, and their daughter, Edith, after Edith Wharton, and how when she was eleven, my friend Edith had arrived at school with her head heavily bandaged and reported proudly that she had fallen out a window at home in an attempt to save an injured bird from a tree branch, and she had received much sympathy from peers and teachers alike until one afternoon three days later, she forgot herself, grabbed the monkey bars on the playground, swung upside down, the bandage slipped, and the gory gash on her forehead that she had described to us in voluptuous detail was nowhere to be seen.

Above the clamor of the bar, I heard Whitney's laugh, and I forgot myself completely in the open mirth of her face, which promptly took over mine and gave me as much polish as I needed.

My new friend wrote poems, but she also made poem-objects from discarded things she found on the street, in parks, alleys, and garbage cans. The find, she said, made the poem. For example, she had retrieved a squashed baby doll from a garbage can in SoHo, its face and arms swirled with the hectic lines of magic markers. On the doll's blank belly, she wrote: "I speak a city ruin / Revived by tilted chance / Put ear to mouth / Put brain to eye / And listen hard—a cry."

We discovered we both loved James Baldwin's *Giovanni's Room* and Djuna Barnes's *Nightwood*, and we both knew that "Jimmy" was in Saint-Paul-de-Vence in France living in a big old Provençal house, but that when he was a teenager he used to go and visit his mentor, the painter Beauford Delaney, at 181 Greene Street, just blocks north of where we were sitting at Magoos, and that "Djuna," dear friend of the Baroness, was also still alive, hiding out on Patchin Place in the

Village, a gated cul-de-sac off of Tenth Street, north of Delaney's old studio, a little alley that had been home to Theodore Dreiser and e. e. cummings and John Reed, although they mattered less to us. And we have never stopped playing this game of time and space and ghostly bodies made of words and pictures. Baldwin and Barnes and Delaney and the Baroness are all dead now, but Whitney and I have charted their paths in New York and Paris and Berlin and turned these cities into imaginary libraries of the garrulous dead.

Around midnight, I told her about Lucy Brite. I did not mention the stethoscope, an element in the story I regarded as truly perverse, but which I later confessed to my new friend only to discover she found my use of the medical instrument hilarious. As I talked, Whitney leaned forward, elbows on the table, knuckles pressed firmly into her cheekbones, an intent expression on her face. She listened to me the way she had listened to Ashbery. After I finished my tale, she held out her arms, raised her eyes to the ceiling, and intoned, "Amsah." It was my turn to laugh and, as I laughed, I felt light with relief. For the moment, anyway, Whitney had disenchanted Lucy Brite, had turned her into no more than an eccentric neighbor, even if that neighbor whistled, moaned, and jabbered through the wall.

But Whitney went on talking. She thought Lucy Brite had great fictional potential. I had "lucked into" a "ready-made crime novel" with a brutal husband, an elusive brother, and the dead body of a daughter. I didn't tell Whitney I found her detachment morally alarming. Without going into the particulars, I had already mentioned I was writing a novel with two young detectives in it, so she was picking up on a theme I had already launched. I had referred to Cervantes, too, and once the great writer's name had entered the air between us, I had instantly felt ashamed. "I must have sounded so pretentious!" was the sentence I recorded the following day in the notebook, but Whitney didn't seem to mind my presumption. "I have a thought!" She was busy parsing the material for my *next* novel. "What if she's the murderer?" Whitney said to me brightly. "Wouldn't that be a good twist?

You know, she's yattering on about the evil husband or son and then she's the one who tossed the girl out the window?"

I looked at my lap. All at once there were tears in my eyes, tears that made no sense, but the weightlessness I had felt a minute earlier had vanished. If the composition book is testimony to anything, it is that my emotions were far more volatile when I was young. In its pages, I bounce from one extreme to the other. I'm up. I'm down. I'm a ricocheting ball of feeling. I had laughed about "amsah," but Lucy tossing her child out the window struck me as horrible. Whitney reached across the table, grabbed my hand, and squeezed it. The gesture of sympathy undid me. I felt a convulsive gasp in my throat, heard an ugly gagging noise, and began to cry. "Come on, Minnesota," she said, "let's take a walk." Whitney paid for our beers, returned to the table, grabbed me by an arm, and pulled me into the night. Out on the street, I sobbed in earnest. I snuffled and choked and honked and shuddered and dribbled saliva and snot into my hands, and I managed to gasp out that I was sorry, and I couldn't understand what had happened to me, and then I said it again, I'm sorry, and she told me to shut up and cry if I wanted to, and I found her words so unutterably kind, I sobbed harder. But within minutes, my first crying jag in New York City had ended, and I had received a nickname that stuck: Minnesota.

Whitney lived in a loft in SoHo, and we walked in the still warm air up the barren, poorly lit streets toward her place. She handed me a Kleenex and a mirror from her purse, and I dabbed the paper on my wet red face. The next day I recorded every twist and turn of the evening when my mind was still alive with the details, but I am rewriting Whitney and me from the strange place we call "now" because it allows me to regard the two young women walking up West Broadway in a light unavailable to me years ago. I recovered quickly from my blast of grief, but I have continued to ask myself what broke inside me that night. It may have had something to do with Whitney's verb, *tossed*, the object of which is frequently garbage. The girl tossed from a window had become an image so strong I had found myself checking for bodies below my window. Nudge. Kick. Prod. Push. Brutal urges.

As I sit here at my desk in the relative quiet of my Brooklyn neighborhood, a plane sounds, and the red clock on my desk has suddenly become audible. My books are a blur of colors in the periphery of my vision. A few early November birds pipe a series of sharp notes, and remote traffic imitates the noise of the wind. Walter is still asleep. I try not to think about the cruelty of the presidential election. I hear the roaring spleen of the white crowd as they spit and scream at the woman. The abomination. Cast her out. Push her hard. And Lindy plummets to the ground in that strange internal space where I remember what I have never seen. Again and again, the heavy body of the daughter falls past the window of an apartment. What is missing from the story is the tosser, nudger, kicker, prodder, pusher—the murderer.

From Mead:

Our conversation returned to poets and artists and what we had read and what we wanted to read. Whitney quoted May Miller by heart, a poet I haven't read, but I memorized these lines: "Logic is a grafted flower / In a changeless bed." It might be nice for Isadora to quote Miller as a riposte to Ian. I will go to Salter's and buy her books tomorrow or one of them. Money. Remember to be careful with money.

Before we said goodbye that night, Whitney said she realized she had sounded cynical about Lucy Brite. She had been excited by a potential plot and had said what first came to mind. I told her it couldn't have been Lucy Brite that had set me off, that I had no idea why I had reacted so strongly, which was true, and then she said something I never forgot. I do not need the notebook to remember her words exactly. She said, "There is something beastly and cold in me."

Near the end of the long entry for September 17, I wrote, "I can't explain it, Page, but her words made me happy. I've never met anyone like her. Somehow she made 'beastly and cold' sound heavenly, and I wanted to be beastly and cold, too. I want to wander around New York City with Whitney arm in arm being beastly and cold together."

CHAPTER FOUR

Every story carries inside itself multitudes of other stories. Let us say, Our Standard Hero, or OSH, is on his way to London in a coach and has stopped at an inn to spend the night. (The reader may fill in all the details of the inn from the countless inns so richly described in novels past.) Here OSH runs into a mysterious gentleman with a limp. (I was partial to limps, eye patches, and scars in my young reading days.) Now, because the plot is still unwinding, the reader does not know whether Mysterious Limping Gentleman, or MLG, is a red herring or crucial to our hero's story. The not knowing is precisely what makes MLG's stealthy movements up and down the stairs with a key clutched tightly in his hand significant. But what if the narrative leaves Our Standard Hero snoring in his bed at the inn and travels to Bath with Mysterious Limping Gentleman instead? MLG is now the novel's hero.

It is possible that a majority of readers would object to a hero switch midstream. From one point of view, this leap would create unnecessary frustration, especially among irritable readers who like their fiction as standard as their heroes. Such a perspective supposes

THE MYSTERIOUS LIMPING GENTLEMAN

that the author of a novel "chooses" her plot. The author is a mastermind, a Sherlock Holmes (SH) behind the scenes who knows better than to run off to Bath with the Mysterious Limping Gentleman. And yet, arguably, life is always distracting us from one story into another, isn't it? Long experience has taught me that the SH theory is wrong. I don't know who is writing exactly, but I often feel that it isn't coming from me.

Sometimes in desperation we tie one tale up with another because it satisfies our lust for meaning. And if we are navigating the strange regions of memory, which we always are, then hops from one hero to another or one moment in a life to another are to be expected. For example, what if Our Abandoned Standard Hero doesn't vanish altogether but finds himself in another story? What if in the middle of the night, an envelope is slipped under his door, he wakes up, finds a key inside, opens a door with it, and walks into a novel set in New York in the year 1978–79? But rather than the hero, he is now a minor character.

In the story of my life, Malcolm Silver played the hero briefly before he shrank to a minor character, entered another plot altogether, and disappeared from view. I spied Malcolm's head before the rest of him in early October at a gathering for the magazine *Semiotext(e)* hosted, I think, by a Columbia professor. I went with Whitney and her friend Gus Scavelli, who became my friend, too. Gus hoped to establish himself as a film critic, a shrewd analyst of the form's "complex visual language," but in the meantime, he earned a meager living as a movie reviewer for various publications around the city. Going to the movies with Gus was an adventure because he was prone to whispering commentary—"Watch this shot; here it comes; great fade-out; did you see it? Look at her face; Vaseline on the lens"—but I must return to Malcolm's head or Gus will open yet another door that I am keeping closed for the moment.

I felt like a foreigner at the party. I had seen the Schizo-Culture number of *Semiotext(e)* at Salter's Bookstore with its elegant cover and grainy, disturbing pictures inside. As far as I could tell, its content celebrated a form of schizophrenia that had nothing to do with the kind my second cousin Alma suffered from, the kind that curled you up in a ball in the corner of the room and made you cry out in terror because the pixies wanted you to die. No, it was a far more abstracted and philosophical madness than the illness that afflicted Alma with her popped-open eyes and jerky gestures. The professor's residence showed no signs of either insurrection or psychosis. It looked like nothing so much as a well-appointed, book-lined, upper-middle-class academic's apartment. While I was taking all of this in and pondering what it meant, I saw a young man staring at me. His eyes were leveled at mine, and his gaze—harsh, critical, supercilious—instantly ignited my groin.

The young man's large head was propped on top of a thin, muscular body—a slight mismatch of proportions. He had cropped dark curly hair, defined cheekbones, smooth pale skin, and a humorless expression. His eyes were enormous, and, after he had turned away, I examined him in conversation with a redheaded woman and concluded that he blinked less often than most people. I felt as if a marble bust on display in the Metropolitan Museum had swiveled to inspect me and then swiveled away. I stepped toward him, paused beside him, and introduced myself. He nodded at the redhead, neck swaddled in a silk scarf, pronounced her name, which I instantly forgot or perhaps never registered at all. In memory, she is hair color and scarf only. His gesture was formal, but the contact between us shortened my breath. He was studying philosophy at the New School. And where had he come from? "I studied with Foucault," he said, "in Paris." I had not read Foucault then, knew nothing except the name—imprimatur of soaring thoughts. In the notebook where I recorded these particulars, I wrote in a language I call Novelese: "Then Malcolm Silver examined his watch, expressed surprise by emitting a faint whistle as his red lips pursed momentarily, turned abruptly from me, lifted his hand in a desultory half wave, and disappeared."

After that meeting, every time a door opened, I imagined Malcolm Silver walking through it. I invented patter for him and for me on philosophical subjects. I read Foucault's book on madness, which struck me as Romantic and overblown in its rhetoric, but I knew I might be wrong. And I masturbated vigorously to the memory of the wonderful head and alluring body.

Whether of the standard or limping variety, the hero preoccupied me then in ways he doesn't now. Lust was a dominant feature of my hero fixation. Unwanted celibacy had turned my lust into pain, an ache of desire I lugged with me everywhere I went as I hoped for relief. My problem wasn't suitors. They circled around me, breathed, grinned, and sent important looks in my direction. But not one of them was hero enough to cure my illness. Had I acted on impulse, I would have chased the young philosopher into the street, leapt on him from behind, and tackled him to the ground, but I was far too well behaved to run after a man. I also remembered, still remember, the one time I grabbed a boy in college. We were sitting on a bed of dry autumn leaves when I lunged at him for a kiss. A moon was up behind the Magnus Student Center, and the air was chilly. But once kissed, the object of my desire turned sour. "I'm the one who's supposed to do that," he said.

Lust is never pure; it is pushed and pulled into various shapes by the mutating forces of fiction that blow over us as surely as the winds on the prairie bend and buckle the trees to their will. I cannot remember that boy's name, but he was tall and sandy-haired and well-rounded, which is to say conventional, so conventional that he turned down a girl he had been sniffing around for weeks because she had violated the man-goes-first rule and scraped his pride, which, in turn, wilted the boner I had spotted seconds earlier at his crotch. Arousal has its own curious logic, one I have never fully understood, but perusing the notebook, I can see that the Mysterious Limping Gentleman with a cold smile and a cruel secret, the one who took over that other story I mentioned above and went on to Bath, held sway over me in ways I was unwilling to acknowledge and didn't understand. The MLG can be linked both to the arrogant person of Malcolm Silver who fled moments after we had met, a fact that made him more, rather than less desirable, and to another cipher: Lucy Brite's husband, Ted. "There were nights you loved me, though. Couldn't get enough of me."

September 20, 1978

Lucy woke me last night again. She called out, "No! No!" And then after squeaking out a few high, unintelligible sounds, she said loudly in a deep voice that might have been an imitation of Ted's, "I dreamed I killed you." It took me a while to fall asleep again.

Perusing the notebook, I see that the second phase of "my new life" pushed Lucy Brite to the margins of my consciousness because doors opened, and I walked through them into private rooms in New York City that until then had been shut to me. I see my former self enter apartments, large and small, elegant and grubby, usually with Whitney because I arrive as "the friend." I did not understand that the polite friend who smiles at the party and talks to this one and that one is not the person who comes home and records what she has seen and heard and smelled and touched in Mead. The writer is someone else. It is only on the page, for Page, that the beastly and cold begin to receive permission to appear. The beastly and cold arrive as small hiccoughs in the writing. It is on the page that I begin to take quiet vengeance for the master script, the script that had been dictated to me for years and years, a barely audible voice in my ear that insisted I obey.

September 25, 1978

Dear Page,

Scene: Crowded book party in dark apartment on West 100th Street.

Man approaches. Handsome face. Slightly yellowed teeth. Radiant expression. Sits down, leans in, nose to nose. Philip Hightower.

Squeezed between Hightower and skinny poet in black shoes with pointy toes discussing Language School in low rolling tones. Hightower is evangelical. Multiple upward gestures, uses the word "REVOLUTIONARY" several times. No, I have never heard of Werner Erhard. No, not the faintest tinkling of proverbial bell in my brain. Shocked expression from Hightower! Mint breath. Spells. "E-S-T." Mentions Nietzsche to no purpose. Explains to me that PAYING participants are imprisoned for two weekends. In a mere four days, Hightower has become HIMSELF! Does not respond to my comment that one does not usually have to purchase this form of becoming. More gestures. Further explanation. I glean a crucial point: NO ONE IS ALLOWED TO USE THE TOILET. The greater wisdom of this strikes me as dubious. I withdraw my head from Hightower nose. "You have to do it! I tell you, you have to do it!" Hightower palm lands heavily on my knee. I remove it. Hightower chin moves back and forth in horizontal direction to demonstrate his disappointment in my lack of judgment. After sixty hours of expensive humiliation, I will no longer shrink from Hightower's hand. I will "cause life rather than just live it." I wave at Gus, stand up, and "cause" my immediate departure.

S.H.

September 30, 1978

Joseph Brodsky attacked one of Whitney's poems in class. She defended it. She says the other students in class are cowering wimps. He mocks and taunts them constantly, but after she spoke sharply to him, he smiled. She's his pet now. Whitney says Brodsky's poems in English "suck."

October 1, 1978

Tonight. East 70s. Army of peons must shine brass trim in lobby daily. Doorman with epaulettes. Squashed elevator ride to penthouse on

East Side with older people who knew each other in a noisy, jokey, chummy way. Sad celery sticks with peanut butter. Pretzels. Miniature hot dogs. Whitney called it "WASP fare." They, people from rich, old, white Protestant families with grand names, don't know any better. They prefer cocktails to food. Whitney pointed out a short man chortling and backslapping in the corner. Norman Mailer. He was talking to a tall man about "the wives." "It's tough on the wives, though." Who are the wives? Didn't he stick a knife into one of his "wives"?

October 3, 1978

Whitney and I were lying on her bed on West Broadway, and she said that when she was little and really angry, she used to go into the bathroom, lock the door, bite on a towel, and hammer the floor with her fists.

October 5, 1978

Alvin and Rosie have a bathtub in their kitchen on Second Avenue. Alvin has a starved look—torn T-shirt, protruding rib cage, leather, studs. Nattered on about television. Incomprehensible. Platinum-haired Rosie, silent as a stone on ripped sofa. Eyes closing. Before we left, she opened her palm and said, "Lude?" These people are idiots.

Whitney translated: Television is a punk band. Lude is a Quaalude, a muscle relaxant that makes your limbs spongy. These people are idiots.

Your own S.H.

At night there was a game to play, and we played it. The game is called Pretty Girls. The game is old, but its rules have been written and rewritten and rewritten again over the centuries:

I remember Whitney hooting loudly as she pranced around her

loft in her bra and panties swinging a sequin dress over her head, shouting, "It's Mata Hari tonight, Minnesota!" The fever hit us, and we dressed up, usually in Whitney's clothes because she had far more of them than I did, and we painted our faces and arranged our hair, as if we were going on stage to play the parts of vixens or femme fatales or bad girls on the loose. The wilder the getup, the more hilarious we were to each other, and then we two strode into the small hours of morning and sashayed past the waiting crowd and watched as the man we called "the Discriminator," the giant who stood behind the velvet rope at Studio 54, lifted it for us to pass and then we danced until four, two indefatigable girl-women twisting and grinding and waving our arms and laughing in the din of disco among the other masqueraders—the looming transvestites in peekaboo costumes, the tipsy models, the rich guys in Italian suits, the famous people who lounged in special zones reserved for them alone.

I never would have ventured out if Whitney hadn't accompanied me, nor would I have known that such a place existed, but once I was there, I gave myself up to its allure. The music danced me, not the other way around. I succumbed to its thoughtless charm, to beat and sweat and thrill. And Whitney was there in my vision when I looked for her, her head back, lips parted and eyes closed, wearing sparkles or feathers or false lashes or all three. She was with me in the driving rhythms that are sex without sex, what the Greeks called *ekstasis*, out to place, displacement, no longer home, lifted up and out and into plurality and boundlessness. This is how we enter the mind of the many, become the beehive, not the bee. I remember feeling blind with bodily motion, and I remember the charged joy of release in the dance. Whitney and I were tireless on the dance floor, and once we fell into a Dionysian trance, we could go on and on until one of us had to pee, and then the enchantment was usually broken.

The Ladies' Room was 54's Underworld, and most of its inhabitants arrived there by the river Lethe. I remember well-coifed heads bent over lines of cocaine at the sink and determined fingers with brilliant nails that hitched up fishnet stockings, and I remember necks craned over naked shoulders to check for wrinkled underpants in the mirror, and I remember all the skirt yanking that went on in the crush of women, that vital adjustment to dresses so tight they crawled up your butt if you weren't careful. Of course, those fierce downward tugs mattered only if the look you were cultivating didn't include a bare ass. I saw several of those. The room was resonant with sobs, titters, howls, and oaths. It stank of pungent perfume and vomit and urine. For the sober, the room was more sobering, and I was always sober. It was too expensive to drink. I hoarded my money for nicotine.

We hopped up and down at CBGB and at Max's Kansas City and at the Mudd Club on White Street, where the boys were thin but the girls were plump, and I got used to the conventions, the S&M leather chic, the razor blade earrings that must have had a safety coating because I stopped worrying about vulnerable necks in the pushy crowd. I never saw anyone bleed.

The differences in clubs, uptown and downtown, the sociology of the music and the types, carefully parsed and analyzed by some, were moot for me. When I wasn't dancing, I saw mostly pathos, and it looked the same. Human beings are desperate to be seen and to see themselves reflected in the eyes of others, to feel the family comforts of "us," the charmed caresses of the tribe, and back then when New York City was crumbling and Ronald Reagan and the AIDS plague had not yet begun their scourges, segments of the city's rich and poor sought an easy route to forgetfulness in collective inebriation and fast fucking.

Whitney was a little disappointed that I adjusted so quickly to our midnight forays into urban decadence.

But my friend began to understand that life among rural and small-town white people isn't now and never was a Hollywood movie directed by Frank Capra. I told her stories:

I had been out with my father on "calls" when I was still a child. I rarely accompanied him, but from time to time circumstances intervened, and I found myself along for the ride. I remember looking at the strips of flypaper black with dead flies that hung from the ceiling in a tiny dilapidated kitchen that smelled of cabbage and the woman with a pinched, angry face in a loose cotton dress who sat across from me and scowled while my father attended to her husband in the next room. "Scared of a few flies, are ya, little girl?" I shook my head. "Don't see them pesky things in town, is that it?" I didn't answer her even though we didn't really live in town. Then she stood up, noisily collected dishes, and muttered, "Think you're too good for us, is that it?"

I remember Kari standing with me outside a trailer with no wheels in the trailer park across from the Dairy Queen one night while my father was inside. After a few minutes, a woman began to howl. When she stopped, my father came out, and we knew the boy was dead because my father's eyes said, "The patient died."

Once, I rushed into a house behind my father and watched him kneel beside a blue woman who lay flat on the floor of her shag-carpeted dining room. He looked at her hard, grabbed her by both arms, sat her upright, reached deep into her mouth with two extended fingers, and pulled out a long piece of beef, which he waved at the woman's daughter who was standing above him. The blue woman coughed, gasped, turned white, then pink so fast I thought I had witnessed a resurrection. The daughter began to burble in a high, excited voice, "I thought she was dead! I thought she was dead!" My father must have stayed and examined the woman, must have talked to the daughter, but I remember none of that. I do remember that my father whistled as Clunky lurched and rocked over the unpaved driveway that led to Highway 19, and that as we drove away from the low green ranch house, he winked at me, and he told me that ready hands were a physician's greatest tools. I received the wink as love.

I entertained Whitney with the pot-roast-Lazarus story before I told her the other story because bringing a woman back to life and breath is wondrously simple. My father had played the role of physician-magician. I had kept the other story secret, not even Kari knew it, because it made me feel bad. It still does. I think I told Whitney because I knew it couldn't hurt her. I was ten years old, which means it was the spring of 1965. Malcolm X had been murdered, and I would guess from my memory of budding trees that the violence of "Bloody Sunday" on the Pettus Bridge in Selma had already happened. My mother cried, and she kept saying, "There were children, children!" So it may have been April, and I had just stepped out of my ballet class at the Arts Guild. My father was there to pick me up, but he was standing with a man who was waving his arms wildly.

"Don't be frightened," my father said to me. "We're going to drive like the wind."

I don't remember the trip at all. I can see the house on the east side of town. In memory, it's painted yellow. My father told me to stay in the car.

I studied the stains my toes had left inside my black ballet slippers and looked through the windshield at pale green branches. I recall trembling sunlight and shade under the trees and, after it seemed to me that I had waited so long I couldn't wait any longer, I found myself walking to the house across the muddy front lawn, fully aware that every step I took was forbidden. I don't remember that I had ever disobeyed my father before that moment. This seems impossible, but the truth is I can't recall ever consciously crossing him. I don't remember opening the door or stepping over the threshold either or exactly what words I had planned to offer my father as an excuse.

I have pictures in my mind that have lasted, but their accuracy is something I can't vouch for. They may have hardened over time, because they resemble a series of still photographs. I see my father bent over Mrs. Malacek. I recognized her right away because she belonged to my mother's sewing group, and her son Brian Malacek was one of the mean stupid boys I ignored in class. But Brian's mother, who looked younger than the other mothers and wore skirts above her knees, had always smiled at me. Brian's mother was leaning back on the arm of a sofa, her bare legs in front of her. She held a towel to her face, and her blouse hung open. I saw her full white breasts over her brassiere and rolls of belly flesh, and I saw blood all over her thighs and a huge dark stain on the sofa cushion beneath her, so much blood I think I stopped breathing, but I'm not sure. I knew I shouldn't be looking at her because she wasn't dressed. It was shameful. They would see me. And then I heard my father's voice. He spoke to Mrs. Malacek in a voice so tender and musical it sounded like a song, but she didn't answer him. Then she let the towel fall and looked straight at me with her red, swollen, misshapen face, but there was nothing in her eyes, no recognition, no surprise, no pain, nothing. Was that when I noticed Brian? I did see him. I know I saw him. Brian had pressed himself up against a wall in the corner, and he was shaking.

"Go wait in the car." My father didn't sound angry, but I turned and ran.

I had seen what I was not supposed to see, but I didn't know exactly what I had seen. I waited in the car for a long time. People came and went. But the coming and going is not articulated in my mind. When my father finally returned, his white shirt was bloody under his jacket. He slid into the car, and I felt the horror of the reprimand I thought would come, but it didn't come. It was as if I hadn't disobeyed him, as if I had not been inside the house, as if I had seen nothing. I could feel the tension in my father's body, could feel his knuckles tighten as he drove, and he hit the brakes so hard at stop signs, I wanted to cry. Instead, I concentrated on the white line in the middle of the highway, and we turned onto Old Dutch Road, drove past the Swansens' barn, and took a right into our gravel driveway. He stopped hard and fast outside the garage and, just after he shut off the motor, he bent his head over the steering wheel and muttered to himself in a low, choked voice, "The son of a bitch."

Around this strong memory there is nothing immediately before or after. I have no recollection of the ballet lesson or what I did after I came home. But I know that on one of the days afterward in school,

I caught Brian eyeing me in class, and pity and embarrassment welled up in me, and I smiled at him, not a big smile, just a small one I imagined was compassionate. But soon after that, he launched his vendetta. Brian's malevolence, which had once been broadly disseminated toward just about everyone, found a single target. For weeks the skinny boy with a crew cut, cowlick, and fingernails rimmed in black followed me in the halls, haunted me on the playground, and, as he shadowed me, he imitated my every word, gesture, and expression. Brian became my exaggerated mirror image, a reflection that turned me into a mincing nitwit.

The day after I told Whitney the story, I wrote in the notebook:

Whitney and I discussed my error at length: *the smile*. She said Brian had fought for his dignity the only way he knew how. He attacked the girl who had barged into his house and not only seen his bloody, half-naked mother, but seen him, Brian, shivering in a corner. Whitney wondered if my smile hadn't been touched by superiority. She called me "Saint Minnesota." It made me feel like moral mud, but do I really know what I felt when I was ten years old and smiled at Brian Malacek?

And then she asked, "Who was the man?"

I said, "What man?"

"The man who brought your father to the house. Who was he?"

Fourteen years after the fact, I realize that I have never taken the man properly into account. I scrutinize my memory for his presence. His arms wave outside the Arts Guild, but he is faceless, ageless—all grown-ups seemed old to me then. We must have followed his car. He had run into the house, hadn't he? Do I actually recall him running into the house? Or am I supplying an image for the question?

Whitney said, "Do you think it was Brian's father?"

Page, there is something uncanny about Whitney's thinking. It never occurred to me that the man was Brian's father, but then, I had never seen Brian's father, only his mother. According to Whitney, the waving, desperate man may have beaten, maybe raped his wife in a rage and then, frightened by his own violence, run for the doctor. On the other hand, the man could have been a neighbor or a friend who heard screams, a man who, once he had brought the doctor to the poor bleeding woman, had vanished from the scene. Or maybe, Whitney said, turning the plot again, the man was her lover. "Maybe Mr. Malacek had discovered that Mrs. Malacek was having an affair."

A man runs through a door and disappears. Does he let himself out by the back door? If someone had come out the front door, I would surely remember, wouldn't I? Or, does the man retreat to a bedroom in the house because he lives there?

"Well, she didn't beat up herself," Whitney said to me. "Where were the police?"

Where were the police? Page, where were the police? There was no police car, was there? Did she refuse to press charges against the man? Whitney thinks I should call my father now, ask him about Mrs. Malacek, and find out what happened.

I never did.

Years later, after my father died, I reminded Whitney of the story, but she didn't remember anything about it.

My silence was fear. I was afraid of heroes and villains and fools, afraid of who was who.

And who is the little girl who stands in the hallway and looks into the room at the bleeding woman wearing no underpants and eyes that can't see and the boy shaking in the corner? Speechless witness? Ghost? Nobody? "I'm Nobody—who are You?" Can Nobody write the story? "The Case of Brian Malacek's Mother" by a Lady. By a Little Girl. By Anonymous.

As I continued to work on my still untitled novel, I noticed that Isadora Simon had steadily begun to nudge Ian Feathers off the page.

———

Isadora is taking up more and more room, and poor Ian is dwindling in ways I hadn't expected. I seem to have no choice but to go along with her rather than him. The ghost of Frieda Frail is a further problem. I have to decide one way or the other on the nature of the phantom. Is the final twist of my story that windmills are in fact giants?

Isadora and Ian decided to interview all three Frieda Frail witnesses. They took Dora's testimony first, and then tracked down Martin Pesky, part owner of the Red Owl Grocery Store, in his office. Mr. Pesky had agreed to be interviewed because the teenagers had lied and told him they were doing a project for school on retail product arrangement and its effect on consumers. Mr. Pesky had held forth enthusiastically on the tricks used to lure shoppers into buying more than they had planned. "Candy bars, gum, and the *National Enquirer* at the cash register. The folks have to idle there behind another customer and that's when the urge hits! More money in the till!" But when Isadora delicately moved the conversation onto the ghost, claiming she wanted to reassure her sister Dora that she had been hallucinating, the entrepreneur was suddenly overcome by an urge to scratch a traveling itch. "Could you describe what you saw in detail, Mr. Pesky?" brought on vigorous thigh scratching, over which he mumbled that he must have seen someone else, and when Isadora said, "You and Frieda were engaged, weren't you?" Mr. Pesky was possessed of a need to attack his own bald scalp with his fingernails, and he vigorously denied any formal engagement. The two of them had "seen each other a little." But the question that made the grocer angry was Isadora's last question: "You knew about Frieda's epilepsy, didn't you?" At this, the grocer's eyes boggled, and he yelled, "Get out of here, you nosy kids! Get out right now!"

As soon as they had left Pesky's office and were striding down an aisle past the laundry detergents, Ian said to Isadora, "I am a brain, Watson. The rest of me is a mere appendix."

"Oh, give Sherlock a break, will you, Ian?" Isadora said loudly, but instantly regretted her impatience because her friend looked deflated. His chin, shoulders, and chest sank inward, giving him the bowed look of a religious penitent, and Isadora patted Ian's hand and asked his forgiveness and then looked down at the notes she had taken from Just Plain Dora, who had been, all in all, an excellent witness despite her forays into the Cheshire Cat, which were to be expected.

Isadora loved Ian in her way. He was, in her mother's words, "a dear boy," and she knew he was far too kindhearted, whatever he might say himself, to develop into a mere Turing machine. She also knew that Ian was lusting after her, probably in the way she lusted after Kurt Linder, two years her senior, the boy with slender hips and a lock of hair that fell onto his forehead and a puzzled look on his face that left it only when he smiled. When she met Kurt in the hallway at school, she froze with desire. Her great love was oblivious to her, however, and Isadora, who was swiftly developing what can only be called wisdom, understood that Lust's arrows fly willy-nilly into a target, without reason or justice.

Even in the land of Conan Doyle, love was important. Isadora had come to understand that the great romance in those famous fictions was between the two men, the doctor and the genius. Watson marries for a while, but Mrs. Watson dies, and the doctor returns to his true love. The landlady, Mrs. Hudson, is tidy, but so peripheral to all the truly significant goings-on, her bodily self is never described. The other women mostly flit mysteriously in shadows or breathe out a couple of words or have been knifed or shot or poisoned (although Isadora felt that Violet Hunter, Kitty Winter, and Irene Adler were exceptions to the greater rule), but because Ian fancied himself Holmes, Isadora had been assigned the role of permanent and inferior helpmeet: Watson. When they had embarked on the Frail case four months earlier, Isadora had been only fourteen, and she had embraced her role as sidekick with enthusiasm. Now that she had turned fifteen, she felt cramped in that persona, and in order to analyze her "character" she had embarked on a close rereading of Ian's sacred texts.

In "The Adventure of the Three Garridebs," Isadora believed she had found her answer. The faithful Watson is shot in the story, a superficial wound that Isadora imagined evaluating, cleaning, and bandaging with great care, but that fantasy had nothing to do with the revelation, which arrived by way of Watson's comment when he sees how upset Holmes has become over the injury: "It was worth a wound—it was worth many wounds—to know the depth of loyalty and love that lay behind that cold mask." Because Isadora had not limited her reading to anatomy but had also read many novels from the past two centuries, she was alert to the grinding conventions of love.

"Oh, happy wound!" Isadora thought to herself cynically. "Were there only more! To know that the object of my heart returns my affection is all that matters! For heaven's sake, Watson is the swooning woman in love!" Our heroine was lying on her bed in her room studying a crack in its plaster ceiling when she wondered if she wanted to assume the Sherlock Holmes role instead, if she wanted to play that cold superior mask. Watson was the doctor and the writer, after all. Without Watson there would be no Holmes stories. And, as for the love question, wasn't she, Isadora, swoonish for Kurt? Wasn't Ian swoonish for her? She was pondering these weighty questions when the second-floor telephone in the Simon residence rang, and she walked into the hallway to answer it. It was Ian. "My dear Watson," he said, "I require your presence immediately."

Mead:

October 7, 1978

I saw the pale young man again. I haven't mentioned him, but it's the third time I've seen him near the building in about ten days. He looks ill, tubercular, in fact, a male Trilby wasting away. His pallor is extreme, and he has deep violet circles under his eyes. All he does is stand there, rubbing his arms in the cold and anxiously surveying the door, as if he's waiting for someone, but when I walk past him, he stares at me as if wants to knock me over with his eyes.

October 10, 1978

The pale young man seems to have taken up permanent residence outside the building. I wonder what he wants. I don't know how old he is, not much older than I am. He isn't begging, but his eyes have a terrible pleading look.

October 11, 1978

I stayed in and wrote last night. I have to hoard my money. Lucy was whistling and pacing. Then she left her apartment for a couple of hours. This is unusual. When she returned she started talking right away. I took out the stethoscope and listened. I recorded scraps, but I don't know what to make of them:

"Nothing in his eyes. Do you know what I mean? An alien. Fearful thing. Thing. Why did you kill that poor little animal? Oh, smiling again. If Lindy knew, she didn't tell. She wouldn't tell. I can't get it out of my head. Scoop it out. Lobotomy. Oh, that's so old. No one does that anymore. How do you get rid of the idea? Help me. Help me. Don't lie to me. I want the truth. You have to tell me the truth. Did you do it? Did you do it? I'm so sad. I'm so sad. He's not there. No. He's dead to me, dead to me. What do they call a woman whose children are dead? It should have a name! [Loudly.] Afraid all my life. Afraid of Jimmy. Afraid of Ted, Ted and Ted. Wiggle my ass. Smile. Lucy, head turner, oh, Lucy, you diva, you. [Scraping noises. Laughter.] Hate you. Pig. You're getting fat. Better cut down on those Mallomars." [Sound of weeping.]

Lucy was on the telephone with someone named Patty. Patty talked a lot, because Lucy said very little for minutes at a time. Then Lucy wailed, "Patty, I don't know what to do. I can't take it anymore! I have to know." She listened again to Patty and made little whimpering sounds.

Page, Lucy is irritating me. Her abjection. Oh, happy wound! Shoot me again! And yet, I was listening, wasn't I? I thought of MS. (No, not my manuscript.)

Am I able to see her clearly now? I see S.H. lying near the wall in the fetal position with her stethoscope listening to the story as it unfolds in fragments. No, she is not our Standard Hero. She is not Sherlock Holmes. No, she is stymied by a narrative that predates her existence. I am creating a picture of her now; I am not really remembering her. My reading of the notebook has generated the image of a character: The writer as a young woman clad in pajamas and curled up on the floor. The pajamas might be the pink-striped flannel ones her mother gave her, the ones that shrank in the dryer so that the pant legs do not reach her ankles. I remember the pajamas.

And I see the Mysterious Limping Gentleman climbing the staircase because he has taken over the story. He has a key in his hand. What the writer does not yet know is that she will have to jump him and knock him to the ground. She will have to take the key out of his clenched fist and use it to open a door.

CHAPTER FIVE

When Malcolm Silver walked through the door of the East Hall Lounge of the Maison Française at Columbia University at a minute or two before six o'clock on November 1, 1978, to attend a lecture by Paul de Man, "Shelley Disfigured: The Image of Jean-Jacques Rousseau in 'The Triumph of Life,'" I had already found myself a seat. The standard if temporary hero found a chair in the row ahead of me, and I reported in the notebook that I had "a view of his neck and the fuzz of tiny hairs that grew in its hollow."

The presence of Silver almost within grabbing distance subjected me to a low-grade genital burn that I tried to ignore as I listened to Professor de Man's dissection of a poem I knew rather well, but I no longer recall how he severed the text or excised parts of it for closer examination, except that his technique struck me as bloodless, and I found myself bored, and my thoughts may have strayed onto the unfinished "Triumph of Life" itself and from there to *Don Juan*, another unfinished poem, this one by Byron in ottava rima, a poem in which the hero is shipwrecked and washes ashore on an island, but *Don Juan* was also the name of Shelley's schooner caught in a tempest that blew up suddenly in the Gulf of Spezia on July 8, 1822, and sank, and it wasn't until ten days later that the body of the drowned vegetarian poet washed ashore, but by then the fish had eaten the flesh from his face and hands, and they identified his corpse from his clothing and the book of Keats's poems still lodged in his pocket and, after burying him under the sand in accordance with Italian quarantine regulations, they dug him up again and burned him in a funeral pyre on the beach.

Dead at twenty-nine, Shelley became a literary martyr because the world loves poets and actors and some novelists who die young and never become jowly, dumpy, and arthritic, and they love them even more when they are tormented, hallucinating, and suicidal because the calm, reasonable artist, of which there are many, doesn't deliver the same frisson. And so we gild their young corpses, hold them up to the light, and watch them glow.

I may have thought of Mary Shelley, too. Three weeks before her husband died, she sat in an ice bath to stop the copious bleeding after the miscarriage that almost killed her. Three of her four children were dead by then, and the author of *Frankenstein* didn't want another baby. I don't really know what I thought because I didn't scribble down my reveries at the time. But writing the sentence about Mary Shelley immersed in icy water a moment ago has made me wonder about Mrs. Malacek, whom I wrote about in Chapter Four. It has made me wonder if I had seen the aftermath of not just a beating but a miscarriage. When I was ten, I don't think I knew what a miscarriage was.

Each one of us had come to the East Hall Lounge to learn from the great man, to listen to his elevated, winding, but rigorous sentences. It is a scene I know well, one that has been repeated again and again over many years of my life: the attentive acolytes, dozens or hundreds or even thousands of them, chins tipped upward toward the genius or the man of the people who stands at the lectern with his thick French or German or Spanish or Italian or Mandarin or English or American accent. The man's talk may be abstruse or it may be lucid. It may be rarefied or crude. It may be innocuous or sinister. He may propound on the blind figure of Rousseau in Shelley or awe his audience by attempting to unite loop quantum gravity and strings. He may read from his latest novel or parade his racist politics. The audience may be silent or may erupt in applause, in shouts, or in violence. But the secret of the great man *never resides in what he says*; it lives in the collective charm wrought by the crowd itself, in its assent to his greatness, in its love. In him the crowd finds a feeling about itself it can find nowhere else, and that feeling is contagious. It was there in the room that day. I could feel it.

No one knew that Paul de Man, highly regarded professor of comparative literature at Yale University, had been tainted by fascism. No one knew until a few years after he died that he had written anti-Semitic articles for *Le Soir* in Belgium when it was under Nazi control, that he had faked his academic degrees, stolen money, abandoned his children, committed bigamy, and lied his way through countless close calls with the authorities. In short, on November 1, 1978, no one in the audience knew that Paul de Man was a psychopath.

In Mead, I dutifully recorded the lecture title, the name of the speaker, my boredom, and the worshipful atmosphere of the crowd:

They loved him. His talk sounded like *explication de texte* to me, but without arriving at some final meaning. It was intelligent, penetrating, but hardly a revelation. Is there something wrong with me? What did I miss? Am I stupid? He had this weary tone that made me sleepy. I listened to him on and off and watched the back of Malcolm Silver's head on and off. I was afraid to stare. M.S. might have felt my eyes. And then the girl in front of me, with her hair in a bun held up by one of those leather do-dads with a stick through it, moved her foot, upset her groceries, and a can of Campbell's Soup (Cream of Mushroom) rolled with surprising speed out of the bag, between my legs, under my chair, toward the back of the room, and hit something—a

NO ONE KNEW THAT PAUL DE MAN, HIGHLY REGARDED PROFESSOR OF COMPARATIVE LITERATURE, WAS TAINTED BY FASCISM.

chair leg, the wall? I wanted to laugh, but no one snickered or even smiled as far as I could see. No one twitched, coughed, or moved his or her eyes. They were all under his spell.

And when it was all over, M.S. spoke to me. Hallelujah! He spoke to me about critical theory and Bacon and Bentham and told me I had to read *Discipline and Punish*, and I felt weak with happiness. Of course I will read it! Oh, Page, dear Page, we are seeing each other tomorrow!

Poor, eager, besotted girl. Of course she would read it! She would read Foucault and Derrida and Lacan and Kristeva and Barthes and lesser lights such as de Man because they were high fashion at the time, and the following fall she would begin her graduate studies and, with her head bent over one book and then another (most of them not at all fashionable) in the reading room of Butler Library, she would read and write and smoke her way to the end of school, and in the spring of 1986 she would defend her PhD thesis on the wondrous pronominal jigs performed by the peerless Charles Dickens in front of a committee of six glum, graying white men, only a year before Paul de Man's past was exposed and symposia were held on what to do about the pain and embarrassment of it all, but as she stood there in a room of the Maison Française, having imbibed Shelley's metaphorical disfigurement by way of Rousseau and perhaps contemplated poor Shelley's actual disfigurement by way of sea and salt and fish, she, not yet twenty-four years old, knew nothing of the lecturer's posthumous shipwreck or the friends who hoped to save him from ignominy in those deep waters we call posterity. No, she was swooning for the philosophy student who had studied with Michel Foucault in Paris.

I wish I had recorded the details of the swoon, which lasted ten weeks, but I did not. I suppose I chose to live it instead. The passages that do exist are either cryptic or exclamatory. The words of the notebook have become familiar, but I am always left wanting more. When I try to push through them and experience the immediacy of bone and muscle and meaning, I fail. I remember, and I forget. I leaf through the pages, and even though I know what's coming, I can't recover the now of it. It is a withered now.

Between November 2 and January 15, I wrote a long passage in the notebook about the great man at Jonestown who held sway over his followers and sent nine hundred of them to their deaths in a field in Guyana. I wrote about the blue chair Malcolm and I discovered in the garbage on West Eighty-Third Street and carried home to my apartment, a chair that after a couple of days began to emit an odd smell, to which I subsequently adapted. I made notes on Lucy's further monologues, meditated on Whitney, Gus, and Fanny, Whitney's flamboyant new roommate, a performance artist who had taken up residence in the loft's second bedroom. I also marveled at how deeply I slept while back in Minnesota for Christmas and recorded a long list of book titles, some with commentary on my reading, but the entire ecstatic, miserable *affaire de coeur* between S.H. and M.S. consists of nine enigmatic entries:

November 6

The too vivid. Blindfold, earmuffs, nose plug, thick gloves required!!!!!?

November 12

Raw. The world is raw. Oh, dear blue head! He called Whit "queenly." I don't think it was well meant.

November 17

Baroness to the rescue!: "'Mind blood!' snapp I—'I'm sick! / Hug me—quick!'" Sick to the quick, old girl, and drowning.

December 8

Wonderful bodies! Our bodies. I-YOU, YOU-I, YI!

December 10

Remote. Resistant. Masked.

December 12

Rolled in him. Smiling.

December 15

Hurt.

January 10

Reprieve.

January 15

Beggar-woman.

The story is old and can easily be turned into a silent movie, albeit an X-rated one: Girl meets Boy. Bliss. Sweat. Saliva. Tongues in motion, up and down. Push in and out, also motion up and down. Oh, the happy bounce as orgasms blast out: one, two, three, four (four for Her, one for Him). But Boy is frightened by Girl's blasting love. He pulls away. He walks out the door. Girl chases wondrous feeling, which means she chases Boy up and down through the streets of the city. Boy begins to run. Girl runs. Boy disappears over hill. Girl stops running at bottom of hill, turns around, and walks home as she weeps copiously into her large white handkerchief. But now that Girl is no longer on his heels, Boy stops, turns around, surveys the scenery from hilltop, and places his hand on his heart, a wistful expression in his large eyes. He discovers he misses Girl. He runs downhill and keeps running all the way to her apartment. Reunion. Bliss. Sweat. Saliva. Happy bounce. More chasing, running, turning, walking, weeping, and happy bouncing. Then again, and again: chase, run, turn, walk, weep, bounce, weep, bounce, weep. It is too much. The film breaks and the running, weeping wheel stops turning.

But what do I actually remember? When I evoke the two and a half months we were together, I find bits and pieces of recollections in various modes that have no particular order—I see the sunlight through his bedroom window, and I smell the radiator beneath it, that winter odor of steam warmth in New York City rooms I like so much. And from that memory of radiant glass and the smell of the warmth that chugs and sometimes whistles in the pipes, I am able to recover something of my inebriated state, the twists in the sheets and the gasps and the moisture of being lost in two bodies, the amazement of touch, and this I can't regret. He made espresso in a kind of coffee maker I had never seen before. He poured water into the bottom of the machine, checked to see that the level was right, spooned coffee into the small round container that fit neatly into the gadget, patted the grains with the spoon's back side, screwed the two large pieces together, and placed it on the stovetop. I can see him in his bathrobe, knees bent, his fingers on the knob as he adjusts the flame. Once he said to me, "You hurry through your food so you can get to coffee and a cigarette." I hadn't known this about myself, and I wondered if it was really true. He had his white shirts laundered and pressed, and when he wore them, he left two buttons open at the top. His body was not hairy, but it was not hairless either, and his skin wasn't white pink but white olive. He wore brief-style underpants, had a narrow waist, and visible ribs. He never spoke quickly, and he didn't laugh often, but when he did, I laughed with him because it gave me a breathy pleasure. I recall he had a pair of tan bucks and wore pants with pleats. He danced badly and stiffly, and I didn't like to watch him dance because I felt him watching himself.

In the very beginning, there was a girlfriend who may have been Dutch and may have lived in Amsterdam and whose name I am certain started with a B. He had a framed snapshot of her standing on a French beach in a bikini, and I took comfort in the fact that her bleached hair and crispy milk chocolate tan didn't look pretty to me at all, but he talked about her with reverence. On the other hand, she was across the ocean, and I was in New York and he was in my bed or I was in his, so I worried little about B. I am not sure which week of the affair the already absent B. disappeared from our conversation, but he wrote her a letter and after that he didn't speak of her.

He gave me one of his papers to read, and I found the prose in terrible knots and wanted to snatch up a red pencil and get to work to untie them immediately, but I was afraid Malcolm would be insulted, and I was cowed by the serene confidence he appeared to have in his powers of ratiocination. I mumbled something about the opacity of the style and suggested clarification for the sake of the reader, which made him smile and, although that condescending smile hurt me deeply, I said nothing. The paper's professor didn't give a hoot about knots either because the invisible, learned New School man, whose name I have forgotten, extolled Malcolm's paper as "brilliant." A lesson learned.

Ian and Isadora and their case amused my temporary hero, who pronounced me talented and witty, but upon reflection I have understood that he had no access to my jokes and ironies because he knew little about the art of the novel or how it grew. He wasn't fascinated by the fat and thin of the thing over time, had no passion for my beloved chameleon and its bag of tricks, no feeling at all for its rhythmic glories, for the way it sauntered and skipped, or slowed to a crawl, and then, without warning, turned flips in the air.

I, S.H., the insatiable student of all libraries, read every volume he recommended, his precious Schizo-Culture and all the books in English translation by his Svengali, Foucault, but also Bataille's *The Story of the Eye*, Sacher-Masoch's *Venus in Furs*, Sade's *Justine*, Genet's *A Thief's Journal*, and Artaud's late, crazy poems. He read none of the books I loved, a truth that has a clarion sound in my ears only when I listen to it now. He found the Baroness wild and pleasing, for example, but I don't think he took her seriously, nor did he sympathize with my adulation of George Eliot or Simone Weil or Djuna Barnes.

I remember standing inside his apartment, coat on, listening to him talk in his deliberate, unruffled way, my eyes on the photograph of a woman mummified in bandages that hung on his wall. Only her eyes were visible. I remember my adamant unease, the distinct pressure in my chest when he said the taboo against sex between adults and children was a "bourgeois construct." And I said loudly, "No, it's not, because big people have all the power, and they always will!" A retort he mocked with curled lip. I left him and walked down Third Avenue and felt bad and confused and walked and walked and thought and thought and after some hours of walking and thinking found myself back at his door.

I puzzled over Malcolm because, you see, he was mostly gentle and always clean. A Jewish boy from a middle-class family outside Cleveland whose father ran a mundane business of some kind, he struck me as an unlikely champion of grown-ups having their way with five-year-olds. And he was an attentive lover who, as far as I could tell, didn't long for ropes or whips or props of any kind while he was in the throes of the heavenly bounce.

More than a decade after M.S. walked out my door and left me a tear-drowned inconsolable human heap on my orange-crate bed, I read three sentences in a book called *I Love Dick* by Chris Kraus, who was once married to Sylvère Lotringer, the Columbia professor who founded *Semiotext(e)*. I remember him because he wore a full suit of leather regalia rather than mere patches of leather on the elbows only, as did most of his colleagues. The author of *I Love Dick* and other works of note arrived on the scene (well after I had left it) to edit a series of books, most of them by women, but time, it seems, had not altered the look or the tastes of the professor's disciples. "Sylvère's fans," she wrote, "were mostly young white men drawn to the more transgressive elements of modernism, heroic sciences of human sacrifice and torture as legitimized by Georges Bataille. They scotch-taped Xeroxes of the famous 'Torture of a Hundred Pieces' photo from Bataille's *Tears of Eros* to their notebooks—a regicide captured on gelatin-plate film by French anthropologists in China in 1902. The Bataille Boys saw beatitude in the victim's agonized expression as the executioner sawed off his last remaining limb."

I remember *Tears of Eros*, and I remember the photograph because I found it appalling and Malcolm insisted on discussing its transcendent meanings at length. Of course at the time I had no idea my boyfriend came in multiples. But I did realize that books were mixed up in our amour. Without books there wouldn't have been a love affair at all. I have never, ever shed tears of eros over a stupid, illiterate boy. Moreover, the love affair crashed in part because each of us had been authored differently and, like the dear deluded knight and the poor misguided Emma Bovary, each of us was drunk on ideas, and therein lay the battle of the books. (Do not think for one instant that I consider myself more Bovarian than Quixotic, quite the opposite.) Malcolm, you understand, wasn't about to saw off anybody's limbs. He liked to imagine he was a dangerous fellow without actually being a dangerous fellow because he regarded himself mostly from the outside, and from that distanced perspective, he had decided that a fillip of purely intellectual insurrection was an attractive addition to his persona. I strove to be a high-minded, saintly, and exceedingly good person because I lived my life mostly from the inside, and from that internal point of view I found myself terrified by the rage, hostility, and violent impulses I sometimes felt stirring within me.

And so, as I near the end of the story of my long-lost passion for

Malcolm Silver, I offer a dream report, not my dream, but Malcolm's. I heard it sometime near the end of our affair. After waking together in his bed and eating breakfast at his small table, he told me he had had a dream that night, in which I had murdered someone and dismembered that person in the apartment. He explained that in the dream he had been desperate to protect me and hide the chopped-up body fragments from the police. He gave me this dream report long ago, and I may have forgotten further details, but I distinctly remember that he said he had found the head of my victim in his wastebasket.

It is true that Malcolm's apartment was somewhat nicer than mine, and he owned more furniture than I did, but while the tryst lasted I slept downtown far more than he slept uptown because he did not like the sound of Lucy. The first time he heard her we were naked and entwined on my bed in the evening hours. He pushed me from him, sat up, looked around, and gasped, "What the hell is that?"

Lucy alarmed Malcolm. Most of all he hated her two voices—the high one and the deep one. "Why don't you pound on the wall and tell her to shut up? Why don't you complain?" It was difficult for me to answer those questions. I had once mentioned to Mr. Rosales that Lucy whistled and talked, but it had never occurred to me take action against my neighbor. I had made room for her voice because I had grown used to it. My accommodation involved a necessary elasticity of soul, a feeling that Lucy's chatter, her audible internal dialogues belonged to me as her listener: *Are you listening?* It was as if I had already answered: *I am listening, Lucy.* Perhaps I should have known that as much as I craved Malcolm's mouth and hands and limbs and dick and as much as I liked our long conversations on various topics, he did not qualify as a true confidant, that he was far more squeamish than I was in the so-called real world, which made it impossible to tell Malcolm the pieces of Lucy's story I had shared with Whitney the first night she and I met, much less to relate to him that with amplified ear to the wall I had recorded Lucy's words in the notebook or that the ghost of Lindy's fallen body remained with me, hovering at that ineffable border between the unconscious and the conscious, a wraith that frightened me but one I needed, too. Ghosts are not easily articulated. No bones.

Conundrums. Paradoxes. Baffling plots. Doors open and close and sometimes slam as the wind shakes the house. Footfalls. A woman whistles as another woman sings. A man whistles as he drives. Night comes early in winter. After she reads and sings the lullabies, my mother kisses me, and I inhale her smell. The smell of divinity, of rapture, of grace is a combination of soap and loose powder and warm mother skin, and then she walks across the room to kiss Kari, and she leaves the lamp on in the hallway and adjusts the door so the crack is just right—a little more, just a little more. Now is that good? Yes, yes, that's good.

The wall beside my bed is splitting open in a long jagged line and now the gaping hole. I am screaming. This terror is a knife. The house is falling. I am trying to hold up the wall. I have thrown myself against it. I press my body into it. Mother comes running and pulls me away from the wall. Kari is screaming now. Mother enfolds me and rocks me vigorously, and she strokes my face hard, and she speaks to me in the sweet voice she uses for the darlings. We are the darlings. And then she runs to Kari and rocks Kari, and then in minutes no one is screaming anymore.

I remember that dream or night terror or hallucination with remarkable clarity. I was five. Almost twenty years later, the child desperate to hold the wall together is fully grown. She has left her parents to fend for herself in the city, and she is convinced that the year she has given to herself, the academic year 1978–79, is crucial to her fate. She imagines she is writing her future. She loves the scenes in old movies when a wind rises out of nowhere and blows each month off a calendar that hangs on the wall—September, October, November, December. Usually the flying pages have musical accompaniment. Time passes. As she approaches her twenty-fourth birthday in the story I am writing, I, her author, have moved beyond my sixty-second. It is frightening here in the present, in February 2017. The house is falling apart. The secret of the great man does not lie in what he says. It couldn't happen here, they say, it can't happen here.

By the middle of January 1979, I was sleeping at home again with only the missing Malcolm Silver and the blue chair with the unusual odor that we had found together on the street as company. As everyone knows who has ever grieved over love or death, an absent person is often larger than a present one, and the ache of the departed-from-my-life Malcolm Silver was complicated by feelings of shame about me, the weeping Girl, the one who had left and then returned and apologized for nothing, apologized because she had wanted the Boy so much, even though she despised the wretched Girl who had actually sobbed out the words, "But I love you! I love you!" and in general behaved badly. How badly had she behaved? Did she call him after he had said he did not want to speak to her? I can't remember, and I did not write it down. When I concentrate and cast my second pair of eyes inward, not the eyes that see the world beyond my skin but those that are meant to conjure the past in floating pictures, I cannot call up a single image, just a feeling. What I remember without any specificity is that she, the once-I, felt herself egged on by the imp of the perverse, a tiny being that scrambled up and down her chest and made it itch, and when the itch came, she had to scratch it until her skin turned raw.

On January 18, I wrote in the notebook: "Broadway on West Broadway last night." And unlike the Malcolm Silver memory-chain, those words about the Broadways bloom with images. I see Whitney hug me and stroke me mockingly under the chin with her index finger to tease me out of my stubborn, morose mood. She jeers, "You like to be sad! You like it! You like it! Poor Minnesota. Oh, oh! Leave her to her misery, and let her enjoy it!" And I see her before me as she adopts a preposterous nasal voice and booms out an improvised song called "There Are Many Fish in the Sea" (a tribute to Aunt Irma, Grand Duchess of Cliché), and I see her palms and splayed fingers wave rhythmically back and forth no more than a foot from my face as she taps her feet in an absurd rendition of that already absurd genre, the Broadway musical, and it is impossible not to laugh. I told myself to remember her, to remember dear "Tilty" singing and dancing, and that may be the reason I have remembered. Whit had parted company with a well-spoken medical student from Nigeria she had been seeing for three months. The alliance wilted for reasons she said were "cultural." If that man had bruised her at all, she didn't show it. Her serenity embarrassed me, and I remember I jumped up from the edge of her bed and sang "There Are Many Fish in the Sea" with my friend, and sometime later that same night, we stood side by side at the window together in the loft on West Broadway, looked out, and Whitney said, "It's ours to eat."

Since the day I had first moved to 309 West 109th Street, my neighbor Lucy Brite had circled her pain as if she were a dog turning in the grass before settling in for a nap. She had gone over and over the same ground: The kitchen. The window. The courtyard. Lindy's body on the pavement. The hospital. The doctors she hated. She had shouted at Ted and then had shouted back as Ted, who, as performed by Lucy, had become, if anything, more vicious. The Ted persona had called her a "worm" and a "sow" and "a pathetic bitch," but as the vituperation had risen between "them," the "amsahs" had diminished, and by late January a noticeable change had taken place in the woman next door. She left the apartment more and more often and sometimes returned late at night. She talked on the telephone with Patty and a couple of other people, whose names, if I had heard correctly, struck me as preposterous: Moth and Gorse. For a couple of months she continually mentioned a man named Sam Haynes. "It's me," she would say in a low conspiratorial voice. "It's me, Lucy."

In early February, a blizzard blew in strong and white and cleared the streets of motor traffic. I remember standing outside the Citibank to watch my fellow New Yorkers glide down Broadway on their cross-country skis or advance duck-like in their snowshoes. When I left the bank that day, I had understood that my money situation was dire. While under the effects of the swoon, I had spent rashly—taking twenties from the cash machine without paying close attention to the bank balance. Severe measures were required. This meant no more coffees and croissants at the Hungarian Pastry Shop and no more meeting friends for dinner. It meant eating my way through the cans of beans and soup and packages of pasta until my cupboard was bare. It meant selling back books to Salter's. It meant trolling Happy Hours up and down Broadway where they served little wieners and cheese on sticks. It meant cold fear about the March rent. It meant inquiring about waitressing jobs. (Not hiring.) It meant regular visits to the help-wanted bulletin board in Dodge Hall at Columbia and calling numbers only to discover the positions had been filled. The day arrived when I had the money to pay the March rent in the bank, but no money to eat with in the meantime. As I look back on it now, I know I was stupid not to call my parents or explain my predicament to Whitney. I also know that both options seemed impossible to me then. I would have had to admit that I had failed.

February 15, 1979

Dear Page,

Today I took a walk in Riverside Park because I was in a flutter—so nervous I couldn't write. My poor book! How can I write a comedy in this condition? I can't even afford noodles. Last night Happy Hour again, but the woman at the bar is getting suspicious. I didn't dare eat more than two tiny pieces of orange cheese as I sipped my Coke very slowly. There was nothing for breakfast, as you know, nothing for lunch. I cannot touch the rent money. It was cold outside, but I let the wind from the river blow over me and the walk had a beneficial effect. My thoughts landed on Hamsun for obvious reasons (*Hunger*) and then on Dostoyevsky, the Norwegian's great influence, and then I thought about home, not the apartment, but home, home, and the view of the field from the front window of our house and the mailboxes along Old Dutch Road with their red flags up, and the cheerful letters I've been sending off to Rural Route #1, and I ached to give it up, Page, just give it all up and lie down and weep for a month. I haven't cried at all, you know. Since my two-day wail after M.S., I have dried up completely. I've been flinty as hell, a goddamned stoic. Whitney is on winter vacation with her family, a good thing, because no explanations needed. She is on an island in the Caribbean. I imagine her gorgeous in a sarong. Anyway, last night I kept walking, and then I saw it—a ham-and-cheese sandwich with a piece of pale green lettuce and a whole slice of tomato and mayonnaise oozing from the roll in a garbage can. The can was full, and the sandwich lay neatly on a bed of wax paper. I examined it. There were bites in it, yes, but a good portion of it remained. I looked around. A couple passed me, and I pretended to search for an object in my purse. A woman was sitting on a bench not far away, but she looked absorbed.

I bent over the sandwich and realized that retrieval required avoidance of a cigarette butt that had already shed ashes on the wax paper. What I had imagined would be a deft, instantaneous gesture turned into a more elaborate job. Bent over the can, I carefully brushed the ashes from the opaque paper and then folded the sandwich inside it. I was excited, Page. I could taste it. But as I raised my head, I saw that the woman had stood up from the bench and was staring at me with an expression of disgust on her face. My eyes met hers, and I felt a tremor in my lips and then there were tears of shame, and I ran. I ran with the sandwich all the way to the apartment and, as soon as I was inside the door, I pushed it into my mouth, and I chewed hard, and I ate it up, and it was so good, and I cried all the way through the eating of it because I was so ashamed. There it is. My degradation. S.H.

February 16, 1979

I've been making the rounds again of the bars and restaurants. Nothing so far. I'm not feeling very strong. *Wobbly* is the word. Headache. Kari called. She's full of her senior year in college. Loves her genetics class. It seems so long ago that I was there, too, in another world. I lied to her. Gus called. I lied to him, too. I am a big, fat liar. I have to hide.

Here is Simone Weil on the problem: "Too great affliction places a human being beneath pity: it arouses disgust, horror, and scorn.

"Pity goes down to a certain level but not below it. What does charity do in order to descend lower?

"Do those who have fallen so low have pity on themselves?"

Do I pity myself? I am sitting here asking myself this question.

Today I drank so much water my stomach sloshes when I walk.

February 17, 1979

The pale young man was outside today, and when I saw him, I realized he has been gone for weeks, and the moment I saw him again, I felt as if I were looking in a mirror, and I knew I had changed. I smiled at him and he smiled back at me—a sad little smile from only one side of his mouth. I walked past him as it was getting dark. You see, I was on the prowl with my flashlight.

It took some digging to uncover my meal, but as I went from can to can, as I shone a light into the dregs and the running liquids and poked the cans and newspapers and butts and bottles with my torch for lurking comestibles, I understood what was needed: another story. The story is entitled *The Introspective Detective.* The heroine of the new story investigates real-life philosophical problems. She, the Introspective Detective, otherwise known as ID—isn't that wonderfully Freudian and suitable?—is prompted by her empty belly to conduct experiments at the very threshold Simone Weil articulated with her incisive honesty—that limit where pity ends and charity begins. ID's adventures go well beyond the mere thought experiment. No smug, armchair, risk-free mental pirouettes for this girl; she is living the question. SHE HAS BECOME THE QUESTION ITSELF. I found ID more than comforting. She filled me with JOY.

And, my dear Page, I met with success: three untouched slices of pizza in a box in one of the park cans! No one saw me as I peered under the cardboard lid and spotted my prize. No one saw me as I shut the box and lifted my treasure into my arms. And, as I strolled jauntily up Riverside Drive and turned onto 109th Street, hordes of people saw me, but what do you suppose they believed? They believed I had ordered my cheese pizza at the pizza parlor, that I had paid for my pizza, and that I, a free and careless young woman with tens and twenties in her wallet, was on her way home to feast on hot baked bread and tomato and thick running cheese. I felt jubilant, and, after returning home and heating one of the pristine, perfect slices of pizza in the oven, I ate it. I ate it, and it was delicious.

After an hour, I ate the second slice.

Earlier today, before I was sated with pizza, I checked the air shaft to make sure no BODY was lying there. I haven't done that for a while. It's compulsive. It's because Lucy is disturbing me. I believe she is plotting REVENGE. I have no idea what she plans to do or how she plans to do it, but other people are involved. Patty is among them. The Introspective Detective is on the case. Isn't that funny? Ian and Isadora are asleep on my desk. I can't write them. My teenagers in Verbum are not up to the job just now. I want to follow them, but I am following Lucy instead. Things will turn around when I get work and money. I'll wake up the two kids and get them off and running again, but my nerves are standing on end, and I breathe too quickly. Mohammed told me to come back tomorrow. They might have something. I also called about three research jobs. Two had been filled. I called the third, but no one answered. I will try again tomorrow. Something will turn up. It's ten thirty now and Lucy is silent. No talk, no TV. She may be asleep already, but she chatted on the phone tonight. She's been whispering a lot, and I can't hear the other side of the conversation so the transcript is full of holes, but here it is, Page. I wish to hell you could tell me what you think of it:

"It's me again, Patty. How are you? [Silence.] I know. It's arrived . . . looks of shadows. When I'm finished, I will let you know." [Silence.] "The crippled gardener is the one to follow, yes, I understand that . . . [inaudible] Old dawn, Sam Haynes, that's right. You know, I want to punish him . . . [Long listening silence.] I live for it. Why do you think I spoke to you? [whispering]. What are switches for, then? . . . No, no, listen to me. What if he's guilty? I can't live without knowing. I can't live. [Silence.] We have to get her back to tell us. We have to call her back. [Listening silence.] I have pictures, documentation. Dolls. You have dolls? [Silence, breathing.] Mmmmmm. She crossed the bridge. I will tell myself. She crossed the bridge. [Pause.] That's all. [Pause.] Yes, I promise. It's helpful. [Silent listening, musical murmurs.] Can you cut the fear out of me? [whispers]. Yes, it may help me. The magical child, ya, ya, tomorrow three o'clock . . . [inaudible whispering] . . . hey, mad Lena, mad Lena, mad Lena . . . [laughter] . . . Goodbye, no, I won't forget. Lavender oil in distilled water, thyme, two and a half tablespoons of vodka. Okay. Yes." She hung up, whistled—not a sad tune but an upbeat something or other—and dialed again. "It's me. I'm ready for tomorrow. Yes, I rehearsed. Can temptation. [?] It's here in the book [whispering]. No, it's true. [Silence.] Until tomorrow, then, dear sister."

I have half a mind to follow Lucy to that three o'clock appointment. I have four subway tokens left.

P.S. I ate the third slice. I couldn't let it sit in the fridge and torture me. It will help me sleep. Good night, Page. I love you. Minnesota.

———

No, I never forgot picking through the garbage for dinner, and, yes, it is still terrible to remember the woman's face in the park because her revulsion was mine, too, and the burn of shame cuts straight through time. And, yes, I pity that girl now, and I move beyond pity to charity because she was young, and I can detect that just under the bright, brittle tone and all those capital letters lies a wail of near hysteria induced by hunger, willed isolation, and stupid pride. Her desperate circumstances did not last, and it is obvious to me that she did not believe they would last either. Her color and class inoculated her from such pessimism. The very next day, she called the number she had taken from the bulletin board at Columbia, a woman answered, and the two of them scheduled an interview for the same afternoon, and by the time she had left the splendid duplex apartment on Fifth Avenue with its view of Central Park and a cobalt-blue Yves Klein sculpture of a headless, armless, legless woman—the sex parts only—on a pedestal that stood in the corner of a room, where she had perched on a grand low-slung white sofa with a cup of aromatic tea and ingested seven grainy biscuits (five while the interviewer had disappeared to answer the telephone), she had a new boss: Mrs. Elena Bergthaler.

CHAPTER SIX

February 1, 2017

"I've been watching TV," my mother said to me yesterday when we spoke on the telephone. "Can that man be president? He's so ill-mannered, so vulgar. He doesn't make sense."

"He's an ignorant, swaggering buffoon."

My mother clicked her tongue and sighed. "I used to follow politics so closely. I forget now. It must be my age. How old am I?"

"You're almost ninety-four."

My mother laughed. "That's old, old, old, my darling, really old. I lie here, and I look out the window. I doze and dream." She took a breath and said in an alarmed voice, "You aren't losing your hair, are you?"

I reassured my mother that hair still sprouted from my head.

"I must have dreamt that, you see. Sometimes I can't be sure if I dreamt it or if it's true." She paused. "I think of Mama." She fell silent. "Sometimes I wake up and think she's still alive." I waited. "And I think of you as babies. You were such beautiful babies. I am looking

"CAN THAT MAN BE PRESIDENT?"

at your baby pictures right now on the top of the cabinet." She paused again. "Did I ever tell you about the day we were having breakfast at home? Oscar was in the Philippines somewhere. We didn't know where, and we hadn't had a letter for a while. We read the papers. Father's heart, you know, his heart was bad. He was awfully winded in those days. The stairs were especially hard. Well, the three of us were around the table one Sunday. The war had turned for the better. I know that. My father had finished his coffee and my mother was just about to pour him another cup when he noticed that the cup had a tiny crack in it—a crack no wider than a hair—and he said to her, 'You should have taken this one. It's damaged.' It wasn't like my father. It wasn't kind. Later, Mama took me aside and said, 'You know, he never would have said that if he wasn't ill and if Oscar were home.' "

"No," I said. "I don't know that story."

"Yes, the cracked cup. It didn't leak, just a hairline. I loved my father, but he disappointed me when he said that. I never forgot it. I wish you had known him. I wish you had known Mama. They died too young. Well, my beloved child," my mother said. "Isn't it funny how these stories come back? There are times when I think Mama is still alive, especially after a nap. I am confused sometimes, but then I'm old. I send you kisses and hugs through the phone. And Freya, Freya is all right?"

"Yes, she's doing well, working hard at her music. We heard her sing last week. She has an album coming out soon."

"Does she have anyone special?"

"No, not now."

"How old is she?"

"Twenty-nine."

I heard a soft note over the phone—neither a sigh nor a murmur, but a noncommittal hum.

"And," my mother paused. "Oh, your husband. What's his name?"

"Walter."

"Of course, dear Walter, and he is still at Rockefeller, and his important work with mathematics and biology—isn't that it?—that's going fine?"

"Yes, that's it, and he's fine."

"And your book, darling? You're writing your book?"

"Yes, I am. It's coming along."

"Well, my dear child, I send you hugs and kisses over the phone all the way to Brooklyn." And, as I listened to her voice, I thought to myself, Kari and I are still the darlings, and the lilt in her words pulled me back, far back to the time when she had supernatural powers.

I told her I loved her and hung up.

The mother I was startled to find sitting motionless on the floor in the kitchen after Kennedy's assassination, the mother who said she would leave for Canada if Goldwater was elected, the mother who shook her fist at George Wallace's image on television, the mother who walked beside me to protest the Vietnam War, the mother who followed the intricate minutiae of the Watergate hearings, the mother who just a few years ago reported on the arcane doings of politicians in her district I knew next to nothing about has disappeared and been replaced by a mother who turns on the television to witness a mass of fluctuating pictures and garbled sounds with confused emotional meanings. "Can that man be president?"

My mother's brain has lost the stretch of now, that temporal yawn that moves us from the immediate past into the immediate present with the expectation of the immediate future, all wholly elusive, receding and reappearing at a rate beyond our comprehension. We live at a perceptual speed that makes me wonder why we don't fly apart. It is this tumbling, unfathomable sequence of experience my mother no longer registers, and it is both fitting and ironic that she will never preserve the details of the new man in power, that as she leans forward and squints at the images on her small flat TV, her fragmenting memory will make no sense of what is, in fact, political obscenity.

A squat, mad, would-be despot rushes up and down the croquet field bellowing, "Off with their heads!" We live in Wonderland now. It does not matter that he lacks decorum, that his sentences are crude and ugly, or that he lies. He is a great man, the hero of the people, and they, "the people," love his swagger and his rage and his fuck-you-fancy-schmancy-city-slickers-who-think-you're-too-good-for-us, for US, the real people, us white people out here on the plains. Yes, the real people swoon for the nullity of his superlatives shouted at the cameras that are all trained on him all the time as he worries in public about size, the size of his victory, the size of his crowds, the size of his hands, the size of his dick. They love Dick.

"Think you're too good for us, is that it?" The little girl who sits in the kitchen with her hands folded in her lap as she waits for her father to emerge from the bedroom doesn't reply because she knows the woman with the thin wrinkled face and pointed nose is not asking a question, and it would be impolite to answer a question that is not a question, but the girl does not forget the fury and hatred in the woman's voice as she mutters those words, and the girl feels shame for the woman and when she feels it, the shame is hers, too. I told my mother that Freya and I marched in Washington the day after the inauguration, but she doesn't remember. The house is going to pieces, Mother. The wall has cracked open: the world of the bad dream has bled into the waking world. It's not what he says, it's what they, the worshipers, feel when he speaks. The feeling moves like an illness through the crowd. The crowd is feeling, and the great man is their route from shame to pride.

I cannot read what lies ahead of us. All I can say is what old Mr. Jensen used to say as he sat on the stump outside his barn: "It don't look good." As for my reading of the past, caution is in order on that front as well. I am a sophisticated narrator, to be sure, mature, learned, mostly kind, sometimes cruel, and as prone to delusion as the next person, despite the fact that I try to keep myself honest by admitting to holes in my own story. I am humming my song in my own way, Madam, humming my way down avenues and back alleys and into buildings where I take the elevator or climb the stairs and open and close doors and, yes, listen at walls with pen and notebook.

We left our young heroine, Minnesota, on East Seventy-Fourth Street in late February 1979.

From Mead:

Mrs. Bergthaler is a woman of uncommon solicitude and sweetness, who has a habit of clasping her hands together just below her chin to communicate joy and surprise. "Let me take your coat, dear." Vigorous yanks at navy peacoat eventually free my arms. Closet door glides noiselessly open to house shabby peacoat and red scarf beside long furs within. Closet door glides shut. Much chatter about bags piled in hallway. I am to pretend large sacks of unwanted clothing on their way to charity do not exist. They are not to be given a second thought as they are soon to be whisked off by helper named Kyle, "a sweet boy," who may ring bell in the next hour and interrupt us, but we two (if her manner is to be believed) have already, in the course of three minutes, become cozy conspirators (she has linked her elbow with mine and has patted my wrist with her free hand several times) and should Kyle, the sweet-boy-bag-snatcher, arrive at the door, it won't take but a second because despite immense workload and responsibilities that would strain even the most organized of humans, Mrs. Bergthaler has everything under control. And then after my maybe future employer has literally pressed me down—with her hands firmly on my shoulders—into the largest sofa I have ever seen outside of *Architectural Digest*, she communicates her eagerness to know all about me, but before I can open my mouth to reply, she calls for tea from a hidden person in the kitchen named Lilibeth and continues to speak. And behind the Klein, isn't that a Giacometti, a small standing woman? And who knew that lemons in a blue bowl on a table could look so beautiful? But even that light costs money,

Page, that bright daylight from the window illuminating the lemons. I hope you are aware of this fact. In the city, light is in short supply and reserved exclusively for those who can afford it. The rest of us creep about in the shadows with the roaches.

I have already forgotten what Mrs. Bergthaler said as she searched for her glasses in order to read my résumé because her speechifying and gesturing made me dizzy, and I couldn't keep track of her meanings. I know she mentioned *The Gin Game*. She had seen the play three times on Broadway before it closed, "so wonderful, so wonderful, and deep," and a short story she had read in *The New Yorker*, also "wonderful, wonderful," and she shot several names in my direction I did not recognize, but as they flew past me I thought perhaps she was testing me. (I did not say I had seen the play and found it bad, but the actors good, or that when it came to the literary arts, I regarded the premier magazine of the city as a purveyor of mostly smug mediocrity.) There was so much Mrs. Bergthaler this afternoon, Page, so much of her and so little of me that I did what I used to do as a child: I turned rigid, watchful, and silent.

After my hostess had secured her reading glasses and directed the short, lithe Lilibeth, who I guessed was Filipino, to lower the tea tray onto the coffee table, she plopped herself down across from me on a magnificent moss-green chair, lifted her head, and again wanted to "know all about me," and I began to tell her about my interests in literature and philosophy and my year given over to writing, but within seconds my lady had slumped back in the chair and her eyelids had fallen to half-mast, and she looked out from under them and smiled in a way that made me feel as if I had suddenly been deported. I directed her to the two-page summary of my life's achievements, snatched a biscuit while her head was down, then another, chewed, and worked hard not to make a single noise of pleasure.

In the momentary quiet of my chewing and her reading, I noted that Mrs. Bergthaler's facial skin is taut and pale, but the skin on her neck and hands is wrinkled and spotted. I concluded that her face is younger than the rest of her. No fat on her at all, a tight, gaunt woman with wildly expensive swooping hair. I examined the perfect cut of her violet cashmere jacket and the collar of her blue silk blouse inside it, and I inhaled her good smell—conifers and citrus and bergamot. (My guess.) Mrs. Bergthaler's eyes widened as she read "summa cum laude," aloud, then narrowed in suspicion as I watched her try to place the institution, St. Magnus—"Where did you say the college is located?" And a moment later, she nodded approvingly and said, "Oh, a fellowship at Columbia this coming fall," which I understood to mean: if that august Ivy League institution has accepted the summa as genuine, why shouldn't I? She must have concluded that the person who marched across those two printed pages, winner of the Greater Midwest Prize for Best College Paper in Philosophy, was qualified to call the butcher and the hairdresser, to run errands and organize her desk, because she smiled warmly at me with most of her perfect teeth on display, leaned forward, and hired me as her part-time assistant at six dollars an hour.

After a phone call that she took in the other room and which allowed me the ingestion of five more biscuits, she broached a subject of a more delicate nature, another possible but more lucrative job. "I hope you don't shock easily," she said. I assured her that thousands of volts of alternating current could be sent through my body without the slightest effect. Mrs. B. looked puzzled for three or four seconds, clapped her hands together yet again, held them below her chin, and gasped, "Oh, you're joking, aren't you?"

Seconds after my attempt at humor, Kyle appeared, and the "sweet boy" turned out to be a glowering teenager with a rash of pimples on both cheeks and, as I thought of him carting away the bags, I imagined an entire wardrobe of silk and cashmere disappearing out the door into the elevator, and I let my hidden heart wince for me.

The extra job, the one that pays more but may shock me, is a book, or rather the beginning of one. Mrs. Bergthaler has written sixty pages of a memoir with the clever title *My Interesting Life*. The project is not going well. "I know what I want to say, but when I sit down at the typewriter, the words don't come smoothly at all, and I change my mind. I just peck, you know, with two fingers, but I am constantly sticking in those little white things to undo the type. Oh, it's dreadful. And I have such lovely stories to tell. You know, my father always said I had spunk." Mrs. B. likes the word *spunk,* and she used the noun and its adjectival form *spunky* several times to describe herself and the quality she wished to communicate to the world in her book, but each time she used it, the word seemed to lose rather than gain meaning, becoming increasingly abstract and therefore alien, and I found myself marveling at the five letters and the ugly sound of the word. In my past, *spunk* has often been applied to cheerleaders, the girls who smile and jump and cartwheel and yell themselves hoarse for the team. Are there spunky boys? Of course there are. Are there spunky men? No. It isn't used for grown men, not unless the word is taken in another direction entirely to stand in for semen, the sticky stuff the Hua men were so desperate to save. Is *spunky* similar to *feisty* but less combative? And isn't *feisty* one of those words also applied chiefly to women, girls, and small dogs? As I sat there listening to Mrs. Bergthaler, I realized that I did not want spunk, and I did not ever want to be called spunky, that *spunk* and *spunky* were patronizing, even demeaning words. On the other hand, perhaps in the mouth of her father, *spunk* had been a term of affection. It may have been uttered in the warmest of warm tones with a smile of approval and therefore, in the mind of Mrs. B., the word had assumed a nobler meaning, one akin to valor.

I came away with the idea that the tale my employer hopes to tell is one that combines spunk and shock. The "shocks" are connected to her four husbands, her continental travels, and her protégées, in other words, to sex with relatives, friends, and strangers. This is where I come in. She needs editorial assistance for her spunky, shocking adventures. She wants ten revised pages by the day after tomorrow and comments on the whole manuscript. She handed over a hundred dollars. A hundred dollars! A little retainer, she said. O blessed retainer! "And please," she said, "call me Elena!" And I told her to call me Minnesota. And she said it was an "adorable nickname," and I felt adorable with a hundred dollars in my pocket, simply adorable. *My Interesting Life* may save my life. If she likes my work, I will make more money. Hundreds of hundred-dollar bills may rain down on my head! Page, oh Page, I am resurrected! Who would have thought it? The Introspective Detective in Riverside Park is metamorphosed overnight into Adorable, imbiber of tea and crumpets on Fifth Avenue!

Love, S.H.

Hindsight gives a shape to what is shapeless as you live it. The man who walks out his door one morning and, as he enters the crosswalk, is hit by a speeding car that has just run a red light and lives to tell the story, but lives with a limp and chronic pain in the leg that was crushed on that day, will give the accident climactic importance in the narrative of his life because the man who left the building that fateful morning whistling and swinging his briefcase, that whole and hale and perfect man, disappeared minutes later. But, let us say, that after his unfortunate accident, our man meets a woman, or a man (depending on his romantic preference), a physical therapist who works with him to get the leg back in working order and, as she or he gently massages the damaged limb, love happens and, just to make it a good story, let us say the love lasts between the man and woman or the man and the man, and that love—simply the fact of it—can never be separated from the hurt leg or even the pain that persists in it year after year.

We are nothing if not the accumulation of what Alfred North Whitehead calls "drops of experience" and, as I sit here writing to you, my imaginary friend, I know that life's sorrows and injustices—the ruined legs and lost teeth and cruel remarks—but also joys—a knee or thigh caressed with tenderness or the word *spunk* pronounced in such a way that it becomes an endearment or five twenty-dollar bills materializing at the moment they are most needed—are part of us even when we don't remember them very well, even when they are forgotten forever. They are part of the mysterious push and pull of a universe that is not static but in motion all the way down to its haunted quantum quarters and their uncertainties that pulse with the beats of mind or a kind of mind. And just last night as I lay in bed beside Walter, who was breathing slowly and regularly, and I was so close to the edge of sleep that our darkened bedroom had begun to shed its thereness, I had the strange intuition that I felt the stirring and heard the rustle of multiple affinities, extended and distended outward and inward without fixed location, and it occurs to me now that my reading of Whitehead from earlier in the day returned in those throbs of awe.

I have traveled in and out of thousands of books in the library, have walked in and out of countless mental rooms and turned down hallways I had not known existed, only to find at their end more doors to open. There is always another door and another room. And I have been writing, too, for decades now, and, as I write, I walk because writing is the perambulation of narration, and it has taken me into the streets of the city and out onto country roads where I tread again on the ground of my childhood. I look out upon row after row of erect or disheveled corn depending on the season, and I note the distances between telephone poles connected one to the other by sagging black lines. Sometimes those wires are dotted with the tiny firm bodies of sparrows, which, at a sound—a shot fired or a car engine turned over—disperse in an instant and punctuate the sky. I have had to go around the world several times without budging from my chair to begin to articulate what I already knew as a girl, felt as a girl in the busy hum of my nervous system attuned to person and tree and bird and horizon and moon and sun. But the gift of storytelling and the further gift of writing those stories down are surely among the myriad shapes time has taken inside me.

I will always think of Elena Bergthaler's memoir, *The Rebellious Debutante*, published in the spring of 1982, as my first published book. Not a single sentence of the 286-page autobiography belonged to the author whose name was so prominently featured on its cover. My lady's sentences sagged. Her diction was banal, her punctuation egregious, and her clauses unruly. When I took the sixty pages home with me, I discovered that she had spent so much time tending and watering the illustrious Bergthaler family tree, with its Jewish roots in Germany and its burgeoning offshoots in America, that she wasn't born until page 59. (After her four marriages, Elena had cut all other names from hers and rushed home to her patronymic.) I reduced the preamble to a paragraph with the flattering argument that it was her story the reader wanted. As long as the reader knew that the peddler of the first generation became the store owner of the second and that the store owner of the second became the department store owner of the third and, although large sums of money had fallen into and out of the laps of the Bergthaler clan as they continued to spawn offspring, when all was said and done, millions remained by the time the spunky heiress was born—all would be well. Although not the sensation my lady had hoped, the book was well received. The *New York Times* praised it for its "insouciant charm," "self-deprecating humor," and "crisp, often cutting observations of New York society."

Working for Elena Bergthaler served me well. The money I earned supplemented my stipend after I started graduate school in the fall. She gave me "bonuses" for no reason, treated me to lunch and the occasional dinner. She threw cashmere sweaters and silk blouses in my direction when the garments made from those precious fibers either didn't please her or she had tired of them. Although we were never friends, I remain grateful to her. At least a year after the book you are reading now ends (despite digressions, anecdotes, and trips into later years for clarification, my story as a whole will not go beyond September 1979), Elena and I sat in her study. I can feel the light in the room. I believe it was spring. I read aloud a passage I had written the night before about one of the lovers she had taken up with in Paris when she was twenty-one, a French count whom she had discovered standing over the bathroom sink in her hotel room at the Crillon, carefully washing out a condom after their tryst. Poor Elena had been justifiably mortified at the time, but listening to the tale from where she lay in her chaise longue in 1980, she laughed until the tears ran. No doubt, she laughed too much. I remember the moment as one of happy camaraderie between us.

On the evening of the lavish book party she gave in her own honor in the spring of 1982, I understood that my employer had subsumed me into her much larger and much richer self and that however much she may have admired my rendering of her life or the many sharp turns and leaps my prose had taken on her behalf, she had purchased my efforts outright. That evening she introduced me to the smiling crowd as her touch typist—"I can only peck, you know, with two fingers, but this girl is a whiz." My boss made it clear to the exceedingly well-dressed white people grinning in her direction that without my secretarial efforts, the formidable task might never have been finished. "Hear! Hear!"

To be entirely hidden is one thing. It is possible to remain a ghost in the wings with a secret, to smile to oneself and take some pride in the doings that are the direct result of one's labors, but to be publicly announced as the book's typist, a girlish whiz of fleet fingers, was a humiliation for which I had not prepared myself. From the distance of years, my guess is that this tactic reflected unconscious, not conscious malice. I honestly believe Elena Bergthaler admired and liked me. There were also moments when I intimidated her. "Who's Christopher Smart?" she once snapped. "You bore me with your references." Hidden somewhere in the subliminal soup of her mind, she must have known that by publicly turning me into her typewriter, she would prompt my voluntary exit from her life, which meant she wouldn't have to fire me. Elena hated to let people go. Not long after the party, I left the job. As a farewell present, she gave me a gold bracelet, which I lost three or four months later. It fell off my wrist.

But the elated young woman who walked onto Fifth Avenue with a hundred dollars in her purse had no inkling about how her new job would end. All she knew on that bright cold February day was that she had been relieved of penury, and the first thing she did was rush to a pay phone and call Whitney, who had returned from vacation, to report the news, and then Minnesota skipped, yes, skipped, to the number 6 train, emerged at Spring Street, and ran—how she could run back then with her long legs and her young lungs (despite the cigarettes)—to West Broadway, and Whitney buzzed her into the building, and she leapt up the stairs, and there was Whitney in the open doorway, looking deeply tanned, and they embraced and laughed and turned each other around and embraced again. And they spent the whole evening together, talking poems and art, and Whitney unpacked an object she had dug up on the island of Antigua, a rusted goat bell with a high hollow clang they took turns ringing in the loft, and each time they rang it, they shrieked with laughter, not because the sound of the bell was all that funny but because they wanted to laugh. Minnesota spent the night with her friend, and the next day after she had returned home to 2B, she wrote in Mead:

I think I am the happiest person in the world. Even thoughts of Malcolm don't hurt me today. I didn't want him forever. If he hadn't left me, I would have left him. There was something tight in him—a coil. Whitney told me she was never really fond of him. I read Laura Riding to Whit:

To-day seems now.
With reality-to-be goes time.
With the mind goes a world.
With the heart goes a weather.
With the face goes a mirror.
As with the body a fear.

I know the weather changes, but today my heart-weather is balmy. We were cozy in Whitney's bed last night, and when I woke up this morning, she was hugging my back and had thrown her arm across my waist. I had to lift her hand before I slid out of bed to make coffee. I thought of Kari. When one of us was afraid, we would sleep together in my bed or hers. I will send my sister a long letter soon. And, good news: My sleuths are awake. Poor Ian and Isadora need a progenitor with a full stomach. They need a fat, happy mother with a good job who makes money and can provide for them. I love you, Ms. Page Mead. I love you to pieces! S.H.

Rather than rush to Ian, Isadora summoned him to her house, and she decided not to bring up the who-was-Holmes-and-who-was-Watson question yet, despite the fact that if he said, "Elementary, my dear Watson," to her again, she feared she might clunk her friend over the head with whatever weapon was handy. Isadora had begun to avoid Ian's house. Although Mrs. Feathers always took herself "out of the way" so as not to "bother you two young people," she announced her out-of-the-way whereabouts at such regular intervals—"I'll keep myself busy in the kitchen"—"Don't you worry about me. I have some dusting to do in the dining room"—"Just let me know if my watering the plants here by the window is interfering with your conversation"—that her out-of-the-way-ness metamorphosed into an in-the-way-ness that sometimes caused Isadora to grind her teeth.

Mrs. Feathers fussed and fluttered and fidgeted and was prone to stream-of-consciousness narration on the subject of her extreme discretion in regard to the "young people," and she conducted this inner speech as outer speech in a high-pitched voice that strayed onto unrelated subjects such as dental bills, the rising cost of chocolate chips at the Red Owl, and the new play at the Arts Guild, starring Ronald Flury and Jeannie Valek, who were always starring in everything, and didn't it seem that they should give someone else a chance, for pity's sake? When Mrs. Feathers wasn't deep in an I'll-just-stay-out-of-your-way monologue with digressions, she roamed the house to do battle with the impertinent enemies of order—coats that lounged with brazen defiance on the banister, library books sprawled nonchalantly on the sofa, silver gum wrappers curled up tightly on the coffee table, so tiny they dared her not to see them, and bowls with the streaky remains of ice cream crusting inside them that taunted her from the bottom of the sink before she took them firmly in hand and wiped the silly grins off their faces.

The truth was Isadora often envied Ian his neat house, all swept and dusted and shiny, every object securely parked in its designated spot. She was particularly fond of the lavender sachet poised on a white shelf in the bathroom, and she liked to put her nose close to the thoughtful little herb that worked so hard to disguise unseemly odors. What troubled Isadora when she visited Ian's house was not its cleanliness or even Mrs. Feathers' soliloquizing, it was a particular look in Mrs. Feathers' eyes directed only at her, a look of worry that was just a mouth twitch away from disapproval. The look was there even when Ian's mother chirped out a gracious welcome, "Hi there, Isadora, and how are your parents?" And if Ian and Isadora retreated to his room to do math, biology, or English together or to discuss the Frail case, always with the door cracked open, Mrs. Feathers would hover in the hallway or rap lightly at the door or stick her head through its opening and call to them in quavering notes, "Cookies, you two?" And when the maternal head and neck had squeezed themselves into that liminal space between decency and indecency, chastity and sexual abandon, the narrowed maternal eyes were turned, not on her offspring, but on her offspring's feminine companion.

The irony was not lost on Isadora. Mrs. Feathers held *her*, not Ian, responsible for Ian's lust, even though Isadora's lust was aimed elsewhere. The mother had probably sniffed out her son's moony, swoony avidity for the young Miss Simon of the swelling breasts, but the idea that her tall, pointy, myopic, Sherlock-obsessed boy might be responsible for his own concupiscence did not enter Mrs. Feathers' feather brain. No, Isadora, with her curves and her large eyes and her pretty pink mouth, was most definitely to blame.

Once situated comfortably in the Simons' smelly living room, also known as the Menagerie, Ian and Isadora found themselves removed from Mrs. Feathers' out-of-the-way attentions, but this did not mean they were undisturbed. Disturbance was built into the Simon household. What it meant was that the disturbances were not directed at them. The disturbers were not spies. Before Isadora could ask Ian what it was that couldn't wait, Theodora swished past them in a ratty black slip that may once have belonged to Professor (Mrs.), a tasseled lampshade on her head, and a clothespin on her upturned nose, impersonating the sixth-century empress of Byzantium for whom she probably *had not been named*, wife of Justinian the First, immortalized as a clever, salacious, ambitious female in Procopius's *The Anecdota*. Theodora was followed by her obsequious subject, Andora, in sacral mode with her head bowed over a book that rested on her flat open palms as she intoned loudly from the historical text in question: "There was not a particle of modesty in the little hussy, and no one ever saw her taken aback; she complied with the most outrageous demands without the slightest hesitation, and she was the sort of girl who if somebody walloped her or boxed her ears would make a jest of it, and she would throw off her clothes and exhibit herself naked to all and sundry those regions, both front and behind, which the rules of decency require to be veiled and hidden from masculine eyes."

At the very instant Andora pronounced the word *eyes*, an enormous cowboy hat draped with several Hawaiian leis made of pink, blue, and yellow crepe paper rushed into the room on a pair of skinny legs in black tights that bagged at the knees. The hat snatched the book from Andora and roared, "Mother said no *Anecdota*!" The ten-gallon headwear then took a dignified march across the room, knelt beside the shelf, studied an arrangement there below, and reinserted the volume. The empress and her acolyte leapt on the hat that suddenly released its charge. Just Plain Dora shot from the room, chased by the two elder Doras into the dining room, where the larger siblings collapsed in a fit of manic laughter on top of the shrieking pipsqueak, and all three rolled around on the floor as if they were puppies, not girls, and were quickly joined by Monk, who excitedly licked their faces and thereby increased both hilarity and hysteria.

But poor Ian hadn't moved a second or an inch beyond the arousing passage from *Mother Said No Anecdota,* a book heretofore unknown to him, a book that appeared to have dashed his consciousness to pieces. A couple of minutes earlier, he had blushed purple on the sofa and, although he was unable to see the hue his complexion had taken, he had felt its heat, and had been obliged to turn his face away from Isadora and had forced himself to meditate on a logical conundrum. Alas, it was too late for logic. The Little Hussy had leapt into Ian's head, and the brave but shameless girl had already made herself at home. Although in the weeks that followed her taking up residence, she would sometimes bend over and wiggle her naked backside at him during lulls at school, she would become most violently active at night when she would put on a gymnastic show the likes of which would surely have panicked his mother. And so it was that Ian's nightly festival of rub-a-dub-dub, which featured the lascivious Roman hussy, circa 550, was inaugurated by Theodora Simon and her history-loving sister, Andora, many centuries later by means of the Simon family library, which included a volume of Procopius's eyebrow-raising, not to speak of penis-raising, observations.

Without knowing it, Ian found himself a foot soldier in what the pious dean of St. Patrick's Cathedral in Dublin, Jonathan Swift, who penned many a sober sermon between 1713 and 1745, along with other works, referred to as "The Battle of the Books." That great literary man, a veritable phallic tower of wit and wisdom, articulated the age-old conflict this way: "And therefore, Books of Controversy, being of all others, haunted by the most disorderly Spirits, have always been kept in a separate Lodge from the rest; and for fear of a mutual violence against each other, it was thought prudent by our Ancestors to bind them to a Peace with strong Iron Chains." By some egregious mistake, the Little Hussy had not been fettered to a cement wall in the Simon basement to keep subterranean company with the mythical alligator Geoffrey, as she should have been, but had been living freely upstairs among the Ps in the classics section, side-by-side with volumes of a far less controversial cast, the *Elegies* of Propertius and the Christian effusions of Prudentius. The great detective with the superlative mind resided on a shelf at some distance from the Hussy, and, as he was not being read by any of the Simons at that moment, he found himself inactive and between cases, which meant he was in a coke haze on a divan at 221B Baker Street and therefore vulnerable to molestation.

It is now necessary to pose the philosophical question as to the exact location of books, to ask straight out: Where do they live? Our Dublin Sage speaks of Spirits, and he speaks the truth. A book on the shelf is asleep; it is the Spirit of the thing that lasts, and only after it has been read and haunts the brain of its reader. And brains are various, which means that when a book is read, it, too, takes various forms, forms that may or may not closely resemble the words printed on its pages. Although Ian's brain had been molded by Feathers and Whortle genes (Mrs. F. had once been Miss Whortle) and by the undoubtedly nervous (if orderly) interior of his mother's womb, it had also been shaped by that asexual, never-to-be-a-father Cerebrum on Legs, Sherlock Holmes. Ian knew that Holmes was a fictional character. He was not one of the naïve believers who insisted that S.H. had actually walked the earth, but the deductive, inductive, and abductive hero had been an intimate part of Ian Feathers for a long time, and the boy fervently desired to keep his man aloft in the unsullied atmosphere of Reason and Science, that pure domain untouched by conniving female flesh. Furthermore, because it was the character he loved, he had paid little attention to his hero's author, Sir Arthur, and had *not liked it at all* when Isadora informed him that Conan Doyle had been an ardent Spiritualist and card-carrying member of The Society for Psychical Research, which smelled vaguely of communism to Ian (an ideology highly repugnant to his father), but in truth, the Spirits of one had nothing whatsoever to do with the Spirits of the other.

While Ian was sitting on the sofa beside Isadora listening to the raucous yelps of Monk, the wild cries of the three Doras, and the excited repetitions of Roger the Cockatoo's "Thy stubbel goos!" he eyed the bookshelves that lined all four walls of the Menagerie, with allowances made only for the three windows that faced the street, and it happened that

The Complete Sherlock Holmes collided with *The Anecdota* in the battlefield of his mind. Such collisions are inevitable. The more one reads, the more promiscuous the traveling from one book into another becomes. Emma Bovary is daydreaming about Paris in Rouen. There is a knock at the door, and who should march into the sanctum of Madame's room but the Knight of the Sad Countenance with a barber's basin on his head, followed closely by the young Catherine Moreland from *Northanger Abbey*.

Veteran readers come to expect these intrusions, but Ian was still young and, although his reading had been vast, it had also been narrow: detective fiction, symbolic logic, mathematics (especially algebra); Ian loved groups, rings, and fields. So we may excuse our bright but limited boy his shock (even though the event that caused the jolt transpired in his own brain) as he watched the Hussy leave the Ps, where the hat had ceremoniously left her, and climb with great agility from one shelf to another until she reached the Ds, and then, after rushing past Dickens, she found the address she was seeking, crept up the stairs of 221B Baker Street, stripped naked before the unsuspecting detective, who lay in an addled but contented state on the divan, did her scurrilous dance of front and back revelations, climbed on top of the great man, and ravished him. It is true that Sherlock was taken by surprise. It is true that thoughts of resistance flitted briefly through the great detective's head, that marvelous head that had never guessed but filled itself with data, data, data, and yet that head with the wonderful machine inside it, that machine supposedly free of the "emotional qualities antagonistic to clear reasoning," was no match for the empress.

And that is why when Isadora turned to Ian and said, "So what was it that you so urgently needed to tell me?" Ian looked at her with a flushed face and a puzzled expression and said, "I can't remember."

...AND THEN, AFTER RUSHING PAST DICKENS, SHE FOUND THE ADDRESS SHE WAS SEEKING...

CHAPTER SEVEN

Can the past serve as a hiding place from the present? Is this book you are reading now my search for a destination called *Then*? Tell me where memory ends and invention begins. Tell me why I need you with me as my fellow traveler, my variously dear and crotchety other, my spouse for the book's duration. Why is it that I can feel your stride beside me as I write? Why is it that I can almost hear you whistling while we walk? I don't know. I don't know. I don't know. But there it is: My love for strangers.

Every book is a withdrawal from immediacy into reflection. Every book includes a perverse wish to foul up time, to cheat its inevitable pull. Blah, blah, blah, and hum-da-di-dum. What am I looking for? Where am I going? Am I vainly searching for the moment when the future that is now the past beckoned me with its vast, empty face, and I cowered or tripped or ran in the wrong direction? Do my memories, painful and joyous, provide tenuous proof of my existence? Do the revolutions of memory, that circling from year eight to year twenty to year fifty-one, provide an illusion of more time? Are they a way of tricking myself into believing that mortality can be put off, and then put off again? Remember this: Scheherazade was a creature of the library. She read philosophy, history, science, poetry, and the pace of her stories kept her alive night after night because the great man listened, and as he listened he shuttled back and forth in time and traveled down many roads until he became someone else, and then the moment comes when all the stories have been told, and the book ends. There is no story without a listener, Madam. I need you as my intimate witness because without you, none of my stories will be real.

Almost every day, my mother tells me she is not ready to die. Then she adds, "But I don't want to live to be ancient and shriveled without a brain cell left. I don't want that." (No, I don't want that either, Mother.)

"How old am I?" she asks me again.

"Ninety-four."

"How old are you, then?"

"Sixty-two."

And she tells me it can't be true that her child has grown so old. She tells me that I was such a beautiful baby, and she has always been of the opinion that infancy is too short. How she loved that time of our lives, both mine and Kari's, and then, as if to correct her idealization, she recalls my convulsions at age one, the urgent call to my father, her desperation, her beating heart, "not just in my chest, in my head," my body clutched to hers as she felt her infant lurch, but by the time my father came home, the crisis was over. Thank God, she says, Thank God. The relief she felt, oh, the relief. And I remember losing the three-year-old Freya at the Central Park Zoo. I had thought she was with Walter and Walter had thought she was with me and for five minutes she is nowhere that we know of. She is lost or taken, and I race ahead in my mind and I see us at the police station and I see us living through days, weeks, months. I cannot breathe. Then I spot her talking in a loud, articulate voice to a woman who has bent down to listen to her.

Yesterday, a few minutes after I had hung up the phone with my mother, I checked the daffodils that have pushed themselves up in the garden behind our Brooklyn house, and I remembered the springs of my childhood that in memory have an excitement and violence missing from the season here and now. When the March winds blew, they blew so fiercely against my face I had to lean forward to keep my balance on the road, and when the many snows of the long winter had finally melted, they saturated the earth and turned the lawn into a bog Kari and I went out to navigate. Did it happen every spring or was it just three or four or five springs? Our feet sank so deeply into the grassy mud that we couldn't move, and immobility was an adventure. I see a rubber boot, upright and disowned, and my partly naked foot, sock gathered around my toes, as it waves in the air above the mucky green shoots.

I remember the first bloodroot in the woods behind the house and the crimson juice that stained my hands. I shuddered with the terrible strangeness of things that are alive and flowers that bleed, and I brought the fragile white blooms to my mother, and she made much of them and much of me. I lived for her kisses then, and they were plentiful. In those days, if she was sharp or irritable because she could be, the sharpness and irritability scraped the inside of my chest as if her words actually had barbs and thorns. Back then, when the buds began to erupt, I felt them break open in my body, and that hurt a little, too. And when the lilacs burst out of a deep tight violet into pale lavender, their perfume attacked my nose and made me drunk and unstable, so I would approach them cautiously, inhale and retreat, inhale and retreat.

My father is in his study reading a medical book on an afternoon in one of those years during one of those springs long ago. I know because in the memory I am looking through the large window onto the lawn greening and the lilac bushes blooming. I am interrupting my father because I have memorized the bones of the body from *Gray's Anatomy*. I hold up my rubber skeleton for my father, and I recite the bones, mispronouncing *femur* because I don't know the "e" is long, and my father smiles. He says kindly, "Oh, you'll make a fine nurse." And I pretend he hasn't sent a blow to my belly. I am bewildered he doesn't know I want to be a doctor. I want to make the rounds. I want to pull long slices of beef out of the mouths of prostrate women and set the femurs of farm boys fallen from haylofts. I want to carry my black bag. I want to pat old men on the shoulder and reassure them about their blood pressure. I want to shake my head over the bodies of people I couldn't save. I want my own Mrs. Stydniki at the office to look up at me and say, "Yes, Doctor H.; No, Doctor H." I want to be a hero. I am not a hero. I am a girl, and it is bitter.

But back then I couldn't organize the bitter feeling into words, although I can still see the lilacs through the window—the flowers of my defeat. And was it then or was it before or was it later that the tiny, bitter seed began to grow within me? No one will take the names of the bones or the muscles or the constellations in the heavens away from me. I will not be told that my mastery of knowledge is not really mastery but a girl's game, not serious because it is a little girl who plays. I will read my way far beyond you, Father. I will read and read and read all the books in your study and all the books in the library at school and all the books in all the libraries in all the world, and I will grow so large, I will be a giant in the earth. The miserable child who stood in the room with her skeleton, doomed to be a nurse, could not have said it. She could not have thought it because the words were unspeakable and the thoughts were unthinkable. The child did not know she was a heretic, but she felt the burn of ugly heretical emotions.

She consumed stories of injustice with a determination and energy that was surely a clue, but neither of her parents noticed or, if they did, they said nothing, and of course who knows what is boiling inside the head of a child? She read Anne Frank's diary and converted to Judaism in her mind, and she tried to imagine the suffering Anne doesn't tell. And it was around that time, wasn't it, that she saw a film called *Hand in Hand* about a Catholic boy and a Jewish girl? I remember little of what happened. But she, S.H., was so moved by the beauty of the friendship and the cruelty of the world that she staggered out of the special screening at the Arts Guild almost unable to breathe.

She read every book she could find on the Abolitionists, even when they were too hard for her. She carried around Booker T. Washington's *Up from Slavery* for a month, read it, but didn't understand it, not really. (I still remember long discussions of technical colleges.) Frederick Douglass was too difficult—what was the great man actually saying? She discovered *Harriet Tubman: Conductor on the Underground Railroad* by Ann Petry in the library at school with a beautiful Harriet in a pristine white dress holding a rifle on its cover. I remember the cover. I remember the rifle. She read it three times, and she dreamed she was Harriet Tubman, magnificent in her righteousness as she led slaves to freedom. That odd little girl was multitudes. She was Joan of Arc on her white steed, and she was Florence Nightingale during the Crimean War, her hands deep in abdominal wounds, blood to her elbows, and she was David Copperfield hurt and humiliated by Mr. Murdstone. She was a panicked Jane Eyre in the red room, and she was Dantès starving himself in despair, ready to die in prison, bereft of hope, forgotten and alone until he hears scraping sounds, the sounds of his rebirth, the sounds of someone digging.

She saw the bloody Mrs. Malacek just before the pace of her reading escalated into obsession. No doubt Mrs. Malacek's blood ran from the bodies of the dying soldiers and the dying slaves she read about, but the blood belonged to her, too. She was the miserable wretch whose dignity and humanity had been assaulted. Over and over again, she died a noble death fighting for the cause—in a grassy ravine, on a dirty military cot, in her sickbed with its ironed white sheets. She was a boy and she was a girl. She was a woman and a man. She was the young soldier who died with a great pitiable gash in his side or with one of his legs blown off. She was incinerated in a blaze as a heretic, poor Joan turned to cinder and ash, or she died pale and beautiful and tubercular with a couple of florid red spots on her cheeks and, after she was dead, tales of her goodness and greatness echoed through the land.

It is easy to ridicule the past self, to condemn that little white girl in a little white town out there on what used to be the prairie and her ludicrous fantasies of unjust suffering. Oh, happy wound! What did she know? And it is easier still to laugh until the tears run down our collective face over the stories and poems of wronged orphans, starving girls, and courageous slaves she wrote in secret. I am kinder to her now than I used to be. Cervantes is kind to his poor knight in the end, isn't he? I wept over his death. Sad man. Sane again. Cervantes is as kind as Flaubert is cruel. The Frenchman tortures his offspring and then he dissects her with the cold glee of a sadistic surgeon who eases his knife into the flesh of a female cadaver and cuts her lengthwise from pubis to rib cage. And the world applauds. It sings. I wonder if it would be quite as much fun if Emma were Étienne?

I take pity on the child-me, who is, after all, a creature of my imagination, and was herself an imaginative creature, as all readers are. We sway to the tunes of others, don't we? We become them when we are quite still and lean back in our chairs and read our way into their lives. I am you. You are I. And some of those foreigners decide to stay, possibly for the duration. Some are quiet, orderly people; others are loud and brutish. I can see now that she had to write, had to relieve the pressure created by the battle of the books in her young body, and if what came out of her scribbling hand were naïve Romantic effusions, that is nothing new. The author of the Mead Composition book, the mother of Ian and Isadora, had been writing for much of her young life, scribbling and drawing away in her diaries and notebooks and on scraps of paper stuffed into envelopes.

But we must return to our story. It is still early spring. The month of March in New York that year had been cold, and the city was slow to bud. The notebook's narrator grumbles about it. March 15, 1979. "Sleety, shitty, and wet." And yet, the overall tone of the entries is marked by a lilt and a swing that betray a cocky mood.

March 17, 1979

Page, I am learning to dance the city dance; it's a tap dance, in case you didn't know, shuffle ball changes and hops and riff walks. I can beat it out with the best of them. I have been practicing my superior and disdainful face in the mirror. You need to lower your eyes and turn your face a bit to one side and make sure you don't smile or, if you smile, it has to come from the corners of your mouth, slyly. Of course, I save this look for jerks. I do not use it on my real friends, never on the gang of five. Whitney does it naturally, of course.

I have no memory of this "practice." And I wonder if the writer is making it up, preening, not in the mirror but in the notebook. I cannot say. The gang of five had been recently formed and consisted of Whitney Tilt, Gus Scavelli, Fanny Cumberland (aforementioned flamboyant roommate), Jacob Ackermann (physicist), and me. (More about the gang and its consolidation in Chapter Eight.)

By then, Minnesota has paid her March rent. She writes about her bank account, which she now checks regularly. Some of her accounting appears in the notebook's margins. She works on the book that is still called *My Interesting Life*, and worries over the direction of her teenagers. She reads Wittgenstein slowly. Whitney is always on her mind. "Whitney is writing a time machine poem; it's a spiral." Our heroine returns to regular, percussive foam-hitting with various phantoms, and keeps an eye out for possible real-life heroes to fill air with flesh. Finds flesh, not hero, on the eighteenth of the month.

March 19

Date report: Twenty-four-year-old law student, D.T. Tall and slender with beautiful arms, long legs, and a round, tight ass. Beseeching eyes, slight hook in nose. Good teeth. Pleasant conversation about legal jargon over Chinese food. Takes me home to tiny apartment. Lowers me onto short cream-colored sofa with large coffee stain, undresses me methodically, neatly hangs each of my garments over nearby chair, arranges my naked limbs to his liking. I am grinning throughout. D.T., still clothed, kneels on floor beside me. It seems that he has mistaken me for a string instrument. He plucks, delicately, earnestly. His soft fingertips dance near sleeping clitoris. I am afraid I will laugh, but I close my eyes. At long last, his technique pays off in small explosion. He unzips, pleasures himself, and it is over.

I cannot fill in the two letters with a first and second name. I see only shadow and sofa, and I vaguely recall my bemused participation in the young man's erotic idea, which was not my idea at all. I submitted to his ritual with good humor because he was kind and handsome and innocuous. I had many lovers in the years before I met Walter Feld, but I have forgotten most of them, and the irony is that they, those panting, straining (or gently fingering) but once so solid persons, are now a faceless, nameless parade of airy ghosts with whom I collided in a city where easy, fleeting collisions were frequent. Is it possible to celebrate or regret what has vanished from the mind?

Lucy Brite, on the other hand, even as she was then, a person I had barely seen and with whom I had never had a real conversation, is vividly present in my memory. I listened as she hustled to and fro in her apartment, whistling and humming, shower water running, hangers rattling, her swift small steps headed for the door. Three times in a single week, I opened my door an inch and watched her leave 2C in a cloud of perfume, a fat manila envelope clutched to her chest, dressed in a long, hooded cloak that billowed behind her as she walked. "My dear Page, It's as if Lucy has become one of those furtive ladies in a nineteenth-century novel who steals into the night to deliver letters to a lover or to a long-lost child born out of wedlock. Where is she going?"

For Page, recorded March 27

"Patty, it's me. Can we talk now? [Listens.] Hmmmmm. I don't get it. You're too deep for me, you know. [Listens.] I repeat. The power of air—whirlwinds, salt and water. Long vowels. I'm learning. [Listens.] Revenge, kiddo. [Listens, sighs.] I'm trying. I don't know how I managed without you. [Listens.] I have the knife. No. I haven't seen him for a couple of days. I told him to leave me alone. [Listens.] I don't want anything to do with him. It was a mistake to talk to him again. Patty. I don't have it. [Listens.] I agree. Yes, for the bat. [Listens.] You're right. I know. I know. I'm trying hard, overcoming. [Listens.] Younger self. Bloomering [or boomerang? Inaudible]. Blood, the blood, yes. I tasted it. Just like you said, before the binding. Are the others in? [Listens.] Moth? Gorse? Moonlight. Do we need it? [Listens.] The needle. Ted. [Listens and laughs.] Tie him up, gag him, cut off his balls!" [Laughter. Listening for a long time. Murmering.] Yes, I see it all in my mind. Lindy. [Voice choking, silence.] I say her name. I say it. Why didn't the doctors think of that? They're so stupid. Dim bulbs. [Silence. Whispers—inaudible.] I'm rehearsing! Of course I'm rehearsing! The circle. [Listens.] No, I love the gardener. Every day without fail, honey. I'm in. I'm in. [Long listening silence.] Feel the rope. Visualize the rope. Tie the knot. [Listens.] Goodbye, my sweet."

March 28, 1979

I was jumpy this morning. Knives and ropes. The crippled gardener drags his leg under a trellis heavy with roses. Undertow of dread as I smoked too many cigarettes and added three more pages to *My Interesting Life*. Elena talks and waves both of her hands. I call her "the great gesticulator." I write. My character Elena bears a family resemblance to the Elena who tells me stories, but no more than that. I have sharpened her outlines considerably, but my lady hasn't noticed at all. The book is an episodic novel, a work of fiction as all autobiography is, and yet I am suspicious of the woman's memories. I think she lies. If Elena had her way, the book's narrator (she or I or a blend of the two of us, depending on how you look at it) would be forever describing the heroine's appearance as "slender" or "winsome" or "doe-eyed." When I pointed out to her that this is a phenomenological impossibility, that no one actually sees herself walk into a room, she frowned but didn't insist. Anyway, as I sailed with E.B. and her parents on a ship in the spring of 1931 to London, I pondered the date, a date pregnant with coming horror, and I found myself tugged around to Lucy's mysterious family: to the two Teds and Lindy dead in the courtyard. Lucy's enigmatic chatter is my bad dream.

When I met up with Whitney downtown at the Cupping Room around five, she looked at me, narrowed her eyes, and said, "What's wrong?" While I related my eavesdropping adventure to her, I knocked my fork off the table, and as it clanked to the floor the sound moved through the nerves in my hand and up my arm. Whitney looked on silently. I read the phone call transcript from last night to her, but I kept my voice to a whisper so the people near us wouldn't hear me, and when I had finished, Whitney snatched the notebook out of my hands and read the text loudly back to me, enunciating the words as if they were part of a poem or an absurdist play. The two men at the neighboring table watched her and grinned. I told her she was being "unsympathetic." Then Whitney leaned close to me and said that if she didn't know me so well she would think I had "fabricated" the whole crazy story, but she knew I hadn't, and she had wanted me to hear the words, really hear them, and then she said: "Your neighbor lady sounds like a demented fairy in some cracked version of *A Midsummer Night's Dream*." She told me I had worked myself up for no reason, and then she said, "Rehearsing. She said 'rehearsing.' What if they're rehearsing a play? Did you ever think of that? Maybe the play is called *The Crippled Gardener*? Maybe she was leaving the house with the script? Maybe 'The Circle' is the name of a theater. There are zillions of little theaters in New York."

She's right, of course. It's a plausible explanation. Whitney is sharp. And yet, she isn't the one who's been listening at the wall. She didn't hear the emotion in Lucy's voice when she talked about tying and gagging and cutting off balls. She didn't hear the way Lucy said "Lindy."

March 29, 1979

On the cover of the *Times* this morning, I read this headline: RADIATION IS RELEASED IN ACCIDENT AT NUCLEAR PLANT IN PENNSYLVANIA. I felt unreal for a couple of minutes. I could hear the city beyond the air shaft. Shouldn't they have evacuated the people nearby? The place is called Three Mile Island. Pretty name made ugly.

April 1, 1979

Page, it's Sunday night. The city is still here. Of course we may die slowly of exposure, all the inhabitants of New York may sicken slowly of one ailment or another and die, a mass evacuation of souls that leaves millions of rotting corpses behind. No one wants to think about it. I made myself rigatoni and stayed home to read. Around seven, I heard people arriving next door. It's eleven now, and they're gone, but Lucy had visitors. They talked over one another in the beginning, and I couldn't record any of them properly. Here are fragments:

"Red for me! White for Patty." [Glass clinks, rustles, laughter.]

"No, you get the cheese."

Lucy: "Oh my God, Moth, don't hog the paté. Give it here."

[Laughter. They talk over one another.] "This is such a great pillow, Lucy. The embroidery."

Lucy: "My cousin in Tulsa . . . [More talking from the others—unintelligible.]

Someone with a high, sweet voice: "How's it coming, Patty?"

[Excited din. Squeals. Laughter. All women.]

Hoarse but low and impressive voice: "Remember this. The mother is the whale of Western philosophy, always quaking under the surface. The whole goddamned tradition constitutes a denial of origin."

Lucy: "I don't really know what that means."

Screech voice: "Melville. *Moby-Dick*."

Someone else: "No women in that novel. None to speak of."

Screech voice: "Mother whale. That would be it, honey bun." [Continues in high, wild voice]: "Of course, we might all get nuked soon by leaking radiation, for God's sake. The great mother oughta strike down those fucking assholes before they kill us all. Gets me worked up, gets me mad. [Exclamations, chatter.] Okay, folks, everybody ready for the cut? Who has the knife? Where is that little critter? I know I brought him. Come on, little man. We're going to bind you tight [singing voice]. It's time! Where are you, my little poppet? Gorse, I tell you he was in the bag."

Shushing.

Lucy: "Not so loud. The walls are paper here."

Sweet voice: "I've got him. I've got him. Do you have the knife?"

Suddenly quiet. Whispering.

Hoarse voice: "Pour out your radiance upon us. The wheel turns . . ."

Someone hisses: "The radio. Keep the secret."

Sweet voice: "I'm naked."

[Giggling. Shushing. Wolf whistle. Laughter.]

They turned on the radio. Jazz station. A drum. Someone is drumming. Someone is drumming in the room, not on the radio.

Page, I couldn't hear well after that. The radio music and the drums interfered. Rumbling voices—chanting and singing, periods of music only. It went on and on, and I was tired. I stopped listening because my arm was tired from holding the stethoscope and my hip started to ache on the hard floor. Around nine, I heard a person crying over Chet Baker. I think it was Lucy. Someone yelled, "Hold her!"

More chanting. The words blurred. Moaning. A voice: "I'm scared. He won't die?"

And then whatever-it-was ended. Someone shut off the radio. The women whispered to one another. One of them cooed. Footsteps. The door opened and shut. Musical farewells: "Goodbye, my sweet. Love you, sister. Love you, too. Sleep sound. No worries now. All is well."

Then Lucy walks. Water runs. Lucy to bed. I hear a siren, the New York ululation. Now it is waning. I am counting to eleven. Now gone. Fanny mentioned "Rolfing" the other day. They massage you until you scream. Gus said he had a friend who underwent "attack therapy." They howled insults at him until he writhed and sobbed. He said it was a thing for upper-middle-class people who seek out humiliation. He's probably right. A city theme—urbanites wailing out their monsters. There is a word for it: *abreaction*. The deep hoarse woman's voice in my head: "The mother is the whale of Western philosophy." That's an intriguing phrase, but in Melville it's an albino sperm whale. Whitney's wrong; Lucy's not in a play. "Come on, little man." It makes me think of elves and fairies. What does it all mean? I hope I can sleep. I wonder what Whitney will say about it tomorrow.

Love, S.H.

Fairies dance under the lamp that hangs above our door. It is evening, and I see their agitated motion through the screen as a wind still hot with sun blows into the house. "They're attracted to the light," my father says from above. Is this a memory? I fill in. I fill in. But I can still walk through the old house, sold years ago to the man with tattoos after my father died, and then sold again to two ecologists with three children. I move one step at a time through the rooms.

Remembering is navigation, is repetition, is a wheel, and I step into the mud hall and see the hanging coats and jackets on my left and the shelf above with knitted woolen caps and my father's berets and my mother's white mohair scarf and various stray mittens, and I pass into the kitchen and there is the oak table and behind it a counter with four stools painted red, and I close my eyes in the light that shines through the window, a light that changes with the season, a light that comes around to its former self in spring and summer and fall and winter, and if I walk around the counter and past the stove and pause beside the sill, I can read the temperature on the thermometer on the other side of the glass. In the first three months of a year it can drop to twenty, twenty-five, twenty-seven below zero, and when the sky is cloudless, the snow glints with hundreds of thousands of diamonds that make me blink as I look outside at the white drifts and the woods beyond and then sometimes I feel the chant inside me, an incantation in my ears—the elves or fairies or goblins are speaking to me. And I stop everything and try to pray over them to God and wait for them to leave me.

On April seventh I left the building to set off for Elena's apartment as usual and saw Lucy and the pale young man in excited conversation to my right. I recall Lucy's stiff upright posture from behind and that she looked small in relation to him; her head reached only his shoulders, but it's the pale young man's face, bent toward hers, that remains fixed inside me. He had wet eyes and a contorted expression on his face. I took a fast breath to steady myself and, as I turned left toward the subway, I heard Lucy's voice rise behind me. "I told you, it's over!" Her cry, pitched sharp, seemed to rap the back of my skull and then echo in my ears as I moved down the street, and with the words arrived the suspicion of a love affair between them. Despite their age difference, the words were intimate. "It's over." That's what people say, don't they? "It's over." Let's call it quits, basta. Splitsville. The End. Close the book. It's finished. So long, Bud. You go your way and I'll go mine. Scram. Make tracks. I don't want to see your ugly mug around here anymore. We're apart now, severed, cut from each other forever and ever. "I am warning you, if you walk through that door, never come back." That's what they say in the movies. "If you walk through that door, never come back."

Aunt Irma used to say, "Never say never." But here is the secret: Never also has time and space, although those coordinates are often forgotten. It may be the Forgotten itself. When you get to the end of the road, take a right, then walk a quarter of a mile until you reach the abandoned house on your left. You will see it. It's all boarded up. They say a woman squats there. I have never seen her myself, but they say she walks with a limp and that she has seen wonders and terrors. They say she walked out of one story and into another.

CHAPTER EIGHT

I was the only member of the gang who had heard my neighbor through the wall, the only one who had ever seen her. For my friends, Lucy Brite was not a human being so much as pages of gibberish transcribed into my notebook over a period of several months, very little of which had any grounding in known facts. Lindy, Ted, Ted Jr., and the hopeless doctors were creatures of Lucy's monologues, which then reappeared in her telephone conversations with the mysterious Patty. I had definitely seen and heard Lucy on the sidewalk with the pale young man. I knew for certain that Patty and at least two other women had been in Lucy's apartment, and while they were there had been up to something that involved drums, a little man, whirlwinds, mother whales, a knife, and a rope.

Each of my friends concocted a possible narrative to explain what was happening to my next-door neighbor. The data were the same; the imaginations were different. Callous as it sounds, the how-to-tell-the-Lucy-story turned into a game we played for our amusement. Although I felt guilty about tossing Lucy around as if she were a tennis ball, I found relief in the various theories that were batted back and forth because I didn't want to live with the mystery alone. I needed my friends to lift me up and out of the violence that lurked in the fragmentary tale still unfolding in 2C.

In memory, I often see us around the table in Whitney's loft late in the evening. A stubby candle has burned to liquid in a saucer, wax brimming around its nearly drowned wick, and when I raise my eyes, I see its unstable light refracted in the curve of a wineglass and watch the cigarette smoke drift above our heads. I would like to be able to listen in on us now, to hear our voices, my own among them. I wonder if the high-flown discussions that delighted me at twenty-four wouldn't sound less than rigorous now. The truth is I am not remembering one dinner but several that have collapsed in memory: 1979, 1980, 1981, and 1982 have mingled in my mind because one dinner after another took place in the same room.

I can't accurately conjure the faces of my friends any more than I can reproduce our conversations, although I can broadly describe each person's features. Language hardens visual memory and, after the image has disintegrated, the words survive. But the picture of the five of us is less important to me than the feeling of us, an air of satisfaction that did not belong to one person but was created among us. We were pleased with ourselves, you see, and that self-satisfaction was derived from just the right amount of self-consciousness—not so much that it stiffened our words and gestures, but not so little that we weren't aware of ourselves as a rumpled, Romantic, lively collection of young artists and intellectuals either.

When we were together, what we had not yet done but surely would do had the power of an enchantment. We were raw youths, and we had swallowed the future whole, which is to say that what we were depended on what we imagined we would become and because we impressed one another, we were illuminated by our mutual admiration. Although human beings are forever projecting themselves into tomorrow, time takes the shape of a funnel as we age. The opening in the distance grows smaller; the passageway narrows. The possible becomes the probable. These days, I clutch the immediate. I am writing toward death.

The only way I am able to enter Whitney's old loft now is as a ghost of myself. I can imagine us around the table, but I cannot relive the particular form of contentment we felt because it was founded on expectations that have since vanished. In the notebook, I use "the gang of five" interchangeably with another, more affectionate phrase.

April 15, 1979

I don't use the expression with them. It lacks irony and reeks of nineteenth-century sentimentality. To be perfectly honest, it smells to high heaven of Dickens himself, but with you, Page, I am entirely free to call them the "Dear Ones." I had dinner with the Dear Ones last night. Everyone has a different position on the Lucy story. I wonder what she would think if she knew that there were five armchair detectives working on her case. S.H.

I gave no further particulars about the dinner.

As I meditate on the many meals merged into one meal, I see Jacob Ackermann lean back in his chair, the sleeves of a sweater pushed up above his elbows, a Gitane between his fingers. Jacob is our physicist at Princeton, twenty-eight years old, blond with a reddish complexion, born and raised in Paris, a Jew with roots in Palestine, often dressed in narrow white jeans and sneakers. Whitney met Jacob at the Castelli Gallery on West Broadway, where they had discussed Jasper Johns with mutual affection. He drove an old blue-and-white convertible of an American make I wish I could remember. Not one of us understood what Jacob actually did at Princeton, but we loved the idea that he was working to extract tiny secrets from our greater universe.

It was Jacob who first used the word *quark* in my presence. He described the fermion particles as "smeary," and he told me the story of Murray Gell-Mann, who had predicted their existence and had named them after a line in *Finnegans Wake*. Jacob also mentioned up, down, top, bottom, charm, and strange quarks. The language made me think less of Joyce and more of Lewis Carroll, and in that moment physics itself seemed to exist on the other side of the looking glass. Four years later, Jacob would introduce me to another physicist, Walter Feld, by saying, "He's left string," a mystifying comment that would be clarified soon after by Walter himself, but in 1979, "Walter Feld" wasn't even a name to me, and its referent occupied no time or space in my world.

At one of those dinners downtown, Jacob informed me that in theoretical physics one had to break through by thirty, do something big or you were pushed to the sidelines. Jacob had published an important paper, but he led me to believe it had to be followed by something better, and I understood that like dancers' bodies, physicists' minds were not allowed to grow old, and this thought made me wonder why certain kinds of thoughts appeared to thrive in young brains while others needed years of tending to mature.

It took me a while to understand that for Jacob much depended on hitting just the right chord in conversation, one that mingled sincerity and cynicism, compliment and joke. I also discovered that along with many of his compatriots, Jacob regarded flirtation as an art. In France the well-turned sentence is sometimes preferable to the acrobatic contortions of the flesh. Bantering with Jacob reminded me that I had traveled far from the Midwest, a feeling of distance I liked. I vividly recall that Jacob once said to me in a voice of measured sadness, "Why do you wear those pants?" and I looked down at the khaki trousers I had always liked to discover that they suddenly disappointed me.

It's not surprising that Jacob's position on the Lucy story mixed jocularity with reason. Lucy, he argued, was delusional, insane. He declared that the two Teds, Lindy, the crippled gardener, Sam Haynes, and the magic children were all figments of a psychosis. Hadn't she alluded continually to "the hospital" and "the doctors"? Jacob argued that she had been on the telephone with her indulgent psychiatrist, Patrick Somebody. When I challenged him to revise his theory to account for the "It's over" revelation on the sidewalk and the moaning women next door, he grinned and said delusions had been known to be contagious and cited as an example the dozen or so people who insisted they had witnessed a statue of the Virgin in some Italian town square shed three tears of blood. (It strikes me now that this must have made me think of Frieda Frail and my troubles figuring out what to do with her, but I really don't remember.) I reacted indignantly. I had seen the pale young man outside the building and had been listening to Lucy for months. I was not hallucinating. Then he patted my shoulder and said, "I know you're not insane, Minnesota, but are you or are you not a *romancière*?"

Even then, it wasn't clear that Jacob believed his Lucy-is-psychotic proposition. He enjoyed provocation for its own sake, had been a Maoist for a brief period a few years earlier (a fact that appalled me, but which he seemed to think had its dashing qualities), and despite his agility in the realm of theoretical physics, his psychological insight was not astute. *Romancière*, the feminine of *romancier*, is inevitably touched by the condescension the French have shown toward writers with the wrong genitalia for centuries, and that is why this sentence that began with the fact that I was not crazy and ended with the feminized noun for "novelist" has never left me.

I loved to play with Jacob, enjoyed the speedy back-and-forth of our talk, although I couldn't match his manner. We are still friends. This apparently innocuous comment hurt me because in it I recognized a familiar, patronizing music. Jacob did not and does not make a habit of looking down on me from on high, but at that instant his voice blurred with other voices I had heard over the years of my then still short life. If that particular tonality had played in my presence only once or if it had belonged to a single person, I am certain it would have vanished from my memory, but those demeaning notes have over the course of the years become a nauseating refrain.

And listen to me closely: In hexed repetition, time loses its direction. It springs backward and forward, bounces up and down. It floats to the top and sinks to the bottom, and it turns on its wheel. The melody echoes and reverberates and reaches a crescendo, and that is when it is truly hard to bear. "You'll make a fine nurse."

I closed the door on August Scavelli in Chapter Four to lunge in the direction of Malcolm Silver, the standard hero who has vanished from this book entirely. I will place Gus across from me at the imagined-remembered table, and I will summon Whitney to sit beside him and conjure up the breeze that blew over us many times through the open window on West Broadway. The street had a distinctive odor, but it is one I can only guess at—gasoline and exhaust and human sweat and newsprint and garbage and groceries and dog shit, but much else, too, until the blend becomes indescribable.

The stout, white-haired Gus I still know has obfuscated his younger self, but I can say that at the time he was neither thin nor fat. His body had the pleasant softness of the well fed and well cared for. He had thick dark hair he kept carefully combed, olive skin, wore glasses over his brown eyes, had a capacious memory, and delivered his communications as fast, detailed bulletins, dense with names and dates, whether they were about his hero of the moment, Wim Wenders, the genius of Eisenstein or Jimmy Cagney, the emotional meanings of camera angles, or the ingredients in his mother's lasagna.

Gus grew up in Tom's River on the Jersey Shore with his parents, his six brothers and sisters, and his paternal grandfather, who ranted in Italian when family relations became boisterous, which they often did. According to Gus, his passion for the movies was launched by illness. The summer after he turned nine, he began to feel heavy and peculiar and told his mother that his "knees were tired." His mother then grabbed his face with both hands, a gesture Gus explained was the maternal method of homing in on a single child among seven, and noticed that the lips of her fourth-born had turned ashen. Mrs. Scavelli hustled Gus off to the doctor, who diagnosed the boy with a rare, but transient, form of anemia, and after that, he had to lie in bed for two long months while his sisters and brothers ran in and out of the house, pushing the light screen door ahead of them or slamming it behind them as they skipped or ran to and from games and friends and the beach. I know about the screen door because Gus liked to dress up his stories with particulars. We knew his mother pitied him and therefore spoiled him that summer, that he consumed large amounts of ice cream and cannoli in bed and, as countless children who grow into artists and intellectuals had before him, Gus found himself a resident of other worlds.

He watched every movie he could find on television and indulged his mania for the Million Dollar Movie, which ran the same picture twice every day for a week. Because he was able to see the films again and again, he told me he would rerun the scenes he liked best in his mind before he slept. "I'd walk around in them," he told us, his eyes bright with memory and humor. Gus's first movie queen was Fay Wray, the screaming, squirming victim–love object of the great ape, King Kong. The film served as a reiterated joke, and we enjoyed arguing about its pernicious meanings. Hollywood, for better and worse, projects a host of fantasies, fears, and prejudices onto the screen, an often grotesque mélange of American piety and lunacy, especially about sex and race. It was Gus who told me that, in 1925, Samuel Goldwyn tried to lure Sigmund Freud to California with an offer of a hundred thousand dollars, but the author of *The Interpretation of Dreams* wanted nothing to do with the Dream Factory.

Whitney called Gus "Dr. Plenitude" because he was prone to providing more information than was strictly needed or wanted on his way to a larger point: exact film release dates, the middle names of actors, a director's eating habits, continuity errors, and disasters on set. These side and back routes were almost always interesting, but there were times when Gus couldn't find his way back to the main road. Whitney regularly pointed out flaws in the people she liked best, and this rude strategy made her more rather than less wonderful to her friends. I suspect it was because her criticisms were founded on a combination of insight and intimacy and, rather than wound, when the arrows hit their human targets, they made us feel distinguished—not like other people—and therefore understood.

Gus didn't limit himself to the movies, however. He was drawn to collective dreaming in many forms and took a great interest in fads. He defended the Lucy-as-member-of-crazed-psychotherapeutic-cult hypothesis. He cited psychic fads that had come and gone: nudist colonies, neurasthenia, corn flakes, and eugenics. Rolfing, primal scream, EST, and Z-therapy were currently in vogue. He regaled us with stories of his own cousin, Maria, who had become a Moonie. Gus insisted that the most unlikely people were vulnerable to the pull of idealism, intense emotion, and charismatic leaders. Look at Jonestown. Jones had offered his followers a vision of racial inclusion. They had gone off to make a new world in Guyana. Gus also mentioned the Sullivanians, who were headquartered in buildings on the Upper West Side. He knew the sister of one of them. Her brother had cut all ties with her and his parents, but after the Three Mile Island accident, he had broken his vow and called to warn her to leave New York. He informed her that he was on his way to Florida with the rest of "the family," that the entire northern part of the East Coast was about to "blow."

Lucy, Gus believed, had fallen for one psychotherapeutic scam or another. Hadn't money been mentioned? Most of these cults ran on their followers' savings. The mumbo jumbo on the telephone and the chanting I had heard through the wall struck him as definitive proof. And who was the pale young man? A member who had broken the rules, been pushed out, and now, bereft without his commune, was imploring the others for readmission.

Whitney stood by *The Crippled Gardener*–is-a-play thesis but embellished it slightly to make room for the additional through-the-wall information by citing Stanislavsky. Hadn't he advocated "emotional memory" as a vehicle for getting inside a role? Hadn't any number of groups taken this idea pretty far? Acting coaches were known to push their students to "express themselves," weren't they? Didn't that sometimes mean yelling and screaming? Patty was Lucy's coach. Lucy wasn't saying "I'm sad" over and over these days, was she? She was out and about with a manila envelope—*the script*—wasn't she? She seemed happier, less self-pitying. She invited friends over to her apartment—actor friends. Weren't they "chanting faint hymns to a cold fruitless moon"? Didn't those women sound like garbled thespians? Maybe the pale young man had been kicked out of the group, and he wanted back in. That surely happened. Maybe he drank or took drugs. Maybe he had missed rehearsal too many times and, filled with remorse, was begging to be forgiven for his lapses. Whitney believed that Lucy genuinely wanted revenge against her ex-husband, but she believed that Patty was "exploring" those ferocious feelings for Lucy's role.

And what did Fanny think? "Lucy wants that prick dead. Isn't it obvious?" Fanny uttered these sentences on April 23, 1979. I am certain because I wrote them down in Mead later that night. Fanny, whom we also called "Tiny"—she measured five foot one—had short brown hair, a heart-shaped face, a large, freckled nose, a wide mouth always rosy with lipstick, and a body with the proportions of a starlet. The curves beneath her chin had secured her work as a stripper and lap dancer while she earned her BA in psychology at NYU. The four friends liked the idea that the fifth friend had so recklessly cast off the restraints of bourgeois nicety that she had actually worn pasties. Fanny had made good money as a dancer and saved for the future, and yet I confess I never liked the thought of some middle-aged man leaning back in a booth, his dick hardening in his suit pants as the barely dressed Fanny undulated over him.

After she left school, Fanny had turned herself into a performance artist with a penchant for forceful nakedness. She hung bells from her breasts, wrote on her body, crawled on the floor, squawked, whinnied, mewed, and loudly recited texts. She quoted regularly from *Anti-Oedipus* by Gilles Deleuze and Félix Guattari, a book she had handled so often and so lovingly it had lost and then regained its cover with the aid of masking tape and super glue. Its innards had suffered as well, becoming badly wrinkled from her regular habit of bathing with the two philosophers. Her quotes from the anti-Freudians never failed to invigorate her small, mostly young audiences: "Shit on your whole mortifying, imaginary, symbolic theater!"

Fanny's intelligence was strong, but it came in fits and starts. She resisted method, logic, and all forms of slow study. She approached learning by the lightning method. She read steadily to be struck down by electrifying bolts of truth, which she then pondered for months. She and I argued about her worship of D&G, as she liked to call them. "Minnesota! Loosen up! Don't you get it? I want to smash things up and kick ass." While Jacob maintained a bemused distance from Fanny's "work," Gus struggled with it. The boy who at nine had fallen for Fay Wray, a "little woman" if there ever was one, wasn't always able to hide his discomfort, and once I remember he spoke to her harshly. "If you think wearing bells on your tits is a wrecking ball for capitalism, think again." Fanny pretended to be tough, but slights pained her, especially when they came from Gus, since I suspected she was secretly in love with him.

One of the great mysteries is where performance ends and life begins. Fanny had not solved this dilemma, nor had the rest of us, but she had a gift we didn't have. She loved an audience, although it may be more exact to say that she loved its love. She could work a crowd up to a high pitch of excitement, and she could work it down to an awed silence, and this power had an intoxicating effect on her. And, as we all do, she played parts offstage where she could be just as captivating—belligerent sexpot, earnest intellectual, stand-up comic. Her plurality allowed her to use her looks in ways Whitney and I never could. I was pretty, Whitney was beautiful, but Fanny, who was neither, had glamor, the magic of a particular kind of narcissism. Fanny's self-love exuded self-sufficiency and abundance, as if she had more than enough for herself and enjoyed giving it away. And in those days, just about everyone seemed to want it.

I will never forget Fanny's ecstatic face after a performance she had given in a friend's loft. Her pupils had grown huge with concentration and her mouth was stretched in a crazed expression—as much a grimace as a smile—and she threw her sweaty self into my arms, roared with laughter, and tried to pick me up off the ground, which she managed to do briefly because she was strong. She had hooked a donkey's tail onto her thong, and I watched it swish on the blond polyurethane floorboards as she jumped up and down. It's odd how vividly I recall the tail.

Over and over, I have found myself returning to Fanny in memory. I see her on stage, her mouth wide open as she bellows a phrase from Nietzsche or Mae West and sticks out her ass or laughs raucously, wearing only a top hat and a huge merken, also known as a pussy wig, which made her look as if she had an animal pasted onto her pubes. I hear her screaming, "I won't eat my peas for those fucking kids in China!" I see her wielding a gigantic phallus as she pounds a baby doll on the floor. The intense discomfort she created was the point, of course. I also knew that if I had performed as Fanny did, my parents would have wept with shame. Her parents were divorced, and she rarely spoke of them. Once, just once, she said, in response to something I had said: "My old man? It's simple. He hates me."

I must add that Fanny's habits were slovenly. She left her clothes lying about the loft. She made smacking sounds when she ate cereal, which she ate often. She drank all the orange juice without a thought for her roommate. She picked her nose in front of us and, when we groaned in disgust, she hooted obscenities. She bit and chewed her nails until they bled, and if Whitney expressed her disapproval and suggested a manicure, Fanny stuck out her tongue and whined, "Yes,

Mom," and "No, Mom." She spoke openly about how much she loved to smell her finger after she had inserted it in her "butt-hole." At the same time, she was intensely affectionate. She hugged us and kissed us and tickled us and made us laugh. We loved Fanny, but our short, pugnacious, unruly friend surpassed our understanding at the time.

Tiny was not fearless. She usually vomited before her performances. She would emerge from the bathroom white and with a sheepish smile on her face and say, "Well, that's over." By definition, the fearless can't have courage, and Fanny had a lot of courage. Only now am I able to see that beside Fanny, Whitney and I were decorous, if ambitious, young women, who mostly stuck to the rules. So, you see, the table of five has changed meaning between 1979 and 2017. *Remembering is change*. Our "Tiny" has grown taller and wiser: "Lucy wants that prick dead."

Unlike Carolee Schneemann or Marina Abramović or Karen Finley, Fanny never became famous or even semi-famous. She had the energy, but she lacked the steel, the metal needed to go on with a show that was more and less a version or multiple versions of her "self." She suffered from funks, too, during which she cried a lot and ran high fevers no doctor could explain. I remember bringing her a cold washcloth after her temperature had hit 103 and, as I placed it on her forehead, Fanny began to blubber that she loved me. "I love you, Minnesota, because you're kind." Whitney was there, too, sitting on Fanny's bed upstairs. She looked straight at me and mouthed, "Saint."

When my eyes scan the dessert plates with half-eaten pieces of a tart on them and the glasses with an inch or two or three of red wine that gleams ruby red in the light of the candles, my inner vision blurs, and I hear the sound of our talk and our laughter as if from a distance. What were we saying? I turn my eyes toward the door, and I watch it open. A woman enters the room. She is wearing a tin-can bra and has a postage stamp carefully glued to her cheek. She has a shaved head and has painted her scalp red. I have already introduced the Baroness to Fanny, and Fanny is in love with her. Fanny calls Elsa "Granny" and "The Crash Creature" and "The Burning Bard." A year later, a line from Elsa became part of her act: "Tinkle I mellow ukulele!"

The Baroness was a femme fatale who tackled the boys to the ground when the desire hit, and she bit them until they bled. She was a brazen beast with wit. She frightened Marcel Duchamp and William Carlos Williams. I watch the two little men run for the hills. "Come on, little man. We're going to bind you tight." The Baroness was a phallic woman punster, arrested in Pittsburgh for wearing a man's suit and smoking a cigarette. As a teenager, her father attacked her, and she punched him back hard and left his house forever. Her mother was dead. When Ida-Marie Plötz went mad, her husband banished her to an asylum where she died of cancer of the uterus. Elsa blamed the great man, her violent, autocratic father. She was convinced his untreated syphilis had caused her mother's malignancy. She remained an avenger of her mother's death all her life.

My bawdy spirit is innate—
A legacy from my Dada—
His crude jest bestowed on me
The sparkle of obscenity

My noble mother's legacy
Melancholy—passion—ardour—
Curbed by gentlewoman's reins
Exiled from castle—spoilt gentility

The Dear Ones are sitting around the table in Whitney's loft. They are all alive, and they are all still young and promising. Elsa is there, too, with her arm draped around Fanny. Maybe they are kissing. They both took girls and boys to bed. Fanny and I kissed once to see what it was like, but then I laughed, and it went no further. Were you disappointed, Fanny? Maybe you didn't care. It seems I like girls more in my fantasies than in real life.

I am writing not only to tell. I am writing to discover. Whitney knows what I want because I have told her about "beastly and cold." I hear her laugh. The Little Hussy climbs the bookshelf. Fanny lies in bed with a washcloth on her forehead. Gus ponders the cheap and flagrant overuse of the close-up. Jacob pronounces the word *romancière*—the Little *Romancière*. Someone wants that prick dead.

There isn't much time left, and there is hardly any money. Maybe she is hungry. The Baroness is writing a letter. "Dearest Djuna, my book of poetry . . . Oh! What may be—it would do for me to keep me—at least *floating*—if I could see it soon! Djuna, it is desperately necessary for me—"

There is no book. There is no book until 2010.

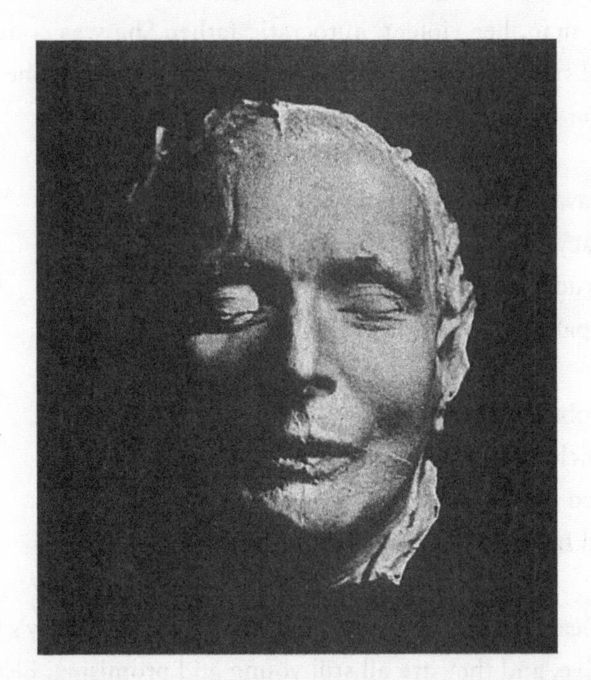

DEATH MASK OF THE BARONESS

REPRODUCED IN *TRANSITION* 11, FEB. 1928

CHAPTER NINE

I am in Minnesota. It's early in the morning. The window is open and it smells of spring. Yesterday, as the taxi from the airport moved along the highway toward Webster, I let the greens of the warm May light inside me, and I felt the slight undulations of the wide flat landscape and its periodic staccato protrusions—the barns, silos, houses, trailers, and the intermittent billboards for food, motels, and Jesus along the road. The visual music of home.

I write until noon, and then I walk down one silent corridor and then another to Sunflower Suites. I press the release button to enter and walk through the common room where the TV is always on, most often to the nature channel, and I catch a glimpse of a mammal's mouth agape, dripping with the crushed body of its prey, or a wriggling oceanic squib that darts in and out of underwater foliage to the sound of a man's voice explaining the curiosities of the animal kingdom, usually in anthropomorphic terms. I push open the door and greet my mother with a kiss, and the vigil begins. I sit beside her in a chair as she lies in her bed. We contemplate the orchids and the photographs on the wall and sometimes the familiar paintings, and we talk. My mother dozes off from time to time and she startles awake and says in an anxious voice, "Are you still there?" And when I assure her that I am, she says, "I'm so glad you're still there, my darling." I am here. By Monday I will be gone.

She asks me about this book, and I tell her I am in the middle of it. "You are writing about your life, your *own* life?" Only one year of it, I explain. "Do you think I will understand it?" And I say yes, and I tell her that she is in the book. "Nothing bad about your mother, I hope." No, nothing bad, I say, and minutes later she asks me about the book again, and I tell her that I am working on it and, yes, it is a memoir, but memory is not fixed. I have always believed that memory and the imagination are a single faculty. "I don't know what you mean," she says. I begin an explanation and my mother sighs. "You read a lot, I know, but then you remember it. How do you remember it all?" And we talk more. And then she says, "And how is your book going?" I explain, and she says, "Oh, yes, I think you told me that yesterday, didn't you?" Is my mother losing time or is she losing the perception of time? Are they one and the same thing?

When minutes and days collapse, does existence lose its tensed quality? Do "is" and "was" and "will be" collide and fall into an undifferentiated heap of time? Does time-telling lose sequence? I climb into bed with her and stroke her hand, a hand that resembles my own. I must do it carefully because of her arthritis. "How old am I? Am I seventy?" And I correct her: "Ninety-four." My mother laughs. "It's embarrassing. You know when I asked you I actually believed I was seventy. Twenty-four years ago! Isn't that strange? At that moment, I believed it." And I think to myself: Her arithmetic hasn't faltered.

I see my mother clad in a canvas jacket and rubber boots leave the house for her daily walk into the woods and beyond, and I watch her as she ambles along the creek, stoops to pluck a flower or a fallen leaf or gather up long grasses, depending on the season, and I watch her cross the water by route of the fallen tree and hasten across it with small determined steps, her arms extended for balance, and once she is on the other side, I admire her as she climbs the steep earthen wall, clutching roots with her hands and securing them as footholds. Now she is crossing the open meadow. She is a small, thin, brisk figure under an immensity of sky—rolling, gray, and moist. "I miss the spring in my step," she said to me yesterday. It was yesterday. Mother, I miss it, too.

I never told her about the night of May 7, 1979. Even if she lives long enough to see the publication of this book, it will sit on the night table beside her bed as a talisman of her child's writing. She will never read it because once she has arrived at the bottom of a page, the meanings of that page have disappeared. This thought comforts me. I recorded the sequence of the events in the notebook the following day.

May 8, 1979

I want to tell it exactly as I remember it. I want to make last night intelligible, if that's possible. I will do my best. At the last minute, Whitney, Fanny, and I decided to go to a party on Prince Street because Fanny was convinced Meredith Monk was going to be there. Meredith Monk was not there. I wore my new blue pants, cobalt blue, purchased at Loehmann's in Brooklyn, marked down three times from $200 to $39.99, and a white blouse, plain but well cut, another bargain, and the pink sweater Mother knit me for my birthday. I wore my hair up. I am providing these details because they become important later. Enormous loft, electric wires hanging all over the place, brick walls, battered floor. A minute after we arrived, Fanny recognized a bald man and ran over to him. "Freddy!" Whitney was accosted by Mark Gold, the painter. He's at least fifty. I've met him several times. He leans and leers and talks about his shows and all the famous artists he knows.

That's when I saw the man in question. Loose navy-blue jacket and a blue button-down collared shirt, uptowny, six feet three inches tall at least. Around my age, I think. Jeffrey, Jeff. He has one of those square-jawed faces that instantly make me think of leading men, straight nose, brown eyes, easy gestures. Handsome. Did I notice anything else? No. I am trying to remember what we talked about first. Italy. He had just returned from Italy, from Milan. Why was he there? His mother lives there. She's Italian. He speaks Italian. I asked him to say something in Italian, a language I don't know at all. He did, but I can't remember what it was. And I said I had been to Florence when I was eighteen. We talked about the Uffizi. I told him I got sick after two hours in the museum: too many paintings all at once. I had a beauty overdose, sickened by color. He laughed. Did I like his laugh? I'm not sure. It's hard to recover my opinion now. He asked me if I wanted a drink. I said yes, and then he steered me to the bartender by gently holding my elbow. Think carefully. Yes, the gesture pleased me. It struck me as masterful.

Go back and try to remember as much as you can. His father is an American, lives here in New York, but he said little about him. His mother worked in the fashion business all her life but has left it to pursue birdwatching. Jeff's mother flies to remote destinations to search for particular species, and she now lives, according to her son, in a state of perfect ornithological happiness. More chitchat. He did not lean or leer. Did I talk about myself? Very little. My job for Elena, that's all. He suggested I accompany him to another party uptown. I hesitated. I know I hesitated. What time was it? Ten thirty, eleven maybe? Did I sense something was amiss? No, definitely not. I accepted. I imagined kissing him, holding his big, lithe body. I imagined him naked. That is a fact. I expected to end up in bed with him. I said I had to inform my friends that I was leaving. I searched the room for Whitney and found her sitting on the floor beside Amanda Blake, who works at the Sonnabend Gallery. Amanda was wearing a purple jumpsuit with wide shoulders. I can see the color now beside Whitney's black shirt, their faces turned up to me. When I pointed out Jeff to Whitney, she made a soft wolf whistle and said, "Adventures in living."

Outside on the street, it was colder than I had expected. I see him as he holds the cab door open for me. I remember his legs beside mine in the back of the taxi and his large hand with its long fingers on one of his knees. The expectation was still pleasant. My window was open and the wind blew in cold. I began to crank it up, but he reached across me and finished the job. "Better?" And I nodded. Jeff went to Yale. Did he volunteer this fact? Maybe. He studied history and economics. I forget most of the exchange, but I quoted Marx: "Money is the general confounding and compounding of all things—the world upside down." I explained to him that I had given up Marxism when I was sixteen, but that didn't mean Marx lacked valuable insights. And he said, "You're a funny girl." A sign of condescension? Why did that comment make me a funny girl?

I remember this, too: He told me he had been on "the heavyweight rowing team" in college. I knew about rowing—English boys in shorts, heave-to, heave-to, or maybe that's sailing—anyway, the term "heavyweight, or open, rowing" was unknown to me. As in boxing, it's about the athlete's weight. He spoke fervently about the annual Yale-Harvard competition on "the Thames," a river that has always meant London to me, but this one seems to be in Connecticut, and, as I looked at him in the murk of the cab, his profile and occasionally his full face, lighting up and then growing dark according to the moving traffic, I thought that the memory of rowing had brought out strong feeling in him for the first time since I had met him.

I didn't register the address. I know it was on the East Side, and it probably wasn't far from the East River, because the cabby took the Drive. Why didn't I bother to note the address? I wasn't paying attention. When I'm alone, I pay attention. Also, I don't know that part of town. I offered him ten dollars for cab fare, but he pushed my hand away. "No, no. I invited you." Did that bother me? No, I was happy to save the ten. We took the elevator to the ninth floor. I can see the button: the round brass disc. What did we talk about? He said I looked like a model but didn't talk like one. People are always saying I look like a model—tall and thin. It was a dull comment. I suddenly wished he were less dull. But then, I am used to being looked through. Why do people look right through me? I also noticed a small shaving cut on his cheek that had become slightly inflamed.

Inside, the big room was dim. The view overlooked nearby buildings—a regular geometry of illuminated windows. Several carefully placed square table lamps gave off a cold white light inside the apartment, and I heard murmuring conversations and chuckles and innocuous low music. Jeff introduced me to "Rick," a man who appeared suddenly, a short person, not fat, but with a small round belly. I recall the fabric of his expensive shirt had pulled open at his paunch to reveal skin and a few hairs. The hair on his head was swept back, and he smelled very slightly of cologne. Rick was friendly in that crisp, perfunctory, impersonal way that has become familiar to me in New York, and he had a high voice, almost womanly. He offered me a glass of champagne. I took it and stared out the window. Jeff had wandered over to a large sectional sofa and seated himself beside a young blond man, whom he seemed to know well. I can see the blond man with his mouth wide open: "Oh my God, Catherine Bales. How could I forget that night!" Jeff's eyes were lit with amusement as he remembered Catherine Bales. I liked him less. Mr. Blond-of-the-Catherine-Bales-Comment let his fist fall onto the big square glass coffee table in front of him for emphasis. A vase on the transparent surface rattled, and a woman with a sleek red bob in the style of Louise Brooks said, "Watch the crystal, darling."

Was I bored or tired or both? I was beginning to feel lonely and restless. It's such an old feeling. I call it "the margins feeling." Maybe it's the gulf feeling—a chasm opens up between me and wherever I am—a great divide of difference that keeps growing and can't be bridged. What is it that separates me from so many people? Is it a slant of mind? I walked over to the table and noticed lines of cocaine carefully cut and isolated on a piece of foil. I watched a man with smooth brown hair sniff the fine white powder through a rolled hundred-dollar bill and then pass the bill to Ms. Sleek Red Bob, who leaned over to do the same, and, as she lowered her head, I noticed that her dress had an open back. I can still see the knobby row of her vertebrae, and I had a sudden feeling of vulnerability—whether hers or mine I don't know.

Once she had partaken, she nodded at me, but I shook my head. I probably smiled to hide my pity for her but also my distaste. The idea of stuffing my nostrils with an expensive drug through a hundred-dollar bill made me think of "compounding and confounding." I had a cold and beastly thought: I have dropped yet again into the land of the idiots, decadent, empty-headed idiots. What was the half-Italian Yale "crew" boy doing here? Maybe they were fashion people, associates of his mother. Ms. Sleek Red Bob pulled me down next to her on the sofa and called me "honey." I saw that her eye makeup had smeared. She patted the side of her nose delicately with her fingertips, sniffed, and began a lecture on the joys of cocaine, "the perfect drug. Really, it is. You feel just marvelous. You feel just like yourself, only better, and it's not addictive."

I noticed Jeff studying me. He looked alert. Mr. How-Could-I-Forget-That-Night beside him also looked alert. I told Ms. Sleek Red Bob that she was wrong. "Why, what do you mean?" I told her Freud had felt just as she did about the drug. He had written about cocaine and its beneficial properties, but then he discovered it was extremely addictive, dangerous. Freud changed his mind. She could find the story in his *Cocaine Papers*. Rick grinned. "I see Jeff's girlfriend is an expert on nose candy." The word *girlfriend* jarred me. I should have said, "I'm not his girlfriend. We just met." But when I think about it, why didn't he address me? Do I remember how many people were at the party? Twenty? It was early this morning and except for Rick, Red Bob, and How-Could-I-Forget-That-Night, the others are no more than hazy, milling human forms. I wanted to leave. For an instant, I considered taking the subway downtown to look for Whit and Fanny. Maybe they were already home and asleep. I would splurge on a cab across town. I had enough money. The thought of three subways at that late hour, the lurches and squeals, the faltering lights, the cars occupied by a louche singleton here and there, half asleep or drugged or crazy or all three, repelled me. I lingered for several minutes anyway as the others talked. What did they talk about? Real estate. Rent. Addresses. Does it matter? Why does it matter? I want to remember everything. That's why. I want to understand it.

I approached Jeff, thanked him, and told him I was going home. I was tired. He stood up from the sofa, faced me, and said, "A girl who comes with me leaves with me. I'll take you home." He smiled, but it was a false smile. I could see that.

What did these words mean? Do I know what he meant by them? Why did they make me feel vaguely ashamed? Was it some macho Italian thing? Was he insinuating that I didn't know the rules? Was I "a girl"? I said nothing for several seconds. Why? I had walked through the door with him, it is true, but we had picked each other up at a party only hours before. I told him it wasn't necessary, but he insisted. I must think carefully now. I must try not to read the past through the present. "A girl who comes with me leaves with me." Did I receive that sentence as a threat? I heard it with some alarm. Then why did I stay? There is something in me I don't understand.

I thanked Rick, shook his hand, and walked toward the hallway that led to the elevator. Behind me, I heard Jeff in conversation with Rick and That-Night. Rick said, "A kiss to your mother." Low talk. A minute later, I heard the three of them laugh, and the harsh melody of their mingled voices made me think that one of them had told a coarse joke, and I asked myself how without listening to the content of the exchange it was possible to guess even the rough meaning of what three people have said to one another. Men laugh in ways they don't laugh when women are listening. This is certain. I waited for Jeff outside the elevator. While I waited, I felt uneasy. Why did I wait? I waited because it was polite to wait, and I am polite. But that does not explain it. There was something else—something more—

wasn't there? I worried that if I didn't wait, it might be awkward. He had been emphatic that he would leave the party with me. He would be insulted, perhaps even humiliated if I left on my own. But why did I care? That is not a full explanation either. Why didn't I get on the elevator and disappear? What was my restraint about? Why did I feel bound by him?

He didn't say much in the taxi at first, but I felt tension, a taut irritation. He was probably drunk. I had seen him drinking bourbon. And yet, he didn't slur his words. His movements weren't sloppy. He was big and could probably swill down a lot. He asked me in an arch voice what I was reading "at the moment." Was I reading Marx or maybe Freud? This seems important now. He sounded annoyed about my reading. My reading seemed to be an affront to him personally. He didn't bother to disguise his sarcasm. He supposed it was something "difficult." I felt annoyed and threw Wittgenstein at him, the *Investigations*. I had worked hard on the book. I had read it slowly, had studied, taken notes. I could quote from it. I was tempted to quote from it, but I didn't. His handsome face had begun to look stupid to me, almost venal. He scratched his nose and the gleam of his gold watch in the shifting light of the traffic suddenly repulsed me. It was a Checker cab, roomy. I remember I moved closer to the door and stared out the window as we drove fast through the park.

I was so glad to see good old 309 West 109th Street that if I had been able to hug the dear, ugly building I would have done it. I reached into my bag and offered him the same ten-dollar bill I had tried to give him earlier. He rebuffed it curtly, and I said, "Thank you. Good night." I am always thanking people. Good God. What is the matter with me? I leapt out of the car, my keys at the ready. I heard the cab door shut, heard the car pull away, took a happy breath, and then stopped breathing when I heard the fast, strong footsteps of Heavyweight Crew behind me. My key had already turned in the lock, and I felt his hand push open the heavy door. I pulled the key violently out of the lock and closed my fingers tightly around it. In the hallway,

I turned to him. I told him I didn't need an escort, and he said, "I will take you to your door." Did I say okay? No, I did not. Did I nod? No, I did not. And yet, I didn't run up the steps ahead of him. I didn't yell for Mr. Rosales or run downstairs to his basement apartment. Did I believe I could "handle" the situation? Was it because I didn't want to make him angry, or rather make him angrier than he already was? Did he know then what he would do?

When I pushed the second key into the lock of 2B, he pressed his body against my back and pushed me flat against the door. I felt his hips move into my tailbone and then his fingers in my hair as he gently tugged at a bobby pin. Didn't he understand me? Now I wonder if these were practiced gestures of seduction. They had probably been successful in the past. I turned around abruptly and looked up at him. He was smiling and expectant. I could see his gums. I found his mouth ugly with its red gums. It's odd that I had time to think about his gums, but I did. My chest was tight with anxiety. I said, "It's time for you to go." He looked down at me, his eyes indulgent, patient. "You don't really mean that," he said. "I'm afraid I do." I must have believed then that my will was still in play. I put my key into the lock, prepared to turn it, rush inside the door, slam it, and make sure to fasten the chain, but he placed his hands on my hips and pushed me through the door, closed it behind him, but didn't lock it.

Then he went on with his strange game. It was as if he hadn't forced his way into the apartment, as if I hadn't told him to leave. "Let me help you with your sweater," he said. He reached for me, but I removed the sweater quickly and draped it over my arm. He smiled and waved at the room. "So this is where you live? Cozy." He eyed the bookshelves to his right and then the one across the room. "Lots of books. I wouldn't have expected anything else." Then he pointed at the blue chair. "Where did you get that, Bloomingdale's?" This sentence strikes me as hostile now. Then I was simply baffled: What did he mean? He paced up and down a couple of times, still smiling.

"I'm asking you to please leave," I said. Did I say anything else?

Am I forgetting something? No, I don't think so. Why did I speak in a quiet voice? Why was I calm? Why did I say "please"? Did I believe I could persuade him to get out? He approached me as if I had said nothing to him. He ran his fingers from my shoulders down my arms to my elbows. All my senses seemed to slow down then, as if they were trapped in a long yawn, and yet, this peculiar temporal lag had the effect of augmenting their preciseness. My vision gained sharpness. I surveyed the books on my bookshelf just to the right of his head and paused on *Journey to the End of the Night*. A fitting title, I thought. I can't understand why I was able to think this, but I did. I also heard him breathing. Was he breathing too quickly?

He placed his hand on my back and said, "Come on, baby, let's dance."

I removed his hand and took a couple steps backward. I was all dignity. I didn't raise my voice. It was as if I were playing a part, reciting the dialogue of a character in a novel. It strikes me now that each of us had taken on a role, but the roles belonged to different stories. "I don't want to dance. I want you to go. Your behavior ceased to be amusing hours ago." I chose those words. I chose exactly those words. I recall every single one. I heard the elevator. Was it coming down? He laughed, gums on show. I thought to myself, His teeth are too small. Why hadn't I seen this before? He didn't hear me. He didn't believe me.

"Come on, baby. I'm asking you to dance."

I ran to the door and opened it. Did I yell? No, but I said, "Get out."

He leapt toward me and shut the door. I backed away from him, but he rushed me and grabbed me by the shoulders. I yelped or squeaked. A high noise came out of me that was not a scream. My throat had almost closed, but I gulped air. Now I have to think carefully because I want to reconstruct what happened exactly. It isn't easy. He pinned my arms to my sides in a bear hug, smashed his face toward mine, and began to slobber, his tongue seeking my mouth. I turned away from him and struggled to release myself, the word *straitjacket* in my head. He was a straitjacket. "You want it," he said. "You know you want it. I saw you looking at me. You were hungry. You want it." I began to wail. The unearthly noise shamed me even as it escaped my mouth. I seemed to hear it reverberate in the air.

He flipped me around violently, covered my mouth with his hand, and hissed into my ear, "Who the fuck do you think you are? You think you can drive me crazy and then ditch me?" Again, I remember every word. They are scored into my consciousness. He dragged me across the floor. I lost a shoe. I felt it fall off, but I didn't see it. I bit into the palm of his hand so hard my teeth hurt. He cried out. I am certain of all this so far.

Then I must have been thrown. He must have thrown me. I hit the bookshelf. My head. I fell. I slid to the floor, my bare feet in front of me. I saw him, the room, the books, all in black and white. I noticed this. He had taken his penis out of his pants—an extremely thin, small, hard one. I saw his penis clearly. Fanny calls it a pencil dick. I had never seen one before. His enraged face. Where did the rage come from? He was panting, face flushed as he stood over me, looking down, hideous penis sticking out from his open zipper above me. The refrain had already begun by then: "Please, no. Please, no. Please, no." There are tears clogging the voice. I can hear the begging, pleading, sobbing voice now, but it was as if I were someone else, some other unfortunate, desperate person. It wasn't my mouth moving. The mouth belonged to her. I was no longer inside me. That poor girl on the floor wasn't part of me any longer. I am telling the whole truth. I am awed by this truth now. She had feelings, but I didn't. She begged. I didn't.

Did the pounding from next door start while the girl was on the floor moaning, "Please, no!"? Maybe it started earlier. Bang. Bang. Bang. Banging on the wall. Lucy's voice, her Ted voice: "Get out! I'm calling the police! Get out!"

I watched the colorless Jeff run for the door. That's all I see in my memory, the back of his jacket above his legs as they make long strides. The door opened. It remained open. He was gone. He was gone, and I felt strangely unconcerned.

Then Lucy appeared in the doorway, clutching a broom with both hands. It must have been the tool she had used on the wall. I remember I examined her purple tunic, her straight black trousers, her hair loose down to her shoulders. She was in color. My black-and-white vision had been fleeting. I suspect that when he threw me against the bookcase, I jolted my optic nerve. Haven't I read about that somewhere? Lucy leaned forward and peered from side to side, then she looked directly at me. "Are you okay?" A large round face with several chins entered the doorframe. The face was surrounded by short gray hair. It had a vehement gaze and a small, almost lipless mouth set between deep jowls. Then the formidable body that belonged to the head arrived. From its broad shoulders downward, it looked perfectly square in its proportions and was covered by a long brown muumuu. The big woman gave Lucy a light push in her upper back and lumbered into the room. She craned her neck to look behind her, and barked: "Moth, why are you cowering in the hallway? Get in here!" I remembered Hoarse Voice. Moth had a face as long and narrow as her companion's was big and round. She scurried into the room on tiny steps, warbling, "Patty, Patty, I didn't know if he was gone." Patty and Moth. Moth was Screech Voice.

I lowered my eyes to my own body. My nice, new blue pants were badly wrinkled, and I saw a dark spot on my thigh. For reasons that amaze me now, I felt upset by the wrinkles and the stain. The trousers were securely on me, however. My blouse had been twisted to one side, so the buttons no longer headed straight down my front, and blood ran from my shoulder onto the white fabric. The blouse, too, I thought. Too bad. I wondered idly if I could get it out with bleach. I felt no alarm about the departed Jeff, however. It's hard to overstate my indifference. I know I said to myself, You are alive, not dead. He did not rape you. You were not raped, but I had no feeling of relief, no gratitude, no nothing. It was merely an observation.

Lucy, Moth, and Patty bustled around me. My attention flagged. I felt nauseated. It's happened before. I thought I might faint. There were tiny white lights twinkling in my peripheral vision. Moth's high voice: "She's bleeding. She's bleeding. Oh my God, she's so pale." Patty had lowered herself onto her knees in front of me, and she took my face in her hands. I felt myself losing consciousness. She said, "We're here. It's okay." I said to her, "I don't want to move. I won't move." No one was going to make me move. Lucy's face came into view again. "You're going to be fine, child, just fine." I didn't faint.

The three ran back and forth between my apartment and Lucy's for supplies. Despite my stubborn refusal to move, they manipulated my head up and down and decided that, thank goodness, the wound wasn't bad, just a small cut near the top of my neck. "Lots of blood, but not serious." Patti pressed it with ice wrapped in a towel, and then Moth, with a pair of scissors and tape, bandaged it, and said repeatedly, "Does that hurt you? Oh, am I hurting you, sweetie?" I had no pain at all. I wondered why. Lucy worried about a concussion. "We have to watch her. If she gets dizzy or vomits, it's straight to the emergency room."

This was followed by police talk. Patty was going to call. I said no. I felt her warm fingers on my cold right hand. She spoke to me in that deep, cloudy voice. "You've been assaulted." I said, "No police." She was on all fours and the size of her body impressed me again. Such a big woman. She had moved her face right in front of mine so I could look into her eyes, her intelligent eyes, and I noticed her milky skin, not a mole or a spot, flawless skin with soft folds of fat. I had a desire to lift my hand and touch it, but I did not want to move. I said to Patty, "I never should have gotten into that cab with him. I was stupid. But he didn't rape me. You stopped him. I'm fine, really."

These facts were eminently clear to me, and my thoughts ran in whole sentences, not fragments. Lucy said that I had time to decide about the police. They had heard me cry out. "We're witnesses," she said. Moth hovered at my ear. "She's in shock now." I listened to a discussion about what to do with me. They couldn't leave me there alone. They would take me to Lucy's. I agreed to move. The three of them helped me to stand up. When I was on my feet, Moth said, "Oh, Lordy, you're a tall drink of water, aren't you?" She straightened my blouse and patted my arm twice, a timid pat. Lucy took my right elbow, and Patty took my left elbow. I began to step forward as the two women looked up at me solicitously, eagerly, and the absurdity hit. I was in a comedy. I began to laugh. "I can walk," I said. "I'm fine." I shook them off. I walked and laughed. "I'm just fine." The whole thing was ridiculous, hilarious. I was, in fact, a little dizzy. My laughter distressed the three women. Patty told me to quiet down in a strict voice, and I did.

There were candles burning in Lucy's dark front room, black candles. I smelled incense, too, which reminded me of Edith Harrington's bedroom in high school. She used the sticks to hide the smell of cigarettes. The three women sat me down on a plush sofa that occupied almost the entire length of Lucy's right wall, turned on a small lamp beside it, its shade painted with bluebells, and then resumed their solicitations. They spoke to one another as if I weren't there. Perhaps I wasn't. "She needs something to sleep in." "I think her color is returning. What do you think? Look at her face in the light." I heard whispering about the police; it should be reported. "Fucking creep, asshole, shit face." Moth kept up a continuous mumble-stream, heavily inflected by cussing. I felt limp and empty. The room was all boxy moving shadows, but I sensed the presence of bric-a-brac, of paintings and drawings on the wall, the scenes and figures of which I couldn't make out, books piled on small tables with invisible titles on their spines. "Just sit there and we'll get you all settled in." I sat. Moth made tea across the room, and it occurred to me that her legs had been stiffened by accident or illness. She had no choice but to take small, hobbling steps. I remember the steam rising from the boiling pot on the stove as Moth hummed and muttered. I let Lucy undress me as if I were a child. For a moment, stripped to my underpants, I stared down at my navel and felt pathetic to myself, but then Lucy deftly pulled a heap of rumpled flannel over my head, inserted an arm into each sleeve, and pulled the loose, soft fabric down to my hips. Patty hauled in a blanket and pillow from the next room. Lucy tucked me into the sofa. Moth handed me a teacup. I looked down at the hot, green liquid. Wilted leaves floated on its surface. Patty said, "There's something in the tea, dear, a sedative. It will help you sleep."

The passage in the notebook continues, but I pause at this convenient interval while Minnesota, my young self, sleeps soundly with the aid of a drug on Lucy's sofa. She has been saved by a broom and by three women who think they are complete strangers to her but are less strange to her than they believe. If she dreams that night, she won't remember her dreams. While she sleeps, her heart beats and she breathes in and out, and a clock in 2C ticks off the minutes and the earth moves on its invisible axis and in the morning the sun will rise and the city will get noisier and people will crowd the sidewalks and the trains. If the past is not a somewhere we can visit, then to wring truths from it is like squeezing nothing from nothing. No, the past is not a place. And, if the past doesn't exist except in the machinations of theoretical physics and science fiction, then what are we left with? Should I say all that remains are fluctuating mental images in people's heads that vanish with them when they die, and historical records, volume upon volume of words and numbers?

It will be two days before Minnesota realizes that she doesn't even know the last name of the man who threw her into a bookshelf. She is a healthy girl and her cut heals quickly. But for seven nights in a row, she will wake in terror after a dream. It is always the same dream with no images, just the explosive sensations of her head against a hard surface and no wind inside her, and a malevolent presence moving toward her. When she has calmed herself, she understands that she is reliving the assault. She has heard about such experiences after plane crashes and car accidents and battles. The dream lasts a week and then it disappears. Years pass, and one night, it returns. Years go by again, and she dreams the terrible dream for a second time and then after more years, it strikes again. Three times. As far as she can tell, there is no rhyme or reason for this revenant. The ghost's meaning lies in what she can't know, buried in the speechless truths of her body that have no one to narrate them.

I narrate now as best I can. Thirty-eight years ago, she wrote, "I will do my best." I will not lie to you. The memory hurts me—hurts me now—and that is how the past stays alive. It isn't a place, but a movement, a surge of then in now. The violence of that night and the sound of a voice saying over and over, *Please, no*, echo across and through and in time, not my time alone. It merges and mingles with other times. Our times. The violence quickened in me before I ever saw Jeffrey, and it is here as I sit writing in the guest room only steps from where my mother is sleeping. She always sleeps late in the mornings. Over and over, I have wondered why he didn't hear me, why he seemed to be a character in another story, and why his story smothered mine. Over and over, I have spoken and not been heard. Over and over, I have been looked through. I see her at the old desk in the little bedroom in 2B. She writes. I write:

There is a knife, and there is a key.
There is a lady who boils the tea.
Open the book and learn the spell.
There is a story I have to tell.

CHAPTER TEN

I have often wondered what Jeffrey of No Last Name thought when he fled my building on West 109th Street. I mean after he had a chance to catch his breath. Did he go over the events of the evening in his mind to make sense of them? Did he feel remorse? Did his own violence amaze him? I could be wrong, but I venture to say: None of the above. "Who the fuck do you think you are? You think you can drive me crazy and then ditch me?" These words are surely a clue to the "Who Was Jeffrey?" mystery. A young man thwarted, yes, but also a young man surprised, a young man who just a minute before he spoke those words had looked almost tenderly at the young woman standing before him and had run his fingers softly down her arms. In his eyes, she had seen his conviction, had seen his firm belief that she would relent, that she would buckle to his charms and give way to the techniques that had served him well for so long. It did not matter that she had told him to get out. His was not a case of universal but rather selective deafness. Jeffrey had listened raptly to Mr. Remember-That-Night-with–Catherine Bales. I have come to pity Catherine Bales. He did not hear Minnesota because her words did not mean to him what they meant to her. Two stories crash inside 2B.

By 1979, the Standard Hero without a surname was solidly Caucasian because, although Irish and Italians a century or so earlier were black people in America, they had by the late twentieth century been white people for quite some time, and so the now standardized hero wanders the streets of the city with impunity to partake of adventures in living. He has money in his pocket and an Ivy League education and fond memories of rowing with the heavyweight team, of drinking with the team, as well as the sexual exploits due to him as a member of the team, conquests he brags about to the team to enhance his status with the team and sun himself in the admiration of the team, which will make up, at least in part, for the small size of his organ, and the girls, oh, the girls, are mostly willing. They spread their legs for his little dick, and they moan and cry out as they climax in orgasms, actual or feigned. They want to make him happy, and they do.

When he first sees the pretty girl downtown, he knows he just got lucky. "Say something in Italian." Bless the stupid girls. But then she quotes Marx in the cab and later she mentions Freud and embarrasses him with that prissy cocaine lecture. Jesus. Who does she think she is? Pretentious bitch. He will stop her mouth when he fucks her.

Or maybe he does not think this at all. Maybe she bewilders him. She tells him she is leaving, but then she waits meekly at the elevator and lets him take her home. She runs out of the cab, but when he follows her, she permits him to walk her to the door. She keeps saying she doesn't want him, but he knows better. Look at that face, that mouth, that body. To look is to know. The words are blather. He's been here before. They come around. They always come around. And, when she doesn't come around, he loses control. He can't help himself. No, it's unlikely that this young man rushes home, throws himself onto his bed in his spacious apartment, and weeps. Maybe he returns to Mr. Blond at the party across town to boast and snicker about the "piece of ass" he just "had," the tall girl who called herself Minnesota, and he and his buddy talk together a little longer and the minutes go by, and a magical transformation takes place. The word *Minnesota* loses its human reference altogether and becomes nothing but a proper noun that returns occasionally as a joke between the guys, a state in the union buffeted back and forth on the gusty winds of laughter along with "Catherine Bales."

Is there pity in me for My Almost Rapist? Must I descend further than pity? Is there charity in me for the Not So Standard Hero or the hero become villain or villain who briefly looked like a hero? No. My soul is not as large as Simone Weil's. I am not a saint. More than anything, I want to banish him from the landscape of memory, annihilate his presence in my mind, but that is not possible. Instead, I am asking him to leave the book now. "And please," I say to him, "close the door behind you." We will not see him in the flesh again. He will not return to defend himself or tell his version of the events as they unfolded. The police never arrive because they were never called, just as they were never called and never arrived for Mrs. Malacek. The only person on the case is the Introspective Detective, and she finds herself on the scene only after the crime has been committed and the perpetrator has fled, and she doesn't have a stomach for pursuit. It's only her second case, after all, and she's still green.

But I, the old narrator, am asking myself why my former self waited. I am so ashamed of waiting. I have been ashamed of waiting for almost four decades now and my humiliation does not end. No, it burns brightly. It is as if I am still there waiting at the elevator for Jeffrey who said that if he came with a girl he would leave with her. It is as if I am still that young woman outside the elevator unable to move. That was the moment when I should have run, but I didn't. Something had already happened to me, to her, by then. Long before she flew backward into the bookcase, long before she slid to the floor and begged, "Please, no," the spell had already been cast. And there she stands, flush-faced and humbled forever.

There must be a way to move her from that spot. The final hours of May 7, 1979, that became the early hours of May 8, 1979, cannot be undone, and the clock keeps turning with its two hands round and round, and the once pretty, smooth face of the person outside the elevator is now wrinkled. But the hand that grips the pen still writes in a notebook, and the secret to that frozen figure on the ninth floor of an apartment building on the East Side of Manhattan may lie elsewhere. Let us not forget that a memory is always in the present. Let us not forget that each time we evoke a memory, it is subject to change, but let us also not forget that those changes may bring truths in their wake. We travel back to the well-behaved child who sits upright in the pew with the other members of the children's choir. She tries not to swing her leg back and forth during the sermon, but the leg seems to have a will of its own and her patent leather shoe hits the back of the pew in front of her. "That's mastabading, you know," Ellie Thorson whispers to her. The girl with the wayward foot doesn't know what "mastabading" is. Whatever it is, it sounds bad, and she stills her foot.

There are many rules to be followed. God is watching to make certain the rules are followed. God is watching along with his flaming partner, the Holy Ghost, who at any moment might fly inside her ear and start whispering or chanting along with the goblins because he's a piece of fire and can go anywhere at any time. He doesn't even have a face. The Son has a face, a pitiable, suffering face. They hammered nails through his hands and feet, and when she thinks about the terrible story, her own hands and feet ache. Jesus is much kinder than the other two, much kinder than the Ghost and the Father, but Jesus is also watching.

"Don't fidget." "Fold your hands in your laps." "Silence. I must have silence." "Line up, girls and boys." "No talking in the lunchroom." She sees the shadow of the principal on the wall. "I want you to behave like little ladies and gentlemen." She listens and she dreams, but she keeps her eyes on the page: "Run, Dick, run." Dick is always running. The children in her reading book have no insides, and she feels this lack of theirs intensely. Their stomachs never make noises and their teeth never tingle. They have no thoughts. The minute hand on the big classroom clock is prone to sudden jerks that she watches closely. The little girl waits for permission. She raises her hand and says, "Please, may I go to the bathroom?" There is no color in school.

But at home she can find the Alice book and study the pictures and dream about falling slowly down the hole, and she can turn to the page with the illustration she loves of the hideous duchess with a huge head and the ugly baby that will turn into a pig and the vicious cook who's put too much pepper in the soup, and she can read the words of the song that warms her thighs with a pleasure so sinister she must take a big breath: "Speak roughly to your little boy, / And beat him when he sneezes." She keeps her sadistic joy to herself, but the silent confusion of those feelings mounts, and sometimes at night whirlwinds of torment cause her to twist and churn and beg to be released from her badness. She is bad, an evil thing, and in the quiet of the room she shares with Kari, who is sleeping soundly on her side of the room, the quaking anxiety rises to a pitch, and she bites down into the pillowcase. Listen to the sound of wings flapping in the closet, as if a great, injured bird has found its way inside. Angel terror.

And then, in the morning, she forgets. The light shines through the crack in the curtains and, if it's summer, there's no school and not many rules. The hours in a single day are roomy enough for both boredom and games. Mother drives us to the public pool. I can hear the running feet on the diving board and then the resonant metallic sound of a jump or dive, followed by a splash against the din of high, shouting voices. I can smell the chlorine, feel the wet, hot cement under my belly. Kari slaps herself down close beside me in her two-piece bathing suit with the red-striped top half and the solid red bottom half, her ear to the hard surface. I look into her round face beneath her short hair slick and dripping with water, and she smiles at me with knowing satisfaction because we will soon jump up and throw ourselves into the deep end all over again. We were always jumping and running and falling then.

Father has lifted me onto the kitchen counter. He washes my bloody knee with a soapy cloth. He dabs gently and looks into my eyes to check my expression for pain. He explains to me that no dirt can remain in "the wound," and the word *wound* makes me feel important. With a pair of tweezers he lifts out the tiniest of pebbles, a black dot in the gash, and holds it up for me to examine. There it is, a "smidgeon of the driveway" that must be removed because driveways and children do not mix. An infection might develop, and we don't want that. I see the Mercurochrome, rusty red on my skin, a pair of scissors in his hand, and the gauze. As he cuts the tape and presses the bandage firmly into place, he tells me that such things must be done right. And then he places his hands around my waist and lifts me into the air and lowers me gently, gently to the floor. When I walk away, I limp to exaggerate my injury. I am the happiest girl in the world.

We are not allowed candy often. The Hershey bar excites me as I sit beside Kari and nibble the brown thinness so that it will last, breaking each square carefully at the line to retain its neat rectangular divisions. She and I compare the size of the bars Mother has offered us as a surprise. We see which one of us can eat more slowly. My father speaks from above, "Let me have a bite." His hand appears and my fingers loosen. He returns the chocolate bar decimated. Kari and I regard these interventions as fate, no different from the dandelion seed that flew into my eye and took a long time to get out or the tornados that blow into Webster from time to time and force us into the basement. Like Mother, we are philosophical: "We all suffer and we all die." After Father is dead, Mother sits across from me and tells me more about him than she ever has before. "He never consulted me about those Sunday outings to Aunt Irma. He never gave me any warning at all. I would see him putting the cooler in the trunk. That was the sign I should start making sandwiches." My mother's memory was perfect then. "I do wish he had asked me." She added, "Of course, a family is not a democracy."

And Aunt Irma speaks about the death of her sister in a low voice to my mother. I remember because I wasn't supposed to hear. I am standing in the next room. She says something about "a death rattle." Yes, she says, my father lost his mother when he was too young, twelve years old, and there are considerations to be made, considerations for the black moods. Evangeline, my father's mother, was ill for a long time before Irma came to stay with father and son. There is the war in Europe, too. Irma is whispering. Terrible things he must have seen, terrible things in Germany late in the war. I wish I could see my mother and Irma, but I can't. But then I hear Irma hiss to my mother, "Sick, it made some of them sick." And the words she speaks next stay in my brain forever. "War neurosis."

There are moments when I conjure the child self, and I see her with her arms out and a handkerchief over her eyes in the game Blind Man's Buff. She gropes the air with her outstretched hands seeking the others who dodge her waving fingers. She is dizzy because they have turned her around and around. Much of life has been like that—trying to feel one's way forward sightless. Then she grows taller, and she reads more and she writes more and she draws more. She is an excellent student, but the teachers don't like her much. They give her papers As, but she smells their irritation and resentment. She writes her poems and stories at home. She writes another paper on slave rebellions because she is inspired, but Mr. Wolf hands the pages back to her. He hadn't asked for "extra credit." And the following year, Mr. Burdock hands her the paper, his face cold, and he says, "This is not your work. I don't believe you wrote this. This is not the work of a sixteen-year-old girl. Your father helped you, didn't he?" She says no. She insists that she has written it. He shakes his head. She weeps.

Yes, and remember the day at the dentist. I am fifteen, slumped over a book in the waiting room. It's late spring and hot. I am wearing cut-off jeans as the fan whirs because something has gone wrong with the air-conditioning. The woman beside me examines my bare legs. I have seen her before, but I don't know who she is. I can feel her disapproval swell as she becomes larger and larger in her chair, a great balloon of a woman whom I feel may burst at any moment. She has identified me without asking me my name. "You're the older daughter?" I nod. "Your father is a great doctor and a great man. One of the best men Webster's ever had. I hope you know that." She speaks to me harshly, angrily, as if I am guilty of not knowing, as if she has detected a malformation in my character that she must correct instantly. I faint. They blame the heat.

Do not be misled. These stories are not extraneous to the question at hand. They are necessary if we wish to understand how we might dislodge our heroine from that miserable spot where she waits for the man who will hurt her, who still hurts her, not because he is worthy of consideration—he isn't—but because her immobility has been inscribed in her as punishment for what she is: wrong, somehow wrong, a misfit and an upstart who must stop calling attention to herself. But the knot in time where she stands paralyzed obeys its own law, one that explodes chronology. In another temporal register, time flows, as William James liked to say, and there is more to tell:

Minnesota woke up at 12:45 p.m. For an instant she was startled by her surroundings, the flowered nightgown with its too-short sleeves, the painting of a brown-and-white spaniel near a basket of fruit on the wall, the sofa and bedding, and all at once her memory bloomed and, with it, shame and regret. She wrote it all down in the notebook later that day, but the text is rather long-winded and will benefit from my brevity. Lucy wasn't in the room. The apartment felt empty. It was, in fact, larger than 2B, but it was so crowded with furniture and objects that its space shrank under the burden. She made two notable discoveries. On an ornate table propped up against a small bookshelf she noticed a simple framed drawing of a pentagram, a five-pointed star inside a circle. Minnesota thought of the Pythagoreans. She knew it had meant something to them. Was it the music of the spheres or something else? She stood up, walked over to the symbol, and tried to remember what she knew about it. The Greeks, too, had used it as a symbol. And the Celts later. She picked it up as if holding it would enlighten her, and as she lifted it from its place, she saw something else: Lying on top of a row of books that had been hidden by the picture was the stuffed body of a little man doll in a navy-blue suit. He was about nine inches long and tightly bound with string from neck to foot. "We're going to bind him tight." "Do you have the knife?"

I don't need to read the notebook to remember that the figure unsettled me. I leaned close to him, but I didn't touch him. Whoever had sewn his clothes had made them carefully, miniature businessman's suit and tie, a little white shirt beneath with tiny buttons, but his face had been drawn crudely onto a cloth head covered with a piece of nylon stocking—eyes, simple nose, straight line for his mouth. He had a shock of light brown hair that looked uncomfortably like real hair. The sound of the key in the door caused me to fumble with the drawing, replace it quickly, and retreat to the sofa.

Lucy entered with a brown paper bag speaking joyously of bagels and lox and asking me how I was and commending me on my long sleep. She whistled as she produced plates and cups and put on the coffee. All the while, the horrible little man lay hidden in the bookshelf, a secret totem, hers but also mine, although she didn't know I had seen him, and it would have been untoward to say, "What is that little doll doing behind the picture? Is it Ted? And if it is, what does it mean?" But when I looked at Lucy's face over breakfast, her green eyes had a radiance I had never seen in them before, and I was taken with the tiny wrinkles around those bright eyes and with her mouth and her lank hair and her funny, small, feminine gestures. She was unusually careful with her cream cheese. After scraping a small amount onto the surface of her toasted bagel with her knife, she took time to spread it gently and evenly, as if it were crucial that the white layer have no unseemly holes that might expose the naked bread beneath. She then neatly pierced her salmon with a fork, folded it onto the bread, and delayed before taking a first bite, nodding several times as she admired her creation.

The blue pants and white shirt I had worried about ruining while I lay on the floor early in the morning on May 8 had become repulsive by the afternoon of the same day. Lucy discarded them and tripped into the room with a violet linen dress on a hanger for me to wear instead. It was too small for her, she said. She had grown fat, and she wanted me to have it. I did have it—for years. My neighbor, tied-up-little-man fetish or no tied-up-little-man fetish, had turned into "the really nice lady" Mr. Rosales had maintained she was. It was Lucy who had returned to my apartment after I was asleep, found the keys in my purse, and locked my door. It was Lucy who insisted on walking me the four steps from 2C to 2B, and it was Lucy who patted my arm and told me I looked "darling" in her dress. And it was Lucy who turned to me after I had stepped inside my apartment and after I had thanked her, who said, "The cuts and bruises don't matter. Beating makes you feel like dirt, like nothing. That's what really hurts."

Around five o'clock, after I had called Whitney and told her the story in a dead voice, which was the only voice that worked for telling the story at that time, and after she and I had arranged to meet for dinner and then for me to spend the night at her house, I noticed that an envelope had been slipped under my door.

Dear Minnesota,

Patty and Moth request the pleasure of your company at dinner next Saturday, May 17. Seven o'clock. I'm invited, too, so if your [sic] available, we can walk together. It's not far. Shall I knock at quarter to? I look forward to your reply and hope you are feeling better.

Sincerely Yours,
Your Neighbor,
Lucy

CHAPTER ELEVEN

Although I thanked heaven for the Three Lucky Ladies of the Broom, and I coldly compared my minor misfortune to the monstrous happenings visited upon countless other people—rape, torture, lynching, war, starvation, flood, pestilence—the lectures I gave myself had little effect on the nauseating repetitions that had taken hold of me, not only the dream that split open seven nights in panic but my studious, obsessive return to the hours of Jeff. Again and again, I dissected the evening, its scenes, its dialogue, its violence, and again and again I was struck by my unconscionable helplessness and cowardice. And here is an irony: Just as I had lost control of the story with Jeffrey *during* the hours in question, I lost control of my thoughts *about* the hours in question. I did not want to think about the attack. The problem was the attack would not stop thinking about me.

And this, I dare say, is how time loses all forward momentum and spins in place. The problem is an old one: Could I have changed what happened? I have read many arguments on the problem of free will. I have consulted with Augustine and Aquinas and wrestled with the famous demon in Laplace, whose intellect surveys the continents of Everywhere and from that ultimate view, guided by the universal laws, foretells all that is to come. I have chased after colliding principles in logic and waltzed with Heisenberg's uncertainty principle, but what I am left with is that we human beings must believe in our own volition, whether we have it or not. We must feel that we act freely or we are finished. And so the ironies thicken: By insisting that I was to blame for my humiliation, I was able to retain some sense that I could decide my fate.

Whitney was a stalwart and tender friend, but in the days after the assault I resisted her sympathy and refused to talk any more about it. I had told her the story. She knew what had happened, and that was that. I now think my resistance came from the thought that Whitney would see me as I saw myself, as a repugnant weakling who waited, and because she waited, she had been turned into the pathetic beggar on the floor. I felt certain, you see, that Whitney never would have waited, never would have capitulated to the if-a-girl-comes-with me-she-leaves-with-me rule. She would have tossed her head and waved him out of her sight. Lucy knew. Feeling like dirt was the problem. The bruises and the cut I sustained were of no importance. It was the man's contempt and condescension I couldn't shake off, his smiling confidence that my words were meaningless, that I did not deserve to be answered, that I was Nobody. The moment he grabbed me I lost my borders because he did not believe in them. What remained after that was an edgeless thing, abject flesh to be penetrated and tossed away. That was his plan, wasn't it?—if one can speak of plans.

It took years for me to reinstate the distance between the two characters in that room and understand that what should have been his shame became mine, that whatever I had done wrong it was not nearly as wrong as what he had done to me. But shame is like a viscous substance with adhesive properties. The derision and disgust I saw in his eyes for me infected my vision of myself, and what I saw from his perspective was unbearable to me. I had become his creature, and that ugly thing he had made was responsible for the silence and sorrow that came between Whitney and me, a cleft I grieve to this day. We repaired it. We repaired it in time, but on the night of May 8, when I lay beside her in her bed and felt her fingers on my shoulder and heard her say, "Don't shut down. You mustn't shut down. If you do, don't you see, if you do, it means he wins," I did not answer her. At the time, I felt I had no choice. I had to stiffen every part of myself. I felt that if I didn't, if I let myself go, if I wasn't as hard as I could be, I would dissolve into something inchoate and unrecognizable, that I would begin to scream or begin to laugh and never stop.

The shapeless thing I couldn't articulate ran away into the dream. Whitney woke up when she heard me gasping and choking beside her. For several seconds I didn't know where I was or who was beside me.

Despite the spinning in place, Minnesota wrote. She needed to write. There are many stories of people, who after the death of a beloved person, are struck by a sudden compulsion to write. There are stories of others who suffer a stroke or come down with epilepsy and find they cannot resist the temptations of the page. Writing as mourning, writing as illness, writing as exorcism, writing as revenge. Minnesota had lost control of her book, it is true. The manuscript had become unruly, a sprawling pile of pages that went in several directions at once. She continued to defer the plot of the Frieda Frail case because she couldn't decide about Frieda's ghost. And yet, she continued to try out passages for the unwieldy novel in the notebook. She returned to Verbum, that mythical small town on the prairie at a mythical mid-twentieth-century moment, a once-upon-a-time that never really was but smelled to high heaven of Webster anyway. I can see now that it was an angry comedy I was trying to write, much angrier than I knew.

The version of adolescence preferred by Mr. Feathers was the one Hollywood had promoted in his own youth, most particularly in the Andy Hardy movies that had been so dear to his heart. Indeed, just as Mr. Feathers had enjoyed thinking of himself as Andy Hardy (played with pizzazz by Mickey Rooney, whose short stature and funny face mattered not a whit because all the prettiest girls in town were in love with him), he now liked to think of himself as the kindly Judge Hardy (incarnated by Lewis Stone on the screen), a man who regularly doled out sound, paternal advice to his son. This was the fiction that guided Mr. Feathers' fatherhood, and he stuck to it, despite the fact that he rarely spoke to his son without the presence of Mrs. Feathers, and when he did, it was to make some benign comment about an article in *Time* magazine, a publication he relied upon for all esoteric matters and through which he hoped to impress his offspring. But Mr. Feathers knew somewhere in the geography of his soul that his son was uncharted territory, a distressing blank on the map that had yet to be filled. He knew Ian was nothing like the grinning, spunky, well-rounded American boy of the movies, but this only made Mr. Feathers cling more tightly to the comforting illusion of himself as Judge Hardy.

Mr. Feathers was therefore distressed when Mrs. Feathers raised the alarm about Isadora Simon and declared he must speak to his son about "protection." Although never a subject in the movies, "protection" belonged squarely in the father-son sphere of action and had nothing to do with mothers. Mr. Feathers had hardly noticed the Simon girl. What did he actually know about her? The girl's mother, whom he had encountered just once at a Verbum town-planning meeting, was an unpleasantly masculine woman who had spat out long, rolling paragraphs dense with hifalutin vocabulary that had given him gooseflesh. The girl's father, whom Mr. Feathers had never seen, was rumored to be a confused casualty of the last war. (Mr. Feathers had been drafted but had fortunately remained stateside and therefore had managed to keep his worldview more or less untouched by all things foreign.) Although his information on the Simons was scant, Mr. Feathers concluded that Isadora was the product of a household gone awry. His wife was right to worry. In the Simon domicile, the proverbial "pants," in which he so fervently believed, had migrated from their rightful if handicapped owner and found their way onto the lower body of a person who had no right to wear them.

While Mr. Feathers pondered how to broach the protection problem with his son and savored memories of his own "wild oats" (a field he imagined as remote from "amber waves of grain" but somehow related nevertheless), Ian romped with the fantastic Hussy and pined for the real Isadora. For her part, Isadora continued to ogle Kurt Linder, who just a couple days earlier had grinned at her widely and said, "Hi, Isadora." This had occurred in the hallway at school just outside the faculty dining room. Isadora could not have known that Kurt was promiscuous with both his "hi"s and his smiles because their paths seldom crossed. All she knew was that his greeting had sent an electrical current straight to her pudendum and that she had been extracted from the great anonymity of the hallway into the spotlight of singular recognition. Frequently described by all and sundry in town as "a winner," Kurt Linder won at multiple sports, achieved respectable if lenient B's in his schoolwork, drove his car too fast, and, in the tradition of Andy Hardy, captured the hearts of all the pretty and not-so-pretty girls at Webster High School, as well as the hearts of some of the boys, but their hearts, of course, were not to be mentioned.

In his own American fashion, Kurt embodied the figure known in fairy tales as a "simpleton." Verbum's hero had avoided books all his life, but he held poetry and novels in particularly low regard as printed stuff for girls and pansies, which meant that he had managed to keep his mind free of all articulations that might interfere with the present glory of himself. Of course he liked girls, but in Kurt's handsome head, there were only two kinds of girls: the girls who would and the girls who wouldn't. Although he liked the girls who would, especially at the moment when would became could, he knew he wasn't supposed to like them. Only the girls who wouldn't were worth anything, and no girl was worth as much in the long run as the "other guys," except perhaps that gleaming figment he imagined he might marry fully clothed far in the future sometime after college, the *Playboy* centerfold with eyes he had described to himself as "dewy" because his relationship to diction made it impossible for him to identify a cliché even when it fell heavily upon him.

Literature, of course, is bursting with love. Without the lover, I ask you, what would become of literature? Imagine if the novel were shorn of love stories. Imagine poems stripped of erotic feeling. Imagine the sonnet without the beats of love. What would it be? Would it be? "Love drives me on, / that loosener of limbs." Isadora had not yet read Sappho, but her limbs had been loosened, and the illness that had attacked her joints had nothing to do with arthritis. But she, Isadora Simon, who had never felt love's bite so keenly as she did when Kurt Linder had anointed her with his "hi" in the hallway, was steeped in love's lore. Tristan and Isolde, Miss Elizabeth Bennet and Mr. Darcy, Jane and Rochester, Cathy and Heathcliff, as well as Watson and Holmes, had become part of her own battle of the books. Dogs and rabbits and even flies may lust and lunge, but only human beings turn lusting and lunging into literary art and then enjoy reading about it. And so it was that, with considerable help from the Simon family library, Isadora's mind had already traveled far beyond the provinces where the intellects of Mr. and Mrs. Feathers and Kurt Linder would probably remain tethered in perpetuity.

Time and *Playboy* had no doubt served the citizens of Verbum well, but those publications so beloved by mid-century Middle Americans could not provide either the tools or the skills needed to release Mr. and Mrs. Feathers or the town's darling, Kurt Linder, from bondage, which is to say that the virginal Isadora knew a thing or two about love from literature, a thing or two the Feathers and the entire Linder clan did not know because they had become attached to a view of love so pinched by the cherished, if contradictory, stereotypes that walked across the pages of their magazines that they had lost the particularity of human passion altogether.

Even literature of a higher order, however, is not a solution to unrequited love. Isadora was young and, although she had already ingested many books, enough to make her fat if literature were literally a moveable feast, the instruction she had received from those books about how to conduct oneself in affairs of the heart was hardly consistent. Isadora had noticed a lot of silly female love objects in books designated "classics," love objects as empty and absurd as Miss February herself. Furthermore, she had noticed that in the world, or rather in the world beyond books, which consisted mostly of school, the admired girls adopted a soft and pliable veneer even when they were not soft and pliable but made of iron.

Isadora's decision to act on her desires for Verbum's paragon was partly due to a conversation she had with her mother. Although Isadora revealed no details that explained her problem directly, her mother, the Milton expert, had little trouble interpreting her offspring's circumlocutions. Professor Simon uttered the following truth: "If a boy doesn't know that a girl is interested in him, he can hardly be blamed for ignoring her." (Isadora had not mentioned the "Hi, Isadora.") No more than a half an hour after her mother had spoken, Isadora began composing a note to Kurt. She rejected one as too moony, another as too cold, and a third as too windy. She settled on a careful, dignified inquiry, which she deposited in his locker.

Dear Kurt,

I am writing to you because you have piqued my interest, and I thought we might get together and talk. If this sounds plausible, drop me a line.

Isadora

Isadora regretted both "piqued" and "plausible" as soon as the letter had left her hand, but it was too late. The next day, she received her answer.

Sure. Meet me in Green Boughs Park tonight at eight. Kurt

Exactly how the three other Doras divined that there was "a boy" in the picture can only be guessed at. It may have been Theodora's glimpse of Isadora's anxious face in the hallway mirror as she repeatedly checked her watch and pressed her palms together or it may have been the moment Just Plain Dora noticed a thin but precise application of lipstick on her oldest sister's mouth. Whichever clue had triggered the discovery, by the time Isadora's watch read 7:50 and she prepared to walk out the door, her three sisters had gathered at the foot of the stairs to send her off with a combination of cheers and jeers. Theodora waved a handkerchief and then mock-sobbed into it. She blew her nose with it in an exaggerated manner and then grimaced in the direction of the departing sister to telegraph her agony. Andora made flourishing gestures with her right arm and quoted one of the Brontë sisters: "Farewell to thee, but not farewell / To all my fondest thoughts of thee." And the littlest Dora jumped up and down in place singing, "Isadora has a boyfriend! Isadora has a boyfriend!"

The reputed boyfriend had posed himself under a tree, and when Isadora spotted his lean form in the light of the spring evening, she felt the quickening of various biological systems she had spent so much time studying, noting in particular dramatic changes in her respiration. Kurt was wearing that puzzled look she had come to know and love. He grinned and, as she stood before him, he plopped himself abruptly down on the grass. She sat down beside him and stared with admiration at his large sneakers she felt certain were at least a size twelve.

Talk, as everyone knows, is a vehicle of seduction. Well-placed words are often far more effective than well-placed hands, especially when two people have never exchanged more than a "hi" in the past. In the old days, this kind of talk was called "wooing." Isadora was not so backward as to think that Kurt should do all the wooing. She was perfectly prepared to woo herself. The question on this particular evening, however, was whom was Isadora wooing? In effect, there were two Kurt Linders: the one Isadora had invented and the one who sat beside her on the grass, a person of many gifts, but not eloquence. To be fair to Isadora, she had not created a hero with intellectual prowess. She had created a hero of kindness and feeling, a hero that fit the way his "hi" and his smile had made her feel that day in the hallway. She knew Kurt was conventional, but having grown up in her unconventional family with three other Doras and Roger and Geoffrey and Monk and the *Anecdota*, Isadora longed for a bit of convention now and then to alleviate her "weirdness." She had imagined strolling the halls with the lanky Kurt Linder, his arm draped casually around her shoulder. She had admitted to herself that it would be nice for a change to belong to the world around her instead of remaining forever outside it.

Isadora launched the conversation with a polite question about Kurt's teams, one she had rehearsed in advance. She asked him about the football team and the basketball team and the baseball team, teams to cover all the seasons of the year, after which she prepared to listen attentively to her beloved's discourse on homo ludens. She smiled at him and wondered how the lipstick looked from his point of view. Kurt began to talk, and as he talked, she heard "ums" and "you knows" invade his speech like so many unsavory loiterers, but more disturbing to her was the smug but oddly blank look in his eyes, as if he were not speaking to her but to the anonymous crowd he had plucked her from with his "Hi, Isadora." He seemed not to see her at all. In fact, he did not look directly at her. She began to wonder what he did see. She made an effort to concentrate on his arm with its low-growing field of fine hairs, such a strong, attractive arm, but the proverbial breezes had already begun to blow in another direction and at a lower temperature. Isadora felt cool. She felt so cool that she thought about Ian. She thought about how precise Ian could be when he explained a point, and she recalled with pain how he had collapsed when she had told him to stop the Sherlock nonsense. Poor Ian, she thought.

In the meantime, Kurt Linder droned on about how funny Jack had been at practice and retold a weak joke he attributed to "Coach." Coach said this and Coach said that. He was apparently devoted to his coach. He then moved on to hijinks various members of "the team" had perpetrated on other members of the same team, uproarious games that involved the manipulation of male underwear, and Isadora found herself staring at the grass. She realized that Kurt Linder was boring, and just as she had pronounced this sad truth to herself, the boring Kurt Linder decided they had talked enough.

Kurt had happily obliged Isadora with some easy words about himself because he knew that girls always wanted to talk until they didn't, at which moment he could make his move and see how far the whole *would* and *wouldn't* business went. Isadora had sent him a note, hadn't she? The note was a come-on, wasn't it? What kind of a girl would send him a note and meet him in the park if she didn't want some action? He knew that Isadora didn't neatly conform to the slut category. She was not easy pickings for his "slut slayer," as Jack liked to call his penis. She was one of those bookish girls, and Kurt knew from experience that the limbs of smart girls sometimes loosened more quickly than those of the dumb ones, although he, of course, had not read Sappho either.

Kurt had no understanding of the fact that Isadora's definition of getting together to "talk" included her side of the conversation. Who was Isadora to Kurt exactly? Just a girl. And that was the problem. Isadora had imagined saying a few words herself, had, in fact, hoped to tell Kurt about Darwin's *The Voyage of the Beagle*, the book she was halfway through, but mention of the *Beagle* was not to be because Kurt Linder leaned toward Isadora Simon and gripped her inner thigh firmly with his hand. This gesture so startled her that Isadora leapt to her feet, after which he also leapt to his feet, grabbed her in his arms, leaned over her, and began to slobber in the general vicinity of her mouth.

The truth was that it was too late by then for Kurt to administer even a gentle kiss on the lips Isadora had so carefully colored pink because boredom had come between them, and from boredom there is no rescue. But the sudden turn in their relations did not bore our heroine. The sudden turn ignited her fury. She pulled violently away from him, gained several inches of distance in the process, and then, with all the strength she could muster, she kneed him in the groin.

CHAPTER TWELVE

By Sunday, May 12, at one in the afternoon, the news of my Monday night–Tuesday morning misfortune had made a full circle: Whitney had told Fanny, who had told Gus, who had told Jacob, who called me at home to deliver a lecture on the male monsters that roamed New York City looking for female prey. There might be another Son of Sam out there right now, and Jacob strongly recommended that I carry mace in my purse. In fact, he was going to buy it for me. I was too trusting. I had to adopt a defensive attitude. Martial arts classes were an excellent idea. I remember the phone call. I was sitting on my bed, Jacob's worried voice pressed to my ear, and, as I listened to him, I said yes and then yes again. I said yes even though I didn't agree with him. I was tormented by own culpability, but his uncynical affection, coupled with his vivid rendering of an innocent, vulnerable waif who had been stalked, tossed about, and nearly ravaged by an urban ogre, a maiden who required armaments and lessons if she was going to brave the roiling seas ahead, touched me deeply, despite the fact that I was not that quaking damsel, and, after I hung up the phone, tears were running down my cheeks, but whether they were for her or for me or for Jacob I couldn't tell. I have discovered that I weep in the face of goodness and sympathy, but never when confronted with cruelty and coldness. The music of goodness opens me to waves of feeling while the dissonance of cruelty shuts me down flat.

Fanny took another approach, although she, too, thought a weapon was needed: "a sweet little switchblade." She went so far as to tell me where I could buy that deadly item Sunday night over dinner. To be honest, until I read about our conversation in the notebook, that evening had turned into fog. I didn't record the name of the restaurant, but it must have been the Kiev on Second Avenue. (Whitney was out on a date with a photographer named George.)

May 12, 1979

Fanny was sparkling tonight, all lit up. For the first twenty minutes, she was so excited about a rat attack on Anne Street, she couldn't breathe well, and it took me a while to understand what had actually happened. According to Fanny, the incident took place on May 8 downtown. "The species is known as *Rattus norvegicus*—your relatives, Minnesota." I protested loudly, and Fanny changed her tune. This is the story: On May 8, a dozen foot-long rats of the species known as *Rattus norvegicus* raced out of a mountain of garbage on Anne Street that had been simmering for some time at the very bottom of the borough of Manhattan. The accumulation of crap is mainly, but not entirely, due to the tugboat strike. When the boats stopped hauling trash off the island, the debris started to pile up and, as it piled up, it began to putrefy, molder, and stink, and on May 8, twelve monster rats emerged from one of those putrefying heaps with their jaws agape, chased a pedestrian down the street, caught up with her, fastened their teeth into her legs, and began to eat them. According to Fanny's sources, the victim bravely fought off the rodents with violent swats, kicks, and purse smashes, after which she finally released herself and ran howling down the street with large chunks of flesh missing from her shins and calves and blood gushing from her wounds. Fanny said it was a real-life horror movie. Fanny said everyone is talking about it.

After she had unburdened herself of the repulsive story and vigorously patted her chest to catch her breath, Fanny lit a cigarette and turned ruminative. She puffed on her Camel with one hand and scratched her upper arm with the other hand while we waited for our stuffed cabbage and explained to me that a parallel architecture of waste has sprung up in the city, is growing steadily, and will soon rival the skyline. "We've got towers of rot inhabited by millions and millions of rats, way more rats than people. People are leaving town, Minnesota, but the rats are moving in. There are two cities now, and those ugly beasties know how to survive a whole lot better than we do. Before long, they're going to eat us alive." In Webster, the only rats I saw were pets—small, white, friendly, and clean. They have nothing to do with the bloated gray rodents that loll on subway rails or scoot along brick walls or appear suddenly out of alleys. The rats brought back an old dream. I told Fanny that when I was still in high school, I dreamed that as I shut the door to my room a rat threw itself into the opening. I slammed the door on it, but its body blocked me from shutting the door completely, and it began to squeeze its way inside, its blubber oozing through the crack.

The real rats led to the dream rat, which led to the crew rat with the birdwatcher mother. "That guy with the pencil dick who tried to rape you," Fanny said. "That guy's a rat, a worse rat than the ones on Anne Street. You know what you need, Minnesota? You need a sweet little switchblade to carve up that fucking ratfuck."

Fanny started carrying a knife in her lap-dancer days in case "things got dicey," and she swears by it. The men run. She told me about a customer who wouldn't leave her alone, and she popped out the knife at him, and he kept saying, "Whoa, whoa now, honey. Whoa." Fanny said he was a bald guy with a fat gut and rings, and he must have been at least sixty. "Now, I ask you, Minnesota, why would that hairless, hideous old fart think he had a chance with a smart, gorgeous kid like me?" We laughed our heads off, Page. It's not so funny now, but it was then, and right after we left the restaurant she pulled me against a brick wall on the corner and took the knife out of her purse to show me, and after I had seen it, she stood on tiptoe, placed her hand on my neck, pulled my head toward hers, and whispered in my ear: "Systems / Equal Steel / Shaped / Female." The Baroness. The knife's thin edge is still shining in my mind. And now, Page, the two are forever linked: the Baroness and the promise of a cut, a stab, a slice. Fanny and I hugged each other hard, and we kissed each other on the lips, and she gave me cab money as part of her dinner treat. I told her it was too much, but she insisted, and I sailed uptown with a friendly driver born in Flatbush, who told me about his son in medical school. I worked up the courage to ask him if he would wait until I was inside the door. He said he would have waited anyway. It made me feel that most people really are kind. I hope I don't have that dream tonight.

Love,
S.H.

I knew that Gus knew, and he knew that I knew that he knew, but when we spoke on the phone, which we did at least a couple of times in the days after my own rat attack, he said nothing about it. Then, on the afternoon of the fifteenth, Gus invited me to the movies. I was happy to go. I liked sitting beside Gus in the darkness of the Thalia at two o'clock in the afternoon. I liked the fact that when there weren't many people in the theater, I could put my legs over the chair in front of me, and I liked the prospect of losing myself for two hours in somebody else's drama. The movie was *Baby Face*, from 1933. During the opening credits, Gus was unusually quiet. He didn't whisper in my ear about the director of photography or point to a portentous shift in the music or interesting cutaway.

Lily Powers, aka Baby Face, played by Barbara Stanwyck, is a tough, smart-mouthed young woman with languorous, deliberate movements whom I admired from the moment she appeared on the screen. Lily's father is a soulless brute, a man whose avaricious plans include pimping out his daughter to a politician, Ed Sipple, a "big man" around town, played by Arthur Hohl, a greasy-haired, cigar-chomping creep. Early in the film, a grinning Ed walks in on Lily in her father's speakeasy, sits down across from her, and starts patting and then fondling her knee. After coldly examining her molester for a few seconds, Lily picks up her coffee cup, pours its contents over the big man's hand, and says, in a voice thick with irony, "Excuse me, my hand shakes so when I'm around you." Then she stands up, straightens her skirt, and takes a leisurely stroll across and out of the room. I remember the stony, vindictive happiness that settled over my body as I watched her. I may have smiled. I turned to Gus. His eyes met mine, and he looked at me evenly for maybe three seconds, a long time. That was enough.

But when Whitney pressed me to describe my "emotional state," I found I couldn't say what it was. The silent understanding Gus had conveyed via Barbara Stanwyck was easy for me to accept. Whitney's searching eyes, on the other hand, were somehow too much to bear. Her compassion threatened to break me. On the fourteenth, I wrote in the notebook, "Whitney says I am punishing myself for no reason, but what does reason mean in my case? I don't know what I feel now. Sometimes I feel nothing. Blank. One story seems to have bled into another, as if I am mixing up lives. I am checking again, going to the window to look for the body. It must be Lindy's, but sometimes I think it's my own. It's sick. I cleaned the apartment today on my hands and knees with a scrub brush. It felt good. I used bleach. I am battling vermin."

When I woke up on the morning of the sixteenth, I realized I had slept through the night for the first time since I had drunk Patty's tea. "No nightmare!" I wrote in Mead that afternoon. "I do believe it's over, Page. Forgive me for saying it, but I think we have turned over a new leaf!" It happened that I was right—the dream would be in hiatus for years—but I could easily have been mistaken. My unfounded enthusiasm for page-turning has a pathetic quality on hindsight, but it also demonstrates that the blank, corpse-checking, scrubbing-on-all-fours person of the day before had not lapsed into depression. And yet, the bulk of my writing on May 16 is devoted to a visit from Lucy. I never forgot that visit, but I recalled it in broad terms with many of the particulars missing. "Lucy was here. She left just minutes ago. It was so strange. I am going to write down everything I remember word for word if I can."

In the passage that follows I quote Lucy at length. I use quotation marks. It is true that I had been recording my neighbor with pen and paper for months, that her voice had entered my head, and yet, why did I write it as if I recalled every word? It is impossible to know. There is no ultimate perspective to which I can refer to answer that question. Even if those patriarchal wizards God the Father, Zeus, and the demon of Laplace exist, I am not blessed with their vision. I suspect that I am reading a text that displays my own early ambition to write in another tone, to experiment with another kind of novel, one taken straight from the events of the day.

May 16, 1979

Dear Page,

After I pushed the note accepting the dinner party invitation under her door, I haven't heard from her, and she has been out during the day and often in the evening. I've heard her whistling but not talking. As soon as I opened the door, I knew she had something to say to me. She had an anxious expression on her face, and her eyes had a determined look. After I asked her to come in, she pressed her lips together and inhaled several times, as if she were preparing to blurt out some closely held secret but wasn't sure how to do it.

After she had taken two or three hesitant steps into the room and I had invited her to sit down in the blue chair, she looked abruptly to one side of the room, then the other, movements that struck me as birdlike, and said, "I forgot." When I asked her what she meant, she said, "There's nothing here. No furniture. Just books and papers." She stared at my notebook, which was open on the floor. The page was mostly covered with doodles, faces and shapes with curling foliage.

Lucy approached the chair and sniffed. She told me the chair smelled, and I said I knew it did. "Chemicals. This chair might be poisoning you." She sat down on it anyway, folded her hands in her lap, examined me, and gave the drawings another sharp look. I sat down on the floor in front of her. She unfolded her hands, gazed at them as if they did not belong to her, and in a small voice said, "Patty wants to know what you're talking about over here."

I stared at her round calves, then up at her face. I asked her to explain what she meant. She had heard me say "strange things about moons and trees," and she wondered what it was all about. Patty was curious. She, Lucy, was curious. I asked myself how this mad reversal of roles had taken place. Lucy was the one who had talked about moons and magic children and the crippled gardener, and I was the one who had listened to her talk about them, not the other way around. I had a familiar floating sensation, that old I-am-not-myself-anymore feeling.

Lucy tried to help me. "Patty is interested in circumference, too, in circles and spheres. She wonders why you talk about those things."

As I shook my head, Lucy said, "It's because Patty thinks you might be one of us."

"One of you?"

Lucy abruptly brought her palm to her mouth and, without letting it drop, mumbled from behind it, "Forget that. Just forget it."

Moons. Trees. Circumference. One of us? I don't know how long it took, Page, but after silently pondering Lucy's remarks, I thought, *circumference*, Emily Dickinson. The poems! I laughed.

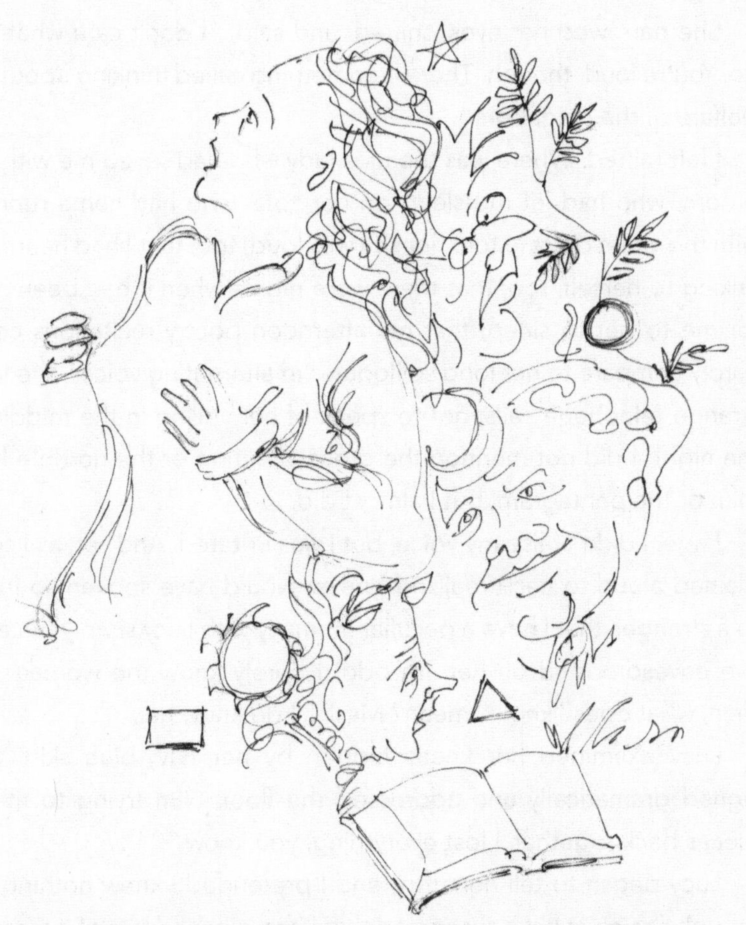

THE PAGE WAS MOSTLY COVERED WITH DOODLES, FACES AND SHAPES WITH CURLING FOLIAGE.

"Oh, Lucy," I said, "I read a lot of poems and sometimes I walk around the room saying them out loud. The rhythms are good for my work."

Lucy waggled her fingers in front of her in a loose imitation of typing. She had heard me typing.

She narrowed her eyes, sniffed, and said, "I don't care what you do. You're loud, though. There is something called thinking about the welfare of the neighbors."

I felt miffed. Where was the nice lady who had saved me with her broom, who had let me sleep on her sofa, who had come running with the violet dress? I told her she was loud, too, that I had heard her talking to herself, too, that there were nights when it had been hard for me to get to sleep, that my afternoon poetry recitations could hardly compare to her long soliloquies in alternating voices, the long strange telephone calls, not to speak of her yelling in the middle of the night. I did not mention the group meeting or the horrible little man or the pentagram, but I almost did.

Page, I didn't raise my voice, but I was irritated. And yet, as I complained aloud to her, I realized I never would have spoken so freely to a stranger, that I have a peculiar intimacy with Lucy simply because I've eavesdropped on her. It's odd. I barely know the woman. But then, what does "know" mean? Maybe I do know her.

Lucy examined her knees hidden by her navy-blue skirt. She sighed dramatically and addressed the floor. "I'm trying to fit the pieces back together. I lost everything, you know."

Lucy began to tell her story, and I pretended I knew nothing, although she must have suspected that I had gleaned bits of it through the wall. Is that why she started talking and didn't stop? Did she want to fill in "the pieces" for me? I learned from Lucy that Lindy died ten years ago. She was fifteen. Ten years seems like a long time. Lucy said she "fell" out the window of the apartment and that her brother had come yelling after she "fell" and that she, Lucy, had suffered more than she ever thought anyone could suffer. I listened sympathetically—but then she abruptly told me that her son is "gone too." And when I said, "Gone?" she looked at me fiercely and barked, "Dead, dead, dead." Then, without telling me how he died, she said that she had been dead, too. "You know what catatonic is?" When I nodded, she ignored me and went on, "I was a statue in a little white room at Payne Whitney, that's the name of the cuckoo bin where they kept me. I went catatonic. I couldn't talk or move or anything. While I was a statue, my husband left me for that stuck-up bitch from Richmond. They've got two kids now, and here I am, practically penniless in this shithole. Pardon my French."

Lucy comes from Lincoln, Nebraska, a new fact among the old ones. I told her I had driven through there with my family on one of our westward camping expeditions, and it was the flattest place I had ever seen, and she nodded and said, "big, bleak, and beautiful," a phrase I liked and told myself I would borrow. She wasn't entirely coherent, but I gathered that Ted had swept her up after a corporate dinner at a hotel where he was a guest and Lucy was working as a waitress, "rotting away after high school." She was twenty-one. A pregnancy ensued. The villain, a standard hero at the time, rising in the company ranks, brought her to New York, married her, went out on his own in ventures connected to real estate, and made his money not before but during their marriage. "It was all a front. You have to look rich to get rich. Do you know that? He'd go out in his fine suits and gold cuff links and buffed-up shoes all for show. Big smiles. Good manners. Well, he fooled them." Lucy lunged from one subject to another. She loves Patty. "I have a new life now because of Patty." When I asked her exactly what Patty had done for her, Lucy said, "She helped me name the shadow and speak the truth." When I said I didn't understand that, she said, "Remember you said to Patty that you never should have gotten into a car with that creep?"

I didn't breathe, Page. I didn't breathe.

"Well," Lucy said, "it was like that for me, too, but it lasted for years, years and years and years. Do you know what I'm saying to you?"

I didn't answer her.

"I still can't figure out why he'd get so mad. I called him tinder sticks, not to his face, of course. He'd march around the apartment and then, before I knew it, he'd catch fire. Oh, that man could yell. We used to say *holler* at home, a hollering maniac. Some men are like that. My dad wasn't like that. He was a quiet man. Never said much. You should've seen him with his dogs. He loved his dogs, didn't like people half as much. Well, Ted seemed really nice at first, traditional, you know, candy and flowers and cards with birds on them. He was living in Chicago then and it seemed like the great beyond. You can believe I fell for the candy and flowers and the birds, too. He called me his little birdie. But I think he hated the baby before he was born, really hated him because that baby tied him down to me, Lucy, the little birdie he knocked up. He could've left me out there, disgraced. It's changed now, but that was a long time ago. They made you feel dirty and cheap. Why is it that men can stick their pecker anywhere and everywhere and it's okay? Ted had a code of honor. He didn't want people talking about him. He wanted to look good, and he wanted to do the right thing. He said that over and over. He was going to do the right thing. And I loved him. Isn't that crazy? I really loved him, but it was all wrong from the start." Lucy paused to think.

"He went to college, but he didn't come from money, none to speak of. His dad was a contractor who did pretty well. Ted sure had big ideas about how it was going to be when we got the money, though. This club and that wine and how I was supposed to look, a mink coat." Lucy smirked. "And how I was supposed to talk. He hired someone to give me speech lessons and get rid of Nebraska." Lucy lifted her chin, turned to her left, and fluttered a hand. "It tied me up inside, you know what I mean? I wasn't good enough. I was never good enough, except in bed. I didn't really mind the lessons. The woman was nice, Sandra Dietrich. 'Now, Lucy,' she used say. 'Now,

Lucy, listen to my *a* sound, ah, as in bah, bah, black sheep. Pa-a-ah-rk Avenue.'"

I laughed, and Lucy smiled at me.

"Well, he got the money from real estate dealing and we got Pa-a-ahrk Avenue. I did it for him because I thought it was right. We each had our rights and wrongs. I waited on him and crept around him, and I never asked for what I needed because I couldn't have any needs, and I just got smaller and smaller." She held up her thumb and index finger an inch apart. "I was about this big." She squinted at the space. "The tinier I got, the madder he got, and the madder he got, the more he yelled, and the more he yelled, the closer he came to hitting me. But I have to be honest, he didn't hit me that many times, just six times over the years, just six times and four of the times were near the end, but if he hadn't hit me those six times, I wouldn't have been so tiny. You see, it's a circle. Patty says you have to look it straight in the face. You have to name the shadow."

Lucy stared at the wall across the air shaft and said, "I wanted him. You can't believe how nice-looking I was when I was young." I wasn't sure how the second sentence followed the first, but I told her I could believe it because she was still pretty, and Lucy grinned. "Well, I played it just right." She rolled her shoulder at me and gave me a bitter smile. "He scared the living daylights out of me and the kids half the time. The other half he was sweet as pie." She looked at me. "Find yourself a nice man."

"I'm not looking for a man," I said.

"Are you a lesbian? If you're a lesbian, why were you with that ass the other night?"

I tried to explain that I wasn't looking to get married, that I wanted to study and write. Lucy leapt from one subject to another. "Have you ever wanted to kill someone?" she said.

When I said no, which is the truth, she regarded me skeptically. I had to insist.

"Well, it came over me kind of slowly," she said. "I had this idea that it was my fault, losing Lindy." (Again I sought the logic between her two sentences but couldn't find it.) She paused. "Lindy was the liveliest little girl you ever saw. Everybody loved her because she was so cute and funny, dancing around the house in her kooky costumes. She had this wand I bought for her. She slept with it at night, and oh, heaven help us if we couldn't find it. She had a little trouble in school early on. It was hard for her to sit still, but she did really well after that. It wasn't until later, I mean, in high school, she got sad. I'd try to get her out of bed, but she'd push me away. She cried all the time, but I could talk to her, not always, but sometimes. The truth is Lindy was the easy one. Teddy, my first, he wasn't right from the beginning. I asked the pediatrician, but he didn't listen to me. Oh, he's fine. He's fine. He wasn't fine. I rocked the baby and I bounced him, but he wasn't there somehow, wasn't okay. I felt guilty about it. I thought it must be me. Ted thought it was me." Lucy leaned forward on the chair and grabbed her knees. "There was something off in his eyes."

I asked her what she meant by "off." It was obvious to me that Lucy wasn't going to stop. The dread I had felt listening through the wall wasn't relieved by the confession I was hearing, if that's what it was.

Lucy said, "His eyes didn't connect. Do you understand what I'm saying? He didn't look back at me right. What do you do then? What do you do to fix it? I couldn't fix it. You know, he said to me, he was four, I think, 'I hate Dad. I hate Dad,' but he'd hang all over his dad, wouldn't let him go, and, when he got older, he started in on me, just like his father. 'You can't do anything right.' That sort of thing. I had to look really hard into his eyes because he fooled me all the time. I believed him and I believed him and I believed him. But my son is the biggest liar I ever knew. He'd apologize and even cry and then he'd tell me some long story about why he failed his test, why they said he cheated, but they were lying, or he'd tell me why they accused him of stealing the tennis racket, but he didn't really do it." Lucy took a breath. "And then he beat up Randolph Burns in school—can you imagine naming your kid Randolph?—anyway, he sent Randolph to the hospital, and they kicked him out of Browning, and you can bet, honey, that the other mothers with their Peter Pan collars and their driving shoes, those gals who had always looked down on me, didn't take kindly to the fact that my kid turned out to be a thug." Lucy kept her gaze on the wall, but she didn't stop talking.

"Big Ted used to grab little Ted by the shirt collar and throw him into an ice-cold shower. He did that for years." Lucy leaned back in the blue chair and turned her eyes on mine. "And I didn't do a thing. You hear me? I just let it happen. I fell down on the job, my job as a mother. He didn't throw Lindy into the shower, but she saw him do it to her brother over and over, and she saw him hit me twice, and the sound of her voice just about killed me." Lucy changed her voice and cried out. She sounded like a child. " 'Please, Daddy, no, Daddy, don't.' And Lindy cried and cried, and I crawled into bed with her and I held her and I told her how sorry I was. Oh, we were a great little family. And then, you know, I remember a couple hours after he gave me a bloody nose, it's like it never happened, and he's there cleaning up the dishes in the kitchen to show he's sorry and telling jokes and laughing, and the kids and I are so relieved, and it's okay again."

Lucy took another breath and looked up as if there were some other listener near the ceiling. "Sometimes I try to remember when it changed. I mean, he got worse. Carolyn Taylor asked me to join her book club in the building, and I did. For some reason he didn't like it. He was always making fun of the women and telling me I was too stupid to read books. I never went to college. What did I know? Ignorant Lucy. And then a few months before Lindy fell, he started locking up his study in the apartment. Before he went to work, he would take out the key and lock the room. He said he didn't want anybody messing with his papers. One day he came home, found a coffee ring on a side table, one of those white circles that you can't get rid of, and he flew into a rage, picked up the table, and locked it in his study."

"He was crazy," I said.

Lucy nodded. "That's what Patty said."

"Patty's right."

"And then, one by one, he started locking things away. The kids watched too much TV. He locked up the set. I had this pair of Swedish clogs I always wore around the house. He didn't like the sound they made. He threw them in the study and locked them in there. When he came home after work, he'd walk around the apartment with his key chain out, looking for mistakes, looking for stuff to lock in the study. Things just disappeared." Lucy shook her head. "I told him he had to stop it, that we needed our things back, and he turned into a savage and he really beat me up then. I thought my arm might be broken. The kids were out, thank God."

"And you wanted to kill him?" I said boldly.

Lucy stared at me. "Oh no, not at all, not then, not for a long time, not until after I met Patty. Once you're in, once you've married him and you've got your kids, you do the best you can. Where was I going to go? My mom was dead. My poor dad was just making ends meet. I couldn't go running home to Lincoln. I didn't have any money of my own. Patty said that you can't see your way out of it when you're inside it. She's right about that, but there wasn't any outside, not really, not until he got me to sign the papers and threw me out and even then most of the time I thought it was my fault."

I asked Lucy how her son died.

"He blew up."

"He blew up? In an explosion?"

Lucy was belligerent. "I don't want to talk about it, okay?"

Chastened, I said, "Okay."

We were silent for a minute and then Lucy said, "We like you. That's why I came over. Patty wanted me to talk to you before the party tomorrow. We like you."

Patty, Patty, Patty, I thought to myself.

"This is one smelly chair," Lucy said. "Before I go, before tomorrow, I just want to say one other thing."

I nodded.

Lucy's eyes looked wet. "You have to listen to me now, without prejudice, as Patty says. You know what's saved me from being dead for the rest of my life?"

I shook my head.

"The wand."

"Lindy's wand?"

Lucy smoothed her hair back with both hands. "No, honey," she said. "A real one. But the imagery is important. The symbol, you know. I found it in a trance, in a trance circle. I found the imagery of the two wands. It spoke to my younger self." Lucy gave me a superior look. "There are two sides of the brain, did you know that?"

I nodded dumbly.

"There are secret ways to get the two sides of the brain to talk to each other. One self can talk to the other self in their different languages and then we can hook into the animals like us and not like us and the reptiles and the fish and even the plants and the seasons as they turn and the fields and the crops and the sun and the moon and the stars, and all of them always make a circle that spins round and round and the circumference of the circle never ends. You see that, don't you? We're born and we die but there's a cycle of getting born and dying. I have to remember that Teddy was inside me and Lindy was inside me, and they were like night and day, you see? I can't do anything about my son now, but he's part of the whole picture, too. Lindy crossed the bridge. And just because the cord was cut, it doesn't mean she's not still part of me—that she's not here and there and everywhere." Lucy raised her arms and extended her two index fingers above her head in a gesture I guessed was meant to signify profundity. "There's no darkness without light. How would we know what the night is if we didn't have day? They go together."

Lucy extended her palms toward me as her voice became more impassioned.

Page, I had no idea what she was talking about.

"We'd just like you to think about it, that's all, because we know you have it, too."

"Have what exactly?"

"The feeling." Lucy straightened her spine in the chair. "When I was in the circle, I saw a wand lit by fire in a night sky, and I knew it was Lindy's wand, too, a sign of the feeling cure."

"The feeling cure?"

"Yes, sweetheart," she said. "The magic, the old language. It's running through me right now."

CHAPTER THIRTEEN

A woman breathes in and out. Are you listening? She parts the ear tips of the stethoscope and fits them into the other woman's ears. Can you hear the heartbeat? Yes. Yes, I hear it. An old woman asks, "How old am I?" And her daughter answers, "Ninety-four."

The narrator takes her position in the night sky and looks down at the city, at all the cities. Something is happening. Something is about to happen. What time is it? It is the time of your reading, Madam, and it is the time of the story, which, of course, are not the same times.

Something is happening in the nighttime of the book. It is happening now. Oh, she said to her sister, remember the stars at home? In New York, the same stars disappear in the burning haze of urban light, hidden by the hubris of the city.

Far below are two tiny figures, two women who cannot see the stars. They are crossing 109th Street on Riverside Drive and walking south. They cross the street in our past but in their present and, as they walk, I adopt the present tense because you and I are with them now. It is May 17, 1979, Norway's national holiday, which, unlike so many national holidays, the tall young woman who goes by the name Minnesota tells her much shorter companion, Lucy, is not a celebration of revolutionary frenzy and stormed fortresses and running blood and hundreds of martyred corpses piled up in the streets, but the day the Norwegians adopted a constitution in 1814. Ninety-one years later, they peaceably voted themselves into independence from the Swedes. Lucy knows nothing or very little of either Norwegians or Swedes, and she nods as the two of them continue to walk toward the apartment that belongs to Patricia Thistlethwaite and her beloved friend, Moth, born Deidre Wood somewhere out West, but Lucy can't remember exactly where, what state, that is, except that little Deidre had polio and spent time in an iron lung many years before she "named the shadow" and became Moth.

As she walks with Lucy, Minnesota remembers lining up in the school gym to receive the sugar lump steeped in a pink liquid that melted in her mouth so she would never get polio or need to wear braces on her legs, the kind Laura Larsen had, who worked at the Public Library built by Andrew Carnegie to display his great benevolence for the immigrant swarms who had pushed out the Lakota and had raised their farms and had sometimes starved or gone crazy out there on the land. Yes, it was only time before the children of those immigrants traipsed in and out of libraries in little towns all across the country.

The stars are foggy and the city pops and drones and whistles and heaves with a cacophony of sounds, and just as the two women pause at a curb, they hear footsteps close behind them, heavy, quick, and determined. The sound is memory, and Minnesota startles. Her hands fly out and her chin bobs as if she has been knocked on the head. She stops breathing, and the man who has been at their heels walks swiftly past them. It was nothing, nothing at all, and Minnesota feels acutely embarrassed. The kind, good Lucy, the Lucy of the broom and the violet dress, not the other less kind, less good Lucy whose temper flares for inexplicable reasons, places her hand on Minnesota's forearm, wraps her fingers around it, and squeezes the flesh for a moment. Lucy parts her lips to speak, hesitates, and closes her mouth.

Minnesota is skittish, easily rattled by noise or shadow or even a passing odor if the smell she inhales doesn't seem to belong to its whereabouts. The explosive dream has stopped coming, but her restive state will continue for months, and she will shy from the sexual attentions of men for a year. Instead she will hit the foam on her cheap mattress in the room with its orange-crate bed and desk and bookshelf and bang safely with various phantoms, more often women than men during the months after the night of May 7 that became May 8. Yes, something is happening to our protagonist. Minnesota doesn't want to be pushed anymore. She does not want to be prodded or kicked or thrown, and yet she cannot say these simple words silently to herself or aloud because her case is not grave enough to warrant that kind of verbal attention. Just think of all the suffering in the world. Who does she think she is? Not a single broken bone.

Minnesota is looking for a story, but it is not among the stories she has been writing. Sometimes her characters meander into the rooms and streets and byways where the larger story is taking place, but her view is too pinched to see the city as a whole. A narrator whispers in her ear. The young woman needs a key. Remember that. She will get a knife, but what she needs is a key.

I am probably the only guest who attended the dinner party on that spring evening who is still alive. I was young. The others were not. On May 18, I inscribed them into my notebook as if they were characters in *Minnesota in Manhattan* or *The Mystery of Lucy Brite*. My eagerness to translate my life into Novelese can in part be explained by the fact that the novel I had hoped to finish was stalled for lack of a driving plot, and desperation had begun to haunt my hours at the typewriter. My original ambition—to pit the artificiality of Holmes-ian reasoning against the unpredictability and irrationality of actual human behavior—had imploded, not because it was a bad idea but because Ian and Isadora seemed to have their own ideas about where they were going and were not at all happy embodying my abstractions. *The Rebellious Debutante*, on the other hand, seemed to write itself. I had firm control over the heroine of that novelized memoir. She came to life via literary conventions that had long been established. She was written to please; her spunk subject to final approval by the boss.

May 18, 1979

As we walked to dinner last night, I knew Lucy wanted to tell me something but was holding back. I could feel her inhibition as a pressure in my own chest. When we reached Patty and Moth's building on Riverside Drive, she halted abruptly on the sidewalk, looked up at me, and said loudly, "I wanted to tell you this yesterday, but I wasn't sure how to read the sign. Now I do." Lucy looked behind her as if someone might be listening. She spoke fast in a low voice. "You know the night you stayed with me? Well, that morning when I came into the room, you were on the sofa sleeping, but you weren't alone." Lucy's eyes looked wet in the light from the lamp over the door. "Lindy was sitting in the chair next to you watching you sleep. My Lindy was there, just as she used to be, unhurt, nothing wrong with her, perfect." Lucy breathed in deeply; then came a shuddering exhalation. "She wasn't angry. She wasn't upset. She looked at me and smiled!" Lucy's lips quivered. "I can't tell you what it means to me. Everything has changed."

"What are you saying?"

"You brought her back. Well, my helping you brought her back. Don't you see? It's all tied together. I saw the circles and faces and vines in your notebook. It took me a while to find the answer, but last night I had another sign." She smiled. "Then I knew it was okay to tell you about Lindy. It's all about that night when you were attacked. I made noise. I yelled. I hit the wall with the broom. I ran over to you. She's forgiven me because of you. Now there's hope. I'm not being punished anymore."

"Circles and faces and vines, Lucy? They're just my doodles. Nothing more."

"That's what you think. It doesn't mean the old magic isn't working. It doesn't mean it's not a sign. You just don't know how to read it."

"But Lucy." I dragged out the S-sound like a hiss. "I made those drawings. You're telling me I don't know what I drew?"

Lucy smiled at me as if she were indulging a four-year-old. "You think that what you think you're doing is what you're really doing? That's naïve, you know."

I gaped at her, my frustration growing. "Let me get this straight. You believe that you saw something in my drawing of circles and faces and vines that's connected to Lindy? You're telling me you saw her ghost?"

"If that's what you want to call it. Ghost sounds a tad primitive to me. I saw her astral body."

Then Lucy glanced at her watch and said cheerfully, "Dear me, we'd better go in." She fluttered her fingers a couple inches from her ears, apparently a signal to hurry. In the elevator I told Lucy that we had to talk more about "all this." Oh yes, we would do that, she said, but right now we were going to a dinner party, and I watched her smooth her hair and then pinch her cheeks with her fingertips.

By the time Moth opened the door, my thoughts were whirling with circles and faces and vines and ghosts. Lindy watching me as I slept. "You brought her back." I did not. Moth was greeting us with shouts of "Alice! Alice! Down! Down!" a reference to the frenzied yellow mutt with a good deal of terrier in her who leapt, ran in circles, and barked at us until I reached down and let her sniff my hand, after which she wagged and licked my fingers. Moth's gray frizzled hair had been pulled up loosely toward the top of her head and she had a multicolored shawl with little mirrors and beads sewn into it wrapped around her shoulders, a garment Lucy immediately declared "festive."

As I stood in the hallway staring at an odd geometric print on the wall with a pentagram at its center and Latin inscriptions, I wondered if the image was another goddamned sign and what the hell I was doing there. My gratitude to the Ladies of the Broom had waned. "She's forgiven me because of you." No, she hasn't.

Moth was warbling about how happy she was to have us and wouldn't we come into the living room and just ignore the piles of books because there was nothing to be done about them. Patty would not be reasoned with when it came to books, and soon they would be pushed out of the apartment altogether because there would no longer be room for the two of them to sit or eat or sleep. It's hard to say whether I was glowering or not, but I imagined I was. People die. They don't evaporate into astral bodies. They decay and putrefy. Ashes to ashes. I had to calm my breathing. Large apartment. Were they rich?

I looked at Moth as she tottered on her stiff legs at great speed with Alice trotting behind her through the maze of volumes along both walls and stacked up in small towers in the hallway. The dog's nails clattered noisily on the parquet floorboards, hammering into my temples. Those nails needed clipping. I tried to focus on the present. Lucy pressed her lips together and smoothed her hair again. I found her gestures so annoying, I clenched my jaw.

Moth ushered us into a room darker than the hallway, and it took me a minute to adjust to low lamplight, candles, cigarette fog, and a faint herbal odor that permeated the room. Books were everywhere, stacked on the floor, on tables, and on a row of straight-backed chairs. All four walls bulged with books, pushed vertically into the tall shelves, but also squeezed in horizontally when there was space above them. A wooden ladder leaned against one of the shelves attached to a rail, and despite my irritable mood, I silently wished for a library ladder in my future life. Moth's excited talk escalated without any interference from us, and I heard her voice rise in a screech of new ardor. She waved toward the far end of the room, "Patty, I have the two of them here. Isn't it lovely?" And then she asked Lucy and me about wine—red or white or rosé; they had all three—and rosé made Moth think of the summer in Provence she and Patty had together, and she could almost smell the lavender, holy shit, it was such a great smell, and Lucy and I declared our preference for rosé, having been swayed by the imaginary lavender, and she rushed off to fulfill the request with Alice rattling and wagging happily at her heels.

When I turned, I saw Patty seated in a chair near the end of the large room, her big smooth face illuminated by a standing lamp, the rest of her bulky form in shadow. The angle of the lamp ignited the planes of her white cheeks and forehead, and I vaguely recalled characters in novels whose skin had been described in terms of marble or alabaster. As Lucy and I walked toward her, the perfume I had detected moments before grew stronger—sweet and green, but with low medicinal strains that reminded me of Aunt Irma's drawers, some lavender perhaps, but mingled with other potent ingredients, a whiff of camphor? The scent struck my nose in waves, and each wave was accompanied by a tug at my nostrils. I felt strangely warm and, seconds later, slightly dizzy. Didn't the others smell it? I had a brief memory of leaves floating in my tea and then a confused thought that ghosts and odors are somehow alike. Lucy was standing beside me. I glanced at her. She had a pleased look on her face that increased my annoyance. And then I became suddenly conscious of my swallowing—once, twice, three times. Don't count, I told myself.

Patty, emanating the strange perfume, looked up at me, and I noted her milk-white skin and her calm gaze as she fixed her eyes on mine.

"I'd like to show you something." Patty's expression was friendly, but I made a point of sealing my own face of all emotion. After Lucy's bizarre confession I felt defensive. "Interpretation," Patty was saying, "is a curious thing, don't you think? Everything depends on how we read the world, and yet we're always misreading it. I think those misreadings often depend on what we've left out, what we've forgotten. We're not operating with a full deck, as it were, but with a few cards we shuffle and distribute to all the players as if it were the whole deck. The players have to make sense of the game, and they do, but they don't realize that cards are missing. They don't understand that if they had all the cards, they would be playing a whole different game." Patty nodded sagely.

The metaphor made a kind of sense, but I didn't know what she was driving at.

Patty smiled up at me from her chair. "Let's say that someone has hidden all the queens, or worse, someone has burned the queens, but it happened so long ago that no one knows the queens ever existed in the deck."

"I'm not sure that playing without queens would make that much difference," I said. "The rules are arbitrary, and they change. There are many games that can be played with fewer cards."

Patty nodded. "But let's say for argument's sake that the deck is standing in for everything, for the whole. Then the suppression of the queens does make a difference." She gestured toward a small table with a burning candle. "The green volume there on top of the pile. I've marked a page for you. But what I really want you to see is the little drawing inside."

As I turned my head in the direction of the book, I felt dizzy again, and I thought I should probably sit down.

"But first," Patty said in her deep tones, "let me introduce my colleague, Alistair Frame." She pointed to her left. There in the relative gloom I saw a bald man, his narrow feet stretched out on an ottoman. He was smoking with one hand and clutching a glass of red wine in the other. An ascot bulged at his neck. Why hadn't I seen him?

"Look in the book!" Lucy's excitement had a tremulous quality.

I picked up the green volume and read the title aloud, "*The Key of Solomon*."

"*Clavicula Salomonis*," Patty intoned beside me. "A grimoire."

"What's a grimoire?" I said. My voice was strong and clear. The sound of it comforted me.

"Magic," Lucy said.

As I stared at the book's cover, I listened to Patty explain that it was an English translation from 1889, but its sources were much older. I think she said the sixteenth century. "The author claims that the wisdom is straight from Solomon, but that's nonsense. What did Solomon know of Christianity? It's a Christian grimoire, an instruction book for how to cast spells. There are many from that period." I was still thinking about the hidden or burned queens, but I opened the book, held it near the candlelight, flipped over a few pages, and began to read. The book's author, whoever he was, was insisting on calm weather. He recommended weather without wind, weather "without clouds running hither and thither over the face of the sky." Without stillness, the spell would fail. I turned to the marked page: "The Construction of the Circle." Take a knife or a quill pen and cut circles within circles—"the second circumferential line."

A knife. A circle. Circumference. I thought to myself, Gus wins: a circle-and-knife cult. "She thinks you might be one of us." No, ladies, I am simply an admirer of Emily Dickinson: "And back I slid—and I alone—A Speck upon a Ball—Went out upon Circumference—"

Lucy put her arm around my waist. "You have to look at the picture in the book! Hold it under the light!" I stared down at a page of mostly unintelligible drawings:

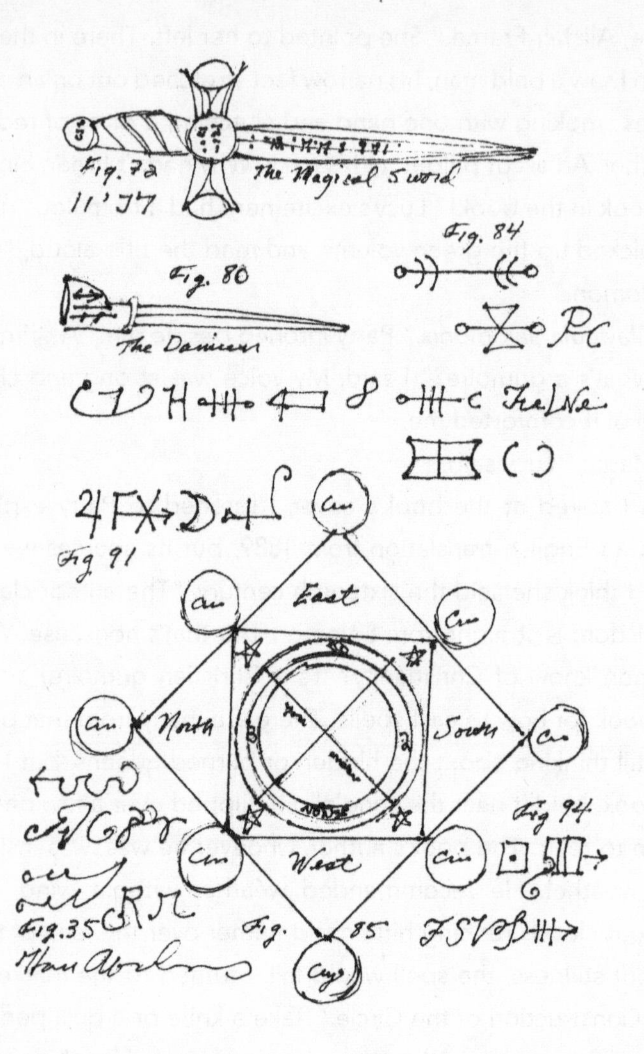

Patty's resonant voice rumbled beside me with further explication, but my vertigo was worse. I carried the book with me to the velvet sofa across from Patty and sat down. Lucy followed me with the candle, holding it over the image. Patty was still talking. She had found the volume in a used bookstore about ten years ago during what she called "the political upheavals." She had bought the book, taken it home, and discovered the small drawing tucked inside it. "That drawing," she said, "helped me to see what was missing. I have no idea who the artist was. It may have been just an attentive reader who drew what she had discovered. I assume it was a woman. I like to think of the drawing as the key behind the *Key*. Solomon's key is nonsense. It's the partial deck. The real key is not in the book at all. It's in that picture. It's there in the glassine envelope."

Lucy handed me the candle and carefully removed the drawing from its envelope and held it out for me.

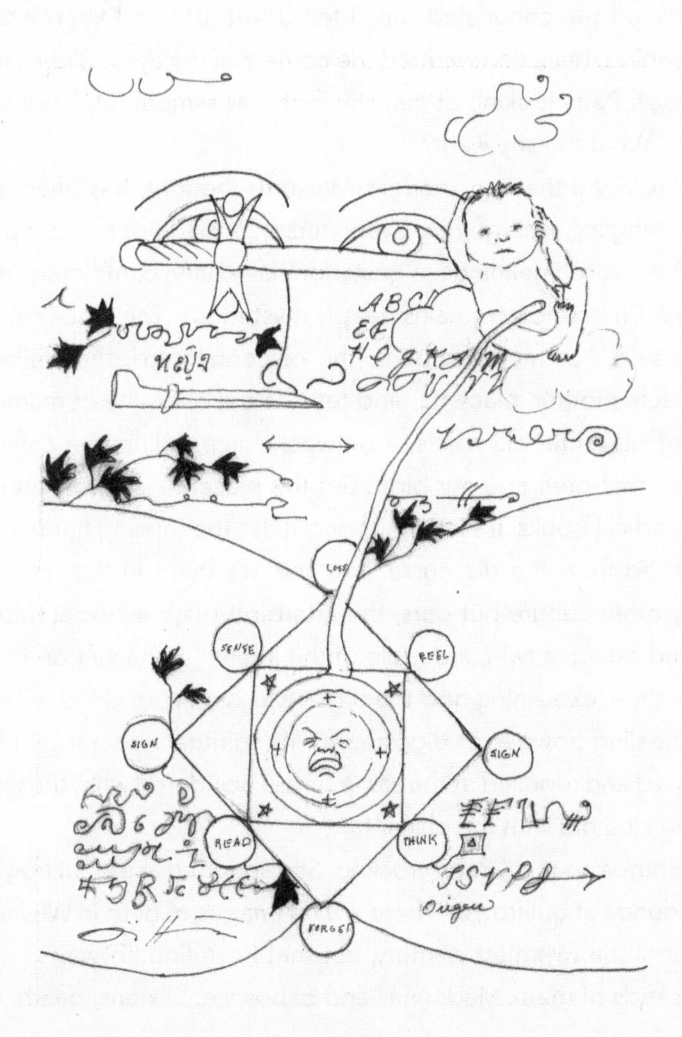

The drawing was obviously a variation on the image in the book. Yes, there were circles and vines and the face of a flying baby on a string and the square, what was that? I wanted to laugh, but there was something disturbing about the image. I watched Lucy slide the drawing back into the envelope and place it inside the volume with a look of satisfaction. She returned the book to the pile and came to retrieve the candle from me. She grabbed it a little roughly, and with the jerk hot wax dripped onto my hand. I suppressed a gasp and, as I examined the purple oval near the bottom of my thumb and began to pick off the congealed wax, I felt upset. Before I knew what was happening, tears had warmed the corners of my eyes. When I looked up, I saw Patty looking at me. Her face was sympathetic, too sympathetic. What did she want?

"I realized that our thought, Western thought, has been a flight from mingling ambiguities. Every person is made of two people, but the theoretical meanings of gestation have been completely misconstrued. Embryology remains deeply mysterious. The umbilical cord," Patty said, "or more properly, the placental cord, the lifeline that connects mother, placenta, and fetus is the ur-reality of mammalian life, of placental mammals, a between force, a link, the connective tissues that prefigure our birth. But the placenta is hardly present in the medical books. It's an afterthought. It's the missing human organ, banished from the discourse. You see, it's there in the drawing. In every other culture but ours, the afterbirth plays a crucial role. It's a second being, a twin, a double of the infant." She went on for quite some time, explaining how the organ was buried, or dried to be used as a healing powder, or digested for its spiritual nurturance. I felt interested and repelled at the same time. I wondered what the woman-hating Hua did with the placenta.

"Think about it," Patty croaked. She sounded like a bullfrog. I love the sounds of bullfrogs. "There are no images of birth in Western art, not until the twentieth century, not that I can find anyway. There are thousands of meek Madonnas and babes, crucifixions, death, dying, battles, corpses everywhere, but birth—nothing." She looked at me. "Unstable borders are intolerable. You see that, don't you? In the beginning, it's not one thing and the other. It's both. It's the mother and a wholly dependent fetus; it's not two people. That's ridiculous. It's not two until very, very late in pregnancy. But just think about it. Every one of us begins inside another human being, attached to her through the magic of a temporary organ science knows little about and hasn't bothered to study. Now, why is that?" Patty looked very pleased with herself.

"Isn't it funny?" Lucy said. "We're all born! Did you ever see anybody giving birth in the Metropolitan Museum?"

"Never," Patty said and laughed.

I remembered Lucy talking about her children then. "Just because the cord was cut . . ." Two dead children. Lindy was fifteen. Her son had exploded somehow. Poor Lucy. Patty had power over her. And now she's seeing the ghost of her daughter. I heard canine toenails approaching and Moth handed us the glasses of rosé. I had the peculiar sensation that I had already been in the apartment for a long time, that Moth's reference to Provence and to the smell of lavender had occurred days ago. I smelled the pink liquid. Alice began to nudge my thigh with her nose, a signal that I should pet her. I did, with my left hand, and the mutt stared up at me with grateful, luminous brown eyes.

Alice wasn't going to accost me with astral bodies, signs, knives, circles, or placentas. She just wanted to be rubbed. I sipped the wine.

More guests arrived. Moth introduced me to Martin Blume, a heavyset man who taught philosophy at NYU, a man in his late fifties, I guessed, in a suitably rumpled corduroy jacket, gray hair swept back from his temples, a large, straight nose, and eyes that glistened with irony. He shook my hand firmly and smiled slightly with one side of his mouth. I must have seen in his expression promise for the hours ahead. Here was a person who would relieve me from the descending cloud of hidden meanings—from ghosts and signs and temporary human organs. The professor bantered with Moth about her shawl, chatted about the David Hockney exhibition at MoMA with Patty, and charmed Lucy by taking an interest in a necklace I had not even noticed she was wearing by asking, "Victorian?"

Sarah Blume had none of her husband's charm. She was a squat woman with a nervous gaze that darted from one person to another, and whenever her spouse began to speak she had a peculiar habit of ducking her head, as if she had been swatted by some invisible presence. Several times I watched her open her mouth, only to give up immediately. I wanted to yell, Speak up, woman! Just speak up! She did manage a few hesitant words about a daughter who lived in Stockholm and worked in some capacity at an institute. The mysterious Alistair remained silent, offering only an intermittent smile and friendly nods meant to illustrate he was listening attentively. The last person to join the company was Gorse, one of the women I had heard through the wall. She had a narrow wrinkled face and a thin body, a little lumpy around the middle, but it was her high sweet voice I remembered from the night of the knife and the little man. Was she the one who had said, "I'm afraid. Will he die?"

I sat on the sofa and listened. Like Alistair, I smiled and nodded. Unlike him, I made a few comments that struck me as appropriate. I was beginning to feel better. My dizziness had vanished. Professor and Mrs. Blume had ushered a comforting, pedestrian aura onto the premises. This was, after all, a dinner party. The conversation was meant to be superficial. I stroked Alice steadily, who had taken up a position near me, but each time I withdrew my hand from active petting, she nudged me for more caresses, and her insistence was beginning to irritate me as well as attract the commentary of Moth—"I hope she isn't bothering you. Alice, lie down!"

Alice did not lie down. Martin Blume, who had seated himself opposite me, looked on with amusement. I felt exquisitely conscious of his eyes. I heard Lucy say to Patty: "I picked it up at the magical child, dirt cheap." It sounded like a place, not a person. I wanted to inquire, but an instant later Alice's nose moved aggressively in the direction of my crotch and, as I pushed her cold snout away, Patty rumbled in her hoarse tenor, "She adores you. I've never seen her quite like this." When I lifted my head, I saw the professor smiling at me; this time he displayed his even teeth. My face felt warm again, and I noticed Lucy glance at Blume, register his expression, and revert to her sniffy, unkind self. She gave me a look that communicated the words *behave yourself*, as if she firmly believed I had arrived at the dinner with the sole intention of seducing the dog and/or the man.

After we were seated at the long dinner table near the windows, which were opened a crack to let in the air, the wine had relaxed my shoulders and produced a pleasant lifting sensation inside my skull. Patty sat at the end of the table to my right and seemed somewhat less fragrant. Gorse sat directly across from me, and I noted that she repeatedly straightened her glasses with both hands, as if she couldn't situate them well enough on her long nose, and that she made a little noise in her throat after each adjustment. Alice, my devotee, who had followed me into the dining room, slid deftly under the table and arranged herself so that her head rested comfortably in my lap. I was glad she seemed to have lost interest in sniffing my genitals. Patty informed me that Alice intended to look longingly up at me throughout the meal to induce my pity and, soon after, my scraps. Patty laughed, a deep rumbling laugh. "It's an effective strategy," she said. "Our Alice is well versed in a silent rhetoric of persuasion."

When I told Martin Blume, seated across from me at an angle, that I would begin my studies at Columbia in September, he looked puzzled. "But it's all men, my dear." I explained that I was going to graduate school in comparative literature, to which he said, "Ahhhhhh." We talked for a while, and *Tristram Shandy* came up along the way, probably because I brought it up. The subject animated him, and he smiled and spoke to me about Hume's influence on Sterne, which I already knew about, but I found it pleasant to listen to him expound. I enjoyed listening to words I understood. We laughed about how long it takes for Tristram to get born, not until volume four. And I quoted the line I loved about the novel's temporal scheme—"digressive . . . and progressive, too, and at the same time." He looked over at me then with benevolent brown eyes, and I felt his attention as if it were a small sun shining on me at the table. It had the quality of a memory I couldn't place, a good memory.

Patty was deep in conversation with Gorse but also seemed to be following what Blume and I were saying to each other because she grinned at me and said, "I see we've returned to birth. Delivering babies, delivering manuscripts, nine volumes, nine months. The book is one long labor!" Some moments later, she quipped, "I'm listening to you. I'm not surprised that you've left out Mrs. Shandy altogether." To which he said, "Never! I always remember the ladies," and returned to his disquisition. I recalled Mrs. Shandy shouting at some point late in the book: "What's this story all about?" I thought it would be nice to mention it, but then Lucy, after giving me a close and critical look, distracted Martin Blume with a question, and he turned away to speak to her.

Abandoned for the moment, I listened to the mix of voices as if the table were a single being with many mouths and then to the constant sound beyond the chatter of cars passing on the West Side Highway. The wine was still rising in my head, and Alistair, seated to my left, had a voice, after all. He was speaking to Sarah Blume in polite tones. I noticed that the skin at the back of his neck was rosy and that the wool of his jacket had pilled. I wondered why I had felt so bad half an hour ago. I noticed that the linen cloth under my plate was badly wrinkled, but when I surveyed the table as a whole, I detected a smooth area toward the middle, as if someone had started ironing and had given up. I remarked to myself that the china and crystal were fine, as were the two heavy silver candelabra with five dark candles burning in them that summoned the image of a frightened heroine in a great black-and-white room with blowing curtains and organ music. I smiled to myself, and thought, Yes, that's the way I've been behaving—like a scaredy-cat. That's what Kari and I used to say. I noticed that the floral arrangement was peculiar—a haphazard collection of herbs that included drooping sage and browning rosemary and comparatively fresh oregano mingled with red roses, their necks fallen. My mother would have disapproved of both wrinkles and centerpiece, but I felt sympathy for the person I strongly suspected was Moth who had begun the ironing job and stopped. I also felt a pang for the roses, as if they were weren't flowers but people hanging their heads in sorrow or shame. It wasn't their fault they were a little too sad or old to stand upright.

But now I must think through why it all went so badly wrong, why the whole atmosphere of the dinner changed and why I acted the way I did. There is much that can't be articulated when several people find themselves in a room together. Bristling as well as warm breezes circulate among those people, and one may find oneself in a crosswind without knowing why. It must be connected to the density of memories in the room. Each person drags his past into a chair with him and then he sits down next to another person who has her past along with her as well—mothers and fathers and aunts and uncles and friends and enemies and hometowns and roads and mailboxes and streets and diners and skyscrapers and bus stops are all there in the events that have stayed with him or her because the thing that happened caused pain or joy or fear or shame, and as I look back on the dinner party, I understand that the memories seated in the chairs along with the guests included dead people like Irma and Lindy and Ted Jr., yes, real ghosts borne into the present by each mind at the table—and when you multiply the pasts and memories and ghosts of everyone in the room, you understand they aren't quiet or contained because they inevitably reappear in the conversation in one form or another, and then they begin to mingle and stir up the rest of the company, one blending into the other, and it's not only the words of the conversation that count but the tone of voice each person uses when he or she talks, and then think of all the looking back and forth that goes on at a dinner table and the gesturing and all the visible information as well—faces that flush momentarily and tiny beads of sweat that form on upper lips and wrinkles that arrive on a face only in a smile, or the various pairs of eyes that appear cool and indifferent and other pairs that are alive with interest, or the same pair of eyes that seem far away one instant and focused the next, and every person is reading and rereading and interpreting all the big and small signals that are whirling about and that can't be kept separate from the memories at all, and I wonder how on earth we keep track of any of it.

I know that Lucy told the awful story about the hamster during dessert. The hamster story was the stillness before the storm, but seconds before the hamster story there had been the incident of Martin Blume's hand on his wife's shoulder. I am calling it "the incident of the heavy hand" because I think it was crucial to the turn that took place and changed everything. Before the heavy hand and the hamster, many subjects had come and gone, most of which I've forgotten. Patty's talk was memorable, however odd, but much of the dinner-table chitchat has vanished. I know that Alice had fallen asleep on my feet, and I felt the steady rhythm of her breathing belly against my bare ankles. We had eaten well. I can still see Moth's long, narrow face, wattled at the chin, and her eager eyes surveying the table, her kingdom for the evening, as she told us "to eat and drink and be merry as hell." She had brought in the aromatic leg of lamb herself for Patty to carve, which Patty did carve expertly, and then Moth had rushed back to the kitchen for small potatoes and asparagus and had said, "Oh, fuck, damn, shit," when several buttered potatoes dressed in bright green parsley had rolled out of the heaping bowl onto the floor upon her return to the dining room, after which Alice had raced from her position under the table and had swiftly lapped them up.

I know that by the time the dessert arrived, a lemon tart, I had discovered that Patty was writing a book called *A Study in Western*

Amnesia, which treated "esoteric works" by women philosophers but also a few men. I had further discovered that Patty and Martin "went way back" to graduate school, had studied in the same program, but that Patty had abandoned the study of "mainstream philosophy" to pursue "the other side of things," a side of things her friend-from-way-back strongly disapproved of as "the province of kooks," and which Patty defended in her deep voice, but exactly what she was defending wasn't clear to me except that it was connected to "the body, feeling, and the sacred imagination" and perhaps the peculiar drawing, the key to the key.

I took Martin Blume's side, as moderately, discreetly, and diplomatically as I could. I was feeling hostile to "the other side of things," whatever they were, because they seemed as diffuse and intangible as the herbal smells in the air. Gorse had informed me that she was an artist who painted "the invisible forces of nature and spirit," a grandiose project of many colors she had piped on about in her sweet high voice between her tic-like relocations of her glasses and nearly inaudible squeaks. I had divined that Astral Alistair was a polite Englishman who sold rare books and had "clients" all over the world and expressed himself almost exclusively in negative terms, a verbal habit that may have been responsible for my first impression of him as dry, a person so parched I feared he might turn to dust if I spoke too forcefully in his direction. "No, that particular edition was not without interest," "I wouldn't call it dull, no, not dull precisely." "It wasn't a scintillating lecture, but . . ." The man eschewed the positive altogether and yet he did it with an affable demeanor, and I sensed that for him negativity was a form of modesty.

I also know that between the appetizer and the dessert, Sarah Blume had undergone a personality change. The doormat had become a flying carpet, encouraged by Moth, who had been pouring a lot of wine at their end of the table and exclaiming, "Well, fuck all that!" a phrase that caused Sarah to yelp with laughter. Lucy, too, was altered. She had taken on a glazed expression as she fluttered, cooed, and smiled at Martin Blume, who grinned back at her with what struck me as genuine pleasure in her company. I could see Lucy was flattering him, but I had also seen his eyes stray repeatedly away from Lucy and onto his wife, toward whom he had sent numerous significant glances. Alistair and I had become keenly aware that Sarah's hilarity had been rising decibel by decibel since the beginning of the meal, although we hadn't said a word to each other about it. Nevertheless, just after Sarah had released a cackle with a little scream in it, Alistair regarded me fixedly for a couple of seconds, as if to say, "That might not be entirely called for. Don't you agree?" My view of the uproarious Sarah was partly blocked by Alistair himself and further by the scarf that bloomed at his collar, so I hadn't been able to see if she had met her spouse's eyes, but from the sound of things his corrective looks had been wholly useless.

At some moment after that, Martin left the table, no doubt headed for the toilet. On his way, he paused beside his wife's chair. I confess I leaned forward to see what he was doing. I watched as he placed his hand on his spouse's shoulder and squeezed it, not hard, but it was then that I, peering at Sarah in profile just beyond Alistair's shoulder, saw her smile vanish and her chin drop. It had startled me—that heavy hand, the squeeze. As I had watched, I had felt the fingers on my own shoulder and along with the sensation a keen sense of shame. What had happened? Sarah had been wild, it's true, and Martin had wanted to stop her before, before what? Before she laughed too hard? Before she drank more? Why had his hand seemed so terrible? Was it that his grip had been so effective?

Moth, too, fell suddenly silent as she watched the husband disappear into the hallway. Lucy, seated directly across from Sarah, had had a better view of the heavy-hand incident than I'd had, and while the professor-husband was passing urine and the tart was being delivered by Gorse, Lucy began a charged monologue on the subject of not knowing who people really are. She insisted "they" can fool you over and over again, and I instantly began to worry about what she might say. "Smiling snakes," Lucy barked at Sarah, who said nothing. As Lucy spat out the words, "liars, cheats, deceivers," Alistair sent me a look of high alarm, which I answered with an acquiescent glance. The table was silent. Lucy forged on.

As was her habit, she veered from one subject to another connected by some emotional string only she could see. Lucy's eyes were ignited with ferocity, and, as she waved her hands, I noticed that her gestures had been further loosened by feeling and drink. She didn't flutter. She flapped. When sober, Lucy's movements had always been petite. "They think they own you! They think they don't have to ask!" Lucy leaned over her tart and eyed me intently. For an instant I stopped breathing, terrified that she was going to tell the story of my near rape at the table. "The bastards," she continued. "They deserve to be punished, stripped naked and hung by their ankles upside down. They deserve to be pinched black and blue, and kicked hard with their own golf shoes." (Did anyone but me know about the golf shoes?)

"Now, Lucy," Patty rumbled beside me. "That is not what we are about. You know that. No harm. We don't do harm." Her deep, hoarse voice had a soothing timbre.

"Well," Lucy said, "they deserve it. That's all I'm saying." And she looked down the table at Patty and said, "It reminds me of the hamster."

"The hamster, Lucy?" Moth said.

"I once knew the mother of a boy," Lucy said, as if she were beginning a fairy tale. I heard Martin's approaching steps as he returned to the room, and a tremor ran through me. What was it? Fear. Was I remembering ten days earlier? Hadn't I startled in the street that same evening? All gaiety had left me.

Lucy continued her story. "She loved that kid, the mother loved him, but there was something wrong with him. Even I could see it every now and again. Oh, he was a charmer, a smiling cute little guy who agreed with everything you said. Now, it was like this." She paused. "His parents gave him a hamster for his birthday." I can't say exactly why, but Lucy's face looked at once excited and bitter. She smiled. The breeze from the window had turned the candles into elaborately spiraled wax bulges, and I was beset by another wave of dread. Martin Blume took his seat beside Lucy and turned to her, listening politely.

"Well," Lucy said, "the boy was really happy and gave it itty-bitty pieces of lettuce to eat in its cage and carried it around everywhere. Its name was Lester. And then one day the boy's mother found Lester dead at the bottom of the cage." Lucy breathed in and looked up and down the table. I had the distinct impression that she enjoyed monopolizing our attention. "The poor little critter. They're kind of weak, you know, but little Lester was dead as a doornail. They wrapped him up in an old hand towel, and the boy prayed over him, and the mother said she would bury him, but he actually went out with the trash and, after a while, the mother forgot all about it. But five years later when she was cleaning the boy's room after he had gone away to a summer program, one of those woodsy in-the-wilderness places for kids who need to shape up, very expensive, she found a little piece of paper taped to the back of his drawer. She pried it loose and unfolded it." I pressed my hands into my knees under the table. Lucy smoothed her hair and breathed in. "It said: 'I strangled Lester today. I don't know why. I wanted to and so I did it.'"

No one said a word.

Then Gorse said, "That's just terrible."

I sensed poor Alistair stiffening beside me. This was not a subject for dry, modest people.

And then Lucy laughed, a high, desperate laugh that cut me just below my rib cage, and the table fell silent again. Martin Blume had obviously decided to lift us out of the land of murdered hamsters and back to dinner-table conversation. He looked at Lucy, nodded sagely, and said, "In philosophy, you know, we have wrestled with the problem of other minds for some time."

"Are they a problem?" Gorse said brightly as she straightened her glasses.

I watched Martin lean back and extend his hand comfortably onto the back of Gorse's chair in a gesture of relaxed colonization. I watched him smile at the painter of the invisible on his left. I watched him turn to the rest of us, his voice rising, and I felt a sudden pressure in my chest. Something was happening to me. I looked at him. Everything I had admired and enjoyed about him had vanished. I didn't like him anymore. The man began a patient outline of the problem. His own mind—Martin Blume's mind, that is—is not a problem to himself, of course; his mind is locked inside himself, as it were, a perfectly sealed container of knowledge in Descartes's mode. "I explain much of my own behavior in terms of causation by mental events," he said to Lucy, who had cocked her head to one side and pursed her lips. Lucy appeared to have forgotten her hang-them-upside-down outburst. She had recovered her piquant, theatrical femininity. Had she forgotten about the heavy hand on his wife's shoulder? Sarah had not uttered a word since. I felt it as a burning silence.

Martin continued, "This is a handy example," he intoned slowly to us, his students at the table. "When I cut my finger and howl in pain, I know I am in pain because I feel the pain, but if you cut yourself and begin to scream, 'I am in pain! I am in pain!' how do I know that you are indeed in pain?"

Lucy smiled ingratiatingly. "You know because I'm screaming and I'm telling you."

"That's right," said Moth from her seat at the other end of the table. "It's obvious."

"Ahhhh," he said, resting back comfortably as he extended his right arm onto the back of Lucy's chair, "but there might be some other explanation altogether. How do I know, for example, that your mental state while you are yelling 'Oh, it hurts! It hurts!' is like my mental state? How do I know that you have a mental state at all? You could be a machine or an alien from another planet. There is a fundamental asymmetry between us, you see. The question is how do I know there are other minds? Why do I believe there are other minds? How do I know I am not unique?"

I stared at Martin Blume. I had traveled this weary road before and dimly remembered reading a paper by a man named Pargetter, whom I had contemptuously called Forgetter. The whole business was wrong from its beginning to its wholly inconclusive end. Gorse laughed and said, "You're saying the boy who strangled Lester might be a robot? Is that what you philosophers think about?"

I leaned forward to get a look at Sarah. She had folded her arms, her eyes on her husband's face, her lips pressed tightly together.

Patty was shaking her head. "Martin," she said. "We're talking about a mother and a son. How could she not know he has a mind?"

"Oh, Patty," he said. "Please, no philosophies from female nether regions. I've listened to your views for years, not that they've been either consistent or logical." I winced. What a mean thing to say. Patty regarded him evenly with a little smile. She seemed wholly unaffected by his hostility. I felt amazed. He then turned to me with a broad grin of self-satisfaction. I noted that only his head moved. The rest of him remained spread to his east—Gorse—and to his west—Lucy. He was speaking to me. "I don't suppose *you* have anything to add to this venerable philosophical debate, my dear?"

I examined him coldly. The man could not have known it, but he had burst something inside me. For a long time, it seemed to me, I had been buffeted and blown by a barrage of condescending smiles, instructive comments, and seductive hints that came at me from all directions. I wondered darkly why everyone was always trying to educate me. No, it was over. I would not let this pass. Alice woke up. Maybe I had moved my feet, but I felt her stand up beneath the table.

As I spoke, I heard the staccato syllables of anger in my voice. "You have just made a statement, but you delivered it as if it were a question. I find the technique dubious, if not reprehensible. By lifting your voice at the end of your statement and adding a patronizing 'my dear,' you imagine you can disguise as inquiry what you regard as fact. You have told me that you suppose, you guess, perhaps you surmise, that I have nothing to add. By doing so you have crossed a bridge that you have been at great pains to deny exists. You have assumed not only that I have a mind; you have assumed that the mind I do have is empty. I can assure you it is not."

I felt Alice slip away and trot noisily toward Moth. Martin Blume had stopped smiling. He looked surprised, then dismayed, which I took as encouragement. The words came fluently. "As for the problem of other minds, it rests on solipsistic foundations, on a Cartesian model I submit is wrong to begin with. When confronted with other people, we may ask ourselves 'What is he or she thinking?' or 'Is that smile unctuous or friendly?' or 'What is he hiding?' But such questions are not propositional questions of belief or disbelief about the presence of a mind!"

I had worked myself up. I felt the hush of suspense around me. My hands began to tremble uncontrollably, and I hid them beneath the table, but rather than lower my voice, as I should have, I got louder. I leaned toward him. "If you think that I am ignorant of the analogical, criteriological, and theoretical-entities arguments, you are mistaken. I am not. All of them begin with the fundamental premise of mental isolation. Although I see the person, watch him move, talk, and yell in pain, I cannot assume that person has a mind. Apparently a mind is something that does not belong to a body. It is distinct, separate, and invisible: 'the ghost in the machine.' Aren't you asking me to produce proof that another person is, in fact, another person? Then again, where does this internal mind of yours that you feel so confident about come from, sir? Why are you so sure of your own mind? Descartes's cogito is an island built on a fantasy of absolute autonomy: 'I think therefore I am.' But what is thinking? Did your thoughts about the uncertainty that other minds exist arrive at the moment you were issued from your mother's womb? Perhaps unlike the rest of us, you were born an adult. Hasn't what you call 'thought,' the contents of that mind of yours, developed over time through other people? Doesn't what you refer to as 'thought' include language, and isn't language by definition shared? I suggest to you on good authority that there is no private language. And would you have acquired the self-consciousness necessary to describe this famous asymmetry between your own mind and the minds of others if you weren't a social being, if you had had no contact with others? Do you actually believe there is an 'I' without a 'you'? Do you believe that your mind could exist without your body or without the bodies and minds of others?

"I refer you to Wittgenstein, sir," I said, as if someone other than I, some satirical demon had taken hold of me and was giving me dictation. I rushed onward. "I refer you to the *Investigations*. I'm sure you remember the section." I smiled maliciously at Professor Blume or I believed I was smiling maliciously at him. I really have no idea what I looked like at this point in my tirade. "Wittgenstein writes, as you remember, I am sure you do, 'I believe that he is suffering'—do I also *believe* that he isn't an automaton?' No, Professor Blume, it's hogwash—your problem of other minds." Was I shouting? I don't know. I don't know. But I quoted Ludwig Wittgenstein, on whom I had spent so many hours: "My attitude towards him, that other person whom I believe to be suffering, is an attitude toward a soul. I am not of the *opinion* that he has a soul." To add further injury to Sarah's husband, whom I understood I had come to detest, I pompously quoted Wittgenstein in the German: "*Meine Einstellung zu ihm ist eine Einstellung zur Seele. Ich habe nicht die Meinung, dass er eine Seele hat.*"

My performance was over. My face was hot. I felt the eyes of the whole table on me, and I felt unwell, terribly unwell. What had I done? My hands were still shaking. Nevertheless, something prompted me to stand up. I did. "Forgive me," I said. "Please forgive me." Then I fainted.

Something wet and cold was being pressed into my neck. I heard voices. I heard voices and a door shut. Loud breaths. Alice was panting close to me. I remembered Alice, and I saw the ceiling I had not looked at before and noted it had no cracks—an excellent paint job. Patty's deep voice: "We're always scraping you off the floor, Minnesota." And then I felt an embarrassment so intense I had an urge to disappear, to wish myself into oblivion, but I pushed myself up on my elbows.

"Alistair caught you!" Moth was standing over me with Gorse beside her. They looked like gnomes. "Are you okay, honey?" Moth was saying. "Your color is coming back. Well, you certainly told him, didn't you? I mean, you should've seen his face! He sure as hell wasn't expecting that speech! Holy shit!"

I sat up. Alice licked me, and I petted her neck. Lucy was sitting in one of the dining chairs and eyeing me rather sadly. Her hair no longer looked perfect, and she had kicked off her shoes. I stared at her painted toes through her nylons as Alistair handed me a glass of water. He looked at me gently, and I felt a rush of gratitude. I drank the whole glass. Moth clapped.

And then, looking from one to the other, I blurted out, "Who's the crippled gardener?"

"The crippled gardener?" Patty said. "I have no idea."

"Well, who are you?"

"We thought you knew," Moth said, smiling down at me.

"No," I said. "I don't know. I don't know anything."

"No matter." It was Patty. I craned my neck in the direction of her voice. She was sitting in a chair behind me. "She has the feeling. That's what matters."

I said it again. "What feeling?"

Moth bent forward at her waist and reached for me. "Give me your hand, honey," she said. I lifted my hand and Moth took it in both of hers. Her old face with its sagging chin struck me as ineffably tender. "Well," she said, looking at the others as if seeking their approval, "it's like this, see. We're witches."

I said nothing. Perhaps I gaped.

"It's true," Lucy said defiantly. "We're a coven."

"The coven is connected," Gorse said, "to the invisible, to the natural forces I paint. The hand knows what the head doesn't. The colors encircle me!" She sounded rapturous. They're nuts, I thought.

I shoved myself backward on the floor so I could see Patty, Patty who hadn't struck me as thoroughly insane. I turned to her. She had settled her large body into a chaise longue and I looked straight at the soles of her oxfords. I had dimly noticed the chair earlier when we had entered the dining room.

"They're quite right," Patty rumbled. It was impossible not to be impressed by her voice and its low resonances. I wondered who she would be without that voice. "We've revived the old pagan beliefs and the worship of the great goddess. We are adamantly opposed to all patriarchal religions, Christianity in particular, because it has shaped the West, has shaped us, has made us hate ourselves, blood and bone and breast and breath and womb." Patty knew her lines. "We stand opposed to patriarchy's hatred of the body and sensuality and nature and woman. We believe in the old ecology, in harmony and healing. We draw on the powers of nature, on the moon and its sacred cycles, echoed in the equally sacred cycle of animal fertility, in birth, in life lived, and in death. Death comes around and we must honor it. Death is part of the circle. And we cling to the deep knowledge human beings hold within themselves, not spoken or written knowledge, but a knowledge that is unbounded, borderless, one that thrives on felt communal truths, truths impossible for the individual alone to attain, truths made possible only among us. We must practice in secret, of course, because the larger culture is not attuned to our faith. We do not proselytize. We find one another."

Moth and Gorse had pulled out chairs from the table and had seated themselves on either side of Lucy. The three were nodding happily like a row of carnival dolls with their heads on springs.

Alistair had pulled up a chair to one side of them, smoking in a slow, contemplative manner, and I had a sudden desire for a cigarette. Alice had lain herself down at Moth's feet.

"You're not a witch, too?" I said to Alistair.

"Well," he spoke to the floor. "Perhaps not entirely as my friends are, you know, but my interest in the occult has not been tepid either."

"Oh, he's a witch," Lucy said.

They burned tens of thousands of witches, mostly women, but men, too. I remembered the terrible book of woman hatred they used to prosecute witches, *Malleus Maleficarum*. "You don't really believe in magic?" I said.

"Of course we do," Gorse said. "But we don't do evil magic."

"The second turn of the key," said Patty.

The second image, the second turn?

"I wanted them to hex Ted," Lucy said. Her bottom lip protruded.

"They wouldn't. All they would do was bind him. Gorse made the poppet and the clothes, but it was fun winding the string around and around him, tighter and tighter."

The little bound man.

Patty spoke. "The magic is already there among us. The candles, the poppet, the geometric figures are symbols that help us along. We simply harness the power that's already there. It's not supernatural; it's natural. You're here tonight because I felt it in you. I had an idea that you knew. I had an idea that you've been feeling it since you were a child, the electrified air, the active currents that move from one person to another to hurt or humiliate or heal. That force can be used, that's all. If there is a clavis universalis, a universal key, it's in the stirrings of the universe itself, and we are not its observers. We are part of that motion. As witches we've learned how to use a little piece of that power, that's all. Some people are more gifted than others. Some of those gifted people are what I call mood readers. I think you're a mood reader. So, you see, a binding spell uses that natural power to prevent others from doing harm. We send out energy that restrains, that blocks the person from harming others. Lucy has been learning to recognize her rage, to fantasize about it and visualize it, but she also knows that she must not turn those feelings into vengeful acts."

Witchcraft as therapy, I thought. Gus really is right.

"Where's Sarah?" I said, looking around. "And, and," I had forgotten his name, "her husband?"

"Her husband!" Moth shrieked. "That's funny. Martin would hate that. He's such a fucking blowhard. Patty, I never understood why you put up with him."

"He leavens me," Patty said in a dark voice. "He's good for me. He can be sharp even though we don't agree. I've known him for a long time."

"He's good-looking," Lucy said.

Moth made a face at Lucy and continued, "Martin and Sarah left when you were coming to. She was furious at him. She dragged him out of here because you were so mad. She called him a pompous ass. I was proud of her."

"Was I so mad?" I felt guilty. The guilt had a strangling quality. Why had I been so mad? Why had I made a scene? I had a confused thought about the hamster and the little piece of paper and then about the mother, philosophy's hidden whale swimming under the surface of the ocean.

"Don't you remember being mad?" Gorse said. I hoped she wouldn't adjust her glasses, but she did, and then made the tiny sound.

"No, I do," I said. "The problem of other minds."

"You spoke German!" Moth said. "Patty knows German."

"Are they witches? Sarah and Martin?" I asked.

"Good heavens, no," Gorse said. "We think we might do Sarah some good, you see. We keep an eye on her. We send good spells in her direction. She needs some propping up. We've tried binding Martin, but so far it hasn't had much effect. I think we need more energy."

Gorse gave Patty an accusatory glance.

There was chatter then about calling it a night. Alistair helped me to my feet. Moth patted my arms and straightened my sweater, as if she were putting me in order for my exit. I didn't mind. Her fussing felt maternal. Patty noted that it had been a long evening and far more eventful than anyone had expected, much wine had been consumed, et cetera.

When Lucy and I were at the door, Patty shook my hand warmly. I realized I was both a little bit afraid of her and drawn to her at the same time. She leaned close to me and looked up into my face. I inhaled the herbs. She spoke just above a whisper. "Don't turn away from your gifts. Don't apologize for them. Don't fear your anger either. It can be useful. And remember this: the world loves powerful men and hates powerful women. I know. Believe me, I know. The world will punish you, but you must hold fast."

Every word has remained inside me as if my consciousness were glass, and the words had been cut into it, but last night I just nodded. I was tired and all I knew was that what she was telling me had a generous tone; that was all that mattered then.

Before we left, I looked over at Alice, who was sleeping near the table, and had an urge to run over and say goodbye to her, but I suppressed it. Gorse remained with Patty and Moth, and Alistair accompanied us out into the cool night. He insisted on walking the few blocks north with us because it wasn't far, and I felt grateful. Lucy whistled a pretty tune I didn't know. I do believe she is the most changeable person I have ever met. I didn't speak. There was a slight wind and a moon. I wondered how I would recount the evening to Whitney, and Fanny, too, but Whitney above all. I could hear myself telling the story: I had dinner with witches. Did you know that a grimoire is a book of magic? And, oh yes, there was this man at the party that I liked and then, all of a sudden, I couldn't stand him. Other minds. It was all about other minds. I got pretty angry, and after I told him off I fainted. I stood up too fast. That would be my explanation. I stood up too fast. Yes, that's how I would tell it. It made perfect sense. But when I talked to Whitney today on the phone, I left out both my fury and my faint.

When we turned onto 109th, I could see the lights from Broadway and the dark figures of pedestrians moving up and down. I remember a pale piece of litter, a flyer perhaps, hop down the street as the breeze from the river pushed it forward. Alistair said he would wait until we were safely inside and then flag a cab going downtown. I used my key, and while I was turning it I heard someone run behind us, and a man's voice shout "Son!" and then, "Son of a bitch!" I pushed the door open and glanced at Lucy. She looked dreadful. She had frozen beside me—her eyes fixed and her mouth open in an expression of terror. Alistair patted her arm. "It was nothing," he said. "Just some idiot."

"I've got her," I said, suddenly heroic. "I'll make sure she's okay."

Alistair left us somewhat reluctantly, mumbling in Latin—I thought I heard "venire ventus"—and I helped a wobbly Lucy up the stairs and wondered if the wine had hit her hard all at once. She had seemed well enough whistling on Riverside Drive. I pulled her key out of her purse and opened 2C. I guided her inside and flicked on the light. Speechless and staring, Lucy let me pull her jacket down over her arms. I laid it carefully over one of her two dining chairs. Then I asked her if she didn't want to sit down. She looked to her left, to her right, and then straight ahead. Without warning, she lunged toward the upholstered chair beside the sofa and reached out for it as if she were a blind person, her hands fumbling over its striped arms. As I stood and watched her, she said in a soft, high, choked voice, "Come back. Come back, my darling. You have to tell me, don't you see? You have to tell me. All you have to do is nod. That's all. Come back. Please come back!"

In a fit of compassion, I walked over to Lucy, put my arms around her, and felt her collapse into my neck. I expected her to cry, but she didn't. She let me hold her for about half a minute, and then she pushed me away, declaring she was okay now and that I should go to sleep. I told her I was happy to stay, but she insisted that I leave. As I lay awake with my scattered thoughts, I felt an ache inside me. "All you have to do is nod." I can't say why, but I thought of the passage in the magic book about quiet weather. No, the clouds should not be running hither and thither across the face of the sky. The winds must die down before the spell can be cast. A hush must fall across the landscape. And then I thought about the sky at home and its vastness, and after that I remember nothing, not even my dreams.

CHAPTER FOURTEEN

A letter is slipped under a door. A knife is sent through the mail in a plain brown box addressed to 309 West 109th Street, Apt. #2B. An artist is bent over a piece of paper in a tiny flat in Paris writing to her friend in hope that the book of poems will not be abandoned. "Djuna, it is so desperately necessary for me!" Years after she is dead, a man's tongue will begin to move, and he will claim her work as his own, and her punster wit and her big laugh that rumbles deep in her diaphragm will be metamorphosed into his dry quips and frigid ironies and will be sanctified by museum curators and art historians who commemorate his name, which reverberates with GREATNESS. And even after busy scholars dig into archives and make their formidable case that it is SHE, not HE, who is the author of *Fountain*, they believe in the Great Man. But she wouldn't live long enough to know that Time's joke is on HER. There is more to come, Reader, about this fracas over a urinal, this transubstantiation of pisspot into God the Father of Modern Art. But now the package has arrived in the mailbox, and inside the package is a note:

Dear Dearest, Darling Chum,

This is a 5½-inch Brazilian stiletto switchblade flick-knife. Picklock closing. It was made just around the time you were born. May it and the memory of the Baroness protect you.

Fat, sloppy tongue kisses,

Fanny

I discovered the folded piece of lined paper tucked into Mead the same day I found the notebook among my mother's things, and when I opened it and read the message in the guest room of the retirement center, I recovered for the briefest of instants what had been wholly lost to me, a feeling I had long ago, a feeling bound up with Fanny and the knife and air and light, not as I have recalled it on hindsight but as it once was—a wild, raw, dangerous happiness. The memory was excruciatingly immediate. I stopped breathing, and then the relived past was gone so swiftly I stood amazed for minutes afterward clutching the letter in my hand.

Do I remember lifting the knife out of its paper towel wrapping? It's possible that I do, but it's also possible that I am writing the memory into being from the stories I have told myself about the knife I would soon come to call the Baroness. The blade must have been locked and folded into its sheaf. In the memory, I let my finger run along its dull side, and I turn the thing over in my hands. Its handle is made of dark horn, and I test its weight in my open palm. Did I pop open the blade then? Did I release it? I don't know, but when I did, perhaps the next day or the day after, it was marked with tiny letters: EIG CUTLERY, ITALY.

I had forgotten that my former self was so rattled by the gift that when she wrote about it in the notebook, she did not even refer to it as a knife. She avoided the noun completely: "Fanny has sent me a present in honor of Elsa. I'm afraid of it. First, I put it behind some books on the shelf in the other room. That made me nervous, so I brought it into the bedroom and hid it behind *Don Quixote*, but that seemed wrong. It's now behind *Wuthering Heights*, which is where it should be."

Which is where it should be. Yes, she understood implicitly what she couldn't say explicitly. I can say it now. When she opened the box and took out the knife, she felt exhilarated for reasons she could not articulate, but the thing she held in her hands arrived as a rush of dizzying truth. For months she had been listening to Lucy's rants, had heard her neighbor's abject self-pity transform itself into murderous wishes. The eavesdropping had affected her, not because she had been privy to a woman's unhinged chatter but because Lucy's story had cracked open a door to a secret that belonged to her own story. "Did you ever want to kill someone?" The young woman had shaken her head, had insisted that she never had. She had not been lying, but with the knife she would begin to cast her own spell, not one to bind, but one to unbind.

In 1979 she couldn't name the shadow, to borrow the language of the witches, and that is why the knife would rise up and out from behind Emily Brontë's beast of a book, a book that was well suited to conceal an illegal weapon because in its pages brutality and beauty are bound up with wind and weather and Eros and reading. The knife wouldn't leave her alone. The thing would find its way out of its hiding place and into the bedroom and then into the second room, as if the dead thing made of horn and steel and nickel had a volition all its own. It would draw the young woman to it over and over again because it burned hot behind the green hardcover volume, and she couldn't ignore it, and before long she had mastered the simple mechanism of the knife that released its deadly blade into open air, and she had figured out how to close it with the picklock, but she didn't record any of these operations in Mead. Her attraction frightened her far too much to write it down.

But I know that she practiced removing the knife from her purse as swiftly as possible, a gesture, at first slow and awkward, that soon improved. She experimented with the knife tucked into the pockets of her jackets and jeans, and she stood in front of the mirror to examine the bulge the knife inevitably made when it was resting in those pockets. She disguised the lump by placing pens or the thin case for her sunglasses over it and, when she felt satisfied the knife had been well hidden, she shuddered with a perverse excitement. And she leaned close to her own reflected face, and she smiled at it sweetly. No one, she thought, will suspect this baby face. No one.

And while she rehearsed the simple gesture of removing the knife from purse or pocket and springing its deadly blade open again and again, she stabbed the would-be rapist, whom she had stopped naming even in her own mind. But she played out the short story again, the waiting and the taxi and the sound of his feet behind her, and she felt him against her and his fingers in her hair and his hands sliding down her arms, and she saw his thin, ugly prick, but this time she had the Baroness with her. This time she backed him against the wall, knifepoint at his Adam's apple just as if she were Errol Flynn, light-footed movie hero in a swashbuckler with his narrow sword, and she did it long before the nameless creep had a chance to take out his dwarfish member, and she watched the tall man shake with terror, and his fear filled her with happiness. And this time she slashed him right along his ugly shaving cut to scare the daylights out of him, yes, the daylights. Whatever daylights are, she wanted them out of him.

Did she know that there were others, other figures, both vaguely and more clearly defined, more or less hidden villains, more and less guilty, with whom she fought in the bare front room of 2B where she leapt and stabbed the air with her knife, cutting them down one by one? When I survey the scene from my narrator's perch, I look down at my former self beset by an imaginary crowd of evildoers, and I wonder if the knife didn't belong behind *Don Quixote* after all. "We don't do harm," said the witch. "You know that." The only harm Minnesota did as she enacted her crazed vengeance on disembodied phantoms from her past was to cut her own hand while pushing the knife back into place, a clean slice that bled profusely, soaking paper towels and turning the sink red.

I never left 2B without the Baroness. She was always on me or near me, a dense little weight at my hip or a pressure on my buttock at the back of my jeans or a lump in the breast pocket of the man's suit jacket I picked up at the Salvation Army especially for her. She was my mentor, protector, my *pòete maudit*, my femme fatale ready to leap and bite hard at a moment's notice.

When I was
young—foolish—
I loved Marcel Dushit
He behaved mulish—
(A quit.)

Before I read what I had written in my long-lost notebook, I remembered my clandestine rapport with the Baroness. I remembered that I thanked Fanny for the gift but didn't tell her that I kept it close to me, and I didn't tell Whitney either until much later. I could have recited the sequence of what happened in late May and June of 1979 because I had told the story to myself, and discrete events are suffused with powerful emotion, but there was amnesia, too, encounters and conversations that had disappeared in the wilds of memory with poor Wanda and her mother.

May 28, 1979

Dear Page, old friend,

Recent updates:

1. Ian and Isadora are paralyzed.
2. The Dear Ones are spouting one witch joke after another.
3. Fanny is dying to meet "the evil sisters" and has been croaking

out "Double, double, toil and trouble" ever since Lucy's "true identity" was revealed. She loves the idea of flying babies like kites on strings.

4. Whitney scolded me for not asking more about the crippled gardener and has made up a list of enemies she wants the ladies "to fix" for her.

5. Jacob prays to the goddess nightly for inspiration to guide him. His goddess looks a lot like Hedy Lamarr. He mentioned in lieu of *Solomon's Key* that the physics version of the clavis universalis is "The Theory of Everything." Many such theories on the horizon. He mentioned strings, but nothing conclusive yet.

6. When I gave Gus the news by phone, he volunteered that the Latin word *cultus* means "worship." He called back two days ago to inform me that there's been "a flurry" of pagan revivals in the Bay Area among a group of California feminists. He also mentioned a recently published book called *The Spiral Dance* on the new witchcraft.

7. I wish I knew how to explain to them that the word *witch*, a word that seems to answer the question—who are they?—doesn't really answer it at all. When I told Whitney the other day about Lucy pleading with the empty chair, she smiled. Maybe Lucy's desperation sounds funny from downtown, but it wasn't funny when I was looking at her uptown. Whit's smile made me feel lonely.

8. I've been thinking about the second turn of the key. It's so silly, really, but I'm unable to shake what Patty said, high-flying hokum, yes, but there's something in it that disturbs me. I can't really articulate it. "Remember this: The world loves powerful men and hates powerful women." Is it true? Why did she say it to me?

9. How did Lindy die? I think about it, Page. What does Lucy really believe happened to her daughter? What happened to her son?

May 29, 1979

This afternoon at the Hungarian Pastry Shop, Whitney read me her poem "Fart" in honor of the Baroness and in dishonor of Allen

Ginsberg. She is sick of "the Big G" swanning around town like a demigod, worshipers in tow, cameras rolling. "I saw the best butts of my generation erupt in farts, gaseous odiferous blasting." She's hardly the first person to parody "Howl." Maybe I didn't laugh loudly enough. Maybe I never cared enough about Ginsberg to begin with. I was always a heretic. The truth is I would have laughed harder a few weeks ago. Everything is going haywire, Page, and I don't know what to do. Whitney said, "What's wrong with you, Minnesota? You're not yourself."

I asked Whitney what she meant by "not myself." Maybe a self is just a bunch of little stories glued together in some haphazard way that we use to comfort ourselves. Maybe it's Hume's tattered fragments, and how could I possibly know what she was talking about? I was doing the best I could. And then I let it out: I admitted to her for the first time that I don't know how to write my novel. I told her I've come to several dead ends. I don't even know what's wrong with it. I've failed.

And she said, "It's not the book." I turned my head away and didn't answer. I felt hard. The Baroness was in my purse under Kleenex, and I could feel her fiery presence just inches away from my elbow. Whitney said it again in a softer voice, "It's not the book." I stared at the pale brown foam in my cup.

"It's me. Remember me? Your old friend Whitney Tilt? We met many years ago at the Ear Inn."

I didn't want to look at her. I sat there, a stone, and then I had a thought that scared me: "I'll never get her back. I'll never get back the person who met Whitney at the Ear Inn."

I'm going to sleep now. There's a lot I have to think about tomorrow. Do I want that person back?

Love, Not Myself.

No, Whitney was right. I, the old lady writer, can see that now. It wasn't the book. It was rage and shame, and it was the Baroness, whom I needed so desperately. The Baroness was more witch than the witches. She wrote, "City stir—wind on eardrum." The Baroness went "moon—riding." She looked up and saw an "appalling sister" in the sky. Where is the Baroness now? She lives in her poems, *Body Sweats*, published seventy-three years too late. She lives in her letters and papers and collages and photos in the University of Maryland archive. She lives in a biography by Irene Gammel. She lives as a character in Djuna Barnes's *Nightwood*.

She shudders and shakes and sings and farts in the objects that survived her, in *Enduring Ornament* and in *Limbswish*; in photographs of her art now lost: the preening peacock object called *Portrait of Marcel Duchamp*. Oh, how he disappointed her. In a letter to Jane Heap, she wrote, "Cheap, bluff, giggle frivolity, that is what Marcel now can only give. What does he care about 'art'?" She is there in the two remaining stills from a ruined film, *The Baroness Shaves Her Pubic Hair* by Man Ray and Marcel Duchamp. "Marcel, Marcel, I love you like hell, Marcel!"

The love cry rose and fell to land in "Dushit."

But there are clues, Dear Reader, multiple clues in *The Case of the Stolen Urinal*. Consider plumbing. She called William Carlos Williams W.C., poet as water closet. She admired corporeal pipes and drains. "If I can eat I can eliminate—it is logic—it is why I eat. My machinery is built that way. Yours also . . . Why should I—proud engineer—be ashamed of my machinery?" She loved the city's elaborate intestinal and urinary tracts. She reveled in scatological associations, so unladylike, so undecorous. She bowed down before running sewers. She dragged around spouts and funnels and tubes. She loved rumbles and groans and gurgles and toots. And recall her FART POEM is a prayer to GOD. For many years her artwork *God*—a cast-iron plumbing trap—was attributed to Morton Schamberg. It seems he mounted it, and then took a picture of it. Now it belongs to her, mostly to her, although they often put his name first. But she was the plumbing master. "Iron—mine soul—cast iron!"

The Baroness is a revenant, and like the Mysterious Limping Gentleman and the old woman squatting in the abandoned house down the road, she walks from one story into another. Her mystery story is tied to mine and to Lucy's and to many others, all the girls and women robbed of their wits and their work. I know that now. The Baroness is a tender fury. I needed her then. I need her still. The year she died, she wrote a letter to Peggy Guggenheim:

"We me posing as art-aggressive—virile extraordinary—invigorating—anti-stereotyped—no wonder blockheads by nature degeneration dislike it—feel peeved—it underscores unreceptiveness like jazz does. But there are a number of bright heads that have grasped fact to their utmost pleasure—advantage—admiration of me."

She knew she was a fist in the face, a knee in the groin, a laughing bomb. She was art aggressive. She knew that the world loves powerful men and hates powerful women. Is it true? Yes, it's true. The Baroness was written out of the story, and that, my friend, is murder. No blood. No broken bones, just an art crime, one that takes years and years to accomplish, a slow and terrible death—the Tears of Eros.

As you may remember, the Introspective Detective did nothing to investigate my almost rapist, but I am calling her back to the story. She's not young anymore. She's gained weight and has problems with her feet, bunions to be exact, and her left knee buckles on her every once in a while when she navigates the city on foot. The woman's been on the job for decades now, sniffing out crimes and misdemeanors, putting two and two together and solving cases one by one, but she also has cases that were never solved because there wasn't enough evidence to track down the perpetrator, cases that were ruled suicides or accidents which haunt her to this day. She's become philosophical. She knows we all suffer and we all die, but she has a taste for righting wrongs nevertheless, even when many years have passed and all the parties involved are dead. She mentions Oedipus. I am a bit tired of Oedipus, the first detective, the one who killed his father but didn't know the man was his father at the time and then set out to find the culprit and the clues led to himself. Nevertheless, she has turned into a wise old woman and, like Oedipus, she's a fictional character, but she isn't blind. She keeps her eyes open. I see her walking in a familiar landscape, one slightly blurred in memory.

I see the road and the mailbox and the field that slopes slightly upward and ends at the horizon, and I experience a strangled sense of being bad and good at the same time—an unbearably tender suspense. It's an old feeling. Don't touch it. It hurts. I can see my grass-stained knees and their scabs. I used to study them with interest and couldn't resist peeling off a loose crust that almost always released a thick slobber of blood down my leg. He walks sleepless in the house at night. I tell myself that the ailments and injuries of the day return to him at night and he lies awake and worries, all the suffering patients, and when the worrying hits, every room hums with tension. The fretful house twists and turns as I lie awake and listen. What am I listening for? I am listening for him to stand up and leave his study and return to my mother. I have seen the bottle of whiskey sitting on his desk in the morning. It helps him sleep. The witch said I was a mood reader. Black moods. His moods were our weather.

I see my father's eyes shift in another direction. He's expounding on ringworm. Yes, he had a case today, and he's explaining it at the table or maybe it's another worm or a glandular problem he is calling to our attention. He leans back in his chair. He settles in. He doesn't hear my question. Such a small thing. No broken bones. He looks through me. I am nobody. The lilacs are blooming. Considerations. Considerations are in order. My mother reminds me to keep my knees together when I sit. Such good girls. Yes, they are such good girls. Smile for the camera. Say "cheese."

You hear your father's voice behind the door of his office. You hear someone crying. It's late afternoon. Mrs. Stydniki was probably there, but you don't remember her sitting at her desk. You can see the office. You can walk up the two steps from the street, push open the door with the inscribed glass window and the letters M.D., proud letters, and look straight ahead at the three floating bookshelves in the waiting room—the worn copy of *Safety on the Farm* is among the volumes with its picture of a man's leg cut off by a threshing machine inside. After you glimpsed the leg, you never opened the book again. The crying gets louder, and you hear your father's low voice, the ineffably sweet melody you recognize, the same voice he had when he spoke to the beaten-up Mrs. Malacek. If Mrs. Stydniki is there with her large silver-framed glasses and her permanent wave, she makes no remark you can remember, but that would not be unusual. Mrs. Stydniki must be used to bawling in the next room; sickness and death are sad, after all. We all suffer and we all die, and it's best to pretend that no one is sobbing on the other side of the door.

You must feel distressed by the sound, but if you were, you don't remember. How old were you? Fifteen? At fifteen you were a fiercely antiwar young feminist eager for love of the carnal kind but a little afraid of it, too, and you were reading Eldridge Cleaver and Simone de Beauvoir and William Faulkner deep into the night, but that is not what you are remembering now. Your father emerges with Brenda Linberger of the endless cheese jokes, her eyes red and her cheeks wet and her black roots showing. She is two years ahead of you in school, and as you sit in the waiting room chair, you see your father take one of Brenda's hands in both of his and say, "Remember, I'm here for you whenever you need me," and she looks up at him as if into the face of Jesus, and your eyes move from her face to his, and you see his eyes ignite in her admiration, in her love, however fleeting that love may be, and then you feel it, an exquisite pain in the hollow between your breasts that mutes to familiar dullness after several seconds, but you do not ask yourself what it is. You don't dare. You don't know. He sees you then, his eyes cloudy. He nods, and you walk together to the car.

Perhaps he thought he didn't need to say that he was there even though he was always disappearing, always leaving, even when he was talking to us. "The pituitary gland is the size of a pea at the back of the brain. A tumor on the gland is tricky to diagnose. The symptoms vary greatly." There was no hypocrisy in him. He meant to be kind, and he was kind, but it was easier with Brenda, with all the Brendas. The distance between him and the patient suited him perfectly—it was an intimacy that is not intimate. I couldn't say, Father, I want your face to light up when you look at me. But I could have said, I want to talk to you. Can we talk? I have something to say to you. Something has been bothering me. Was I waiting for a clear day without clouds running hither and thither across the face of the sky? How I loved it when he whistled. "You know," my mother said after he died, "I told him once that I thought he shouldn't cut me off in midsentence, you know, not in front of other people, that it hurt my feelings. He didn't speak to me for two days. I put your father on a pedestal. Maybe that wasn't right."

Years and years and years had to pass before I understood that my father wanted my mother to wear Brenda's face always. If her expression betrayed criticism or hurt, he couldn't bear it. Perhaps every one of us wants adulation day in and day out. But there is a difference: He believed she owed it to him. When it didn't arrive, he punished her.

And so it is that one story becomes another story and one time is also another time, and "once upon a time" is a way of not telling time at all. But something is happening, and the Baroness, the woman-knife, has become a vehicle of enchantment in the story of not only myself but of others, a person-object that carried what I couldn't say or even allow myself to feel. It is so ordinary to rage at our beloveds, to rebel and scream and succumb to fits of anger, but a looming faceless figure made me silent and rigid and guilty. Who is that figure? "What are you afraid of, child?" That's Aunt Irma speaking. After my grandmother died when my father was twelve, long before I was born, Irma, the maiden aunt, stepped in for her sister. "What are you so afraid of, child?" Aunt Irma speaks to me in a voice full of curiosity. How old am I? Seven? Eight? She probably said it several times to me over the years. I can't answer. I don't know.

"And you wanted to kill him?" I asked Lucy boldly, and she answered, "Oh no, not for a long time, not until after I met Patty." Yes, here are more clues for the Introspective Detective. One by one, a man begins to lock things away in his study. He tells his wife that she is too stupid to read books. Ignorant Lucy. A man settles back in his chair. He stretches his arms out onto the backs of the chairs on either side of him. A man strides toward the lectern and begins to speak: "On April 9, 1917, just over a hundred years ago, Marcel Duchamp achieved what was perhaps the most brilliant and absurd art event of the twentieth century."

On April 9, 1917, a porcelain urinal turned upside down, placed on a pedestal, and signed R. Mutt was submitted to the exhibition of the American Society of Independent Artists. The committee rejected it. Duchamp resigned from the committee in protest. Alfred Stieglitz photographed it, and then it was probably tossed out with the trash. But the urinal would rise again. It would rise again on the winds of bluff and baffle.

"Your father is a great doctor, a great man. Are you aware of that?"

"This is not the work of a sixteen-year-old girl. Your father helped you, didn't he? He wrote it."

"I can only peck, you know, with two fingers, but this girl is a whiz."

"Why is it that men can stick their peckers everywhere and anywhere and it's okay?"

"In the last available text, itself frozen into place by Shelley's accidental death, the hierarchy is quite different: Rousseau is now set apart quite violently from the representatives of the Enlightenment . . ." (What kind of an idiot would use "quite" in one sentence and then the next?)

"A girl who comes with me leaves with me. I'll take you home."

The Introspective Detective leans toward me and asks, "And you wanted to kill him?"

"Oh no," I answer, "not for a long time, not until I started going around with the Baroness, and even then I didn't really know what I was thinking or feeling. I just wanted her near me."

"Violent feelings are not criminal," the Introspective Detective says as she looks at me across her desk, squinting a little. It's not a modern desk but an old scratched one made of oak, and I have placed a manual typewriter, probably an Underwood, on its surface, a superannuated machine to be sure, but I am free to decorate this psychic interior as I please.

"I know that," I say to her.

My character folds her spotted hands on her desk and continues, "I'm sorry I let you down. Back then, I mean."

I say, "It's okay. We were young and foolish."

And she says, "The preponderance of scholarly evidence has long been on the side of the Baroness, you know. One, we have the letter Duchamp wrote to his sister, Susanne, two days after the urinal was rejected. It wasn't discovered until 1982. In it he wrote, 'One of my female friends who had adopted the pseudonym Richard Mutt sent me a porcelain urinal as a sculpture.' Two, we know that a newspaper reported *at the time* that the artist Richard Mutt was from Philadelphia. The Baroness was living in Philadelphia *at the time*. Three, we know that it wasn't until after the Baroness and Stieglitz were both dead that Duchamp assumed full credit for the urinal. Four, Duchamp maintained he had bought the plumbing fixture from J. L. Mott Ironworks, but J. L. Mott Ironworks did not sell the model that was submitted to the exhibition. There are those who say he must have misremembered, but that is unlikely because his explanation for R. Mutt is that Mutt is a derivation of Mott. It's an oddly clumsy transposition, don't you think? He then claimed Mutt was intended to summon the cartoon character Mutt, of Mutt and Jeff. That also lands with a thud, doesn't it, a quick cover-up hardly in keeping with the Frenchman's usual wit. But Gammel notes that R. Mutt reads as *Armut*, the word for poverty in German, and that backward it reads as *Mutter*, mother. She was always playing with words and sounds: *A quit dushit.* Louise Norton discussed the urinal as 'Buddha of the Bathroom,' but by the time Stieglitz took the photo, it had metamorphosed into 'Madonna of the Bathroom.' Mother Mary Urinal Uterus. The Baroness's mother was deeply religious. Her father disparaged both her mother and religion. The Baroness was endlessly evoking God and souls and the body's honking machinery. Five, she loved dogs. Did Duchamp care about dogs? She used to walk the New York City streets with several. They lived with her, her mutts. Six, look at the writing of R. Mutt—then examine the letters she used for her poems. R. Mutt is in the same hand."

"I have," I said. "I was in the archives."

"Yes, of course," she said. "I remember."

"Duchamp stole it, all right. It doesn't even resemble the rest of his work. The man was nothing if not refined, elegant, decorous, a fop giggling delicately over his little jokes. Mr. Chess. *Fountain* doesn't fit in. But the museums haven't changed the attribution. It belongs to him."

"But what if the Baroness had always been known as the brain behind *Fountain*?" said the Introspective Detective, her expression wry. "Then it wouldn't have become what it is. It wouldn't be great. Except for a few marginal characters, who would care about a wild woman poet who turned herself into a work of art and signed a urinal as one of her pranks? Duchamp allowed the lost urinal to be reproduced years after it was trashed. By then, he held the key in his hand, and it was easy to push it into the lock, turn it, open the door, and rush into the future story already taking place in the next room: The Great Father of Conceptual Art. In 2004, five hundred specially selected, highly credentialed art-world professionals in the UK voted *Fountain* the most influential artwork of the twentieth century.

"In fact," the Introspective Detective continued, "he owed his 'female friend' big time." My character pounds her desk with her fist and upsets a pencil that rolls in my direction, and the small distur-

"DUCHAMP STOLE IT, ALL RIGHT."

bance makes me happy. "He knew. He said himself the Baroness 'is not a futurist. She is the future.' But he ran ahead of her into that future and locked the door behind him, and she was abandoned in a room called *Armut* in Paris with the little stove that killed her, and the room has a name!" The Introspective Detective's eloquence is rising now. She lifts her right hand off the desk and points her index finger at the ceiling. "The Never Room.

"Notice, too, that Duchamp refers to the urinal as a 'sculpture' in his letter, not a 'ready-made,' the word he was already using for his found objects. Duchamp's *Bottle Rack*, the *first* ready-made, is from 1914. The Baroness must have called her urinal "a sculpture." But she, too, was in the ready-made business. In 1913, a year before *Bottle Rack*, the Baroness, who was not yet the Baroness, was on her way to City Hall in NYC to marry the Baron and become the Baroness, and she spotted a rusted metal ring, scooped it up, and named it *Enduring Ornament*.

"But then," the Detective sighed, "a thing is never just a thing, certainly not that discarded potty. It's a thing enchanted by the aura of the great man, the great dry God of Art, Duchamp; it's urinal as pure disembodied idea, a Platonic form robbed of the flesh altogether. The art world is Quixote blinded by the masculine myth. And so, Elsa's complex bathroom joke, her virile Madonna, her smutty, jazzy, slavering, anti-stereotyped Mutt-Bitch, has been murdered by the Blockheads."

"Amen," I said.

The Detective looked at me shrewdly. "But it goes on. The controversy isn't over." She lifted a piece of paper from her desk and waved it at me. "Listen to this bright fellow: 'Certainly, Freytag-Loringhoven had created broadly similar scatological works but nothing that held the *thinking* expressed in Duchamp's piece.'" Then my Introspective Detective smiled, her cheeks wrinkling into a hundred tiny lines. "Well, we all know women can't *think*. I don't suppose *you* have anything to add to this venerable philosophical debate, my dear?"

"I did and I do," I said. "But I'm still mortified that I fainted."

"Patty saw it. I do believe she was a witch. She knew you were terrified by your own rage."

"Yes," I said, "she knew."

"It was the Incident of the Heavy Hand that did it, you know."

I close my eyes and feel the hand on my shoulder. I feel the large fingers squeeze the bones beneath my shirt and skin, and I cannot breathe. It is a gesture of authority, of correction, of superiority, of condescension, and I cannot breathe, and I want to kill him.

The Introspective Detective is smiling at me when I open my eyes. I notice that she has let her hair go gray. There is very little of it—just a couple of inches of choppy hair styled to look charmingly messy. She smiles more broadly. "You wanted that prick dead. It's good to know, good to say it."

"They silenced the Baroness and then they killed her. "

"Maybe you and the others are writing her back into the story," she said brightly.

"Have you forgotten that this is November 2017 in the United States of America? This is the age of hatred. This is the age of a powerful man yowling obscenities about Muslims and blacks and immigrants and women to vast crowds of adoring white people."

She looked grave. "I think we can be thankful you didn't use the Baroness to slice You-Know-Who into little pieces." Humor returned to her eyes. "I would've had to investigate the murder."

"You're ahead of the story."

"In memory," she said, "there's no ahead and no behind really, is there? Memory wells up in the now, in vertical time. And remembered time, as you know, is shot through with imagination. Who am I, after all?" She opens a drawer in the desk and pulls out a fat volume. "You forgot this," she said. "It was never returned to the New York Public Library." She slides it across the desk. I recognize the book: *The Female Quixote; or The Adventures of Arabella* by Charlotte Lennox.

"I was attracted to the title," I said. "And the century—the eighteenth."

"You left it on the subway."

I take the book and slip it in my bag. "Thank you so much. You are indeed a great detective."

My character grins. "Let's take a walk. I'll accompany you to the corner."

We take the elevator to the ground floor and when we step outside it is June 1, 1979, and Morningside Heights is shabby, shabby, shabby. She walks down to 109th Street with me, and I ask her, "You're not the narrator, are you?"

"Of this story, you mean?"

I nod.

"Good God, no. What gave you that idea? I thought it was you."

"Well," I said. "Sometimes I think I am and then at other times I have my doubts."

We shake hands, and I watch her cross Broadway. She has a waddling gait now, and when she reaches the middle of the street, she loses her footing for a moment. It's her knee. She recovers, but she limps the rest of the way. I wonder if she is on another case. When I turn to look at my filthy building, good old 309, I see the pale young man at his post. It is still light out, but not for long. And, yes, I feel the Baroness in my back pocket. Do I remember if there was a wind that day? There were winds that blew from the Hudson River and swept across the highway and onto Riverside Drive and traveled down my street and ruffled my hair and the hair of other pedestrians who were out and about back in the old days when I was young and they called me Minnesota. I mention the wind because "with the heart goes a weather." It stormed for a while, and then it cleared up.

CHAPTER FIFTEEN

The young woman is writing. She is writing in her room the day after she has had an encounter with the pale young man. She has been trying to read the signs, but she knows she has gotten them mixed up, and she wants desperately to know what this story is all about.

June 2, 1979

I hardly know how to write this to you. It's so confusing, almost hallucinatory when I think about it, but I am going to write it as it happened. I hadn't seen the pale young man since the day Lucy was yelling at him, but he was outside the building yesterday when I returned from Elena's rather late, around seven thirty. It was still light and warm. Not a good day at work, Page. My Lady was disappointed in the chapter. I had neglected her wardrobe. I tried to explain to Elena that describing her outfits in detail slows down the narrative—to which she said, "But I must have more Dior!" I need the job so badly I am all patience, but more Dior will wreck the book. And I care about the book. Maybe she will forget about the clothes. She often forgets. I am looking forward to her leaving for the summer. I need the job, but I need the distance, too.

And so when the pale young man nodded at me politely and then humbly asked for my help in front of the building, I was not in the mood to talk to anyone. (All I wanted to do was go inside and boil up some noodles and read *The Female Quixote* on my bed *all alone* and lose myself in Arabella's misreading of Everything.) The young man was carrying a military-style duffel bag over his left shoulder, a bag heavy enough to crunch his posture into that of a very old person with lumbago. When I told him I was hungry and exhausted and didn't have time, he insisted that he speak to me. He insisted it was a matter of life and death. He used those words, "life and death." He said, "Please." His eyes looked hurt, and his whole being was disheveled, and I felt the pull, the tug, the arc that moves from the inside out, that sympathy or curiosity or vicarious pain or whatever it is that answers the call of life and death, even though it probably isn't a call of life and death *at all*. He said he was "desperate" to come into the building "just to talk." I said no, and he said "Please" again, dragging out the long "e" sound as if he were a child of six begging for a candy.

Yes, I was attracted to the story, to the mystery of the words spoken on the sidewalk, "It's over." Maybe he was a witch, too, or a warlock or an alchemist or a ghost. He looks like a ghost. I took him to Tom's. It's a public place, and it's cheap. After we had sat down in a booth, I glanced across the table at him and at his duffel bag, which was sitting upright beside him as if it were a speechless third party. The pale young man struck me as even more sickly than before. I examined the blue-black circles under his eyes and his gaunt, colorless, cleanly shaven cheeks. A bony, spectral boy in a shirt that looked expensive, but I noted it had a rusty stain on the sleeve. In fact, when I looked closely, I saw a constellation of tiny stains near the cuff. I offered to buy him a sandwich, and he seemed so happy that it lifted my spirits. We both ordered BLTs. He ate his fast, and I looked away several times so as not to witness his greed. I examined my own sandwich and glanced at the duffel bag, which was filthy, and somewhere near what would have been the neck if it had been a person and not a bag, I noticed a dark stain. I didn't talk while he ate because I pitied him, and I knew a little about hunger, in the short term anyway, so the pity I felt was partly for myself, but after he had licked up every bit of mayonnaise, scrap of lettuce, and tomato seed on the plate with his last crust, I asked him what was so urgent.

"I have to see Lucy Brite."

I said, "Why?"

And he said, "Every son deserves to see his mother."

I felt a spasm in my lungs. I remembered Lucy's fury on the sidewalk, remembered her talking about her son's eyes as a baby. I remembered her own glittering eyes as she told the story about the dead hamster at the table and the cold showers and the boy named Randolph, although the memories didn't come in that order, and not one of them existed separately from the others. They were a felt tumult, an emotional jumble of knowing and not knowing, of dread. And as I sat there I was hearing Lucy through the wall again with the stethoscope—it seemed as if my listening had happened long ago. I was more afraid of my eavesdropping than I had ever been before, and I stared down at my sandwich scraps, and at the same time I might have held my breath for some seconds. "She's afraid of her own son." She had said that. I had written it down. I believed him. I believed him because Lucy hadn't wanted to talk about him, because she had been so strange about the dead boy now come to life before me. "All you have to do is nod." What had he done? Lindy. Lindy. Lindy, a name that sings. An awe fell over me then, and I thought about the drawing in the glassine envelope and the winding string. Page, I thought about the fact that this sick-looking person had once been inside Lucy's body, an embryo. I said none of this, of course. I asked to see some identification. I asked him for an ID.

The driver's license lay on the table: Theodore Brite.

I kept my face as still and blank as possible. I spoke calmly and slowly. "She told me her son was dead. She used the word *exploded.* Why would she say that?"

His bottom lip trembled. I looked away from him into the restaurant and concentrated for a moment on the clinking music of cutlery and the voices in the diner and the dusk through the windows. It would be dark soon. I'm safe here. I said it to myself. No one will hurt me in Tom's. He began to tell me about Lucy's illness, that she had been "removed" to a hospital.

Without looking directly at him, I told him I knew about the hospital. I also knew about the divorce and the new wife and the new children, and I knew about Lindy's fall.

He leaned forward. "What did she say? What did she say about Lindy?"

I turned my face to his, trying to interpret his expression. "She said she died ten years ago."

I don't know whether his emotion had colored mine or whether the story of Lindy's death had been inside me for so long that I felt Lucy's grief as if some of it were mine, but a tremor crossed my mouth, and I know that he saw it because his hazel eyes grew focused, and then he seemed to relax. I wondered why. I told myself to remain steady. The Baroness was in my back pocket. I touched her several times as I listened to him.

It was really and truly sad, he was saying, but his "mom" had "mental health problems." She was "delusional and paranoid." She imagined all kinds of things. It was incredible the stuff she came up with. The neighbors were after her. License plates on Park Avenue had secret messages in them. She had been really, really sick and for a while they were afraid she would have to live in an institution forever. "Dad thought we'd have to lock her up and throw away the key." He said it exactly that way. I remembered Jacob expounding on the Lucy-is-psychotic theory. I looked in young Ted's eyes. Could I see anything in them? Lucy had said, "It's over!" What did it mean not to want your own son?

He talked about Lindy then, about how much he had loved his sister and how pretty and sweet and kind and gentle and adorable she had been. "She was a dreamy little kid, like me, a really creative little kid. She loved to play dress up and draw and write plays. I used to let her put me in all kinds of crazy costumes. I even let her put makeup on me. I taught her checkers. I taught her how to whistle."

I didn't want to hear it. Why was he telling me this? The whole family whistled, apparently—whistlers and more whistlers. Why was he talking about Lindy as she had been as a little child? Where was the depressed fifteen-year-old? There was something wrong with his story. I stopped the eulogy. I told him I had passed him and Lucy on the street several weeks ago. I had seen their fight. I asked him how he even knew Lucy and I were "friends." It wasn't the correct word, but I used it.

"We've talked on the phone," he said. He looked directly into my eyes as if to demonstrate his sincerity.

"There's a phone booth," I said, pointing toward the window. "There's a booth right outside on the street. Call her now and tell her you're coming over."

"She won't let me in."

"Why?" I said.

"She's sick, I told you, but I need to see her. I need to make it better between us. She's my mom." The word *mom* sounded like a wail.

"That's for Lucy to decide. Why should I mix myself up into it?"

He smiled a sad smile and shook his head. "Because I think you care," he said, his eyes wide. "You have a nice face. I can tell. You're a good person. We could go in together. I just want to see my mom." He dragged out the "o" in "mom" again and blinked away a tear.

And then I thought, I'm not a good person. Why do you think you know that I'm a good person? She's such a nice girl. She has such a nice face. At the same time, my doubts about Lucy were rising. What was true and what wasn't true? She was erratic. She had a couple voices at least. I recalled her pushing my arms away when

I was holding her in the apartment. I couldn't ask him about Lindy's "fall." What if Lucy had invented or imagined parts of the story? I worked up my courage. Why it took courage I can't say, but it did. "Did your father lock away your things in his study?"

He looked at the duffel bag and then at me. He pressed his lips together tightly. He said, "It was a kind of game he played."

I said nothing.

He continued, "He wanted to teach us a lesson about taking care of our property, you know, a lesson in responsibility. It was for our own good."

I wondered if he believed this.

And I said, "When you say 'our,' you mean you and Lindy?"

"Us and Mom. He locked up a lot of her stuff, too."

I was silent. He was silent. I thought about the words "It was for our own good." Lucy wasn't a child. She was his wife, an adult. And it made me sad. I looked at him beside his overstuffed duffel bag with the big stain and my sadness grew. Page, the world seemed terrible to me at that moment, so terrible that all of Tom's and Broadway and the whole Upper West Side sank into sadness, but such thoughts are unspeakable. I said, "You look ill. Are you seeing a doctor?"

The moment I finished pronouncing the word *doctor*, the tears began to spill over his lower lids and leak down his face to his chin. He sniffed and covered his face with his long white hands. "I'm broke. I don't have anywhere to go. My girlfriend kicked me out of the apartment a couple of hours ago. I've just been wandering around with nowhere to go."

I ripped some napkins from the dispenser and handed them to him.

He blubbered into the paper, and I felt the eyes of the two men at the next table upon us.

"Why don't you go to your father?"

"He's too busy with Wendy and Peter." He spoke the names in a self-pitying tone that shrank my sadness. His whining repelled me.

"His other children?"

He nodded pathetically.

I studied his face. His expression struck me as oddly lax. It was as if his features had never been sharpened by experience. He looked like an infant.

I spoke to him gently. "But why won't your mother see you?"

"I told you," he moaned. "She's paranoid."

I remembered Lucy's happy face as she held the purple dress in the air. I remembered her eyes fixed on her bagel. I remembered the little man doll. I remembered her rushing at the chair. Did I even like Lucy? I wasn't sure, but I didn't know anything about this pale young man with his driver's license that said Theodore Brite. Why would I trust him?

After explaining that I couldn't let him into the building, I promised to tell Lucy I had seen him.

Of course, Page, it was cock-eyed—the whole business. It wasn't hard to get into the building. People came and went all the time. If he had really wanted to see her, he could have slipped in without much effort, but I didn't think of it then. I don't know why.

I paid the bill, and before I closed my wallet, I handed him a twenty-dollar bill. It's a lot of money. I didn't think about it. I just did it. I can see now that I must have felt enhanced by the gesture. I liked being the one to give away money. He took it without a word and stuffed it in his back pocket, but later he thanked me more than once. Outside, night had fallen. Broadway was illuminated by neon and electric lights and lots of pedestrians were moving along the sidewalks. The people made me feel safe. We didn't say anything to each other until he said he would walk me back to the building. He promised he wouldn't ask to come inside. I hesitated. I touched the Baroness a couple times. I noticed that he carried the bag more easily, that the lumbago had vanished, and he had a spring in his step—the sandwich, maybe—and then, as we arrived at the building on my side street and we stood under the lamp above the door, he told me had forgotten something. It was important. He wanted me to take it to his mother. I began to breathe more quickly. I had my key in my left hand. My right hand was free.

He knelt, unzipped his silent partner, and began to rummage inside. I looked down at the visible contents of the bag, and, as I watched him, I realized I didn't want to take anything to Lucy. I didn't want to be a go-between. I wanted to run inside, wanted to escape his abjection, his pathetic need for his "mom." I wanted to say no, but I just stood there, staring idly at his balled-up shirts, a pack of condoms, a paperback, the title of which I couldn't see, and then he tugged open the bag a few inches further, and I saw the stains. I knew it was blood, blackening, viscous, still-drying blood. I knew blood from my father's office. I have seen a lot of old blood. I looked down at a garment that oozed congealing blood. Seeing the blood went fast, faster than I can write this, faster than anyone can read this. He was removing something from the bag, a blue stick, and there was blood on the stick. What had I been thinking? I didn't know who he was. "She's afraid of her own son." I panicked.

Oh God, Page, I seized the Baroness from my back pocket, popped the spring, and aimed her straight at his head. I growled, "Stand up." His eyes looked huge and young and terrified, and his fear gave me pleasure. I didn't wait. I acted. I watched him rise tentatively to his feet, one of his hands raised, its palm toward me. I saw spittle coming from the sides of his mouth. He made a gagging noise. I didn't budge. Then I noticed the stick in his other hand, a blue plastic stick with a star at its end. I felt extremely clearheaded. I felt cold and beastly. I felt magnificent. I held the knife a couple inches from his belly.

My voice was commanding. I said, "There's blood, blood everywhere. What the hell have you done?"

"No, no, no," he whined. "No, please, put it away." He was gasping. "Listen, listen to me. I had a fight with my girlfriend."

I stopped breathing. I thought murder. I thought body parts in the bag. I thought to myself, This is real. This is happening now. He's carrying around the girl's dismembered body. I moved the knife closer to his shirt. "Tell me now," I said, "or I'll push it in."

"We haven't been getting along."

I grunted at him, "Why is your fucking bag bleeding?" I don't talk like that. Was it the Baroness speaking? No, it was a man in the movies. That's what men in the movies say.

He was gasping for breath. "I was shaving. Ally was so angry, she yanked at the razor, so I would listen to her, and it cut me bad and I bled all over the bathroom. I was crying, but she didn't care, and she kicked me out, and I grabbed a towel before I left. I had to clean myself in a diner and change my shirt. The lady was nice about it. She gave me some Band-Aids but they bled through. It's the truth. I swear. I swear. There was so much blood I thought I would pass out. I had to press the cut for about an hour to get it to stop."

"Where's the cut?"

The pale young man lifted his chin. I looked at the fresh gash underneath it, two inches long and deep. It looked as if it could easily start bleeding again.

"I should have thrown it away," he said, "but I stuffed it in the bag. I had to see someone. I didn't know what to do with it . . ."

"Get out the towel," I said, moving the Baroness back and forth near his gut. "Take it out of the bag."

He knelt down again and extracted the soaked towel from the bag.

"Now open it up and let me see what's in there."

There was nothing in the bag, Page, but the mess from the towel and his miserable belongings.

"You need stitches," I said. "It will heal badly without them. It will open and bleed again." I slowly and carefully closed the Baroness.

He began to shudder, then he gagged, and I thought he might throw up, but he didn't. He gulped the air, squeezed his eyes shut, and rocked himself back and forth as if he were regaining control of his body. Then the motion stopped. He opened his eyes. He stared at the thing in his hand. "I still want you to take it to her. Okay?"

"What the hell is it?"

"It's Lindy's wand. It was lost for years."

I didn't answer him.

"It was at Dad's. I found it."

I took the wand. I remember he crouched over his duffel bag to zip it closed, and he pushed the bloody tumor of a towel back inside it, and I turned away from him, put my key into the lock, turned it, and pushed the heavy door open. If he had wanted to, he could have rushed in with me, but he didn't. It wasn't until I had made it inside 2B that I saw that the star attached to the wand wobbled precariously and had been reattached with a thick application of duct tape.

Minnesota would not see the pale young man again. She could never bring herself to call him Ted for some reason, not after she had threatened him with the Baroness. She might have killed him, and for many years she thought about that particular horror story, which might have happened but didn't. She saw him lying on the sidewalk bleeding, and she saw herself, an unhinged murderess wailing at the night sky, bloody knife still in her hand, and she heard the sirens blast in her ears, and she dimly made out the crowd of policemen in their blue uniforms before she fainted, and she imagined the trial and the prison where she lived with hundreds of other women and spent years and years studying their hard, unforgiving faces. When she was optimistic, she wrote many books during her life sentence, but when she was pessimistic, she dwindled away in her cell to next to nothing, a wan and wasted being, drained of the future altogether.

She did not see the pale young man walk down 109th Street and turn left at Broadway and walk one block north to descend into the subway at 110th Street and ride off into the sadness of the Upper West Side and beyond. She didn't know then that the pale young man was a heroin addict, that he lied to and stole from and cheated all the people who loved him or had loved him, including the enraged Ally, who had troubles of her own, but whose story in this book ends when she shuts the door on her boyfriend's bloody face.

Minnesota didn't know until months later that on the same night that she was brandishing the Baroness at Lucy's son, the witches were casting a spell from the apartment filled with books on Riverside Drive to bind the pale young man, Theodore Brite Jr., an exploded lost young man without a future or without much of one. It was Patty who told Minnesota the story, and it was Patty who would tell her years later that he died of a heroin overdose on a sofa in a friend's apartment in Orlando, Florida, in April 1987, a town I cannot think of anymore without speeding ahead to June 2016 and the massacre in a nightclub called Pulse. I live in the United States of Weaponry, land of the lone gunman, armed, as they say, "to the teeth."

Another spell the witches cast that spring night was intended to heal Lucy, who wrestled with ghosts and demons, or maybe astral bodies—as you prefer. Lucy, officially a member of the coven, was sitting on the floor in a circle with Patty and Moth and Gorse and Alistair, and they were chanting and burning candles in a thick cloud of herbal scents as they rocked back and forth to the rhythms of the greater universe. Minnesota never found out whether they were naked or not on that particular evening, but sometimes they were and, as the weather was warmer, they may have been, and she couldn't help but find this a little ridiculous. She couldn't help but imagine their old bodies and cringe, but then she was young and foolish, and perhaps her feelings were only natural for someone her age.

On June 2, before the female Quixote, also known as Minnesota, sat down to write the extended passage in her notebook, she washed the wand carefully and dried it carefully and walked over to Lucy's around eleven thirty in the morning. She felt that the plastic stick with its black duct tape and unstable star had the quality of a relic. It was an object irradiated by grief and madness, a dead child's toy that could unleash an emotional tempest if she didn't act with great subtlety and tenderness before she handed it over.

I was nervous, Page, really nervous, and I knew I had to tell Lucy everything, and I knew I couldn't just wave the wand at her without warning, so I decided to leave it outside in the hallway and then retrieve it if she wanted it. When she opened her door, Lucy looked different. Her hair was wet, therefore darker, but I also realized she had no makeup on, which gave her features a wan, younger appearance. The bathrobe she was wearing had a monogram on the breast pocket, LBC. I wondered what the C stood for. Her eyes were shiny just as they had been on the morning we ate bagels. After I had stepped inside, Lucy chirped, "The door, the door." I closed it, left the wand alone, and hoped no one would grab it. She seated herself on the ghost-of-Lindy chair. I sat on the sofa, my onetime bed, and I asked how she was, and she said, "Fine," and I said that something had happened, but I didn't exactly know how to tell her about it.

She stared at me. Then she said, "Fire away, honey."

"I met someone yesterday who said he was your son. He had a driver's license. Theodore Brite. You said that he was dead."

"He was dead, dead to me."

"That's not really the same thing, Lucy."

Lucy looked away into the room. "You can't know," she said. "You're too young. You don't have children. It's probably wrong to say he's dead. I know that now. Last time I let him in here, we talked, and I thought he was better. He stole a hundred dollars from my purse. It's not the stealing, though." Lucy clenched her jaw. "I took him to see Patty. I thought she might be able to look into him and find out what's true and what isn't. I've begged him to tell me, but Patty says I'll never know. She says that Lindy won't come back and tell me, and I have to stop thinking she will. She says the magic can't do that."

"What, Lucy? What can't the magic do?"

Lucy walked over to the little table with the pentagram, picked it up, and pulled out the little man I already knew was hidden there. Then she lifted him into the air for me to see. I drew a breath. The thing wasn't the same—different hair, different clothes—another little man tightly bound with string. She put the doll in my lap. It was wearing blue jeans and a sweatshirt.

"Lucy, I saw a doll the morning I was here. It was behind the picture and I looked at it."

"That was the father. This is the son."

"Poppets?"

"One poppet. Gorse made new clothes for him. Senior and Junior cut from same cloth!" She laughed. "It's just a symbol, you see, a thing we use. I thought we could force it out of him, do a kind of long-distance hypnosis by breathing into the doll. I really did, but Patty says that's too much to ask. She said the magic can't do that. It can't get it out of him."

"Get what out of him?"

Lucy took a deep breath. She pressed her fingertips against her mouth and then released them. "Patty says I'll never know if he pushed Lindy out the window or not. He was in me, but that doesn't mean I can control him. We can't read people perfectly, not even our own children. Patty thinks it's wrong to think we can. And then she asked me what I would do if I knew he had really done it. What would I do?"

I had a curious sense of relief. I said, "Lucy, do you think he pushed her? Do you believe that?"

"I don't know!" There was a cry in her voice. "I think he could do anything. That's the problem. He's like his father. He hides behind all his smiley and sad and sorry faces. He never felt guilty about anything. He doesn't really care about anyone, so I can't tell what's in there. I don't know. That's the torture. But I'll bet Daddy-O is kicking around that slut from Virginia right now. She got herself a real bargain. And I wanted that bargain! I wanted it. Can you believe it? It's disgusting."

I examined my knees.

Lucy kept talking. "And me? And me? I just keep wrapping up Lester and throwing him into the trash under the sink." I looked up. Lucy blinked and slowly shook her head. The rest of her face remained rigid. "Patty says that it was awful to kill his hamster and that it shows he hasn't been in his right mind since he was little, but it doesn't mean he pushed Lindy." And then, as I looked at her, I saw it, or rather I saw him in her—the resemblance between Lucy and her son. It vanished in an instant, and I couldn't retrieve it. I wondered why I hadn't seen the similarity in their faces on the street or at Tom's or when we were standing outside the door with the bleeding bag, but I hadn't. Lucy closed her eyes and grimaced. "I thought I would die if I didn't know," she said. "I thought I would die. She was here, you know, Lindy was here, right in this chair. And she forgave me."

"What was there to forgive, Lucy?"

"I stayed in that place. I stayed with him in that place, and I didn't save her. I should have taken the kids and left, gone somewhere. But it was like I couldn't move. I was stuck. That's the shadow, my shadow. There are days I forget all about it. I feel okay. I made brownies with Moth yesterday and I felt so happy. We ate them all up. They were yummy. And then, I remembered." Lucy made the birdlike movement with her head. "Moth told me to lie down, and she chanted over me, and she stroked my arms ever so gently."

"That sounds pleasant." It was all I could think to say.

"It was," she said. "But, you know, there's a big hole in the world where Lindy was, and it will never get smaller. The best I can do is walk farther and farther away from the hole. It's still there, you see, but I'm not as close to it, so I'm less likely to fall in."

I had a strong feeling that this metaphor belonged to Patty, but I said nothing.

"Distance," Lucy said. "It makes you stronger. But then there's Teddy, my own kid who's alive, not dead. Remember after the party when you came in with me, remember there was someone in the street, right outside?"

I nodded.

"Remember he yelled 'son of a bitch'?"

And then Lucy growled at me in her other voice. "That was him."

And I thought, the insult is about origins, about coming from an inferior mother, an abject cur. "Oh, Lucy," I said. "I'm sorry."

Lucy avoided my eyes. "Don't be sorry for me," she said sharply, "I'm leaving this dump at the end of the month. I gave notice a while ago. I'm moving in with Patty and Moth. They've got a whole big room for me. Patty inherited that apartment, you know. It's just the maintenance we have to pay, and it's nice over there. I can't see him again. I'm afraid of him. I don't want him to know where I am. Don't ever tell him. I'll bet he played you, too, sweetie. He plays everybody."

I remembered the deadly edge of the Baroness in the lamplight.

And so, Page, by the time I told Lucy about my encounter with her son, it had diminished, had become a coda to the bigger story. I explained about going to Tom's and the twenty-dollar bill and the duffel bag and the walk back to the building. I told her that I was carrying a knife because I'd been afraid of an attack ever since the night she and Patty and Moth saved me. It was true, and yet while I talked I felt as if I were lying. Telling the story of the Baroness in the simplest way possible—young woman sees blood in bag, is afraid, pulls knife, which is on her person to protect her person from new assault after old assault, discovers blood is from shaving-girlfriend injury, puts knife away—all those were facts, but the facts were oddly remote from the actual story.

After I had finished, Lucy looked at me and smiled broadly. Her face lit up with malicious mirth, and she began to shake with laughter. At first, I didn't know what to do. She scared me, to be honest, but she looked so jubilant, I felt vindicated. "Oh my God," she said, "you must have scared the bejesus out of him!" I smiled, and then I laughed. I found the whole story with the bag and the Baroness suddenly comic. I hadn't jabbed him, after all. No one was hurt. Lucy slapped my arm and then rubbed it vigorously. "You're just full of surprises, aren't you?" She laughed so hard tears spurted from her eyes. When we had recovered from laughing, I told her about the wand.

I looked closely at Lucy. "Do you want it? It's just outside the door. I'll bring it in if you want it. He said you had been looking for it."

She folded her hands in her lap; all merriment had left her face. Her eyes narrowed. "You say it's in the hallway?"

"Yes."

"Then get it."

It looked forlorn as it leaned against the wall, its star-head hanging on its chest. I took it by its handle gently and walked into 2C.

When I held it out to Lucy, she took hold of it, looked at it critically, and in a loud voice, said, "That's not it!"

I sat back down on the sofa. "He said it was, Lucy."

"No," she said fiercely. "It's old and broken and ugly. Lindy didn't love this, this stupid thing." She threw it on the floor. I was tempted to pick it up, but I didn't.

She looked at me, her face hard.

I turned my head away from Lucy. There was something mean in her, but I pitied her, too, no, more than that. I had charity for her. What would I be like if I had her story? Who would I be? How would I live?

On the little table beside Lucy I saw a book. The words on its spine read: *Witchcraft Today*, Gerald Gardner.

I pointed at the book. "The gardener," I said. "Maybe that's what I heard you talking about."

"I read it every day," Lucy said solemnly. "It's a very important text for us."

"The crippled gardener," I said.

"Crippled?" Lucy said. "He's not crippled."

I wondered how he got crippled through the wall.

"You can go now," she said. "And take that thing with you."

It's funny, Page, I'm used to Lucy, and her harshness didn't bother me. I picked up the broken wand and walked to the door.

Just after I had opened it, Lucy said, "They want you in the coven." Then she corrected herself, "We want you in the coven."

I turned around and smiled at her. "It's not for me, Lucy, but thank you. I'd like to see you again though, I mean after you move out."

She spoke loudly. "You think you can be a witch all by yourself?"

The question surprised me, but an answer came quickly to mind: "I'm already a witch, Lucy. I've been a witch for a long time."

Those are the last words on Lucy Brite in Mead, the end of the writings that turned into a little novel dense with dialogue I couldn't possibly have remembered word for word, a never-published novel called *The Mystery of Lucy Brite* or *The Woman Through the Wall.*

In July, a graduate student moved into 2C, a short, plump young man with a beard, who smelled of high seriousness, carried around books by Willard van Orman Quine, and made no noise whatsoever.

I would see Lucy, Patty, Moth, Gorse, Alastair, and Alice the dog again, but not until after the notebook ends. The Three Ladies of the Broom lived together until March 1981, when Lucy suffered what was then called a "nervous breakdown." She didn't return to the apartment on Riverside Drive but became a resident of a psychiatric halfway house, where she made some trouble but not so much trouble that they didn't allow her to stay. The members of the coven visited her. I didn't. Several times I said I would join them, but I always called to cancel. I felt guilty about it, but Patty said to me wisely that she didn't think Lucy cared all that much one way or the other. We like to think we're important to other people, but we aren't always that important.

I didn't see the witches often, but I stayed in touch with them during my years at Columbia. Every three months or so I would find an invitation to tea in my mailbox marked with a subject. "The Crisis of Western Epistemology," "Healing Womanhood," and "The Animal Self" are three I remember. I accepted from time to time and would find myself among the books and herbs, with other guests of different ages, mostly women but not exclusively, who had come to listen to Patty's disquisitions, which were at once erudite and peculiar. We drank unusual teas and bit into little white sandwiches with thin fillings that Gorse and Alistair had made. I often left the apartment with a book Patty had loaned me. She also sent me a gift in the mail: *The Book of the City of Ladies* by Christine de Pizan, a defense of women against misogyny published in 1405. When the book opens, Christine is in her library reading. She has become increasingly miserable by the attacks on women she discovers in the volumes that line her shelves written by supposedly learned men. She falls into despair, and then with help from three beautiful ladies, Reason, Rectitude, and Justice, Christine builds a fortress city to house virtuous women of the past, present, and future. It is a real city that is also an imaginary city. I still have the edition she gave me on my shelf. Patty inscribed it with the following words: "The magic happens between and among us."

At the time, I thought of Patty as a person whose brain had simmered so long over unanswerable questions that it had boiled over into witchcraft. Whitney and Fanny accompanied me to tea only once. The subject was "The Problem of Leakage." Patty lectured us on menstruation, birth taboos, the fear and hatred of the female body and its fluids, and generative powers, which she insisted have shaped the Western tradition, and she pounded away (metaphorically) on her favorite organ, the placenta, and held up illustrations in medical texts to demonstrate how it had gone missing, and she told us the whole philosophical tradition turned on a denial of origin, a fantasy of fetal independence from the mother, a homunculus lie propagated through the ages, and before we left, she offered us herbs in little packages—valerian and Saint-John's-wort and myrtle and bay leaf and dragon blood and elderflower and hazel mandrake. (I saved the neatly labeled bags.) After we had left the apartment and had stepped out onto Riverside Drive, I remember we stood looking at one another in amazed silence, three friends holding our herbal gifts. Whitney looked at me and then she looked at Fanny, and I looked at Whitney and at Fanny, and Fanny looked at me and at Whitney and then, as I looked at Whitney again, I saw the corner of my friend's mouth move upward, and she smiled and her eyes lit up with mischief. She began to dance and hoot on the sidewalk, and Fanny buckled over in laughter. I laughed, too, but not as hard as the two others. In that mental image, there are dried leaves on the ground, but I can't tell you exactly what year it was.

I had and still have little use for props and herbs and spells, but Patty had access to secrets I didn't know about then, secrets I have reconfigured and rethought, but she is right: we forget. Patty looked in places most of us don't. She looked between the lines.

CHAPTER SIXTEEN

The sad and sorry wand Lucy had rejected, and which Minnesota firmly believed had belonged to Lindy (and no one could or can prove otherwise), stood in a corner of the front room in 2B for three days. The idea of tossing it out with the trash seemed cruel, and so the young writer decided to rehabilitate it.

She covered the blue end with strips of gold paper. Working with white glue, she fastened one piece after another over the plastic tube. Little by little her technique got better. She learned to use exactly the right amount of glue. She learned how to flatten the paper quickly and evenly. She peeled off the duct tape, a laborious enterprise because the tape was so old it had welded itself to the handle, but she used turpentine and then sandpaper to clean the remnants, and she carved a new wooden neck for the wand that slipped neatly over the tube and grasped the star with two thin wire clamps to make it stand upright. She bought thin silver paper at a craft store and glued it over the star's pointed surfaces. After days of working every afternoon on the project, she looked at it closely but wasn't entirely satisfied. With a tiny brush, she began to paint signs on the handle with her acrylic paints. She discovered that shades of purple and green were felicitous. She then added touches of yellow and red. She painted circles and pentagrams and swirling foliage that connected one sign to the other.

The handle, she told herself, is a world in miniature, and then after examining an untouched swath of the wand, she decided it needed an inscription. She stole bits and pieces of poems and made a whole poem from them, and she gave the Baroness the last word. It took her many hours to inscribe the text, which turned around and around the handle. She worked with a magnifying glass, and she smiled to herself as she painstakingly, slowly, obsessively formed each letter. She called it the witch hymn.

Where wert thou, Mighty Mother, when he lay in darkness,
Drowned, perjured, murderous, full of blame?
Thou, our general mother of dews and rains,
Lately made of flesh and blood?

She weeps out her division when she sings.
If it was only the dark voice of the sea,
Logic and lust together,
All is in an enormous dark. Drowned.

The king is dead. Brown eyes and toothed gold,
Out of the cradle endlessly rocking,
A firstborn, set at the mercy of the wind.
I grow old, I grow old.

I am sick. I must die.
Look in my face; my name is Might-have-been.
I am also called No-more, Too-late, Farewell.
Cut, cut in white, cut in white so lately.

The dread voice:
You forget, madame—
that we are the masters—
Go by our rules.

And when the poem had been written onto the wand and she had recorded its stanzas in Mead, she shellacked the wand's surface and let it dry and shellacked it again and dried it again. She shellacked for seven days and she dried for seven nights, and while she labored over the wand, she thought often about Kari, about lying on the floor beside her sister drawing, and she could almost hear their mother's steps somewhere near them in the house and she could almost smell the house itself.

And the day after she had finished restoring the wand and had hung it by two nails from the bookshelf in the front room near the kitchenette and decided that it was beautiful and mysterious and that she loved it, her teenagers woke up. She wrote them back to life. Minnesota had wondered repeatedly why she hadn't murdered Frieda Frail to begin with and thereby given herself a nice, clean murder plot for Ian and Isadora to solve. But, no, she was too ambitious for that. She had read too many books for that. She was after something she didn't really understand. She was after a story that sang inside her. She wanted to break the rules, and she knew for certain she didn't want her old self back. It was way too late for that.

On the night in question, it was snowing, and there had been talk on the radio of the coming storm all day. The blizzard began to blow around seven in the evening. Professor Simon (Mrs.) and the four Doras did not know that Professor Simon (Mr.) had disappeared until Just Plain Dora, who was sneezing and coughing and running at the nose and aching in her bones from acute rhinopharyngitis, also known as the common cold, wandered out of her sickroom draped in a red blanket carrying a wand in her hand that she had fashioned from cardboard and vast globs of glue earlier that day in her bed to look for the patriarch at around eight o'clock and discovered that his room was empty. Because the Chaucer specialist was known to flee from himself, or rather to flee the part of himself that knew himself to be himself, the five remaining members of the Simon family mobilized for action. Each Dora was assigned a part of the house to search. They searched but no father was found.

Isadora had not spoken to Ian about the nefarious adventure with Kurt Linder in the park. She had not informed him either that her role as Watson, like her paisley shirt from last year, didn't fit her anymore. She should have told him, but instead she avoided him, which made her guilty, and the guiltier she was, the more she remained aloof. She made excuses when he called and returned to Charles Darwin, her only love interest at the moment, and that is why an interval of several months had passed since the friends had talked seriously, months that had pinched and pained the heart of the pseudo-Sherlock almost beyond endurance. But after her father went missing, Isadora picked up the phone and dialed her old friend's number. When Mrs. Feathers answered the call and started in on her false and simpering platitudes, Isadora shouted, "It's an emergency!" words that quickly brought Ian to the line. Isadora told him that he must come immediately because her father was gone, and they needed all hands on the Simon deck.

The telephone call effected a marvelous change in the young detective, who in order to relieve his depression had been in his room paging idly through college catalogues, in which verdant lawns, astrophysics, and coeds mingled seductively with the promise of escape from the here and now of the Verbum winter. He sprang to attention, leapt down the stairs, grabbed his hat and coat and scarf and mittens and boots from the downstairs closet that smelled so heavily of cedar he had to stop breathing, flew into his winter gear with great haste, tripped over the settee in the hallway but didn't fall, and, despite the icy sidewalks, ran the three blocks to the Simon residence, during which he displayed a speed and form that would have pleased both his father and his mother had they witnessed their son's heretofore hidden gift for track and field.

While Ian ran, Professor Simon (Mrs.) called the police station. The officers of the law in Verbum, a town of six thousand residents, spent untold hours investigating the disappearances of lawn dwarfs. They dutifully checked on the suspicious persons Mr. Babic called in, persons who lurked or skulked or sneaked in and out of driveways or appeared suddenly from around corners or crouched beneath windows to peep inside. They checked on these shadowy characters even though not a single one of them had turned into an actual suspect, not to mention a bona fide criminal. They answered countless complaints about loud music from various record players and radios, Verdi included, beloved by the Dahl family, but hated by Don Esterhauser, who claimed to be driven out of his head by vibrato. Almost every night they tested the equilibrium of youthful Verbumites, who climbed out of pickups and station wagons and sedans and obediently staggered along the line in the middle of the road and failed to locate the noses on their own faces with their own index fingers. In short, a missing person in Verbum had an allure that would have been lost on flatfoots in Los Angeles, Chicago, and New York. The dispatcher promised that Officer Knuckler would drive around town to see what he could see. The call ended ominously: "Hope the professor comes home soon, Mrs. Simon." (The lawmen never referred to the womanly half of the academic pair as "Professor.") Then the dispatcher added the obvious: "The snow, you know."

The Milton expert ordered Ian and Isadora to "hold the fort" and to look after Just Plain Dora and to call the police department the moment Percy wandered in. She directed Theodora and Andora "to bundle up," and she swaddled herself in her old beaver fur, the lining of which was ripped, but it was the warmest thing she owned. She topped off her outfit with a massive rabbit trapper hat that had belonged to her late father and, with two of her daughters in tow, she started up the old Citroën—the only vehicle of that make in all of Verbum—and as she backed out of the garage, she shouted to them that she would check the college library first and move on from there.

After the dramatic departure of the mistress of the house and two of the Doras, Ian turned to Isadora with a stern, important face and inquired whether anyone had heard Monk bark that evening. No, Monk hadn't barked. "Not a kidnapping, then," said Ian, squinting as wheels turned in his brain.

Isadora did not say aloud what she was thinking, Who on earth would kidnap my father? Have you ever heard of a kidnapping in Verbum? She knew that Ian was eliminating possibilities, just as Holmes did. She indulged him.

Ian then asked if the man's coat had gone with him, and they checked the downstairs closet and the hooks in the hallway and the kitchen where he sometimes dropped it, but the overcoat wasn't in any of those places, a bad sign to be sure, and Isadora imagined her father in one of his fugue states frozen stiff on Highway 3 or Highway 19 as a drift slowly covered him over, which meant that no one would find him until the snow melted, perhaps not until March, even April. Her heart beat faster. Just Plain Dora, who was looking up at her oldest sister, had tears in her eyes that appeared not to be viral tears, although when she blew her nose hard an instant later, the tears and snot and phlegm from her cold and the dribbling caused by her emotion mingled indiscriminately.

Ian, still maintaining a strict military posture, took it upon himself to search the paternal study as Isadora and Just Plain Dora looked on. He stood before the desk and surveyed its surface with eyes full of meaning. He then dipped his finger into the cup of coffee that stood half drunk on the green blotter. "Not yet room temperature," he pronounced. "How does your father like his coffee?"

"What does that have to do with anything?" Isadora said.

"We could approximate how long ago he left the house. The rate at which the coffee cools is proportional to how much warmer it is than the room temperature. Newton's law of cooling."

"It's a good clue, Ian, but I think it's enough that the coffee's still warm, don't you?" Isadora said. "He can't be that far away."

Ian blushed. Isadora patted his arm.

Ian, with an "aha" glint in his eyes, plucked a red thread from the floor and twirled it between his thumb and forefinger. He then laid it on the blotter for future reference. He crouched to examine the position of the desk chair—did it appear to have been moved in haste? Were there any marks on the floor? Yes! Were any of them new? No. Dirt had seeped into each and every scrape. He stood up, bent over the desk with his hands folded behind his back, and sniffed the volume of Webster's dictionary that lay open on the blotter to a page among the Fs and was startled to see the word *frail* right under his nose. Of course, it was only one of many F words the professor might have been looking up. Coincidences were not clues. Ian said aloud, "I never guess. It is a shocking habit—destructive to the logical faculty."

As Isadora watched her friend scrutinizing her father's study for clues, she sighed without making a sound. She realized that she hated Ian's posing as Holmes. Along with countless other gullible readers, Ian seemed to have missed the fact that the great detective is always guessing. He does not solve every crime because his logical reasoning is impeccable—it most certainly is not. She had pointed this out to Ian, and she knew he was far too bright not to recognize that her skepticism was warranted. Take a single example from *The Sign of the Four*, she thought. Watson returns to Baker Street, and Holmes yet again overwhelms his befuddled doctor friend with the powers of his superior logical mind. Because Holmes notices soil of a reddish tint on Watson's shoes and Holmes has noticed red soil outside the post office on Wigmore Street and nowhere else, he "deduces" that Watson has been to the post office. But Mr. Holmes, Isadora thinks, Dr. Watson could have walked *past* the post office. Even if the only soil in all of London with a reddish tint was outside the post office on Wigmore Street, another person could have tracked the reddish soil from Wigmore Street to some other street, which then might have found its way onto Watson's shoes. Dirt travels, Mr. Holmes. This "deduction" in *The Sign of the Four* is a guess, an educated guess, but no more than that. No, Isadora thought, Sherlock Holmes is always right because Conan Doyle, his maker, has arranged a fictional universe in which red soil and red threads and markings on the floor and opened dictionaries inevitably lead to a solution. In the real world they most definitely do not. Ian's identification with the so-called genius had made him obtuse. Ian was in thrall to a hero who is always right, but that rightness is the result of a wish, a flawed and frankly silly wish.

IAN'S IDENTIFICATION WITH
THE SO-CALLED GENIUS
HAD MADE HIM OBTUSE.

After Isadora had silently condemned her friend's fanaticism and Ian had not deduced her father's location from any of the myriad "clues" in the study or anywhere else, there was nothing to do but wait. Eight had become nine, and nine had become ten, and ten had become eleven. Just Plain Dora had fallen asleep in her bed with her wand as she steadily dripped snot onto her pillow and coughed intermittently, and Ian sat beside Isadora on the sofa in the living-room-cum-menagerie in a posture of defeat, a posture made more pathetic by his great height and striking thinness. Monk dreamed on the rug at their feet, and Roger in his covered cage slept, too. The phone had rung three times, and each time it had rung, Isadora had answered it and told her mother there was no sign of the man yet, after which she had returned to the sofa and imagined her father's dead body encased in ice. The wind whistled and whined and rattled the house, and beyond the porch light there was little to be seen but white and more white in hectic motion. The clock ticked loudly as it always did, but they usually didn't hear it, blocked as it was by ordinary domestic hubbub.

Isadora told Ian in a quiet voice that she didn't really know her father and that he rarely listened to anything she said, although he was usually kind and occasionally patted her arm. She said that her mother hoped time would cure what ailed him, although what ailed him was probably the war, about which he had never said a word, and possibly other events that may have occurred in his childhood. Her mother had hinted at happenings way back when, but she knew nothing about them either. And Ian confessed that his father was a cipher, too, even though he knew the man took his paternal duties seriously and sometimes slapped his son on the back, a gesture that was meant to convey a jovial masculine attitude but most of the time just hurt Ian's shoulder blades. The boy detective then offered a further wistful comment. He told Isadora that he had long hoped his mother would say what she thought instead of what she didn't think. And they sat for a minute or two in silence, after which Isadora began to cry. Ian put his arm around her and was tempted to kiss her but decided against it, which was a sound decision because if he had moved his lips anywhere near hers, she might have punched him.

And then along with the sounds of Isadora's sobs and the ticking clock, they heard light footsteps trip down the stairs and into the hallway, and seconds later Just Plain Dora stood before them in her pink-and-white-striped flannel pajamas and chenille bathrobe, her now-crumpled cardboard wand in her left hand. She dropped the magic equipment to the floor, looked at them with electric green eyes, and spoke in a serious if rather loud voice. "Father's in the basement. I have the key." She opened her hand and in her small palm, flaked with dried white glue, they saw an old brass key.

"You mean the door that leads down to the little room? We lost that key long ago," Isadora said. "You know that. It's been locked for years. There's nothing down there. We just joke about Geoffrey. He's not real, Dora."

"But where did the key come from?" said Ian.

"It was probably a dream," the girl said, her face lit with confidence. She coughed, removed a Kleenex from the pocket of her robe, delicately dabbed her inflamed nose, and then blew into the thin paper, not at all delicately.

Just Plain Dora picked up the wand, gestured for them to follow her, and walked into the dining room with the dignified gait she used whenever she hoped to rise above her runty station in the family hierarchy. She passed into the kitchen with Ian and Isadora close behind her. After failing several times, Dora managed to wrench the key into a sideways position and then, strangely enough, she turned it twice, opened the door with a kick of her slipper, and below them they saw a dim lightbulb dangling from the ceiling, 15 watts, according to Ian. The three children made their way cautiously down the old stairs, covered with inches of gray dust that would have made a wonderful clue not long afterward, had they needed it, because the family would drag that ashen powder from room to room for days, but then it would seep into the corners and crevices of the house and remain for years, and all hope of distinguishing it from other dust would be futile.

The professor was lying in the fetal position, wrapped in his large overcoat on a stained tarp. His eyes were closed and he was breathing noisily. His always-disheveled hair stood up from his head in wild sticky bunches. Beside him, they saw the cage that held his seven white rats, the sight of which made Ian blanch because he realized he had forgotten to account for the animals in the menagerie. Isadora spotted the bottle of whiskey near her father's hand and snatched it just before Dora crouched down to pet her father's face and coo in his ear and drip her fluids on him and wave the crooked wand ceremoniously over him several times. Ian called the police to take them off the case, and then all three of them put the man to bed, although he seemed not to understand much of what was happening. He moaned, snorted a couple of times, and quoted Chaucer as Ian removed his shoes, which sounded like more grunting to the boy detective. And, as Isadora heard one paternal shoe and then the other drop to the floor, she vowed that she would never devote herself to a great man as her life's work, even if that man was a genius. That went for Darwin, too.

Professor Simon (Mrs.) returned home soon after they had covered the basement adventurer with an extra blanket. She rushed in from the porch in a blast of cold air and blowing snow, her cheeks and nose blazing red as she vigorously stomped her ankle boots trailed by the two frightened Doras, their faces almost as red as their mother's. And for an enchanted period of seconds only, hats and shoulders and mittens and boot toes and every eyelash of the three explorers in the hallway were dusted white. But then the melting started and rivulets of water ran hither and thither across the floor. The wife was so relieved to hear the husband was safe that she threw herself onto the stairs without removing what remained of the poor animals she was wearing and, with a sob in her voice, exclaimed to Ian and Isadora, "I think people really can die of mere imagination."

Isadora whispered to Ian that the line from Chaucer her mother had just uttered was well known. It popped from the mouth of a silly character in "The Miller's Tale." She added that it was surely appropriate to the occasion.

Ian wanted desperately to find out how Just Plain Dora had acquired both the key and the secret to her father's whereabouts. But Isadora was weary of all of them, weary of Geoffrey Chaucer and John Milton and Sir Arthur Conan Doyle, and she sent Sherlock on his way. As the tall, thin, would-be hero walked through the flying snow that stung his exposed nose and cheeks and chin, he may or may not have remembered the dream he had dreamed months earlier, the dream about the living key and the girl on the stairway, the dream that ended with semen in his bed. Narrators aren't always omniscient, and therefore I am unable to pronounce on the boy's memory with absolute certainty.

Isadora hugged her mother and her sisters firmly, turned down their offer of hot cocoa, and walked upstairs. She tiptoed into her youngest sister's room and sat at the edge of the bed. Dora was almost asleep, but the young patient smiled when she felt Isadora's hand on her arm.

"How did you know?" Isadora whispered. "How did you know?"

"Frieda Frail. It was Frieda Frail." Just Plain Dora coughed and then she coughed again.

Isadora stroked her sister's forehead and kissed her slimy cheek and thought to herself that a cold wasn't too high a price to pay for this particular kiss. Besides, she knew that she, the oldest of the four, was famous in the family for a formidable immune system.

Isadora didn't believe her little sister. She didn't believe that Frieda Frail's ghost had solved the mystery of the disappearing father. There were many other explanations for how the girl might have known about the key to the door that led them to the slumbering, inebriated veteran in the basement. And some of those explanations involve long stories and multiple digressions that would take up many volumes if we were to deliberate on them properly.

Isadora didn't shut the door completely. She left it open a crack so the hall light would shine through the opening because that's the way the littlest Dora liked it, and then, just before she turned toward her own room, she heard her sister's voice say, "I told you ghosts were real."

CHAPTER SEVENTEEN

•

We all suffer and we all die, but you, the person who is reading this book right now, you are not dead yet. I may be dead, but you are not. You are breathing in and out as you read and if you pause and place your hand on your chest, you will feel your heart beating, and there must be light in the room where you are, a light from a window or a lamp or a screen that illuminates the page and part of your body as you read.

Doors have been opening and closing and memories have been coming and going and would-be heroes have left the story one after the other. The Mysterious Limping Gentleman arrived in Bath long ago, but the MLG may be worth following even if it turns out he's the wrong man. Life inside and outside novels is crowded with wrong men and women, one misleading character after another, whose wooden legs, eye patches, crutches, scars, beards, and spectacles may or may not be part of a disguise. But a man or woman doesn't need a wig or a false nose to deceive. He or she can do it just as ably with a smile or placating words or a friendly manner. We are still following several persons who may or may not have keys to the story. When I listen, I can hear their footsteps in the streets of the city I imagine as I write and you read.

To write a book is for all the world like humming a song or whistling a tune or striding down the street, skipping a little, and then breaking into a run before returning to a saunter. The most important thing of all is to keep time.

A voice says loudly, "Just the facts, Ma'am. Get a hold of yourself and tell it just the way it happened." It's a man, of course. He speaks with the voice of authority. I answer him that I will do my best because the stories in the book aren't quite over.

The Gang of Five remained together until time and space pried them apart. Nothing is more ordinary than a group of young friends growing older and each one going off on his or her own to work and love, to fail and succeed, but to quote Kurt Koffka, "the whole is other than the sum of its parts," which means that a gang is something different from the five individuals that make it up. My old gang can only be reconstituted in memory, and when I remember us whole, I am seized by nostalgia, not for the past but for the future, a future to be conquered by the more-than-just-five we were then.

Gus is a rotund, reasonably contented, widely respected man of the cinema who lives not so far away from Walter and me in Brooklyn. His thoughts still meander on back roads before they arrive on the freeway, and he still notices scenery other people don't. For years, he wrote for *The Village Voice* and then for the *New York Press*, as well for more esoteric film journals. Movie buffs recognize the name Scavelli. Gus bemoans the decline of art house theaters in New York—they're almost all defunct—and the cultural amnesia for films in general that do not feature superheroes, although Gus has no prejudice against superheroes, a theme he can elaborate on for hours if he's given the chance. He teaches a film criticism class at NYU and after an extended history of heartbreak fell in love at age fifty with a gynecologist-obstetrician named Adi Badour, a hardworking, wisecracking doctor with spectacular cleavage.

In 2006, Gus and Adi invited me and Walter over to their house in Cobble Hill for dinner and a DVD. After the meal, Gus gave a prolonged introduction to the unnamed film we were going to see. In 2004, an archivist at the Library of Congress had discovered an uncensored version of the movie that had been lost for years. When the original film was released in 1933, the New York Board of Censors demanded cuts. Gus announced that we were about to see the "real reels" of *Baby Face* with Barbara Stanwyck and George Brent directed by Alfred E. Green and that we should look out for a very young John Wayne in a bit part. He explained that to comply with the censors, a full five minutes had been hacked out of the original, a brutal quotation from Nietzsche's *Will to Power* had been replaced by moral treacle, and the ambitious heroine had gotten her comeuppance in a new ending. After 1934 and the rise of the Hays Code, punishment for bad girls would be de rigueur. Gus is a peripatetic film archive all to himself, and I wasn't at all sure that he remembered our afternoon at the Thalia almost forty years earlier. He did not mention it.

It was only when we arrived at the hot-coffee-over-molesting-hand scene, a movie moment I had hoarded in my own mental catalogue, that I began to suspect Gus remembered. As was his habit, Dr. Plenitude directed us all to look closely. The scene was longer than I recalled. After dousing the villain with coffee, Lily Powers ambles from the room with a gait of dignified weariness, her hips and shoulders swaying slightly. When the big man follows her into a bedroom, Lily tells him to "haul" his "freight outa here." But the man doesn't listen to her. He smiles. He knows. He knows what she is: "the sweetheart of the night shift." He throws himself on her. "Come on," he says, "everybody knows about you." "Well, you ain't goin' to," she fires back, smacks him hard, and he lets go of her. Lily doesn't run. She walks into the next room, takes a beer from the table, opens it, and pours the foaming liquid into a glass. But the big man is back in the picture. Still grinning, he mounts an attack from behind and reaches around her to maul her breasts. Lily grabs a beer bottle from the table, and still in his grip, turns, aims the weapon, and smashes him in the face with it. The creep stumbles backward out of the frame, and our heroine returns to what she was doing. She calmly lifts her glass and takes a large swig of beer.

"We didn't see the beer bottle, did we?" I asked Gus. He said no and then asked me if I'd like to see it again. I think we watched it seven times. Before we left that evening, I hugged Gus hard. All he said was, "That rewind button comes in pretty handy, doesn't it?"

Jacob lives and works in Paris. He publishes papers and attends conferences around the world. He and Walter e-mail each other about symmetries, argue about the future of string theory (which Walter believes is hopeless), engage in vigorous pun competitions in French and English, and gossip about other physicists, including a handful of young women who appear to have crashed the men-only gate. Jacob is a conscientious father to his twenty-two-year-old daughter, Jeanette, and his nineteen-year-old son, Jean, but an air of melancholy hangs over him these days. Last time Walter and I saw him for dinner in New York, I felt sad after we parted. He is still slender, has all his hair; his charm is intact, but his wife of many years left him two years ago, not for another man but for herself, a turn of events that Jacob can't comprehend.

Our Fanny is dead. She died of an aggressive breast cancer when she was fifty-four, one year older than the Baroness. She had been out of the city for many years by then. She moved back to California because her mother was ill, got herself a degree in social work, and devoted herself to psychiatric outpatients in Los Angeles. Whitney and I were a little surprised at first, but we realized that her insurrectionist spirit and benign narcissism had simply taken another route. The patients loved her, and she fought for them. When she died in 2009, Fanny was living with a woman named Grace whose lucrative occupation Fanny described as "hairdresser to the stars." I don't know what has happened to Grace, but I vividly remember a moment from the ceremony on the beach. I was the only one of the gang who was able to fly to the coast to attend. I see Grace walking toward the water, her fist in the urn. I am a few yards behind her with other people, none of whom I know, and then I see the pale ash and the white bits of bone fly from her hand in a cloudy stream, her blue silk scarf aloft, pulled south in the hard wind. As I watch, I remember kissing Fanny. I remember, Dear, Dearest, Darling Chum. I remember her tail on the floorboards. Grace falls to her knees in the sand. I hear her wail, "Oh, Fanny, Fanny! My own Fanny!"

Whether it was Whitney who called me or I who called Whitney is a fact that has never been established between us because each of us remembers differently, and neither of us sat down and recorded the events for posterity. Whitney remains convinced that she called me from a pay phone on one of those days in late June 1979. In her version, she had been looking up a book in Butler Library and as she sat reading she found herself worrying again that I was not myself. She insists she was driven to act, and that after she had hung up the receiver, she rushed down to 109th Street to talk some sense into me. I remember that I called Whitney. I remember telling her it was important that we talk. In my version, Whitney hopped on the train and traveled all the way uptown to see me. How the meeting happened, however, is less important than the fact that it did happen. We are certain it happened, and yet, what we said to each other that night neither of us can remember. All we agree on is that whatever we said, we closed the distance that had come between us. Admittedly the distance between the characters in this instance wasn't great—it was, in fact, small—but if we hadn't acted, it might have grown slowly and separated us forever.

Why didn't I write it all in the notebook? What was wrong with me? I didn't write about that evening because I couldn't have predicted the meanings our friendship would accumulate over time. Whether it was on that night or on another night that I told Whitney I envied her, that I envied her confidence and her courage and her clothes and her money, I cannot say, but I did tell her. I knew she wouldn't have waited at the elevator, and I envied her that fiercely. But I have come to understand that before we met, Whitney had waited more than I had imagined, had suffered more than I had imagined, not as I had but in ways I hadn't understood because for me she was a being enchanted by the fairies. But she, too, has had to fight for her work, has faced those who want to shrink her talents and undercut her strength. She, too, has had to buck hard against the stories that are already written, the fixed narratives about the woman artist and what her work is supposed to be.

She flew off to Berlin to escape the New York art world's "pricks and prigs." Germany is different, she soon realized, but no better. She stayed anyway. I see her in the gallery in her soft jeans and loose T-shirt. I see her with her hands on her hips, grinning. I see her strong biceps from all the lifting. I see the words in several languages on her large sculptures. I see her pregnant years ago. I hear her complaining about how often she has to pee in her eighth month. I see Freya riding Whitney's knee and I hear the sound of my daughter's excited laughter. I hear Whit telling me she has left her lover, Theo. I hear her telling me she has returned to Theo. I hear her quoting Sylvia Plath: "Every woman adores a fascist." Love-hate. Whitney says we should have a word for it, for that feeling. I hear her shout, "*I lovate you, you bastard.*" These pictures and words are all Whitney. I cannot disentangle the images and sounds and feelings in time. What was is and what is was.

—

John Ashbery died on September 3 of this year. Whitney sent me an e-mail the following day with the words, "A winter morning. / Place in a puzzling light." It is from the poem "Some Trees" in his first book, of the same title, published in 1956.

Whitney teases me about my philosophical bent, about my insatiable reading in many fields, and about some of the obscure journals that publish my nonfiction, which she mocks roundly. "Really, Minnesota, *Lebenswelt: Aesthetics and Philosophy of Experience.* How arcane." She has read all my novels, however, and I have kept close track of the evolution of her art, from the small early poem works to the much larger tunnel installations one has to crawl into and read as one makes one's way on hands and knees from one end to the other. Children can walk upright, and Whitney had a wheelchair available for adults who are unable to make the trip either bent over or on all fours. My favorite was a piece that included the sentences: "Think about being born. Where are you? Do you love me yet?"

I remember Whitney looking out the window on West Broadway and saying, "It's ours to eat." We ate it. It was bitter, and it was sweet. I loved her then. I love her now, but while I was in the throes of living it was impossible for me to know whether a moment would be significant or whether it would vanish into oblivion along with so much else. Whitney never married Theo. At some point in the last decade they arrived at a state of affectionate truce. Whit had lots of lovers over the years, as did Theo. Their daughter, Ella, was a wild adolescent but is now an orthodontist in New Jersey with a good practice, a husband in finance, and two small children, whose images I see regularly in text messages. "Life is strange," Whitney says. It is. It is. It is strange.

And what about Kari, the person I saw when I looked up during the long years of the childhood we lived together? Kari is a geneticist now—epigenetics is her field. She's at Johns Hopkins working on something called methylation that may help us understand how some diseases function and cure them in the future. I am told her research is "cutting edge." But today, as I write this, I am not worrying about methylation. I am looking forward to the days just after Christmas when we will see each other in Minnesota. Freya will meet up with her cousins, Stefan and Kai, and Walter and my brother-in-law, Caleb, will schmooze about baseball, and we will all spend time sitting beside our mother or mother-in-law or grandmother in Sunflower Suites and asking her questions and listening attentively even when she is a little confused, and Kari and I will have a chance to talk and remember what we haven't remembered for a long time. We may remember the hollow scraping sound our skates made when they cut into the ice, such a good sound, or maybe we will recall pounding our white figure skates inside the warming house to nudge our numb toes back to sensation, or perhaps we will remember that when it was perilously cold the air gave us a special headache we called ice-ache. Why is it so pleasurable to remember together? Why do we always laugh when we summon necklaces made from snake grass or the dozens of little red nodules that rose on our thighs from burning grass?

I know Kari remembers Gertie, the old lady we never saw but once heard jabbering about "bloody murder" in a high whine when we were passing the abandoned Petersen place up the road. It was hot summer and the tar was baking under our bare feet and the moment we heard her we ran home so fast we had stitches in our sides, or at least I did. The other kids said she had appeared one day out of nowhere and that she was bad and crazy and had strangled her own baby. Mother said we mustn't listen to the nonsense we heard from other children, but Kari and I listened anyway. In those days, we lived for wonders and terrors.

I am going to tell you a secret now: There is a doctor in this story, but she arrives much later, well after the millennium has ended. I am writing here in my study on November 29, 2017. The doctor is the book's hidden character, the one who never appears and never speaks. I know it and she knows it. But back in 1978–1979, I had no idea that I would tell her secrets in a room behind a closed door where secrets are securely kept forever. I went on talking for a decade. In that room ghosts are real, and Never has both time and space, even though its coordinates are often forgotten. The room contains the forgotten itself. But I can tell you this, too. Inside the four walls of that room, regrets gather: regrets for waiting, regrets for what never happened, regrets for what was never said, regrets for the books that were never written and never published, regrets for being nudged and prodded and pushed and kicked. Long ago, a poet identified the woman in the room: "My name is Might-have-been. I am also called No-more, Too-late, Farewell."

Maybe, if you ask nicely, you will get what you want. But you must ask nicely, politely. You must smile, and you must not put yourself forward. And remember this: there are rewards for asking nicely, for sweetness and light, for bowing and scraping and raising your eyes to the great man: The Triumph of Life.

Please don't cut me off in midsentence.
Please don't grab my arm.
Please leave now.
Please do not call me dear.
Please, no.

A young writer is listening at the wall with her father's old stethoscope and she hears her neighbor in 2C say "Amsah" and then "I'm sad" and then "I was your bitch to kick," and she hears the same woman speaking in a man's angry voice. He calls her stupid. The words bruise the listener's ears. They wound her ears as if she is the one being called stupid. And she keeps listening. When she discovers that a girl has fallen or jumped or been pushed from a window, she finds herself looking out her own window to make sure that the daughter isn't there discarded on the plot of ground at the bottom of the air shaft where a few weeds and coarse grasses struggle to grow. In a moment of clarity she knows that the pain and fear are somehow also her pain and fear. But this is odd, isn't it? Minnesota wasn't all that sad and she wasn't called stupid, not often anyway, and yet, she knows that she is bound up in the words she hears through the wall.

She imagined most of Lucy's story. Ted Senior and Lindy were always offstage. If one doesn't listen carefully to what has been said, the two may easily become stock characters: the evil father and the angelic daughter. But then, neither Lucy nor her son was a trustworthy narrator. Lucy was unstable, and her son may have been a pathological liar. Each of the Dear Ones had an interpretation of the Lucy narrative, each correct in its way. My neighbor did belong to a cult and, if not psychotic all the time, she had probably been psychotic some of the time. Whitney wasn't wrong either. The Wiccan religion is performance, as all forms of worship are, with their rituals and relics and prayers. The witches belonged to the Circle Theater. And Fanny knew Lucy wanted that prick dead. "And you wanted to kill him?" I asked Lucy. "Oh no, not for a long time," she answered. Her rage grew slowly. Together the interpretations create far more meaning than any one of them alone. I, the old writer, have spent years studying the clouds that blur the neat lines we like to draw between one thing and another. I have immersed myself in ambiguities. The winds blow and the sky changes and the waters rise and interpretations blend one into the other.

Remember that Minnesota had already filled her imagination with everything she had read, enchantments, battles, challenges, wounds, tales of love and its torments, and a good deal of philosophy and history before she arrived in the city. Remember, too, it was a dangerous city then, a city of knives and guns and roaches and rats and towering heaps of garbage, but it was a city that burned with ideas, and ideas shape our perceptions and our memories. Then, ugly was beautiful.

This book is a portrait of the artist as a young woman, the artist who came to New York to live and to suffer and to write her mystery. Like the great detective who shares her initials, S.H., the writer, sees, hears, and smells the clues. The signs are everywhere—in a face, in the sky, in a book. A letter is slipped under a door. A knife arrives in the mail. Footsteps sound in the street and in the hallway. She turns her key in the lock. The women are chanting in the next room. Unlike Holmes, however, Minnesota cannot depend on Conan Doyle to arrange a perfect world for her, in which clods of red earth inevitably lead to the guilty party no reader ever suspected: the crippled gardener.

Minnesota's would-be hero detective, Ian Feathers, IF, is wrong, and Isadora Simon, IS, is right. IF proceeds as if every sign is the route to a solution. IS knows this is nonsense. We are always reading the signs, but what do they mean, the smiles and the stars and the strings and the letters? I remember my old bewilderment. Why are you looking at me like that? What have I done? Why did I wait at the elevator? Can I find the logic behind it all? No, it can't be reduced to true and false, to algorithms or even fuzzy logic. It's not mathematics. There are rules, though, lots of rules and regulations that parade as the one true logic. The rules and regulations are about narration and authorship and who gets to tell the story and in what way. The Baroness wrote, "You forget, madame—that we are the masters—go by our rules." Sometimes those rules are sheer madness. A would-be despot with a red, angry face runs back and forth on the screen howling, "Lock her up! Off with her head!" And the crowd looks up at the hero, the great man who expiates its humiliation and shame with purifying hatred of all the others. The Baroness wrote this, too: "thought tangled—of waste barren, unfertile—violent action—noise—clamour: American lynchings."

___

Lynch and hang and burn.

I am interpreting the clues differently now. I am reading the stories differently. I am remembering differently. I am changed. A man unlocks the door to a room and throws, carries, or pushes objects that belong to his wife and children across its threshold. Then he locks the door with his key, puts it in his pocket, and goes to work. Months pass. One by one, things disappear, a table, a chair, shoes, the television set, hats, mittens, books, pens, the toaster, toys, and after a while the apartment begins to look barren, foreign. And no one in the family asks why he is the only person with the key. They do not think to ask him. The question "Why are you the one with the key?" does not form in their heads. They do not have the words to ask the question. One has to be fully conscious to recognize that one deserves to ask. One has to be fully conscious to be enraged.

But I will tell you again that one story leads to another story. One story becomes another story, and many stories are somehow the same story.

"Certainly, Freytag-Loringhoven had created broadly similar scatological works but nothing that held the *thinking* expressed in Duchamp's piece." The question of mind is not for you, dear. The joke is on you, dear. Your art is not your own, dear. It belongs to him, dear. I'm sure you have nothing to add, dear. You are too stupid to read those books. You'll make a fine nurse. No, Lucy didn't know she wanted that prick dead. I didn't know how angry I was, not at all. And the masters aren't always conscious of what they are doing and saying either. The story of their superiority has been written into them, blood and bone and muscle and tissue, into their very cells. I remember the professor's surprised face, and then the look of dismay that came over it. Why are they always so surprised and dismayed? Over and over and over I have seen that look of surprise and dismay.

I do not faint anymore. If one is able to remain conscious and face one's adversary, what follows the looks of surprise and dismay is the look of anger: Who the fuck do you think you are? And the man's stuttering fury, that one man who is also many men, is made worse by the woman's steadfast calm. These days I am always calm. I am as calm as Patty was. I am a calm, learned old lady.

You forget, madame, you must go by our rules.

No, I will not.

In my world Wittgenstein is still a knife. In fact, my library is chock-full of verbal weaponry. Wittgenstein, however, even when quoted in the original, is no help at all if a man throws you into a wall of books.

I needed the Baroness. She was so desperately important to me. I knew nothing about the Madonna of the Bathroom then. I didn't know they had locked up Elsa in the Never Room. But I gave Fanny's deadly gift her name. She was my instrument of wordless rage. It is lucky, very lucky that my adventures with the knife can be described as a comedy of errors, that I did not slice the pale young man into little pieces. I am sorry for him. He was not one of the masters. He murdered his hamster. Did he push his sister out the window? We cannot know. We will not know. If he pushed her, did he tell himself later that he had not pushed her? Did she taunt him and leap? Did she jump in despair? Lucy said Lindy cried and cried. She was so unhappy. We cannot know. I pitied him. I gave him money. But then his abjection repulsed me. Now I feel for him what Simone Weil called charity, and therefore I believe I held the knife on the wrong man.

I remember the Introspective Detective smiling at me across the desk. Yes, she is my invention, but I am remembering her smile. That is how our mental imagery works. We often remember what never happened. And now I can smile at my former self, a little sadly, perhaps, but I can smile. There she is prancing around 2B with the

Baroness, letting herself go, popping her switchblade to release her fantasies of bloody revenge. She wants that prick dead.

Watson is happy with his bleeding wound because it upsets Holmes, and that upset is a sign that love lurks behind the cold mask. Mrs. Malacek has bled all over the sofa. There's a lot of blood, and there is something wrong with her eyes. It's as if she can't see anyone or anything. Blind. "Every woman adores a fascist. / The boot in the face, the brute, / brute heart of you," wrote Sylvia Plath. What happened to the man? Did he run into the house? Did he run out of it? Was he the boot in the face, the brute, brute heart, the boot brute son of a bitch? Mary Shelley sits in an ice bath to stop the bleeding. The miscarriage almost kills her. Three of her babies are born and die. One lives. She is listening to the men talk in a house in Switzerland. The weather is bad. Why does it never stop raining? Does she feel the fetus stirring inside her as the great men talk about poems and politics? Mary Wollstonecraft Godwin Shelley is nineteen, four years younger than Minnesota when she first arrives in New York. She finishes *Frankenstein*, a book about a terrible birth and terrible loneliness before the body of her husband, the tragic poet hero, burns on a beach in Italy, but Mary doesn't see the flames. She wasn't there. Apparently, it wasn't the custom for women to attend cremations. Their sensibilities were far too delicate for that. The ironies of time and place: Have you forgotten they burned witches, the great majority of whom were women?

In Louis Edouard Fourier's painting of the seaside funeral, the dashing Lord Byron stands in the foreground with Leigh Hunt and Edward John Trelawney. The dead poet, untouched by fish and salt and sea, the dead poet, not disfigured at all, lies on a smoking bier, his beautiful face turned heavenward, a young hero-god preparing for his posthumous resurrection in our collective mind. If you look far to your left, you will see her in the background: that minor character, the wife. She is on her knees humbly praying for God knows what. One story becomes another.

The last time I saw Lucy was in May 1986. By then I had met and married Walter and had defended my dissertation. Patty and Moth surprised me by making a dinner in my honor for the degree, not the marriage. Patty sent me the invitation: "Dear Dr. H.," it began.

Back then Walter was not the potbellied, gray-headed oldster he is now. He's turned seventy and likes to walk slowly. "What's your hurry?" he says to me. "This isn't a race, is it?" Then he was a young, slender, redheaded, nearsighted physicist with strong thighs, a sweet, straight, almost-always-at-the-ready dick, and a raucous approach to lovemaking that sent me into near delirium. When I remember our first two years together, I sometimes see us from a great distance in our first apartment as if I am high in the sky looking down at two naked Lilliputians of the past. I see the little naked woman chasing the little naked man down the stairs. I see the little naked man chasing the little naked woman up the stairs. I see the little naked woman playing the Hussy and showing her little naked backside to the little naked man in the room where they keep all the books. I see the little naked man leaping onto the bed, his arms wide as he beckons his own, his darling, his beloved to hop in beside him. I see their four naked arms and four naked legs and their two hairy heads locked in a kiss. I see them doing the heavenly bounce on the mattress of the four-poster, on the rug, on the kitchen floor.

Walter and I are old lovers now. We have done the heavenly bounce thousands of times. Over and over again, my fingers have slid down his naked chest and made their way to his soft sleeping cock that I have then felt grow and change in my hand. Over and over, I have handled the silken skin of his balls and have felt the slight burn of his beard against my cheek and my breasts and between my legs. I have lost myself in the feeling of him so often that the man couldn't be ousted from my body even if I wanted him gone. Our flesh is mingled now. Our thoughts overlap. We have taught each other much but can't always remember who taught whom what. We grow old, and

I know each of us dreads the other's death, although we rarely talk about it. Time will tell. Unless we explode together, one of us will die first.

Love drives me on, that loosener of limbs.

I was five weeks pregnant at the dinner. Only Walter knew of my suspicions.

"I remember," my mother said just the other day, "I remember that first flutter. I remember where I was—at Emma's house. We were having coffee, and I felt it, the very first sign, the very first sign of you."

The young Walter was grumpy about the prospect of dinner with a cabal of witches. He knew Lucy's story because I had told it to him, and he found it unpleasant, as anyone would. He came along with me mumbling about superstition, and although I have forgotten much of the evening, nothing remarkable happened. We recall the disastrous in far greater detail than any event that goes more or less as expected. I do remember that a couple days after the dinner, Walter told me that he had found Patty arrogant with all her rolling pronouncements. His comment bothered me, but I couldn't say why, and yet, because it bothered me, I remembered it. Now that I have reached the age Patty was when I first met her, I realize that she was no more arrogant than Walter himself or countless men I knew and know. In us women, confidence is often mistaken for arrogance.

Walter probably enjoyed Alistair's negative convolutions and Moth's food, and he probably worked to keep his face still when Gorse explained her theories about the greater universe, but I must be honest: I don't remember. I do remember that Lucy looked older and plumper and that she was in her buoyant, flirtatious mode that night, her eyes alert from second to second. And yet, I felt that her face was not as radiant as I had remembered it. She seemed slower, less prone to sudden shifts of temper, a change Patty said was due to lithium. I remember lithium because I looked up the element and its medicinal uses in psychiatry. I also remember that Lucy charmed Walter that night. She laughed at his puns and nodded meaningfully after every sentence that left his mouth, and he sunned himself in her admiration. When I think back on that last dinner with Lucy, I have a hunch that my husband's face looked very much like my father's face when Brenda looked up at him outside his office that day when I was still a girl.

Just Plain Dora turns the key twice, and the three children descend the stairs to the basement to find the father lying in the fetal position on an old tarp with a whiskey bottle in his hand. What an odd little comedy Minnesota was trying to write. She must have sensed that unknown stories had been locked in a metaphorical cellar inside the man who was her father. But there was another father mixed up in the story, too; Edith's father, Professor Harrington, who used to wander in and out of the living room murmuring quotations from classic works and occasionally looking wild. Harrington had been a tank commander during the war in Europe, and Edith told me he had kept a pet rabbit in that tank. One never knew about Edith's stories, but the tale of the bunny must have lodged itself in me years earlier and then, when combined with Laurence, the sheep dog, and George the cockatoo, had burst out as the Simon zoo.

In her never-finished novel, Minnesota shrank the fathers. She shrank the great men and the self-important boy-men down to size. She shrank them with comedy. She shrank them with pity. She didn't know what she was doing, but then writers rarely do. We know only a part of it. The rhythms rise and fall and take us along for the ride.

I am sorry for the little sleeping man on the tarp.

When he was dying, I sat beside my father and held his hand in the small hospice room. I remember the cold light through the blinds and the vase with dried hydrangeas my mother had placed on the windowsill. I remember the sound of the oxygen machine breathing in and out loudly and the tube in his nose that made his nostrils red and sore. I remember the small jar of Vaseline on the rolling table beside his bed. "They don't know squat about the endocrine system. Did you know that?" he said to me. "It's just one goddamned mystery after another." My father liked to chuckle about medical ignorance. He liked to lambast Republicans. When he was happy, he liked to whistle in the car. The old soldier was not afraid of death. He was afraid, desperately afraid, of being pitied. Aunt Irma used to say, "Aren't we all human?" Well, aren't we?

Near the end of that dinner in 1986, Lucy stood up from her place beside Walter, walked up to me, leaned over, and whispered in my ear, "Honey, I think I want Lindy's wand now. It's about time." And I thought to myself, Heaven help me. I didn't tell Lucy that I had mended and decorated and inscribed the wand or that I had mounted it on the bookshelf, just above the shelf where I had hit my head hard and then slipped to the floor. I asked her if she remembered Bianca, Mr. Rosales's little girl. And she said yes. I said that the ceiling of my closet had collapsed the winter after Lucy left the building. Mr. Rosales had come to fix it, and Bianca had come with him, and she had been fascinated by the wand, had wanted to hold it, and I had let her, and she had waved it back and forth over her head and had skipped across my front room and had chattered to herself in Spanish. "Lucy," I said. "I gave the wand to Bianca."

I expected Lucy to scold me, but she didn't. She just nodded and said the coven had been sending spells in my direction for years and the magic had obviously worked. In April of 1994, Lucy died in her sleep—myocardial infarction. The witches sent out a death announcement with circles and vines on it. Patty included a handwritten note at the bottom: "I have been reading you with admiration. Patty." From that card I also discovered that Lucy's middle name was Catherine.

Sometime after the millennium had turned, I found a remaindered copy of *A Study in Western Amnesia* by P. S. Thistlethwaite at the Strand bookstore and bought it. When I looked at the flap copy, I discovered that Patty had died in 1997. The book was published a year later. I wish I could tell you what happened to the others. I could perhaps discover their fates on the Internet, but I have chosen to stay ignorant. I like to imagine Moth, Alistair, and Gorse, all beyond their hundredth birthdays, chanting and rocking back and forth in a circle sending spells hither and thither. And I like to imagine the ghost of Alice the dog lying somewhere near them.

I remember the last triumphant push. I pushed and as I pushed, I roared. I pushed the small, wet, bloody body out of my body. I see the tiny agonized face, the vital kicks and flailing arms. I hear the sharp-pitched cry of a startled foreigner in a new world. I remember the green and violet colors of the long gelatinous cord that bound her to me. I can't remember the cut, the clamp, or the placenta.

I feel my fingers on the keys. These are the keys Minnesota needed. It wasn't a single key. It wasn't the clavis universalis. It wasn't the theory of everything, but an entire alphabet of living keys. And, as in a Sufi tale, they were there all along. All she needed was a little more time. I am writing now, writing against time, for time, with time, in time. I am writing out of my time and into yours. There is magic in this simple act, isn't there? For you it may be next year while for me it is still this year. To Page, on the page, the dead speak to the living. Remember, the restless spirits rise up and out of the library to haunt us. Remember the battle of the books. And remember that we forget. We forget. *A Study in Western Amnesia* is about the forgotten, those pushed out of the story, the muffled, the gagged, the raped, the beaten, the killed. No More, Too Late, Farewell. Malcolm Silver had a picture of one of those women on his wall. I hated that picture.

My mother's pregnant ghost, Eva, stands at the window, and she seems to want to speak. She moves her mouth the way singers do when they are warming up before a song, but the song doesn't come out. The words don't come out. Are you listening? I want you to listen. Frieda Frail is haunting Verbum. Her ghost is popping up all over town. She places a key in Just Plain Dora's hand, and she whispers in the girl's ear.

My mother forgets. She forgets what I just told her, but she remembers Eva. She remembers the cracked coffee cup. She remembers I am writing a book. She remembers the very first sign of me. She was drinking coffee with Emma. When I call her today, she will ask me how old she is, and I will say that after Christmas and after the new year, in deep midwinter, on February 19, she will be ninety-five, and she will tell me that's old, very old, and I will agree with her, and she will ask me how old I am, and I will tell her. I grow old. I grow old. Freya was born thirty years ago. My daughter sings, and when she sings, she shakes the people in the back of the room. A child waves a wand over her head and skips out the door.

Long ago, I came to New York looking for the hero of my first novel. I didn't find the person I imagined, but then, life is like that. Things change. I changed. "Maybe you and the others are writing her back into the story." The Introspective Detective's hope might not be entirely unreasonable. Even now, during what seems to be the worst of times, I feel the wind at my back every now and again. I didn't know then that I had brought my hero with me to the city. But here she is: Her scalp is painted red, the tin cans at her hips are rattling, and two teaspoons are swinging from her ears as she walks her mutts in Greenwich Village. She laughs loudly, and she farts loudly. She enjoys frightening the neighbors. She is not ashamed of her machinery, and she writes sound poems in her head as dusk falls on the city. The city is New York, Berlin, Paris. It is a real city that is also an imaginary city. Watch her as she takes a piss in her urinal before she flies off on her next errand.

Something is happening. Something is happening in the now of the book. Something is beginning to happen as you read this sentence. Her feet are leaving the pavement. She rises. She moves up and up. She sails high above the metropolis. She is waving a knife over her head—a five-and-a-half-inch Brazilian stiletto switchblade flick-knife. The Baroness is airborne, and there among the lowering clouds she takes her place beside her appalling sister.

And who is the appalling sister who has taken flight before her?

I will tell you who it is: your narrator, the author of this book. I am not waiting anymore. Hold out your hand. I am giving you the keys.

One story has become another.

ACKNOWLEDGMENTS

Over a hundred years after she came to New York City, where she wrote poems, found and made art, and was herself an insurrectionist work of art, the Baroness, who had longed to see her poems collected as a book, was granted her wish. In 2010, MIT Press published a beautiful edition of her texts: *Body Sweats: The Uncensored Writings of the Baroness Elsa von Freytag-Loringhoven*, edited by Irene Gammel and Suzanne Zelzano. Quotations from the poems are all from this volume. Facts and events from the Baroness's life mentioned in *Memories of the Future* are taken from Irene Gammel's excellent book, *Baroness Elsa: Gender, Dada, Everyday Modernity, A Cultural Biography* (MIT, 2002). Gammel's biography also includes her systematic and persuasive argument for the Baroness as the artist behind the famous *Fountain*, for which Marcel Duchamp took credit well after her death.

The fight to attribute the urinal to the Baroness has also been waged by the art historians Julian Spalding and Glyn Thompson, whose article "Did Marcel Duchamp Steal Elsa's Urinal?" was published in *The Art Newspaper*, volume 24, issue 262, in November of

2014, followed by their exhibition, *A Lady's Not A Gent's*, that was part of the Edinburgh Arts Festival at Summerhall in 2015. Although Duchamp as the mind behind *Fountain* continues to have defenders, the evidence for reattribution of the work to the Baroness strikes me as overwhelming. For an exhaustive treatment of that evidence, as well as a correspondence between Spalding, Thompson and Sir Nicholas Serota, who was then director of the Tate Museum (which owns a replica of *Fountain* purchased for 500,000 pounds in 1964), see "Marcel Duchamp's Fountain…he lied!" in *The Jackdaw* magazine, November-December, 2015.

I also want to thank my friend, Jean Frémon, the writer, art scholar, and president of Galerie Lelong, for putting me in touch with M. Didier Schulmann, the director of the Bibliotèque Kandinsky at Centre Pompidou, who kindly granted me permission to reproduce the photograph of the Baroness's death mask, published in *transition 11*, 1928, which Gammel credits to Marc Vaux. The person who made the death mask remains a mystery.

S. H.